THE GRECIAN MANIFESTO

ERNEST DEMPSEY

ENCLAVE PUBLISHING

JOIN THE ADVENTURE

Visit ernestdempsey.net to get a free copy of the not-sold-in-stores short story, RED GOLD.

You'll also get access to exclusive content not available anywhere else.

PROLOGUE

R ome, 50 B.C.

A GUST of wind whipped through Gaius Julius Caesar's already tousled hair as he stood on the deck of the ship. The long wooden boat seemed almost empty, aside from the rows of oars and the single linen sail that flapped in the coastal breeze. The only people who remained were the emperor and his trusted general, Servius Galba.

"Is everyone off the ship?" Caesar asked, uncertain if they were alone or not. He turned his head around to confirm it.

The day was hot, and he'd removed his helmet, holding it at his side under his armpit. Even though it was late in the afternoon, the bright sunlight seemed to superheat his armor. He wore the legion uniform he'd donned so many times before, through battles, hardships, and scenarios mere mortals could never imagine. Some of the metal plates bore the scars from those occasions, a tribute to Gaius Julius Caesar's abilities as a skilled warrior, and leader.

"Yes, General. All the men have gone ashore for supplies and to rest for the night," Servius answered. "They will return in the morning to bring the ship the rest of the way home."

Caesar had been a consul for nearly a decade, but his friend Servius still called him by his former military title. He didn't mind. Caesar had adapted to the political arena out of necessity, but his natural domain was in the military field. "Excellent," he said with a careful grin. "Show me the relic."

"Right this way, General." Servius extended his arm, pointing the way to the back of the boat.

The galley was shorter than the trireme ships the Roman navy had originally used when the republic rose to power. Their more modern boats were also lighter, more maneuverable, which helped them establish a strategic advantage over many seafaring nations. Caesar had served in the Roman navy for a short time, and he knew how important controlling the seas was to the country. Rome's naval power had struggled for decades to establish a strong presence. The Carthaginians had mocked them at first, and beaten them on several occasions. Rome, however, eventually did what it did so well. It adapted.

Now, the navy was as strong as any on the planet. Walking across the wooden planks of the ship's deck, Caesar was reminded of his days at sea. He'd been captured by pirates once and held for ransom. The story had become the stuff of lore with his soldiers and fellow legionaries. When the pirates asked for a certain sum, he balked at the low amount they requested and demanded that the pirates ask for more. When the ransom was paid, Caesar warned them that he would be back and they would all pay dearly for their actions.

The pirates scoffed at his threat, but he followed through, capturing every single one and punishing them by slitting their throats before publicly crucifying them.

Caesar hated thieves. And pirates were the worst of the sort. Rome needed supplies from Africa and the Middle East, Greece, and Spain. Pirates threatened that supply line, therefore piracy would not be tolerated.

Servius pulled back a red curtain near the back of the boat where a small alcove provided shade from the late afternoon sun. That was the first time he laid eyes on it. The mechanism was unlike anything Caesar had ever seen before. It was a complex combination of bronze gears, wheels, and levers, contained within a bronze box. It stood about two feet high and half that wide, with a depth of maybe eight inches.

Caesar stepped through the curtain, and his friend let the drape fall, concealing them both within the small cabin. Servius stood just inside the fabric, watching Caesar's reactions.

"Where did you find it?" Caesar asked, moving around behind the pedestal on which the relic stood.

"Exactly where you predicted it would be, General. It had been concealed in one of the ancient temples near the coast of Crete." Servius seemed pleased to relay the information.

With questioning eyes, Caesar looked up from his inspection of the mechanism. "I trust it wasn't too much trouble to acquire?"

"We searched for several days before finding the location. Once we found the temple, it was a matter of locating where it had been hidden. As I said, it was right where you predicted. Once we extracted the object, no one even noticed us taking it. I believe the locals had forgotten that it even existed, much less where it was hidden."

"Excellent." Caesar raised an eyebrow and smiled. He bent his knees to get a better look.

Inscriptions adorned several gears, and more had been carved into the soft metal around the outside edge of the box. Caesar ran his finger along the grooves, his lips moving slowly as he read the ancient words.

Servius seemed slightly perplexed. "We couldn't understand what the words mean, General. It's old Greek, but everything is jumbled. None of us could make sense of it."

That was exactly what Caesar had hoped Servius would say. He'd taken a risk sending others to retrieve so powerful a device, but he put all his hopes in the fact that his men would simply obey and not ask too many questions. His assumptions had been correct, including the one that no one would be able to decipher the code written upon the bronze gears and its container.

"I beg your pardon, General, but what is that thing?" Servius asked. The hardened commander's voice sounded like that of a confused little boy when he spoke.

Caesar straightened up and clasped his hands behind his back. "This, Servius, is an ancient relic known as the Eye of Zeus. There are only three known to have been created in history."

"Eye of Zeus?"

The great leader nodded. "Yes. One of its uses is as a navigational tool for sailors. It works by plotting your position and path with that of the stars."

Servius seemed more confused than before. "So, you sent us on a secret mission to bring back a navigational device?"

Caesar nodded. "It can only be used at night, but with this object, our navies will be nearly unstoppable. We will be able to outma-neuver any fleet in the world under the cover of darkness, and strike at will."

"If you say so, sir."

Servius still wasn't convinced, which was exactly what Caesar wanted. The real power of the mechanism was something he would have to keep secret from everyone, even his most trusted advisor.

He had served with Servius Galba through the Gallic Wars, and the man had been a good friend. However, Caesar knew Rome, and he knew its politics. Romans in the position of power had a constant tendency to seek more; a trait his friend Servius could easily acquire.

Caesar had stumbled upon the existence of the ancient device from some scrolls he'd discovered after sacking a Greek village, a few hours' ride outside of Athens. It was by mere chance that he'd found the little library, hidden beneath a crumbling temple. He'd never been a very religious person, finding that he had more influence on the things in his life than a bunch of stone statues did.

He remembered standing in the decrepit place of worship, looking around with cynical eyes. He had laughed at the forms of the Greek deities that occupied the space. They were no different from Roman gods; only the names gave them any degree of uniqueness.

As he'd stepped toward the front of the building, Caesar's eyes moved to the base of a statue at the front. It was the famed patron deity of Greek culture. Zeus's long beard, flowing robe, and stern face still struck a chord of reverence, even for a nonbeliever. If there was a deity who had created the world, Caesar thought that god must certainly look something like the image of Zeus. At the base of the statue, he had noticed a chunk of stone had been broken away. Out of curiosity, he'd taken a closer look, only to find that the plinth was hollow and it appeared to contain something within. After a few minutes of hammering away at the sacred pedestal, Caesar had stumbled upon a small cavity filled with three tiny scrolls, stored in separate clay jars.

Servius brought Caesar's mind back to the present. "If you won't be needing anything else, General, I will take my leave."

Caesar's head twitched up. He waved a dismissive hand. "Of course, old friend. Go join the men. You've done well."

Servius snapped to attention for a moment before giving a quick nod and disappearing through the curtains. When he was gone, Caesar's eyes returned to the little bronze box. He had already decided he would keep the truth about the Eye of Zeus to himself. He hadn't lied to his friend; the device could be used to navigate the seas, and he would certainly use that to his advantage in the naval battles to come. However, Caesar knew the real power behind the relic, and he did not intend to let anyone else obtain that information.

He ran his fingers along the outside of the metal case and shifted one of the levers. The gears inside moved a little, rearranging the symbols and how they lined up with those on the exterior edge. Caesar took a step back from the relic and admired it. "An absolutely brilliant creation," he whispered to himself. "To think I have the power of a god at my fingertips."

The ship would reach the main harbor in less than two days. Once the mechanism arrived in Rome, there would be no one on Earth who could stop him.

1

DESTIN, FLORIDA

Sean knew there was trouble as soon as he saw the four men in the black suits and matching black ties. Guys dressed like that rarely showed up to bring good news. Usually, they brought trouble with them. Sean let go of the blind he'd been peeking through and pulled away from the window.

He had heard the black Denali drive into the parking lot of his little surf shop and thought nothing of it, merely glancing out the window as he went through some of his financial figures. His attention was roused when the four men with look-alike government haircuts closed the doors of their SUV.

A quick look at the front of the vehicle revealed no government-issue plates, which meant they were either some kind of secret operational group or they weren't with the government at all. Sean reached under the cash register and grabbed the Springfield .40-caliber XD he always kept nearby. During the years he'd worked for the Axis Special Operations unit, Ruger had been his weapon of choice. During a previous course of events that had resulted in preventing a global virus outbreak, he'd found a liking for the new gun and made the switch. Something about the balance and weight of the Croatian-made piece felt almost natural in his hand.

Sean took a step away from the counter toward the rear of the store. He had thought that after retiring from the International Archaeological Agency these kinds of situations would stop arising. When he'd attended the University of Tennessee in Knoxville, Sean had never really expected his life to go the way it had. When he graduated from college, Sean found himself working as a covert agent for Axis, a new branch of the federal government. He was part of the initial group of only twelve agents who met all the rigorous standards. Axis was designed to remain extremely small, thus retaining control of all facets of the operation with discretion and relative ease. While administration of the agency had been fairly smooth, being a field agent was anything but.

Sean felt like the few years he'd worked for Axis had probably taken a decade off his life in terms of the stress it caused. He'd been shot several times, and shot at many more. Some agents had been captured and tortured; something he was thankful to have avoided, but the possibility was always there.

When Sean's longtime friend, Tommy Schultz, had offered him a new life working for his archaeological agency, he'd taken it without reservations. Sean rested easy, knowing he'd served his country well and was ready to take on a new lifestyle; one he hoped didn't involve international intrigue.

However, that hadn't been the case. There'd been many more incidents involving guns, power-hungry criminals, and hired assassins. Sean didn't want to spend his thirties running from bullets and hiding from people who wanted him dead, so he told Tommy he was walking away from it.

Until now, retirement had been good to him. He had made enough money over the years to live comfortably for the rest of his life, without having to worry about an income. His cabin in the mountains of southern Tennessee was nearly finished, and his kayak and paddleboard shop had been doing well enough to support itself.

The little shop in Destin, Florida overlooked white sandy beaches leading down to the Gulf of Mexico's clear, bluish water. Sean hadn't bought the place to make money. He'd always enjoyed sea kayaking and had an interest in paddleboarding too. Now, he rented and sold to both tourists and locals, spending his early mornings and late afternoons out amid the waves.

He'd trimmed his shaggy blond hair, preferring to keep it shorter while residing in the hotter area of the country, and his skin had taken on a light bronze color over the top of his usual freckles.

The back door to the shop beckoned out of the corner of his eye as Sean watched the suited men approach the front entrance. He wondered if it would make a difference if he ran out the back. Whoever they were would find him eventually. It wasn't like he was trying to live off the grid. Sean simply hoped to avoid harrowing circumstances.

He gripped the gun tightly, keeping it low behind the counter so the men wouldn't be able to see it when they entered.

A little bell rang from the front of the store as the first, a tall, lean black man opened the door and walked in. The other three followed and immediately began assessing their surroundings. One went to the far corner in the back, the other two spread out accordingly to cover each point of escape. The first went directly to where Sean stood behind the register. His fingers tensed slightly, but he relied on old experience and training to keep his nerves calm.

The dark-skinned man stopped a few feet from the counter. His head turned one way, then the other, taking a second scan of the room for possible danger. When he was satisfied there wouldn't be a problem, he spoke in a flat, American tone. Sean couldn't be sure, but it sounded like Maryland's Eastern Shore. "You won't be needing that weapon, Mr. Wyatt," the man said coolly.

Sean raised a suspicious eyebrow. He wondered how the guy knew about the gun, but he also wasn't so sure he wouldn't need it. He shrugged. "Maybe. Maybe not. I guess that depends on why you gentlemen are here. If you're interested in renting a kayak or a paddleboard, I'd say you're right."

The man snorted, almost derisively. "I heard you liked to be a funny man sometimes. No, we are not here to take one of your boats out on the Gulf, Mr. Wyatt. I am agent Gerald Yarbrough of the

United States Secret Service. We are here by order of the president. He requests your presence immediately."

Sean's curiosity deepened. The president? What could he possibly want? Sean had met the president once, at a gala in Washington, D.C. He'd gone at Emily's request, despite a strong objection to the whole thing. He doubted the president would remember the occasion, and it certainly had nothing to do with his personal guards showing up in Destin on a Tuesday afternoon in the spring.

"I'm sorry, would it be too much trouble to ask for some identification?" he asked.

The Secret Service agent's face never flinched, and he remained perfectly still.

Sean continued his request. "It's just that you came in here with your Denali that, I might add, definitely looks like something our government workers would drive. However, I noticed there aren't any plates on the front. So again, I'm just going to need to see some ID." He emphasized his point by slowly raising his hand that held the gun, placing the weapon on the glass countertop. His fingers still wrapped around the grip and trigger. "If you know anything about my past, you'll understand why I'm a bit skeptical of anyone who shows up and tells me they work for the government."

Out of the corner of his eye, Sean noticed one of the men reaching for the gun inside his jacket. The other two on the far side of the room were about to do the same before Agent Yarbrough spoke up and stopped them. "At ease, men. No need to get antsy. If Mr. Wyatt wants to see my identification, there is no problem."

He reached into the right breast of his jacket and withdrew a thin, black wallet, and unfolded it in front of his face so Sean could see the badge. It was legitimate.

Sean's momentary relief was soon replaced by new concerns. The Secret Service didn't just show up randomly to talk to people. If the president wanted to see him, something serious was going on.

The lead agent glanced down at the gun Sean still grasped on top of the counter. "If you don't mind, Mr. Wyatt," he nodded at the weapon.

"Oh, I'm sorry," Sean said, blushing a little. "Force of habit, I suppose." He put the gun back out of sight and placed both hands on the surface. "Now, you were saying something about the president wanting to speak with me. What could he possibly want with me?"

"I'm not authorized to give you that information, Mr. Wyatt." The man's deep voice remained almost robotic as he placed the wallet back in his jacket.

"Not authorized?" Sean probed.

"All I can tell you is that you are to come with us immediately. The president will brief you himself when we rendezvous with him this afternoon."

Sean's eyes drifted around the room. "You know, I have a shop to run here. I can't just up and leave it."

"You have five minutes to lock up. The president will make sure you are compensated for your time." Yarbrough looked down at his silver watch's burgundy face. "The clock is ticking, Mr. Wyatt."

Sean sighed. Just when he was getting used to a relaxing lifestyle, another strange occurrence was thrown his way. "I'll need to bring my gun," he said.

Yarbrough seemed thrown off for the first time since he'd entered the building. One of his eyebrows lowered as he considered the request. "You may bring it with you, but not when we meet the president."

"Fair enough," Sean answered with a short nod. He picked the gun up and stuffed it in the back of his pants before walking to the back door and twisting the lock. His fingers flicked off a few light switches and he headed for the front door. "I'm going to hold you to what you promised about the compensation, Gerald. Is it okay if I call you Gerald?"

The agent gave no response, instead waving to the others to follow out the door.

Sean had met the Secret Service on more than one occasion. They were rarely social, probably because of the intense focus their jobs required and because of their training. After locking the front door to the shop, Sean walked over to the front passenger's side of the Denali and waited for Agent Yarbrough to unlock the vehicle.

"What are you doing?" the agent asked as he fished the SUV's keys out of his pocket.

"I'm riding shotgun. You can't expect me to ride in the middle of the seat back there. That's no way to treat a guest of the president." Sean offered a smart aleck smile, but didn't move.

One of the other agents cast a questioning frown at Yarbrough who shrugged and motioned for them to get in the back.

Sean opened the front door and hopped in. The scent of the black leather interior filled his nose, and he noted how the vehicle was impeccably clean. He wondered how often a government vehicle like that was detailed. He pulled the door shut as the other men climbed into the back of the vehicle. Yarbrough eased into the driver's seat and revved the engine to life.

"So, I guess we're heading to the airport and flying to D.C.?" he asked, buckling his seatbelt.

Yarbrough shook his head. "No. We aren't going to Washington." He put the vehicle in reverse and started to back out toward the busy road known as Highway 98.

Sean cocked his head to the side. "Camp David?"

"No."

"Then where is the president?" Sean seemed bewildered.

"Kiawah Island, near Charleston, South Carolina."

2

CORFU, GREECE

Dimitris Gikas was not a man who was accustomed to being disappointed. People, whose net worth ranged in the billions rarely were. However, at the moment he was extremely frustrated.

He finished chewing on a piece of lamb in rosemary burgundy sauce as he listened to his head of security describe what had happened. Gikas had sent Thanos to the United States on what he believed would be a simple errand. All he had to do was fly to Florida, pick up Sean Wyatt, find out what he knew about the Antikythera Mechanism, and then kill him.

If Wyatt knew nothing about the device, it was not a problem, so long as he ended up dead.

Gikas sat on his stone patio, looking out across the northern Ionian Sea. He held the phone close to his ear while Thanos explained what happened. "Four men got to Wyatt before we could do anything, sir."

A gentle sea breeze rolled up the grassy hill and through Gikas's short, black hair. It was a perfect day in the Ionian Islands, near the border of Greece and Albania. Days like today he loved to spend outside with his dogs and a good bottle of wine, produced at one of the many vineyards he owned across the region. Thanos's call had ruined any possibility of a relaxing day.

He stood up from the iron bistro table and paced along the stones to the edge of the grass. His head turned sideways for a moment, and he gazed across the wavy hills of grape vines extending far to the east. "What do you mean before you could do anything? You have men under your command. Could you not ambush the group and do what I asked you?"

Thanos had worked for Dimitris Gikas for over a decade. When Gikas expanded his financial empire to the tech realm, it had become apparent he would need an enforcer to help keep some things in line. Being no stranger to the seedy underworld of organized crime, Thanos had come highly recommended. His reputation for cruel efficiency had been a trait Gikas had admired in himself, and was one he certainly wanted for the person in charge of security. Of course, head of security was a title that hardly fit the work Gikas had Thanos carry out on a regular basis.

The tall, muscular bodyguard had come from the Greek army and would have made an excellent soldier. When he couldn't play by the rules, the military kicked him to the curb where Thanos began to make his own rules in the underbelly of society. He worked a few legitimate jobs as a nightclub bouncer, but it was hardly the work he was meant for. When he got a little too aggressive and nearly killed a man with his bare hands one night, the courts were about to send him to prison for a long time. Gikas made sure that never happened. With a few political donations and a little persuasion, Thanos had been released from jail. As soon as his feet hit the pavement, a black BMW 5 Series with darkly tinted windows picked him up.

In the back had been a short man with a stubble-covered face, dark hair, and a broad torso. Gikas remembered seeing Thanos for the first time and thinking he was the tallest Greek he'd ever set eyes on.

He pushed aside the memory and listened to his chief bodyguard's explanation. "They appeared to be U.S. government, sir. I don't know which branch. If I had to guess, I'd say FBI, but they could be something else."

"And you had no way to take out the vehicle?"

There was a pause on the other end. "No. The roads are too crowded down here. Too many witnesses." Thanos's raspy voice sounded as frustrated as Gikas felt.

"Where did they go?" he asked, rubbing a free hand across his sweating forehead.

"We aren't sure yet," Thanos answered. Knowing the response would anger his employer further, he continued. "We are still following them. I sent the men in the other car into Wyatt's shop, though, and had them search the entire place. They said there was nothing but a bunch of kayaks and boards in there."

Gikas drew in a long breath and sighed. What were federal agents doing apprehending Sean Wyatt? The timing was strange, too strange to be a coincidence. There was no way the United States government was aware of what was happening; at least that's what Gikas forced himself to believe. He knew their tentacles reached far and wide across the globe, but Gikas had kept to the shadows, carefully orchestrating everything from behind the scenes.

While the Greek economy continued its downward spiral, Gikas had continued to make enormous amounts of money from other places in the world. He was careful to keep his assets where they couldn't be touched by his greedy government, who desperately sought to snatch up everything they could from the few wealthy people left within their borders. Gikas had no intention of leaving his homeland. To the contrary, he had his sights set on the highest prize possible.

The death knell was about to ring on the Greek government. The country's reckless spending and lack of a stable gross domestic product meant they sent way more money out than they had coming in. Importing things from all over Europe and the United States had resulted in a leaky economy that no one could fix. Most of the wealthy people in Greece had under-the-table deals with government officials. They'd allowed their federal deficit to swell despite knowing the problems that would ensue. What did they care? They would be rich, and rich people could figure out a solution later. Gikas knew that it was only a matter of time until the outcry of his people would lead to a change in regime. When that day arrived, he would be ready to give them a leader and return the ancient country to its former glory under a new monarchy.

It would be a glorious tale, too. When he was just a child, Dimitris Gikas spent long days in his parents' vineyards and wineries. At the tender age of six, both of his parents had been killed in a car accident. Young Dimitris was sent to an orphanage, where he first learned the hard lessons that life had to offer.

He was small for his age, and was regularly picked on by many of the other boys. What he lacked in physical stature, though, he made up for in wits. By the time he was nine, Dimitris was making a few dollars a week selling cookies to people in town. He'd discovered a local baker who threw out cookies at the end of each day, knowing he would be unable to sell them the next. Dimitris had never been shy, and asked the baker if he could have the cookies. The man was happy to give them to the child, since he was only going to throw them out anyway.

Dimitris took the cookies down the streets of the city, selling them to every person who passed by. Each day he would make his way back to the orphanage with a pocket full of money. It was always a precarious proposition to sneak past the other boys without them noticing. Every night when he went to sleep, he dreamed of the day he could return to the family land where the vineyards rolled through the countryside, and the ocean sea breeze washed over the land.

Dimitris never took a keen interest in school and didn't excel. He didn't understand why it was important to learn things he already knew about, or didn't need to know about. He did, however, continue his entrepreneurial ventures. He'd taken his little cookie business and expanded into other products. When he reached his seventeenth birthday, Dimitris Gikas had four different businesses going simultaneously, and they all brought in more money than some of his teachers made.

Even with all the early success, Dimitris Gikas was never satisfied. One of his teachers had told him they'd never seen such an ambitious young man before. He took offense to the comment, but said nothing. Dimitris didn't want to be looked at as some charity case who was doing something cute with his businesses. He wanted to be the wealthiest person in all of Greece. Because of that, he had developed a desperate thirst for power.

Maybe his quest for control and absolute authority had come as a result of several instances where he'd been beaten senseless by other children. The fact that he had successful businesses at such a young age brought a great deal of undesirable attention to the young Gikas. At one point, some of the boys in his school had beaten him so badly that he feared he might go blind from the wounds to his face. When he didn't, he swore that someday he would get his revenge.

Now, he was worth billions, and the boys who had beaten up on him in school were working menial jobs in his companies.

His thoughts returned to the present. There were only two other men who could challenge him for a position as sole ruler of Greece. One, Kostas Maragos, had built his wealth through the dairy industry. While Maragos had a considerable amount of money, it was far less than Gikas. Maragos, however, had ties with the current government. Those ties could potentially prove problematic if it came time for a new election. Gikas was done with elections. It was time for a return to the old ways.

The second man actually wanted the same thing as Gikas. Vasilis Leventis believed in what some of the ancient Greek philosophers taught, which was that the only stable government was a monarchy. Democracies and republics were temporary forms of government at best, some of the ancient sages had written, and would eventually crumble to the whims of popular opinions.

While Leventis was ambitious, he also had his own set of problems. Through an extensive amount of research, Gikas discovered some of his opponent's deepest, darkest secrets. They were weaknesses that Gikas could use to his advantage. Leventis would be easy enough to eliminate. Maragos, on the other hand, would take a little more discretion. The dairyman was as squeaky clean as anyone Gikas had ever come across. Getting Maragos would be tricky, and they were running out of time. The government's total collapse was imminent and could literally happen any day.

"We are following the vehicle Wyatt is in, sir," Thanos said. "For the moment, they are heading east. I will keep you informed of any further developments."

"Make sure that you do. We need to find out if he knows anything that the girl isn't telling us, but if that isn't an option, you know what you need to do."

"Of course, sir. He will be taken out of the picture."

Gikas ended the call, set the electronic device back down on the table, and looked across it at his dinner companion. She was beautiful, with a slender, athletic build and hair like dark chocolate cascading over her right shoulder. Her pinkish-red lips were plump like thin berries, and her lightly tanned skin looked like creamy mocha.

She said nothing, though in her eyes Gikas could tell she wanted to yell a million things. Actually, she probably wanted to jump across the table and snap his neck, something he knew she was fully capable of from his intel on her. The deadly set of skills she possessed were the main reason Gikas had three armed guards watching her around the clock.

His patience was wearing thin with her. He'd tried to be cordial, despite the fact that she was his prisoner. All he wanted was some information that he believed she possessed. For the last three days, though, she had produced nothing and seemed as though she intended to keep whatever knowledge she had a complete secret.

"I just got off the phone with my men in the United States," Gikas said, plucking the glass of wine from the table and holding it out with his arm half cocked as he sat down. He crossed one leg over the other in dramatic fashion, exposing pale feet that dipped into black slip-in shoes. "They said that someone else got to your boyfriend first. I wonder who else he might have angered."

The woman in the chair opposite him remained silent, her arms crossed over the tight gray T-shirt she wore.

Gikas took a long sip from his glass, and then set it back down on the table. "You haven't eaten much," he said and motioned to the lamb and vegetables in front of her. "I assure you it is not poisoned. If I wanted to kill you I would have already done it. You must be hungry, so please, eat."

She stared at the food for a few seconds, contemplating. She'd fasted before, but it was going on the third day since she had eaten anything. Water had been the only sustenance to pass her lips since she'd been taken captive. Her instincts gave in, and she devoured the food, first tearing into a piece of bread, and then some of the meat. In a few minutes, the plate was completely clean.

Gikas watched with a creepy smile, as if he were staring at a caged animal eating the morsels from his hand. "That's better."

Her eyes darted up from the plate, and her face washed over with guilt. She wished she hadn't had to eat his food, but she couldn't let herself starve. She wouldn't give him the satisfaction.

He folded his hands and placed them on his knees. "Now, tell me everything you know about the Eye of Zeus, Miss Villa."

3

FLORIDA PANHANDLE

S ean pulled the iPhone out of his pocket and entered the pass code.

"What are you doing?" agent Yarbrough asked, casting a wary glance out of the side of his eye, at the same time keeping focused on the road ahead.

Sean's thumbs flew across the digital keypad with speed and accuracy. It only took a few seconds for him to finish the text to Emily and hit the send button. "Just doing a little background check on you." He flashed a mischievous glance at the driver. "I hope you don't mind."

Yarbrough turned his head and looked directly at Sean with a quizzical expression. "Background check?"

"I know you showed me your ID back there, but I like to be thorough. Figured a guy from the Secret Service would appreciate that." He smiled wickedly and looked out the windshield. "Don't worry. Just a friend in the Justice Department who can tell me if you're legit or not."

The driver shrugged. "Would it make a difference at this point? You don't really have a lot of ways to escape now."

It was a valid point, but one Sean had already considered. His training and experience taught him to always look for an out, always keep your eyes open and be ready for when a window could appear.

"Probably not," Sean agreed, while eyeing a grassy field that zoomed by. His phone vibrated, and he glanced down at the screen. There were only two lines.

"He checks out. You okay?"

"Emily says you're okay, Yarbrough. Guess I'll have to make my escape some other time." His eyes took a moment to peer into the rearview mirror. There were so many cars out on the road between Destin and Pensacola, but Sean had seen one in particular that caught his eye for the last hour. It wouldn't have been strange, given the fact that there were hundreds of thousands of vacationers in Florida at that time of year. The black BMW sedan had remained several cars back over the course of the last forty minutes, almost as if they were trying not to follow too closely. In their attempt to remain inconspicuous, the driver of the sedan had made it obvious as to what they were doing.

Sean looked back at Agent Yarbrough with a blank stare. He waited for a second, as if hoping to get a reaction. When Yarbrough said nothing, Sean spoke up. "You do realize that you're being followed, right?"

Yarbrough's face contorted into a frown, the kind that people get when they feel like something they just heard is crazy. His eyes took a quick peek in the rearview mirror. "Who's following us?" he asked finally. "I haven't seen anything unusual."

"Maybe not," Sean said, slipping his phone back into a pocket. "But that black BMW five cars back has been five cars back ever since we left Destin."

Yarbrough took another look in the mirror. "So? There are a lot of cars on this road."

"That's a 5 Series, Ger. Those things were made to run. When was the last time you saw one of those driving so slow?"

"Maybe it's an elderly person behind the wheel?"

Sean raised a skeptical eyebrow. He noticed a convenience store ahead, which gave him an idea. "Pull into that gas station up there on the right."

"Mr. Wyatt, we really are in a hurry. I appreciate your concern, but—"

"A. don't call me Mister Wyatt. You can call me Sean. B. just trust me. Wouldn't kill you to top off the tank anyway. If they don't follow us in then we pull back on the road." His rationale made sense, especially considering the implications. "You lose thirty seconds at worst if I'm wrong."

The filling station was approaching quickly. Agent Yarbrough had to act fast. Sean stared at him from the other side of the car, as if willing him to do what he requested.

"Fine," Yarbrough said and flipped on his blinker. "But I do believe you're being paranoid."

"Maybe I am," Sean said and leaned back in his seat. He cocked his head to the side to watch the rearview mirror to see what the BMW would do.

As Yarbrough slowed down and steered the SUV into the gas station, Sean watched as the black sedan continued down the road. He couldn't see through the darkly tinted windows, but within a second the car had passed on down the road. His heart sank at being wrong, but he also felt a twinge of relief.

Agent Yarbrough noticed the BMW passing the entrance to the station and shook his head. He pulled the SUV into one of the pumps and switched the car off.

Sean expected him to say something about being paranoid, but instead Yarbrough let it go. "We need to get gas anyway. It will just take a second." Sean was glad to see the younger man was respectful enough not to gloat.

The other guys in the back were not so forgiving. "Probably a good thing you hung it up with the Justice Department a few years ago, huh?" one of them said.

Sean didn't even turn around. He'd seen young guys like that before. They were cocky and arrogant, but the most important thing they seemed to forget was that they were in a job where their lives could change within the second. Maybe they got used to it, always being in the line of fire for the president. Sean never got used to it, which was why he walked away from Axis after only a few years of service.

He stared at the leather dashboard for a moment, ignoring the laughter from the backseat when he caught something out of the corner of his eye. Sean turned to the left and saw the black sedan turning into a fast food restaurant a few hundred feet down the road. He peered through the window as the BMW looped around behind the restaurant and disappeared on the other side.

Agent Yarbrough finished pumping the gas and got back in the car. Sean looked at him and wondered if he'd seen what the driver of the other car had done.

"Yeah, I saw it," Yarbrough answered the unspoken question.

"Saw what?" asked the disrespectful guy in the back.

Sean turned halfway toward the rear. "The car that was following us pulled into that burger joint over there." He pointed in the direction of the restaurant.

All three of the men in the back twisted their heads to the left. "So? Maybe they're hungry," said the one in the middle.

Yarbrough interjected. "You don't think it's odd that they skipped the drive-through and all those empty parking spots on this side?"

No one said anything else. Yarbrough started up the engine. He flicked his head in the direction of the right side of the dash. "There's a nine-mil Sig in the glove box. You might want to take it." His face became immediately concerned. "Looks like you were right, Sean. And the only thing they could possibly want from us is you."

Sean opened the glove box and removed the black weapon. He'd always liked Sigs, though his loyalty to Ruger and Springfield were well rooted. "Always good to be wanted," he said jokingly.

Yarbrough guided the vehicle back onto the main road, heading in their previous direction. He watched out of the side of his eye as they passed the fast food restaurant, catching a glimpse of the black sedan waiting on the other side. The windows were darkly tinted, but not enough to keep the car's occupants completely hidden. Sean saw the four men as well, appearing as if they were waiting on something.

"Any idea why they're so interested in you?" Yarbrough asked and jammed his foot on the gas pedal.

"I'm still not sure why the president is interested in me. Care to fill me in on that one?"

The agent merely shook his head.

Sean wasn't surprised. "Of course not. So, I have two groups of people after me, and I have no idea why. At least when I worked for Axis I knew why I was being chased, and who was doing the chasing." He stared into the rearview mirror, observing the BMW as it pulled back onto the main road, several hundred feet behind them.

Yarbrough's eyes shifted to the mirror on the windshield. "We will be at the airport within five minutes. I hope we don't have to hold them off. On a crowded road like this, there are too many civilians."

Sean had considered the same thing. Collateral damage was something he had always tried to avoid, especially when the collateral was people's lives. He took another peek in the side mirror to make sure the sedan was still back there. It was four or five cars back and impossible to tell what the men inside looked like. He scanned the road ahead and saw the fencing of the airport.

"Almost there," Sean said with a hint of relief.

"Yeah, except the entrance is on the other side. We have to turn off the main road to get to where our plane is." Yarbrough's explanation dispelled any sense of reprieve Sean may have felt. The driver touched his earpiece and spoke again, this time to someone inside the airport. "Ballard, get a car to the front of the gate. We've got a tail. As soon as we pass through, blockade the entrance."

Sean didn't hear the response but he imagined that somewhere inside the airport fencing, another group of Secret Service agents were hurriedly carrying out the order.

"There's the access road," Yarbrough said, pointing to a street that shot off the main highway.

"Looks lonely," Sean said, looking at the side street. "Which is probably just what they want."

He heard rounds being chambered by the men in the back of the Denali. They held their Sig Sauer's close and at the ready.

Yarbrough switched on the blinker and veered the vehicle onto the side road. As the broad side of the SUV swung around, Sean got a better look at the trailing BMW, but still no visual of the men within it.

"Hang on," Yarbrough barked, and then mashed on the gas.

The Denali lurched forward, forcing the occupants' heads back a little as it accelerated. A quick glance back in the mirror told Sean exactly what he'd expected. The sedan turned sharply onto the road and closed the gap quickly, despite Yarbrough's quick trigger on the gas. In mere seconds, the much faster Bavarian car was on the SUV and tightening the space between the bumpers. Thick flatland forest blurred by outside as the two cars sped along the deserted road.

The BMW merged into the left lane, intent on pulling up next to the Denali. Yarbrough repeatedly glanced out the side of the vehicle as both of the sedan's passenger windows began to open. When he saw the black barrels protrude through the openings, he didn't wait for the men to fire. Instead, the Secret Service man slammed on the breaks and let the German car push ahead.

The driver of the BMW adjusted and slowed down, which turned out to be a mistake. Yarbrough punched the accelerator and the Denali hurtled forward again, slamming hard into the tail end of the sedan. The front vehicle shimmied for a second, but the man at the wheel corrected and sped up, getting clear of the SUV's grill. As soon as the car had opened up a small space, two men with handguns leaned out of the rear windows. The one on the left, a blond guy in a white polo, opened fire first, sending a volley of metal into the windshield of the Denali. A few white streaks splashed across the glass as the stray bullets deflected harmlessly away. The guy leaning out the right window of the BMW began firing as well, aiming low at the vehicle's grill and tires. Sean ducked for cover as the rounds continued to pound the front of the vehicle.

"Bulletproof glass," Yarbrough said and stomped on the brakes.

"Yeah, but the tires aren't," Sean said, sitting back up in the seat.

He yanked the slide back on the Sig Sauer and rolled down his window.

"Sean, get back in the car. Let my men handle this."

His order fell on deaf ears. Sean had been out of the game for a few years, but not so many that he was useless in a gunfight. "Old habits, Agent Yarbrough," he said with a smirk.

"Sean, I'm ordering you to stand do—"

It was too late. Sean leaned out the window, and Agent Yarbrough took the cue to speed up again.

"Hold it steady!" Sean shouted above the sound of the wind ripping through the Denali's cabin.

The men firing from the BMW paused for a moment and ducked back into their vehicle to reload fresh magazines. Sean used the second to his advantage and fired a single shot. The bullet found its way harmlessly into the trunk of the sedan. He started to squeeze the trigger again, but the SUV hit a pothole in the road. The bump jarred the vehicle, causing Sean to lose his balance. He shot his hand out toward the grip just inside the window. His body's momentum nearly carried him through the open window, but three fingers hooked around the handrail and steadied his fall.

He imagined Yarbrough's face twisted into a disapproving glare, but he didn't check. Instead, Sean leaned back out the window and trained his sights on the back right tire of the BMW. The two men were climbing back out, their weapons fully loaded and aimed in Sean's direction.

This time, he fired off a quick sequence of shots, the third of which caught the target squarely in the center of the wide rubber piece. For a second, the car wavered slightly, and then began to slow. Sean expected the driver of the sedan to lose control, but he didn't. Sean had an epiphany as the men in the back of the car launched another salvo. *Run-flat tires.*

Sean hoisted himself back into the SUV as the next hail of bullets cracked against the heavy glass. Yarbrough slowed down again, repeating his maneuver. It had the same effect, creating space between their car and the black sedan.

"Sorry," Sean said as he checked his magazine. "They've got run-flat tires."

"That's okay," Yarbrough said. "We're at the gate."

The Secret Service man slammed on the brakes and watched as the BMW sped by. He turned the wheel sharply, whipping the big vehicle into the drive and through an opening between the fence and a small guard shack. They zipped by a similar Denali that moved in to block the gate.

"This is a military airbase," Sean said, realizing where they were headed. "Lot of special ops missions come through this place, if I'm not mistaken."

"Sounds like you're pretty informed."

"I did used to work for the government, you know."

"Yes. We know," Yarbrough smirked.

Sean's eyes darted around the quiet airbase. It certainly was convenient to be able to use an asset like this when it was needed. His gaze went to the driver. "Good to have friends, huh?"

Yarbrough's eyes didn't leave the tarmac as he sped toward a lonely hangar off to the right. "Never hurts."

4

CORFU, GREECE

"What do you mean, you lost them?" Dimitris Gikas slammed a balled fist on the kitchen counter. A round tumbler, half-filled with Scotch, shook for a second after the sudden close call with the hand. The other held a cell phone to his ear.

"They turned into a military airbase, sir. No way we could follow them in there."

Gikas knew what the consequences would be. He didn't need his underling to explain anything in that regard. What he did want to know was how Thanos and his men had allowed Wyatt to get that far. "Why didn't you stop them before they could escape?"

"We tried, sir. I accept full responsibility. We attempted to shoot out the tires but they were equipped for that. Also, you should know their vehicle had bulletproof glass." Thanos's answer didn't please Gikas, but it gave him a clue as to whom they might have been up against.

Bulletproof glass wasn't extremely difficult to come by, but its weight and expense made it an irrational option for most people. The luxury wasn't optional for most consumers; extraordinarily wealthy business people were one market, world leaders another batch that would make the short list.

Based on the description his man had given earlier and this new information, the list grew even shorter. He released his anger and lowered his voice. Night had fallen over the Greek island, and the sounds of evening began to carry through the open windows, various insects, birds, and the constant crashing of the sea in the distance. "These men you described earlier; tell me again what they looked like. What were they wearing?"

"They all wore the same suits, sir. Every one of them looked alike. They all had short haircuts too. One was a black man; the rest were white."

Gikas rubbed his chin for a moment then grabbed the glass from the counter and took a long sip of the golden Scotch. He swallowed hard, letting the burn soothe the back of his throat before setting the glass back down. "You mentioned that they went to the airport, but turned in through a private gate. Correct?"

"That is correct. And," Thanos's raspy voice added, "another vehicle was waiting at the gate to block the entrance."

Gikas processed the additional information for a second. He paced from one end of his extravagant kitchen to the other, stopping at the stainless steel Sub-Zero refrigerator. He spun around and stared across the room, looking out at the wooded hill behind his the estate. "They're definitely U.S. government," he said. "From what you described, it sounds like they are most certainly Secret Service."

"The protectors of the United States president?" Thanos sounded doubtful.

"Agreed, but that is the only thing that makes sense." Gikas trailed off.

There was a tense moment of silence between the two men. Finally, Thanos broke the quiet. "Why would they want Wyatt?"

"It could be anything. He's a loose cannon. Perhaps he did not pay his taxes," Gikas stopped to think about another possibility. It was doubtful, but certainly possible. Was the president looking for Wyatt's help with something? And if so, what?

Gikas had read Sean Wyatt's dossier. He knew exactly what the former Axis agent was capable of. According to his file, Wyatt had gone to work for the International Archaeological Agency after leaving the Justice Department. Instead of a relaxing job doing research, he'd been involved with securing lost artifacts and getting them safely to whatever museum or analytic facility needed them. On more than one occasion, Wyatt had found himself in sticky situations, but he'd always come out clean on the other side.

In recent forays, the former Axis man had made the discoveries of a lifetime, finding what was the final resting place of Noah's ark, and supposedly the last remains of the Garden of Eden. In the course of the events leading to the incredible finds, he had killed several high-end mercenaries. "Keep your ears open. If you hear anything through any of our channels, find the leak and plug it."

"Of course. I'll handle it personally." There were another few seconds of silence before Thanos spoke up again. "What should we do about Wyatt? There's no way we will be able to get to him."

"Forget about him for now. If he is with the Secret Service, he likely has his own problems. Besides, I have the girl here with me."

Thanos laughed subtly. "Has she told you anything?"

Gikas could picture the man's thick face, twisted in a sickly grin. "No, but she will. Everyone has their breaking point."

Another chuckle came through the earpiece of the phone, a little louder the second time. "And what will you do with her once you have broken her?"

Gikas looked over at the door to the basement. He'd sent his prisoner to her cell as soon as dinner was over. He was done being cordial. It was his modus operandi for everything. It had become expected of him with both his friends and his enemies. When Dimitris Gikas wanted something, he did his best to get what he wanted without any trouble. More often than not, a simple exchange of money took care of the request. Sometimes, however, there were troublemakers, people who were too proud to bow out quietly. Whether it was a business deal, or as in this case, information he needed, Gikas was a man who was used to getting his way. Anyone who tried to keep that from happening usually met their end in a very slow and painful way.

Thanos had developed a less-than-gentle touch over the years. He seemed even more vigorous when it came to his lustful instincts. Gikas knew what kinds of twisted things his head of security was capable of. It was a big reason he'd put the man in charge. Thanos's reputation for cruelty was something Gikas had needed to make sure things always went his way. He was also the only person on the planet that Dimitris Gikas felt he could trust.

Through the years, he had paid Thanos a small fortune, making the man powerful in his own right. Never forgetting who had given him his break, Thanos remained fiercely loyal to Gikas. That loyalty was a stronger bond than anything anyone had ever thrown at the two men. From time to time, Gikas allowed his second in command a little leeway with his debauchery.

"This one?" he said into the device. "I may just let you have your fun with her, my old friend."

5

CHARLESTON, SOUTH CAROLINA

T he flight from western Florida to eastern South Carolina hadn't taken long. Through the years, Sean had tried to grow accustomed to the luxury of flying on private jets, but it was something that never got old. Every time he was forced to fly on a commercial airline, he longed for the decadent comforts of the IAA Gulfstream G5.

Even though the airport was relatively close to the president's location, the drive out to Kiawah Island was a slow, tedious cruise through the flats leading to the inlets and shallow waterways of the coast. Spanish moss hung from the ancient Southern willows lining the roads, casting the asphalt in an almost permanent shade. The sun's rays peeked through in a few spots every now and then, shining brightly onto the side of Sean's face like a strange, yellowish strobe light. He'd never really had a chance to head to Kiawah in all his visits to the historic town of Charleston. The city was one of his favorite places to visit when he wasn't working. Being surrounded by all that history plus good, Southern cooking and hospitality made it a definite stop on his travels each year. Sean frequently described Charleston as the Boston of the South. Seeing as how the city dated back to colonial times, that description wasn't too far off the mark.

Many of the homes dated back a few hundred years, and the graves in some of the old cemeteries held the remains of several influential people from the Revolutionary War.

The aesthetically designed exterior of the facility instantly impressed when the convoy of Secret Service vehicles arrived at the resort known as *The Sanctuary*. Its unique combination of Charleston brick, cream-colored stucco, wood, ironwork, and copper were complemented by the dark slate roofing. Sean had never grown tired of staying in a nice hotel. From the looks of this one, that truth seemed unlikely to change anytime in the next twenty-four hours.

He turned his head from side to side, letting his appreciation of the resort's design take over. The men from the Secret Service unloaded several pieces of luggage, and then let the driver cruise away in search of a parking space.

Yarbrough took a few steps in Sean's direction and motioned toward the entrance. "This way," he said blankly.

"Lead the way." Sean didn't even try to hide his amusement.

Even though the men who had peacefully abducted him were pleasant, it was still difficult for Sean to actually acknowledge the fact that he was about to speak with the president of the United States. Apparently, Sean was the only one in the group who would find any appreciation of that fact. It must have become trivial to the men who surrounded the powerful leader twenty-four hours a day.

The group strode swiftly through the entrance, a set of glass doors underneath an enormous, pyramid-shaped awning made of poplar. Inside the lobby, the building opened up to high ceilings and wide thoroughfares. An ornate chandelier hung from the ceiling, showing off thousands of crystals. Directly ahead, several large windows and glass doors opened to display unobstructed views of perfectly groomed Bermuda grass that stretched all the way to the oceanfront. The facility's two guest wings wrapped around the centrally located lawn like the lower end of a tuning fork.

A seating area designed to look like a big living room sat between two bars. The bar to the right was decorated daintily with nineteenth- and early twentieth-century art that featured feminine overtones.

Glass cases were filled with fine china, lacey tablecloths, and fine dresses. On the wall behind the bar, a portrait of a nineteenth-century woman in a fashionable dress hung as a symbol of the lady of the manor. Directly across from it, beyond the sitting room, was a second bar. It was adorned with masculine trinkets like old sports memorabilia, antique guns, hunting portraits, and cigar cases. Mirroring the women's bar, a portrait hung over the bar on the men's side. It featured the man of the house, a burly, handsome character with a thick mustache and a commanding glare.

Sean remembered reading about how, in the old days, a man had his side of the house and a woman had hers. The two bars and the sitting area were a new tribute to a time nearly long forgotten.

He glanced down at the floor made from old, reclaimed wood from several old mansions and factories in Charleston. He admired the thick, dark beams and wondered what stories the gashes and grooves might tell if they could.

Yarbrough and the other two men turned left and headed toward the eastern wing of the hotel. A grand staircase wound up to a second floor sitting area. A sign at the base of the stairs indicated that the famed Ocean Room restaurant was located above. Sean had heard of the place. He hoped he'd get a chance to eat there at some point, but he had the sneaking suspicion that his stay at The Sanctuary would be a short one.

They continued down the corridor and turned right into a narrower hallway. They passed an elevator on the left and walked almost halfway down the passage before stopping at a closed door on the right.

Sean frowned. "The president is staying in a normal guest room?" he asked, finding the notion somewhat odd.

Yarbrough nodded. "The president stays where he wants. This was the room he wanted."

"Interesting."

The agent rapped on the door twice. A second later, it cracked open revealing another black-clad agent just inside. A young, white male with his head nearly shaven clean and dark stubble on his face smiled through the opening. "He's waiting for you."

The door opened wide, allowing Sean and Agent Yarbrough to pass through. The man inside closed the door as the other agents in the hallway continued to scan their surroundings for any potential security threat. The interior of the room was as nice as anything Sean had seen before, at least for a hotel's standard guest room. It was no surprise that the resort had been awarded the prestigious Five Diamond Award for excellence.

At the moment though, the room wasn't what was on Sean's mind. It was the man at the table in the corner. The closest he'd ever come to meeting a president was when he was a child in the 1980s. Ronald Reagan had flown to his hometown for a brief visit, but Sean had only caught a glimpse of the man from a distance. Now he was standing fifteen feet away.

John Dawkins had experienced an odd rise to the oval office. He was born in Spartanburg, South Carolina, to parents who both worked in the education system. His father had been a physical education teacher, his mother a high school science teacher.

Dawkins had attended small public schools throughout his life, always blending in with the crowd, never really standing out in sports, or academics. That all changed when he arrived at college.

He'd attended the University of South Carolina on a meager academic scholarship, but eventually had earned a full ride due to merit. By the time Dawkins graduated with a degree in political science, his grade point average was a perfect 4.0, and he had served as an intern for a local congressman over the course of two summers.

His experience gave him a thirst for politics, but more than that, a desire to change the way things were in Washington. Dawkins had been severely disappointed to see how the political system actually worked. People all around him had taken money from special interest groups in exchange for their votes on certain issues. Often, the things they voted on directly opposed what their constituents would have wanted.

Dawkins took a stand against the corruption. At one point a

senior statesmen warned him about what he was doing, basically threatening Dawkins that if he didn't get in line, things could get ugly for him. One friend implored him to follow the lead and just do as he was told. After all, Dawkins could do more good in other areas as long as he played the game, but if he rocked the boat too much, he would be out come the next election.

His wife had always told him that he never listened, and this time was no different. He insisted that the politics of the United States government change for the better. During his first term, he accomplished little in the way of getting anything passed, but he won a second term and decided to take things into his own hands.

Congressman Dawkins built a website and posted questions to his constituents about the things he was to vote on. He asked them which way they wanted him to vote on every issue, giving the power of decision back to the people. He spent hours deciphering the language of complicated legislation so that the common people in his district could understand it and make an informed decision for themselves. Dawkins stood true to his new plan, voting the way the people wanted every single time.

The story about Dawkins spread like wildfire. The congressman who had returned the power to the people became a national phenomenon almost overnight. Millions of people began to ask why their representatives weren't doing what John Dawkins was doing. As a result, many were not re-elected to serve another term, and were replaced by those willing to be innovative and unselfish.

The presidency was something Dawkins had never really believed possible, especially considering the fact that he was an independent, unaffiliated with any political party. When the election came, he ran against two men who had both been enemies on Capitol Hill. Typically, Dawkins was a mild-mannered man with a quiet disposition and a nose that was constantly at the grindstone. Something changed when he entered his first presidential debate. He fiercely attacked the other two candidates, ripping apart their scripted retorts and firing back almost insulting comments that exposed the men for what they really were: puppets.

Now in his second year as president, Dawkins had already had a successful term by any standard. His leadership had resulted in a prosperous run for the country. His approval ratings were higher than that of any other president in history. No one wanted to run against him in the next election. They knew it would be fruitless.

Sean Wyatt stood silently as President Dawkins finished signing the last of several forms at the dark-brown table. Dawkins laid down the pen and removed the reading glasses from his sharp nose. His light-brown hair was still thick and cropped neatly atop a young, boyish face. A few lines creased his skin around his eyes, the only clues to the president's age. What Sean hadn't expected was to see the man in a pair of board shorts and an old T-shirt.

Dawkins set the glasses down on the table and stood to greet Sean. The man was an inch taller than Sean, who was a six-footer himself. The president crossed the room in two strides and extended his hand.

"Sean Wyatt? I'm John Dawkins. It's a pleasure to meet you." The president said it with a smile, but his voice told Sean that something troubled him. It had a sense of urgency to it.

"It's an honor to meet you, Mr. President," Sean said humbly.

Dawkins motioned to an empty chair across from where he'd been sitting at the table. "Please, have a seat. Can I get you anything? A bottle of water? A Coke?"

"No thank you, sir." Sean shook his head. "I'm fine."

He sat down in the proffered seat as Dawkins returned to his. Sitting closer to the patio door, Sean could see there were two agents standing just beyond the glass, keeping watch.

"I hope you don't mind my casual dress," Dawkins commented as he crossed one leg over the other knee. "I just came back from the beach."

Sean smiled weakly. "Yeah, I've never pictured the president in board shorts and a T-shirt before. Not going to lie, it's good to see you're human. Though I always thought you were." He chuckled as he said it and got the same reaction from Dawkins.

"I'm definitely human," he agreed. Dawkins thought for a

moment before continuing. "Sean, if you know anything about me, you know that I don't beat around the bush very much. I like to be direct, and I prefer to put things out there as quickly as possible so that solutions can be found and the job can be done. I look at everything that way."

Sean nodded. He knew that about the man. It was another endearing quality Sean appreciated.

The president swallowed hard and folded his hands. "When was the last time you heard from Adriana Villa?"

Sean's eyes narrowed. The question of how the president knew who she was flashed in his brain. The leader of the free world could likely get any information he needed or wanted in a matter of minutes. Sean had a bad feeling about where this line of questioning was headed.

"I don't know. A couple of days ago?" He answered with a hint of uncertainty. "She's investigating an ancient artifact she believes is located somewhere in Greece. We talked on the phone a few days ago, but I haven't heard anything from her since." Saying it out loud, Sean realized how long it had been. He hadn't been worried about her. Adriana knew how to take care of herself. She'd saved his life more than once. The fact that the president was asking about it, however, did present cause for concern. "What's going on with her?"

Dawkins took a deep breath and continued. When he spoke, his Southern tenor voice commanded the room. "I'll come back to that, but first, I need to ask you another question. Have you ever heard of a relic known as the Eye of Zeus?"

Sean bit his lower lip and shook his head. It didn't ring a bell. He thought for a few seconds, but couldn't recall ever hearing about such an artifact. "No," he said finally. "I don't think I have. What is it, and what does it have to do with Adriana?"

The president reached over to the far side of the table and picked up a manila folder. He passed it over to Sean and sat back. On the cover was a white label with two words Sean had seen before, though only in passing.

Antikythera Mechanism.

Dawkins knew Sean recognized the name immediately. He pointed at the folder. "That's what most historians call the Eye of Zeus," he said matter-of-factly. "Ms. Villa was looking for the Antikythera Mechanism, correct?"

Sean nodded slowly, beginning to connect the dots in his mind, dots he didn't want to bring together. He knew a little bout the device. It was named for a Greek Island near where it was discovered aboard a shipwreck. Based on what he'd learned through his own research, as well as Adriana's, the device was used as a means to predict solar eclipses and other astronomical events. The Antikythera Mechanism was discovered in 1901, and ever since, scientists and researchers have marveled at the intricate design of the device. It essentially proved that the ancient Greeks were an incredibly advanced civilization, far beyond what the history books tell. Sean got a creeping feeling in his gut that he was about to hear more about the story than he'd read so far.

Dawkins sat up straight, resting his elbows on the arms of the chair. "This needs a little backstory, so I may as well share that with you. The Greek economy has been in a nosedive for the better part of the decade. Their gross national product brings in less than what they import, jobless rates are soaring, and crime is beginning to rise."

Sean knew about all that. He didn't watch the news often, but he kept up with it enough to be aware of the current events going on in the world around him. He kept that to himself and simply nodded, listening intently to the president.

"The European Union is kicking them to the curb. Their government could collapse at any point, and when it does there will be a mad dash for the seat of power."

"That's the way it usually goes," Sean interjected.

"Yep. As far as we can tell, there are three major players in line to take over. One of them is a guy named Dimitris Gikas. He's a wealthy businessman living near Corfu, one of the Ionian Islands near Albania. Gikas made most of his money in real estate and land development, but he has investments in everything. About six years ago, he started buying up tech companies and vineyards, and even owns a significant amount of stock in American and Japanese companies. His net worth is well over four billion dollars."

"Sounds like a guy that might be able to straighten out their economy," Sean quipped.

Dawkins snorted a quick laugh. "He would be, if it weren't for the fact that he's one of the most ruthless men in Europe. Some of the businesses he purchased weren't for sale. Let's just say he made them an offer they couldn't refuse. And if they did refuse, the owners met an unfortunate end."

"Of course, the authorities won't do anything to a guy like that. Sounds like a modern-day Capone."

"Exactly. Everyone's on the take. Gikas is planning something big, we just aren't sure what it is or when it will happen." The president folded his hands and leaned back.

Sean opened the folder and removed the contents. There were a few pictures of the Antikythera Mechanism that resides in a museum in Greece. It was the only one known to be found. Adriana believed that there could be another one in existence and had taken it upon herself to find it. There was a small description of the device in the folder, explaining what historians believed it was used for. Sean had seen that stuff before.

He scanned the text, and then put all the contents back in the packet before handing it over to Dawkins. "I've read all that stuff before, Mr. President. I don't mean to be rude, but what does any of this have to do with me? I've been out of the espionage business for more than a few years now. If you need someone to go in and find out what this Gikas guy is doing, it isn't me."

"Actually," Dawkins said, "you couldn't be more wrong." He stood up and strode over to the entertainment system, where a bottle of water was sitting. He picked it up and took a big gulp, letting out a refreshing sigh after swallowing. "Have to stay hydrated down here," he commented, setting the bottle down again.

"South Carolina can be warm," Sean added, still not sure where this whole conversation was going.

"Sean, we believe that Dimitris Gikas is looking for a second

Antikythera Mechanism, and we also believe that the device may be the key to an incredible power."

Sean frowned. "Power? You mean like magical power?"

The president shrugged. "We honestly don't know. But we do know he wants it desperately."

"Maybe he's a collector of Greek antiquities," Sean offered.

Dawkins acknowledged what Sean had said by tilting his head to the side for a second. "He is certainly that. His home is filled with such things. But this one is different. Most of the relics he's purchased came at auction or through a well-known channel. Not to mention, there isn't a fully functioning device like that, at least not one we know of. He's become obsessed with it."

"I'm sorry, sir, but where is it again that I fit in to all of this?"

Dawkins sat down on the edge of the bed so he was closer to Sean. "Your friend, Adriana, was searching for the Eye of Zeus. The one that has not yet been found. She believed there is another one out there, correct?"

Sean nodded. "Yeah. She thought it was possible there was another one on land somewhere, one that would be intact. She also didn't buy into the idea that the device was only used for navigational purposes."

The president leaned in closer. "And what did she believe about the relic?"

"I don't know. She found some old diary about it. The thing was written entirely in ancient Greek, which Adriana can decipher. She said something about how it aligns with the stars and planets."

"That is correct. All of the research suggests that one of the purposes for the Eye of Zeus was for navigation by the stars. There is something else, though, that you should know." The president paused for a moment. He glanced over at the Secret Service agent next to Yarbrough. "Tyler, could you leave the three of us alone for a minute?"

The young man seemed uncertain at first, but Yarbrough gave him a confirming nod that everything would be okay. He slipped out onto the patio where the other two stood watch, and closed the door.

Dawkins turned back to Sean. "Only Agent Yarbrough and I have seen what I am about to show you, Sean. Outside of us, there are but a handful of scientists whose eyes have taken in this information."

Sean was skeptical, but his curiosity was piqued. Moreover, he was still wondering about what this all had to do with Adriana.

Before he could say anything, the president went on as he handed over another folder to Sean, similar to the first. This one, however, had the words *Classified Antikythera Mechanism* on the cover.

"Classified?" It had been a long time since Sean's eyes had passed over anything that had been classified for government use. For a second, he felt that sickening tug at his stomach, as if he was being pulled back into a life he'd tried so hard to get away from.

Things had been good for him lately. Running the surf and paddleboard shop had been the most relaxing job he'd ever had, and every day he was able to get out on the water and just reset himself.

Sean opened the file and looked through the initial page of text. As he shuffled through to the next, he saw symbols written in ancient Greek, matched with a translation on the right side of the page. The third document was an artist's rendering of the Antikythera Mechanism as it may have looked if it were completely intact.

"It contains a sequence of numbers and letters," the president interrupted Sean's thoughts.

"And the interpretation of the sequence was never released to the public," Sean finished the president's commentary. "So, this must be the mysterious information that tells us what is on the device."

"It is. And more."

Sean raised his eyebrows. "Let me guess; some of your scientists messed around with the relic."

"Not the relic itself. We don't have a working copy of it. However, they were able to get enough information from the original to run a few simulations."

"Simulations?"

"Yes," Dawkins answered. "They tested out what would happen if they plugged in certain numbers and letters. At first, they discovered nothing of note. One researcher had the idea to ask the mechanism questions based on the alignment of certain stars."

"You mean like astrology?" Sean huffed. He didn't believe things that bordered more on the side of hokum.

The president shook his head. "Not really. More like astronomy. The scientists matched up the reproduction of the Antikythera Mechanism and programmed in the date of the experiment. What they found was incredible. At first, the researchers didn't believe what they were seeing, but as they continued to enter places and dates from the past, the device continued to give them answers."

"What kind of answers?" Sean asked, thinking he already knew what Dawkins's answer was going to be.

"The relic was able to give names, events, and details that were a spot-on match to things that happened in history. In other words, the Eye of Zeus is able to tell the future."

6

NORTHWEST FLORIDA

T hanos ended the call on his smartphone and slipped it in his pocket. He stood outside the black BMW at a gas station on the side of the road. The late afternoon sun beat down on his bald head, causing little droplets of perspiration to dribble down the side of his face. He'd encountered problems before. That was why Dimitris Gikas trusted him. Thanos took care of problems. Usually, he took care of them quickly and efficiently. On this occasion, the problem was bigger than he ever could have expected.

He removed a handkerchief from the back pocket of his black pants and wiped the sweat from his brow. He missed one bead that found its way across the scar on his left cheek, but quickly dabbed it with the cloth.

The old wound didn't hurt anymore. It hadn't for a long time. He told his employer that it had only served to steel his resolve in life, to live it aggressively, and never to be afraid of anything.

The scar had come from a rival business leader in Athens. He was only sixteen when he'd begun serving the man known as Gilapos. The enemy wanted to send Gilapos a message. When he'd caught Thanos, the man's errand boy, he thought it was the perfect opportunity.

The act of cutting the young boy's face had not resulted in what Gilapos had intended. Thanos was already very strong, even in his young age. When the blade sliced through his face, he did not cry or scream. Instead, the pain only enraged him. In his short life, Thanos had faced far worse than a little cut. The insult, however, was something that he could not abide.

The man who held the knife had also been the one that tied the ropes binding Thanos to the chair. He'd only done a halfass job, thinking the young boy wouldn't be any trouble and that fear would do most of the work to keep him down. The man had thought wrong.

Thanos slipped his hands from the bonds in short order, even before the man with the knife had done his work. The sixteen-year-old knew that he needed to let the cutter do his work for his plan to work. As the man with the knife stepped back, Thanos sprung from the wooden chair like a rabbit. Skills he'd learned on the street kicked in, and he snapped the man's arm back at the elbow, breaking it in what was surely a painful angle.

The knife clanked to the floor as Thanos spun around and drove his elbow into the butcher's larynx. The man dropped to the ground, grasping at his throat with his good hand. Thanos knew he would be dead within a minute, so he left him and scooped up the knife.

The memory of that day lingered for a minute longer as the forty-year-old Thanos stared down the long, straight road. Pine trees blew in a strong coastal breeze. He smiled, remembering how the rival boss had begged for his life. The bulbous man had made the mistake of thinking he wouldn't need additional guards for a sixteen-year-old errand boy. Even as he bled out onto the concrete floor of the abandoned warehouse, his face was awash with shock at the turn of events that brought about his demise.

Thanos's employer had rewarded him for his loyalty and his bravery. He promised him that he would someday be the number one man in his organization, so deep was the trust of Dimitris Gikas toward Thanos.

For the last five years, Thanos had relentlessly served Gikas. So far, he'd never let the man down, but this situation with the Secret

Service was his biggest challenge yet. He didn't want to admit it, but they'd been lucky to escape with their lives. He let that notion go. Thanos didn't believe in luck. He relied on his strength and wits, and making his own fortune.

A major question, the only question that was on his mind right now, was what the Secret Service wanted with Sean Wyatt.

One of his men in the BMW opened the back door and stepped out. He was one of three hired guns Thanos had brought on. This particular man was Italian, with tightly cut, almost-black hair. His accent was thick, making his words somewhat difficult to understand.

"We have the president's location. It appears he's on vacation," he said.

"That would mean he's in Camp David. No chance of getting into that place." Thanos squinted one eye as he considered the information. The only plan now was to sit and wait until Wyatt left the presidential vacation compound.

"They aren't there, sir. The American president is in South Carolina. From the sound of it, he is in a public resort on one of the islands."

The new information caused Thanos to raise an eyebrow. "What would he be doing there?"

"I do not know the answer to that, but my source is good. And they said that the president has a guest."

It had to be Wyatt. Even if it were, there would be no way to get to him now. Secret Service agents and a security detail would surround him. Thanos knew they would have to be patient. It was likely that the president's visit with the former Axis agent would be short. They would need to act quickly to get to where Wyatt was headed. The problem with that being they had no idea where he was going.

Thanos thought for a moment as the Italian mercenary stood close by with hands on his hips, waiting for a decision. "Wyatt will go after the girl," he said with near certainty.

"How does he know that we have her?" the Italian asked.

"The United States government must have eyes on our employer," he said, casting a look around the area with a suspicious stare.

"Why would they be watching him?"

Another wind gust rolled across the flats, kicking up a swirl of sand and dust. Thanos squinted hard against the dust devil until it passed. "The eyes of the world are on Greece right now," he said as the wind died down once more. "The United States always meddles with other people's issues. They, no doubt, are interested to see what happens with the Greek government. If that is the case, they know that our employer is one of the leading candidates to become the next leader."

The Italian seemed pensive for a moment before asking his next question. "What is our move, then?"

When Thanos answered, it was with a sinister tone. "If Wyatt is going to come looking for the girl, it would be wise for us to leave him a trail to follow."

"And lead him into a trap?"

"Exactly."

7

KIAWAH ISLAND, SOUTH CAROLINA

S ean had trouble believing what he'd just heard. He knew that President Dawkins was an intelligent man, and in his career he had seen a lot of unbelievable things. An ancient hunk of metal that could tell the future, however, seemed a bit on the far-fetched side.

As if reading Sean's thoughts, Dawkins spoke up. "I know that is a little out there, but the numbers our scientists ran are pretty accurate."

Sean thought for a moment then raised a question. "If you guys can predict the future based on the computer model, you wouldn't need the device. No one would. So, why bother with finding it?"

Dawkins smiled. "I knew you were smart, Sean. I've heard a lot about you. Our tests are incomplete because much of the original Antikythera Mechanism was damaged. We were only able run trials based on the few symbols that were available."

"Did you try completing the Greek alphabet and subbing those letters in?" Sean asked, thinking that was the obvious solution.

"We did. It threw everything off. Some of the symbols that were unreadable do not come from the standard Greek alphabet, or the ancient one." Sean thought they had probably tried that, but it was worth asking. "Needless to say, a working version of the Antikythera Mechanism would be the most valuable device on the planet. In the wrong hands, it could be incredibly dangerous."

That went without saying. Sean's immediate thoughts went to a dictator type, like the leader of North Korea, or even a terrorist organization. With something like that in their possession, they could take over the world in less than a year. Nations would crumble. Billions would die. Sean could see the potential danger, but he still had doubts about whether or not the thing was real, or even if there was another version of the relic still out there.

"So, what is it that you want me to do, exactly?" he asked after a few moments of silent contemplation.

"We need you to find the Eye of Zeus," the president said plainly. He leaned forward a little farther with his elbows still on his knees.

Sean laughed out loud for a split second. "No big deal. Just find a three-thousand-year-old artifact with no idea where to start, and no leads." His comment brought him back to the questions about Adriana. She knew more than any of them about the Eye of Zeus. She'd been investigating it tirelessly. There was still something the president wasn't telling him. "Where is Adriana?"

John Dawkins looked Sean straight in the eyes, never flinching, barely passing a glimpse of sympathy to him through the ether. "She's been kidnapped."

The words struck Sean like a lead ball to the chest. Now it made sense why he hadn't heard from her in the last few days. He went over their last conversation concerning where she was and something she was going to investigate that day. Rome, if he remembered correctly. She'd been in Rome, researching some ancient documents regarding the Antikythera Mechanism. Sean squinted hard, hoping to recall the name of her hotel. Another question popped up in the back of his mind, distracting him from his focus for a moment. Why had she been in Rome searching for a Greek artifact?

He shook his head and refocused. Adriana was in trouble. That was all that mattered. He had to find her. Her face appeared in his mind's eye for a moment: passionate, caring, and full of courage.

"You will have any resources you need," Dawkins said, pushing the conversation forward. "I know that this news probably hurts. She's your girlfriend, correct?"

Sean had never called her that. He just assumed that was the case. "Yeah," he said in a choked voice.

"Sean, I know this is troubling, and you have my deepest sympathy. If it makes you feel better, we have reason to believe that she is still alive. The man that took her wants information, information that Adriana possesses. You'll need to move fast, though. I don't know how long Gikas will keep her around if she doesn't give him what he wants."

The thought flicked at Sean's heart. He'd been tortured once. It was the worst thing he'd ever endured in his life. Fortunately, he had escaped and made his way back to safety. He doubted Adriana would have the same opportunity. He pictured her in a dark room, bound and gagged, undergoing intense questioning. The idea tied his stomach in knots.

The president went on. "If you find the Eye of Zeus, Gikas will bring Adriana to you."

"Let me guess, you want me to work out a trade."

Dawkins nodded. "You catch on fast."

Sean knew how government types worked, even if they weren't really government types at their core. "Of course, I assume you won't be letting the Antikythera Mechanism get into the hands of kidnapper."

"We will have men on standby. As soon as Gikas presents her, they will move in."

"That means you will need to be in a neutral place," Sean's mind was already working.

"Precisely."

"This is all working on a huge assumption, Mr. President. What if I can't find this artifact? It may not even exist."

Dawkins stood up and clapped both hands on his thighs. "Sometimes you have to have a little faith, Sean. I am putting my faith in you that you'll get the job done. We cannot let Dimitris Gikas get his hands on the relic. It must be kept from him at all costs."

"Sounds like you believe this thing does exist," Sean said with a hint of cynicism.

The president didn't hesitate. "I do. And for the sake of your girlfriend, you should, too."

He made a good point. Sean knew he was right, too. A plan was already formulating in his brain. He would first need to find anything Adriana might have left behind regarding her research on the Antikythera Mechanism. From what he recalled, she constantly made backups of information she'd gleaned, sometimes digital, sometimes as low-fi as handwritten notes on napkins.

Sean would need help too. He would need an all-access pass to Europe. Getting his gun across borders wouldn't be an issue, but if he got caught with it he would need insurance that he wouldn't be incarcerated. On top of all that, there was one more thing Sean felt he needed.

"I'm going to need to bring someone else on to help me with this," he said after a few seconds of looking down at the floor silently. He raised his eyes and met with the president's.

Dawkins tapped his fingers on the Antikythera Mechanism files. "This is highly classified information, Sean. We cannot let any of it get into the hands of the public. I'm sure you can appreciate the sensitive nature of it."

"The person I'm talking about is used to working on delicate things like this, Mr. President. I need him. He has an intricate knowledge of ancient languages, cultures, and history. He's also handy in a fight. I trust him like a brother."

The president narrowed his eyes suspiciously. "What's his name?"

Sean smiled broadly. "My buddy from the IAA. Tommy Schultz."

8

CORFU, GREECE

Adriana lay on her side, staring out the lone window of the wine cellar. The chilly room was almost pitch black save for the pale light of the waning moon coming through the narrow window. A palm branch occasionally waved across her view, blowing in the breeze that rolled up the hillside from the sea.

The man who had abducted her had provided a military cot for her to sleep on, with only a thin sheet to provide her warmth. She fought to keep from shivering, knowing that two cameras were watching her at all times from the corners of the room. She wouldn't give them the satisfaction.

She cursed herself for being careless enough to get caught. The men had been waiting in her hotel room in Rome. She'd just returned from a locker she'd secured at the train station. Leaving all the eggs in one basket was something she'd avoided since getting into her sometimes-dangerous line of work.

When one of the ambushers stepped out from behind the door, grabbing her from behind, she'd dropped the locker key to the floor. As she sidestepped the stocky attacker, she kicked the key under a leather club chair in the corner with her left foot.

The man attempting to grab her took a knee to the groin as she used his momentum against him and pulled him toward her. He dropped to the ground instantly, moaning in agony. Unfortunately, there'd been a second man in the room. She heard the hammer of the pistol pull back.

She'd had no choice but to surrender. The man with the gun had been smart enough to keep his distance, but remain close enough that there would be no chance of missing his target. A second later, she'd felt a small prick on her thigh. The drugs worked fast, knocking her unconscious within a minute. Adriana didn't remember anything after that until she woke up on the strange island.

She'd heard the man in charge speaking in Greek a few times; his guards had done the same. Since there were only a few places where that language was spoken, it was safe to assume she was somewhere in Greece. The view of the Ionian Sea had confirmed that.

At first, she wondered if the men were human traffickers, just looking to nab another young woman. It was soon apparent that selling sex slaves was not the agenda of the men who held her. They were after the same thing she was, a fact that almost scared her more than the other notion.

Adriana had been researching the Eye of Zeus for months. Much of her knowledge regarding the relic came from an old book she'd discovered, a journal handed down through the decades. The origin of the diary was uncertain, at least at first. It had taken many hours of digging to discover the place that it had called home.

The Benedictine Monastery of Santa Croce was located in a region of Italy known as le Marche. Throughout the year, the place received visitors, mostly tourists, wanting to see a working monastery. The construction on the abbey was completed around A.D. 980, making it one of the oldest operating monasteries in Europe. Adriana had admired the structure, as well as its mountainous surroundings. The views from almost everywhere there were nothing short of astounding.

The builders of the monastery had included special windows in the scriptorium to allow light into the room throughout the day, thus providing the monks with the means to work longer hours on their translations.

It was in that scriptorium where a monk had created Adriana's journal several hundred years prior. Giordano Bruno had been an astronomer and historian in the early 1500s. His studies led him on a fascinating journey through the annals of time, landing on a piece of history he'd never been aware of before.

It seemed that the ancient Greeks had possessed a small cache of relics they'd used during the prime of their empire. When Bruno had discovered the history of the devices, fear filled his heart. The Antikythera Mechanisms were mechanisms that had supposedly been created by the oracles of ancient Greece. Bruno knew that if he documented the artifacts, and alluded to the manner in which they were created, he could be accused of heresy. To cover his tracks, he wrote everything in his journal in a language long forgotten to nearly everyone. Only one other monk in the abbey could speak old Greek, and that monk was twenty years Bruno's senior.

Adriana had found the book in an old bookstore in Copenhagen on a corner of the Strøget, a pedestrian street in the heart of the city. The storeowner explained that he had never encountered anyone able to read the book, and was glad that someone who could actually read it had wandered in.

Now, as she lay in the shadows of Dimitris Gikas's wine cellar, she wondered what was going to happen. She'd left Bruno's journal in a locker at the train station, along with something even more important. The diary had led her to a chain of extremely old documents that dated back over two thousand years to the time of Julius Caesar, and she believed that those papers were the keys to finding the last resting place of the Eye of Zeus.

Adriana hoped the men who'd taken her had been in a hurry to get out of the room. She figured that if they had discovered the key they would have already asked her about it, or would have found the locker and the contents within. Since they hadn't mentioned it, that meant at least the location of the mechanism was safe.

It was folly to hope for rescue. But there was no way to let anyone know where she was. Her phone had been taken, probably when she was unconscious, leaving her with no communication with the outside world. In her most desperate moments, she envisioned fanciful scenarios in which Sean burst into the cellar and took her away. She forced herself to focus on the situation. Thinking about ridiculous things like that would only make her predicament worse, and they were less than productive.

Adriana reminded herself that everyone slipped up from time to time. She simply had to wait for one of the guards to make a mistake. Even the tiniest of opportunities could be opened wide to a window of hope.

She closed her eyes and let exhaustion take over, trying hard not to think about what the next day might hold.

9

ATLANTA, GEORGIA

At first, President Dawkins had been hesitant to let Sean bring someone else on for the mission, but after getting his explanation as to who Tommy was and why Sean needed him, the president had been willing to make an exception. Dawkins knew of Tommy's exploits as an international treasure hunter, though Sean defended that insinuation.

"He's not a treasure hunter, sir," he'd said to the president. "A lot of the world's governments trust his agency to take care of their priceless artifacts. He's providing a good service at a premium price. He doesn't sell the things he finds. That's what treasure hunters do."

"Just make sure you keep a tight lid on this," Dawkins had said as Sean was leaving the hotel room.

Dawkins had given Sean full use of a small private jet, which Sean was happy to accept. Even though Tommy had the IAA company plane, Sean didn't want his friend to have to use it if it wasn't necessary. They'd be harder to track this way.

Sean knew Tommy would be in town since the two had exchanged a few text messages the previous morning. A new team, comprising Joe and Helen McElroy, was carrying out the IAA's current projects. Tommy had brought the couple on after Sean retired, needing to fill a void in the artifact recovery section. Joe had been instrumental in the discovery of Noah's ark, and Helen had helped take down the Biosure Corporation and its plot to infect the planet with a new super virus. The two made for the most logical replacement of Sean and were both happy to take the position. From what Sean had gathered, they were somewhere in Denmark at the moment.

When the airplane door opened, Sean was glad to see Tommy already there, waiting on the tarmac with two suitcases, a laptop bag, and a ridiculous grin. He'd let his oak-brown hair get a little longer, now just past the bottoms of his ears. He had on a white polo and khaki shorts, a common staple for him in the throes of an Atlanta spring.

Sean descended the stairs, followed closely by Agent Yarbrough. The president had insisted that Sean allow the Secret Service agent to accompany him on the mission. Sean had resisted, but he knew the president would have the final say. It also wouldn't hurt to have another gun along for the ride, though Sean hoped it wouldn't come to that.

Tommy let go of the rolling suitcases and opened his arms to give Sean a quick hug. Wyatt responded by slapping him on the shoulder, as was his usual greeting.

"Good to see you again, my friend," Sean said, grinning as he slipped on his Oakley sunglasses.

"Likewise, buddy," Tommy replied. "How are things with the bait and tackle business?" He chuckled as he asked the question.

"Very funny. The surf and paddleboard shop is doing fine, though it looks like I'm going to lose a few days of business." He glanced back over his shoulder at Yarbrough as if subtly blaming him for the occurrence.

"Who's your friend?" Tommy asked and stepped forward with a hand extended.

"Agent Gerald Yarbrough," he answered for Sean.

Tommy was impressed. "You really weren't kidding, huh. You met the president?"

Sean rolled his eyes and shrugged, making like it wasn't a big deal. "It wasn't my idea."

"That is so cool. Is he on the plane?" Tommy asked, sounding like a little boy.

Sean shook his head in disbelief. "No. He has his own plane. And I'm pretty sure that he's got better things to do than jet around the globe with us."

"Fair enough," Tommy surrendered.

Sean took one of the suitcases and hefted it up the steps to the cabin of the plane. It was similar in size to the G5 the IAA flew, but the interior was decorated very differently. Dark wood furnishings and tanned leather seats complemented the richly adorned walls.

Once everyone was aboard, the flight attendant closed the cabin door, and the engines whined, pushing the plane along the tarmac. Tommy sat across from Sean and Yarbrough, and crossed a leg over one knee.

"Where's Adriana?" Tommy asked abruptly, completely unaware of what had transpired.

Sean hadn't told him over the phone what was going on. He preferred to tell his friend in person. "She's been kidnapped, Tommy."

The words caused Tommy to scrunch his face, not sure if Sean was joking around or serious. "What?" He stared at Sean, searching for a crack in the armor. There was none. Sean's eyes told the truth.

Yarbrough cut into the conversation. "We believe she was abducted within the last forty-eight hours. The man responsible for this is one of the most powerful people in Greece. His name is Dimitris Gikas."

Tommy shook his head. "I'm sorry. I'm a little confused. If you know where she is and who has her, why haven't you gotten her out of there yet?"

"It's...delicate," Yarbrough said in response.

"Delicate?"

"She is not a citizen of the United States. You have to understand that we cannot just go into a man's private property with guns blazing and attempt a rescue. There are politics to consider." Yarbrough's answer didn't seem to help curb Tommy's frustration.

He held back his next question as the plane suddenly accelerated down the runway and began to lift off the ground. It tilted to the right and straightened out, still climbing at a dramatic angle.

"How do you even know this Gikas has her? Where did you get that little tidbit of information?" Tommy asked finally.

"We've had our eyes on Gikas for some time now. As one of the wealthiest, most ambitious men in the country, he is a likely candidate to become their new leader if the government breaks down. The president believes that Gikas is helping fuel the government collapse from within. We know he was formerly involved with organized crime in Athens, but now everything seems to be legitimate."

"Seems to be?"

Yarbrough folded his hands and put his elbows on his knees as he leaned forward. "Let's just say that Dimitris Gikas always gets what he wants, even if someone else doesn't want to give it to him."

Tommy seemed to accept the information for the moment, but was still troubled. "Okay, so we can't go after Adriana. What are we going to do?"

Sean had been listening quietly to the exchange and finally interjected. "I told you on the phone that we were heading to Rome to look for the Eye of Zeus."

Tommy nodded. "That's the thing Adriana was looking for, right? The Antikythera Mechanism?"

"Yeah. As it turns out, this Gikas character is looking for it too. And you're not going to believe why."

Tommy raised a curious eyebrow. "Try me. You and I have seen enough to believe almost anything."

Valid point, Sean thought. "The Eye of Zeus wasn't just a navigational device. Gikas believes that it could actually tell the future, based on celestial positions in relation to where the device was on Earth."

For a few moments, the only noise in the cabin was the low hum of the jet engines outside the plane. Tommy considered what Sean had said and leaned back in his chair.

"Okay," he said after a long breath. "So, this device can tell the future." Tommy sounded skeptical. "I could see why someone who wants to take control of a country would want to have something like that. Any idea where it is?"

Sean and Yarbrough passed each other an uncertain glance. It was Sean who answered. "No. We don't even know if we have any leads. The only thing I could find was the hotel Adriana was staying in and her room number. I just hope she left something behind that the kidnappers may have missed."

Tommy stared at Sean blankly. "You mean we don't have the slightest clue as to where this Eye of Zeus thing might be, haven't got a single lead, and we're flying halfway across the world on the slight possibility that we might find a breadcrumb?" He tried not to sound incredulous, but it was hard not to.

"Yeah, that's pretty much it," Sean shrugged. He was trying to be as calm as possible, but the truth was that inside he was worried about Adriana.

Tommy could tell his friend was upset, despite trying to hide behind his usual carefree mask. "I'm sure she's fine, buddy. Don't worry. We'll find her. Knowing Adriana, I'd be more worried about the guys who took her." He laughed at the thought, and Sean had a quick chuckle too. Yarbrough didn't get the joke and remained his usual stoic self. "So, I guess the plan is find a clue, recover the relic, draw out the bad guys, offer to swap said relic for the girl, and then kill them all."

Sean's face darkened. "Exactly."

"Well," Tommy hit the recline button on the side of his chair and eased the seat back, "sounds like you're coming out of retirement."

10

ROME, ITALY

Thanos squinted against the rising sun as the car wound its way out of the airport and toward the city.

He'd made a move, going with a gut instinct that told him Sean Wyatt would try to retrace Villa's steps. Based on the information from the phone conversation Wyatt had had with his friend Thomas Schultz of IAA, it was a solid gamble. Dimitris Gikas's private jet had flown through the night to reach the ancient city on seven hills as fast as possible. Thanos wasn't sure where the United States president fit into the scenario, but it didn't matter at this point. If Wyatt went back to Villa's hotel, Thanos and his men would have him cornered with little chance of escape. It was a good plan, unless Wyatt knew the IAA phones were tapped, and wasn't headed to Rome at all.

No. Wyatt would try to save the girl. There was no question in his mind. The only place to start would be in Rome, where she'd been staying during her research.

Thanos had texted his boss before the plane took off, letting him know the plan. Gikas had simply responded with one line. *Alive if possible.*

He hated it when his employer limited his options. It was much easier to transport a corpse than a living, breathing person. The living caused problems, tried to get away, or simply wouldn't shut up as they begged to be released. The dead couldn't offer any information, which was why Gikas wanted Wyatt alive, but the dead were much more convenient. Thanos knew that his boss needed Wyatt alive, though, and he would do his best to accommodate his employer's request.

The black sedan weaved through the increasing traffic, heading farther into the madness that was Rome's city streets. It wasn't one of Thanos's favorite places to visit. He didn't care much for history, and the millions of tourists annoyed him to his core. There were times when he wished he could just strangle some of them. Something about visiting vacationers got on his last nerve.

At least Rome had good coffee, he thought. It was one of the few saving graces the old city offered. They merged into another lane, now surrounded by scooters, motorcycles, and small cars. Thanos couldn't handle driving in the mess. He preferred that task be delegated to one of his men, leaving him to worry about more important matters.

Twenty minutes later, they had arrived at the hotel where some of Gikas's other men had set up shop to watch Adriana Villa's room just a few days before. They'd tracked her movements, waiting patiently for the perfect time to break into her room and lie in wait.

The men had reported finding nothing of interest in the room, information that had disturbed Thanos. There should have been something there regarding Villa's work in her quest for the Antikythera Mechanism. He'd made sure the men had double-checked, and they assured him that they had given the room a thorough look.

There was nothing he could do about that now. Thanos had become good at letting go of things that couldn't be helped. All he could do was focus on what to do in the future. For now, he and his men needed to get set up and put twenty-four hour surveillance on the hotel where Villa had been staying. If his instincts were right, Wyatt would come looking for the last place his girlfriend was known to be. If he was wrong, they'd lost nothing but a little time. As long as Wyatt was with the president, there was nothing that could be done anyway.

A valet in a burgundy-and-tan uniform opened the car door for Thanos, and then another swung open the entrance to the hotel in anticipation. Thanos stepped out into the musty city air, thick with the smells of car exhaust, Italian cooking, and the mild stench that always seemed to accompany historic cities. He strode gauntly through the entryway and into the hotel. One of his men from the earlier assignment was waiting inside. He wore a tight, gray v-neck sweater with a white shirt and black tie. A shiny belt buckle stood out from the top of his black jeans. Even though he was inside, the man had on sunglasses.

"We haven't seen anything today," he said, handing over a key to one of the hotel rooms they'd booked earlier.

At this time of year, getting accommodations could be tricky, that is unless you worked for Dimitris Gikas. It hadn't been coincidence that a few cancellations popped up at the opportune time.

The men entered one of the elevators just before its bronze doors closed. A minute later, they were on the sixth floor in one of the suites. Thanos had been specific about getting a room that was high enough to see over the fountains in the square between their hotel and the one Villa was using, but not so high that they couldn't get a good view. The sixth floor had been perfect. Thanos and his assistant walked through the room, past the gilded lamps, a neatly made bed with a deep-red comforter, and an oak dresser, and stopped at the doors to the balcony. A small telescope had been set up, making it easy to keep an eye on their target on the other side of the park.

It wasn't completely necessary, the opposite hotel only being a few hundred yards away, but the telescope provided a more detailed perspective in case it was needed.

Thanos examined the space for a moment, twisting around and scanning the room. He cast another glance across the park and gave a quick nod. "Well done. Have a man on this window every hour of the day. Make sure they turn their phones off. We can't risk them missing our quarry because they wanted to check the football scores."

"We'll take care of it, sir. We have also arranged the room next door for you. You'll be the first to know if we see anything suspicious." The man stood erect as he finished giving the report.

Thanos appreciated having reliable helpers. They were difficult to find in this day and age. It was one of the reasons he knew that Gikas appreciated his services. In turn, Thanos appreciated the young Italian's attention to detail. "Excellent work. Take the first shift and rotate out every hour with the other three. That way none of you will get so bored that you start looking at the birds flying around or the buttocks of a ripe young woman on the sidewalk."

The Italian gave a single nod and stepped over to the window. He picked up a pair of binoculars that rested on top of a round wooden table and began staring through them at the opposite hotel. Thanos left the room and went next door to his own room. When he entered, he found it similarly decorated, and with a pair of binoculars provided just like in the other room. He was pleased at how thorough his assistant was.

He closed the door and removed his jacket, hanging it on the back of the chair at a little desk. Thanos stopped at the door to the balcony for a few seconds, and then opened it wide, letting in the smells and sounds of the busy city surrounding him. Tourists and citizens mingled in the slow dance around the shops, cafes, and fountains of the piazza. Mist from the elaborate fountain spewed into the air, evaporating quickly before it reached the windows of the surrounding buildings. Children played in the water, some held by a parent's guiding hand, others not. Hundreds of other people sat in chairs at small bistro tables sipping wine, beer, and even a few coffees. Thanos stared at Villa's hotel across the way and took in a long, slow breath.

"Your move, Mr. Wyatt."

11

ROME, ITALY

Getting into the city of Rome is an exercise in patience at any time of the day. On this particular morning, it seemed inordinately perilous. Vehicles swerved in and out of tiny openings, whipping around the ones in front of them and repeating the stunt all over again.

The driver of the car Sean and his companions were in seemed perfectly at home with the chaos, which was no surprise since he had been serving the American embassy in Rome for the last year. He was a man in his early fifties named Carl. The remaining ring of shortly cut hair on his head was mostly gray with smatterings of black, a reminder of the way it used to look in the man's younger days.

Carl didn't say much, other than asking where the group was headed and how fast they needed to get there. "As quickly as possible," had been Sean's response, which resulted in a tad more reckless driving than he was comfortable with.

After more near misses than Sean could count, and about forty minutes later, the car arrived at the gray, palatial building where Adriana had been staying. The structure was only fifteen to twenty stories tall, but it occupied a huge footprint on the city's landscape.

Sean and the others exited the white SUV and grabbed their

luggage out of the back. Yarbrough led the way to the front door with the others in line behind. Tommy looked around at the scenery, admiring the architecture and grandiosity of it all.

"I do love coming to Rome," he said with a smile as big as a billboard. "So much rich history and culture here."

"Yeah," Sean agreed hesitantly. His eyes panned through the scene, searching for something he wasn't sure was there or not. "And so many dangers lurking in the shadows."

Through the mist of the fountains, he thought he noticed something in one of the buildings on the other side of the street, something out of place in one of the windows. Was it a silhouette? Sean wanted to believe he was just being paranoid. Paranoia had saved him on more than one occasion, though. A bread truck pulled up next to the curb and cut off his line of sight. He shrugged it off, but stepped back over to the SUV before Carl could pull back into traffic. Sean spoke to the driver for a minute before the man nodded and drove away.

When he joined Tommy at the hotel entrance, Sean attempted to wipe away the concerned look on his face before his friend said anything. "Everything all right?" Tommy asked, beating him to the act.

"Yeah," Sean lied. "Why wouldn't it be?" he cast his friend a mischievous glance.

The metal-and-glass doors opened into a vast atrium, featuring a bronze water fountain in the center that portrayed two mermaids. Red and gold tapestries dangled from the second floor on either side of several marble columns that decorated the room. The matching floor tiles covered the entire span of the area. Tourists were filing out the door, ready to begin their day of discovery in the ancient city.

Yarbrough was already inside, talking to a man who appeared to be one of the local authorities. The meeting had been arranged before they had landed at the airport, an easy trick when you worked for the president of the United States. The olive-skinned man was much shorter than Yarbrough, and the Italian's pointed nose seemed much more elongated as he stared up at the secret agent. He nodded several times and then ushered Yarbrough over to the concierge desk.

After a short conversation with the brunette woman behind the counter, Agent Yarbrough was handed a plastic key card, which he accepted with a smile and nod. A moment later, the two men joined Sean and Tommy in the middle of the lobby.

He held out the key for Sean. "The room number is on the back of this. The concierge said the room was paid for through to the middle of next week. Whatever your friend was looking for, she was prepared to spend a great deal of time finding it."

Sean looked down at the room number and felt a twinge of nausea in his abdomen. He wished he'd gone with her to Italy. She'd invited him to go, but he insisted he wanted to get things set up with his new life in the Florida Panhandle. He knew that standing there letting regret wash over him wouldn't save her. What would save Adriana was trying to find a clue, anything that could lead them to what she was researching.

Yarbrough looked over at the Italian man with the pointed nose. "Thank you for your cooperation. The president appreciates your help."

The short man held up both hands and shook his head. "I assure you, it is no trouble at all, signore. Your president has been very helpful to our government during this difficult time in the economy. It is the least I can do."

He was right. President Dawkins had pushed hard for reinvestment into new Italian companies and businesses. He pooled his network of powerful allies together and managed to raise over five billion dollars in venture funding. Having a strong belief in entrepreneurship helped Dawkins start business incubators all over the United States, a move that resulted in a huge jump in the gross domestic product, not to mention the lowest jobless rate in history. Thanks to John Dawkins, the Italian economy was beginning to experience a smaller, but similar growth.

Sean was grateful for the help as well. "Thank you, signore," Sean said to the man, who nodded with an appreciative smile.

The three headed to the nearest set of elevators and slipped in to an empty one before the doors closed. Tommy noticed the Italian had stayed behind in the lobby. "He not coming with us?" Tommy asked.

Yarbrough hit the button for Adriana's floor. "In these kinds of situations, we find that discretion is the best course to take. The less our friend knows the better." Tommy gave an understanding nod.

A few moments and a short ride later, the doors opened and they stepped out into the long, narrow hallway. Sean glanced at the room numbers to the left and noted that they were descending in that direction. "Her room should be that way," he stated.

He started to the left, walking hurriedly down the corridor, passing the golden wall sconces and various paintings of Tuscan scenery. The art had a prefabricated feel to it, as if the artists had just created it en masse for a paycheck. Sean stopped at a door on the right and paused for a second. The *Do not disturb* sign hung from the doorknob.

He frowned and looked over his shoulder at Yarbrough. "Has no one even been in here to check out the room?"

The agent pointed at the sign on the door. "If the men who took her put that on the handle, it's unlikely that any of the hotel staff meddled with anything, especially since the room is paid for through to next week. They'd technically be obliged to obey the request."

"Good." Sean inserted the key card and turned the latch.

He pushed the door open cautiously, an old habit he fell back on when going into an unfamiliar space. He peeked into the first corner on the right, then back to the left toward the window. The place was empty: empty, and completely trashed.

Whoever had gone through there was definitely looking for something. Sean stepped forward, remaining cautious and moving slowly. He reached over to the inner wall and flipped on a light switch to get a better view of the mess. Two dresser drawers lay on the floor, the bottom one hung halfway out of the cherry furniture piece. Adriana's clothes were scattered around the room as if desperate hands had aimlessly tossed the articles. Bed sheets and pillowcases had been strewn about as well, some thrown onto the floor. A small closet next to the bathroom was open, displaying a few of Adriana's shirts, one yellow sundress, and a pair of her shoes.

"What were they looking for?" Tommy said in a reverent tone. He peered around the room at the chaotic scene.

Sean shook his head slowly. "I'm not sure, but whatever they wanted, they wanted it fast. It looks like a tornado went through here." He fought back the lump in his throat. There was still a faint scent of Adriana's perfume lingering in the air. To him, the room smelled just like her. He winced at the thought.

Agent Yarbrough walked over to the window. The drapes had been pulled together, blocking out most of the natural light from the morning sun. He started to pull one of them back, but stopped when he saw Sean staring at something behind the door. One of Adriana's jackets lay in a heap on the floor near the doorstop. Sean reached down and picked it up, letting the scent of it fill his nostrils for a few seconds. He let out a deep sigh, and then frowned. A solitary key attached to a green rubber key ring was sitting on the thin carpet under a leather chair. If he'd not picked up the jacket, Sean wouldn't have noticed the little object.

Sean cocked his head to the side and knelt down to get a closer look.

"What is it?" Yarbrough asked, taking his hand away from the window shade.

"It's a key," Sean said, picking it up. He eyed it curiously and turned it over to see the writing on the other side of the green piece. *Stazione Termini, 57* was stamped on the back. "It's a locker key from the train station."

Tommy took a step closer and examined the object. "You think she dropped it?" he asked.

"Maybe," Sean shrugged. He stared at the key. "But I don't think it was an accident."

Yarbrough still stood near the window. "Why would she leave a locker key?"

Sean knew the answer. Adriana believed he would come for her, and she also believed that Sean would know what to do. At least, that's what he hoped. If Adriana had left him a breadcrumb to follow that meant there was something she wanted him to have, something important. What it was he didn't know, but he knew he needed to find it.

"We need to get to the train station and see what's in that locker," Sean said as he stuffed the key into his khaki pants pocket.

"How do you know there isn't anything else to find here?" Yarbrough said, turning back to the window and reaching for the drapes.

"Because," Sean began, "they searched the room before she came back."

"How do you know that?" Yarbrough asked, flinging open the curtains as he spoke.

Sunlight poured into the room, brightening it significantly. "Because this key would not have been on the floor here under her jacket." He visualized what happened as if he'd witnessed it himself. "There was a struggle. She slipped out of the jacket and dropped the key with it onto the floor so that the men who took her wouldn't see it. She knew I could come to find her."

"That's a big assumption," the agent said dubiously.

"It's all we got."

Tommy butted in. "I'm with Sean. They would have already checked everything. If that key was lying on the floor, they would have easily seen it."

Yarbrough put his hands on his hips and stared out at the square, stretching slightly. Something clicked from that side of the room, and the window suddenly cracked like a dozen spider webs. Agent Yarbrough instantly clutched his left shoulder and dropped to the ground. "Get down," he shouted in agony.

The sickening realization hit Sean almost instantly. Someone was shooting at them from the outside.

12

CORFU, GREECE

Eight men sat around the long, heavy table in the dim, candlelit room. An iron chandelier hung from the center of the ceiling above, providing the only electric light to the space. Seven of the men stared to one end of the table, where Dimitris Gikas sat with his hands folded on the surface. His face expressed compassion and patience, but inside his temper was brimming with rage.

A fleshy, round-faced man at the other end of the table stared at him vapidly. "You cannot just take over a country, Dimitris. And for you to think that we would all swear allegiance to you as our king is absolute insanity." He crossed his chubby arms over his bulbous chest, hands barely able to reach beyond the girth. A toothpick hung loosely from the man's mouth. Even though the room was a cool seventy degrees, the fat man perspired profusely.

Gikas stared quietly at him, forming his rebuke carefully. Before he could say anything, a slim, bald man named Michael Thropopolis spoke up from the other side of the table. His sloping nose and deeply receded eyes gave him a well-aged appearance. "He is not wrong, Dimitris. Greece has not had a monarchy in centuries. The people would not likely take kindly to the idea of being ruled."

Dimitris Gikas had heard quite enough. "The people," he inter-rupted before Thropopolis could continue, "have made a mess of this once-great nation. Like little children given the run of the house, there are broken toys everywhere. The economy is in shambles. Crime is rampant. Tourism, our main source of income for the coun-try, is on the decline. The people need someone to lead them back to prosperity."

The words hung in the room nearly as thick as the smoke drifting up from the cigars a few of the men had been puffing.

"And I suppose that you just have the best interest of the people in mind, eh, Dimitris?" Thropopolis was still skeptical.

He let a smile slip out. "In any government that has ever existed, the leaders always got their fair share."

"You mean the lion's share," the fat man at the other end chimed in sarcastically.

"I mean what we deserve. And not just me, Niko; all of us. If you back me, you will all become the richest men in all of Greece. Your power will reach across all of Europe. As part of my council, your legacies will live on for all of history."

Some of the men turned their heads, looking at each other as if to see what the others were thinking. Thropopolis seemed satisfied with the answer to his question.

The fat one, a man named Niko Teridis, appeared to be the last obstacle in the room. "I am already one of the richest men in Greece, Dimitris. We all are." He splayed his hands out wide, displaying the others in the room. "And we already have power." Niko leaned forward and put his hands on the table. "You think you have some-thing we need, but you are wrong. This government may fall apart, but it has been good to all of us. It has made us all rich men. Now you seek to undo this? Why not just let things take their natural course? We will be fine no matter what happens. We all have enough money to weather any storm that comes our way. And when it is over, we will still be in control of everything."

Gikas had known the man would be a problem. Niko Teridis was a tyrant of a businessman, and he'd built his real estate empire in a short amount of time. Brilliantly, he'd moved most of his assets over to precious metals and technology investments before the Greek economy began falling apart. Now, he was one of the wealthiest people in the entire country, second in the room only to Dimitris himself, a fact that surely festered in Niko's mind.

The truth was that Gikas didn't need him. Teridis would be more of a liability than any of the others, who all seemed anxiously willing to get in line and do as they were told. Gikas had meant everything he'd said. He would make the men in that room wealthier and more powerful than they'd ever hoped to become. And he would expand the Greek empire to the greatness it deserved. Gikas had not revealed the last part to anyone except for his trusted right hand, Thanos. For a second, his thoughts wandered to what his second in command was working on. Gikas needed the Eye of Zeus. With the relic secured, Gikas would be able to plan every military move with flawless precision. Within a few years, Europe would kneel beneath him.

Teridis snapped the silence abruptly. "I must be going. I have many things to tend to before I leave the country this afternoon." He shook his head. "I will not be a part of this ridiculous venture, Dimitris. My money will be kept where it is. I recommend all of you do the same."

The rotund man pushed his chair back and stood up. His lone bodyguard stepped to his side quickly and escorted him to the door.

"I wish you would reconsider, Niko," Gikas said, giving one last attempt. "But I understand. If you must go, I do not hold your decision against you."

Teridis cast him a sarcastic smile, and then turned and left the room. The remaining men turned their gaze back to Gikas, perhaps expecting a less-than-cheerful reaction to the interaction.

Gikas would give them no such thing. He'd spent much of his life honing his emotions so that they would always be under control when the situation called for it. Like a great poker player, suppressing all external signs of distress, Dimitris Gikas buried his thoughts and feelings deep inside.

"Well, gentlemen," he said after he was sure Teridis had exited the building, "Niko is right. I'm sure many of you need to return to business matters. I do thank all of you for coming to meet with me."

Thropopolis stood up and looked around the room. "I cannot speak for the rest of these men, but you have my allegiance, Dimitris. Please do not take it lightly."

A sinister grin inched its way to one side of Dimitris's face. He knew if Michael Thropopolis would commit, so would the others.

One by one, each man in the room stood up and announced their intention to be a part of the new leadership of Greece. *Lambs*, Gikas thought quietly to himself as the men committed their resources and blood to the cause. One always follows the other.

"Thank you all," he said after a moment of reflection. "Your loyalty will not go unrewarded. I will be in touch with each of you soon to give you an update on our progress and to reveal something I have been working on behind the scenes."

The last sentence piqued the curiosity of every man in the room, but Gikas wouldn't give away that last little morsel. Not yet, anyway. They would all be made privy to it soon, but he had to know who he could trust. "For now, carry on with business as usual. You will know when the time has come."

Thropopolis appeared uncertain. "How will we know what to do when this time comes?"

"You will know, old friend. However, if it will ease your mind, I simply need all of you to publicly support me as I push toward a new government. If we stand together, we will not fail."

They all nodded, and then proceeded one by one out the door until Gikas was the only one left. He waited until he heard the door click and slid the cell phone out of his pocket. A second later, it was ringing.

"Yes, sir?" the masculine voice said on the other line.

"Do you have Niko?"

"Yes. We grabbed him and his bodyguard as they were about to get in his car."

Gikas smiled. He'd let the chubby man leave of his own free will, knowing full well that Teridis would never acquiesce to the notion of making Dimitris the new king of Greece. Niko TeridisTeridis was a proud, stubborn individual. Gikas had always disliked him, feeling that his rival had been born into a world of advantages. Sure, he made some smart financial moves to get where he was, but that didn't change the fact that he'd had a significant head start.

"Hold onto him. I'll be right there."

"What about the bodyguard?" the man on the other end of the conversation asked.

"Kill him."

13

ROME, ITALY

Sean and Tommy stayed low to the floor and belly crawled over to where Yarbrough was leaning up against the bed. The agent clutched his bleeding shoulder, trying to keep pressure on the wound.

Yarbrough grunted through clenched teeth, trying hard to fight off the pain. "Get out of here, Wyatt. Both of you." He barked the order at the men.

Neither of them had any intention of leaving the Secret Service man behind. "Sorry, Gerald. It doesn't work that way." Sean smirked at the grimacing agent. "I appreciate the offer, though."

"Yeah," Tommy agreed. "Leaving a man behind isn't really our style."

"I don't care what your style is, get your stubborn asses out of here."

"No can do," Tommy said. "Although, our stubbornness has nearly gotten us killed on more than one occasion."

Sean's grin widened. "We like to think of it as an endearing quality."

Yarbrough could see the argument was going to get him nowhere.

Another round pierced the window and thumped into the wall on the other side of the bed. "We need to get out of here," he said. "Our driver won't be back for half an hour, though."

Sean shook his head. "That isn't entirely accurate." At the quizzical glance the agent gave him, he was compelled to explain. "I may have told him to circle around and come back in five instead of thirty."

"Why would you do that?" Yarbrough asked.

"Call it a hunch."

Tommy nodded. "He's good with hunches."

Sean refocused the group. "Whatever you do, stay low. I'm going to close the curtain so they don't have a clear line of sight. You two start crawling for the door. I'll be right behind you."

Yarbrough agreed with a nod and rolled over onto his stomach. He let out a short grunt, clearly in pain from the bullet lodged in his shoulder. He made himself keep going, inching toward the door with Tommy in the lead.

Sean slid over to the wall and yanked on the stick connected to the drapes. The room went dark again except for the lights on near the doorway. Another bullet found its way through the window and into the far wall, harmlessly sending a puff of drywall powder into the air. Sean removed the handgun from the shoulder holster Yarbrough had given him on the plane. Sneaking weapons into the country was easy when you were on a private jet chartered by Uncle Sam. The Sig felt comfortable in his hand, despite his preference being Springfield's selection of arms.

He caught up to the other two men, who were waiting at the door. Tommy had pulled out his own weapon. He leaned against the wall space next to the doorframe, holding the gun tight to his chest.

"Thinking the same thing I'm thinking?" Sean asked, already knowing the answer from the gun in his friend's hand.

"They're sending someone to the room?"

"Mmmhmm," Sean confirmed and rose up on one knee, carefully holding his weapon at the ready.

"I thought you said they swept the room," Tommy interjected. "Why would they come back?"

Sean didn't like the answer, but he was strangely comfortable with it. There was only one possible reason the men who had taken Adriana would come after him. They didn't know about the key. If they had, they'd have already taken it and been gone. Whoever was shooting at them needed information, information they believed Sean possessed.

"They're here for me," he said in a grim tone.

Yarbrough frowned. "I thought you said you didn't know anything about what your girlfriend was looking for."

"I don't." He shook his head slowly. "But they don't know that. I'm betting they think I know something she doesn't. Or at the very least, they might want to take me to coerce one of us to talk."

Tommy pressed his ear to the door, listening for any movement outside. He jerked his thumb at the door. "They're outside," he mouthed in an attempt to stay silent.

"How many?" Sean whispered, almost inaudibly.

"Not sure. At least three or four."

"The second we turn that doorknob, they're going to open fire," Sean hissed. The other two nodded.

An idea hit him.

"Yarbrough, get in the bathroom and wait." Sean pointed behind where Tommy squatted. The bathroom was immediately to the right of the doorway. Sean got up and stepped into the toilet. A rack of fresh towels hovered over the water closet. He grabbed one of the towels and moved back to the coat closet slightly behind the point of entry. His hands worked quickly, tying a knot around the handle of the door's latch, making sure there was enough slack to reach into the edge of the closet.

"Tommy, hide in here. When I give you the signal, open the door with this." Sean handed him the towel, which his friend took reluctantly.

Tommy lowered his eyebrows. "What are you going to do?"

"Create a diversion, and then kill everyone in our way."

The other two cast a questioning glance at each other, wondering what diversion he was going to create.

Sean moved as fast and as quietly as he could to the desk near the television. He stayed low, aware that the sniper could unleash another volley at any second. When he reached the desk, he slid open the top drawer and found what he needed. He removed the small box of matches and a note pad, and then proceeded to the center of the room, squatting down at the foot of the bed. Tommy watched from the closet, realizing what Sean had in mind.

With a quick strike of a match, Sean held the tiny flame to the notepaper and raised his hand beyond the top edge of the bed. Bluish smoke began to drift up to the ceiling and the fire alarm situated over the bed.

The door latch shimmied for a second. The attackers were trying to get in. Sean figured they would gain access in less than a minute. He waved his makeshift torch around a little, causing the paper to burn faster and produce more smoke. The door's latch continued to jiggle, harder this time. It stopped for a moment, bathing the room in an eerie silence. Suddenly, a loud crash pounded the door, startling Tommy and Yarbrough, but Sean's hand remained steady, holding the burning paper in the air, his other calmly gripping the Sig.

The alarm began to sound, beeping repeatedly in quick succession. The irritating noise was a welcome relief to Sean, but he didn't relax. Water began to pour out of the sprinkler system overhead, soaking the entire room in a matter of a few seconds. It was the diversion he'd needed. "Now!" he yelled at Tommy.

His friend yanked the towel down and back, jerking the door wide open in one sudden movement. The three men outside were caught off guard, looking around at the deluge and stunned by the piercing alarm in the hallway. Sean squeezed the trigger, plunging two rounds directly into the abdomen and chest of the man closest to the doorway. He moved the barrel to the second, missing the man's neck with the first shot, but landing the next two in the throat and shoulder. The initial two targets had been easy due to the fact that they were distracted. The third, however, dove out of the way as soon as Sean's third bullet had been fired.

He yelled something in another language, telling Sean that there was at least one other guy in the hallway. Sean noticed a barrel poking around the right side of the doorframe. He fired another shot, causing the man on the right to pull back. A moment later, the barrel began to creep its way back into sight. Sean sent another round at his target, sending it harmlessly into the interior wall the room. This time the man on the left retorted, using his partner on the right as a diversion. It was clever, and Sean wished he'd considered the attackers might try something like that.

His only move was a quick dive to the side of the bed nearest the window, narrowly missing a barrage of bullets ripping into the floor and drywall.

One of the men said something in Greek. Sean wasn't entirely sure of the translation, but from his vague recollection, he thought it meant they were coming in the room.

There were a few seconds of silence that caused Sean's anxiety to heighten. He lay on his back with his head against the wall, gun firmly clutched in both hands, ready if the intruders came around the bed or over it.

His finger remained loose on the trigger, a habit he'd developed through the years. Sean considered it more of a safety precaution than anything else. Too many people were willing to shoot first and apologize later. He'd always preferred to just not have to deal with it. His motto was to always make sure the target was the enemy, and he'd gotten extremely quick at it.

Three loud pops blasted from the entryway followed by the sound of a body hitting the floor, then a second. There was another precipitous moment of silence before Sean heard a familiar voice.

"All clear at the door," Tommy said in a firm voice.

Sean slid around and peeked by the edge of the bed. The two assailants were on the floor, one piled on the other. A thin line of smoke seeped out of Tommy's weapon.

"You can come out now, Sean." His barb was accompanied by a snide grin.

"Nice job, buddy. You're really getting the hang of this sort of thing."

Tommy stared down at the two corpses. "That's not necessarily a good thing. Means I'm finding myself in sticky situations way too often."

"Would you two mind if we left now?" Yarbrough interjected from just inside the bathroom. Blood was soaking through his jacket, mingling with the water from the sprinklers.

"Good call. I just hope our ride is back," Sean said with a hint of uncertainty.

He and Tommy helped Agent Yarbrough to his feet. Sean grabbed a washcloth from the sink and pressed it hard into the agent's wound. "Keep this pressed against it," he said.

"Yeah, I know the drill," Yarbrough nodded.

Sean passed him a sly grin, and then moved back over to the door. He checked his magazine, confirming there were only a few rounds left. That small supply plus the one extra clip he had in his belt wouldn't last long if they had to shoot their way out of the building.

Outside, sirens began sounding as fire trucks and police arrived in response to the alarm. Sean knew the chaos in front of the building would be the perfect cover for their getaway. The sniper would likely not have a clear shot, but they'd need to move fast.

He stepped into the hall and checked down both sides of the corridor, making sure the coast was clear. "It's good," he said to Tommy. "Head to the elevators. I'll stay in front. Keep Yarbrough between us."

"Gotcha." Tommy confirmed.

Sean darted down the hallway, sloshing his way through the wet mess. When he reached the elevator doors, he mashed the button hard, but got no signal that it was heading their way. Then he remembered; the elevators probably shut down automatically when there was an alarm. A door closed thirty feet away, and Sean spun around with the barrel of his Sig aimed into the empty space. It was the door into the stairwell. No one was there, which likely meant one of the other guests was trying to get out of the building.

Yarbrough and Tommy reached the elevator a second later. "What are you waiting for?" Tommy asked incredulously. As soon as he'd spoken, he had the same epiphany Sean had experienced a moment before. "Oh, right. Stairs."

Sean darted over to the stairwell door where the passageway came to a head and split off in two directions. He checked down both ways, again making sure there were no threats. Satisfied, he took a big step to the door and barged it open. His weapon aimed up the stairs first, then down. "Clear," he shouted back at the other two.

He held the door open while Tommy and Yarbrough slogged their way quickly to the stairwell. "Go ahead," Sean said. Once the other two were headed down the stairs, he let the door ease shut.

Sean was glad they didn't have far to go, only four floors to reach the bottom. Tommy and their wounded companion were already on the landing of the second floor when Sean arrived on the platform just above them. The third floor door suddenly swung open, and a Glock barrel stuck through the opening. Sean ducked to the side just in the nick of time as the weapon fired a round into the stairwell. Instinctively, Sean took a quick side step, grabbed the man's arm, and pulled him into the stairwell.

The attacker's body flung against the railing, jarring him momentarily, just long enough for Sean to wrest the gun from his hand. The respite didn't last but for a second. The man's knee swung around and planted firmly into Sean's abdomen.

Sean gasped at the sudden jolt, dropping his own weapon between the rails. The gun clattered down the steps below, evening the playing field for both combatants. Sean didn't have time to hurt; he jerked backward, narrowly dodging a roundhouse kick from the stranger. He instantly squared up, ready for another attack, and got his first look at the face of the man who was trying to kill him. The assassin's graying hair was trimmed close to his skull, masking the fact that he'd gone bald several years before. His angular nose and narrow face made him appear like a bird of prey. His black turtleneck seemed a little clichéd for mercenary work, but Sean didn't think the man cared what he thought of his ensemble.

"You don't have to do this," Sean said in an almost sympathetic tone. "You can walk back through that door and go on about your business."

The man's mouth contorted in a sickly grin. "You don't have to be afraid of dying, American. I'll make it quick for you." His accent was distinctly western European. Sean was fairly certain from Czech Republic.

"I wasn't begging," Sean corrected. "I was offering you a chance to live."

The mercenary snorted and lurched forward. His fists swung hard at Sean's face, first left then right. Sean easily dodged the first and blocked the subsequent attacks. The assassin swung his knee up in an attempt to catch Sean in the midsection again, but this time the target stepped to the side and grabbed the man by the calf. In a swift move, Sean used the man's weight against him and lifted hard with the leg before the attacker could get loose. The maneuver sent the man flipping backward over the railing. Sean watched as the body plummeted down the chute between the stairs, hitting his head violently against one of the lower railings before coming to a sudden stop at the bottom.

Tommy and Agent Yarbrough's heads poked out from one of the lower platforms and stared down at the motionless body. A little pool of blood was already starting to form around the head of the prostrate form. Tommy looked back up at Sean. "Where'd he come from?"

"Third floor. Better be careful leaving the building." Sean answered as he bounded down the steps, two at a time. "I told him he could leave if he wanted to."

"Did he know you meant alive?"

"Guess not," Sean said. "Let's get the agent here to some help. I just hope our ride is still waiting outside."

Sean opened the exit door and entered the first floor hallway. It was chaotic, filled with guests who were hurriedly heading toward the main lobby and the front exit. The walls and carpet were soaked from the sprinklers, drenching every person in the building. Sean turned to the right and began heading in the direction of the rear of the hotel.

"The exit is this way," Tommy tried to correct him.

"Yeah, but our ride is out back."

14

CORFU, GREECE

The daylight still burned Dimitris's eyes as he strolled down the pathway toward the cliffs at the edge of his property. A gentle breeze brushed through his hair, unable to move it due to the amount of product he used on a daily basis. Two of his guards followed several paces behind. When Gikas walked, he preferred to walk alone. Having people around him crowded his personal space. Times like today called for a little extra space.

Niko Teridis had sealed his fate. Gikas had given the fat man every opportunity to join the new regime that would soon take over all of Greece. Such a union would have made Teridis a great deal of money, and the risk was so low. Treason? It was a small price to pay to return the country to its former greatness. When the government fell apart, who would enforce the law anyway? There would be no one to accuse them of treason, and no one to prosecute. Gikas had weighed the risks long ago, and found them minimal at worst.

Teridis didn't see it that way. That, or perhaps he wanted to be the one pulling the strings. Gikas had known him for several years. Teridis had always been stubborn, and constantly vying for a bigger piece of the pie. He was no leader, though. Rumors were that he'd lost a fortune from the bad business decisions he'd made in the past. His only redemption was that he'd made a few brilliant ones that covered up the mistakes. Men like that were already running Greece. If Niko Teridis was in charge, it would happen all over again, probably worse. There would be a massive coup and civil war within the first three years.

Men like Teridis could not lead.

Dimitris Gikas was certain he was the only man fit to re-establish Greece as a world power. The rest of the men at the table were sheep, willing to follow a strong, confident shepherd. Gikas was that shepherd. Sometimes, however, a shepherd had to defend the flock against danger, even if the threat was coming from within.

He made a sharp right on the stone path. The walkway led away from the mansion, easing its way down the gentle slope toward the sea. He made another turn as he reached a row of bushes and shrubs that lined the outer edge of his property. Gikas stared down at the foamy waves crashing into the rocks below. Those great stones had saved his family's land many centuries before. Enemy ships tried to bring their invasion force around the cliffs to enter Greece from the east. High winds and ripping tides pulled the wooden ships to their destruction, splintering the invaders' boats into pieces and drowning their men in the churning waters.

Up ahead, a small circle of stone benches and wooden chairs surrounded a fire pit made from the grayish stones of the cliffs below. Four of his men stood around one central figure who was on his knees with head bowed low. The blubbery man's breaths were coming in great heaves, a fact that told Gikas his men had done a good job. The four guards took a simultaneous step back as their employer approached. Gikas had loosened the black tie he'd worn to the meeting and rolled up the white sleeves of his shirt as if he were about to do some manual labor. He had no intention of doing any work himself. Those days were gone. Now he had hired killers to do his dirty deeds.

Niko Teridis lifted his head as the bodyguards stepped away. At first, he wondered why they were moving, but soon realized it wouldn't be to his benefit. His eyes were swollen and red, tears streaming from the corners. There were cuts on his cheeks, and blood oozed from a gash on his lip. His thick nose was bent at an awkward angle, also leaking dark-crimson liquid.

His eyes flared angrily at Gikas as he stepped into view. "You have no idea what a mistake you have made this day, Dimitris. Hell will rain down upon you. My supporters, my family, my friends will avenge this."

Gikas smiled cynically and shook his head in a mocking fashion. "I seriously doubt that, old friend. Most of your supporters now support me and my efforts to establish a new monarchy. As for your family? They will be easy enough to pick apart one by one."

Teridis snarled. "You will not touch them! Stay away from my family!"

"Well, that all depends on you, my dear Niko." Gikas raised an eyebrow and reached back to the guard closest to him. The man produced a small roll of papers from his jacket and placed them in his boss's open palm.

"What is that?" Teridis's eyes narrowed.

"It's the paperwork for all your land, all your businesses, basically everything you own in this world. You are going to sign it over to me."

Teridis let out a short laugh that was accompanied by a reddish mist. Gikas's men must have gone to work on the man's lungs. "I will never sign over such a thing to you. You can rot in hell, Dimitris." He spat on Gikas's black Italian shoes.

Gikas took in a long deep breath. "Why did you do that? These are the finest shoes the Italians can make. Now I'm going to have to get them cleaned."

One of the guards stepped forward to strike Teridis across the face, but Gikas held up a hand, signaling him to stop. "No, my friend. You've roughed him up enough, don't you think?" The stout guard gave a quick nod and retreated to his former spot.

Teridis appeared momentarily confused, but remained unyielding. "You think I need your mercy, Dimitris? I need nothing from you."

Gikas shrugged his head to the side. "You see, my old friend, that is where I believe you are wrong. I believe there are actually several people in your life that could benefit from my mercy."

The comment caused Teridis to narrow his eyes a little tighter.

"Your young wife, for instance. She might be interested in a little mercy from me."

Teridis had married a beautiful blonde woman who was nearly half his age. He didn't care about the reasons she married him, nor that everyone in the region speculated about the oddly matched couple. He knew what he liked, and he always took what he wanted. Deep down, though, she was just a trophy to him. "Do as you please to her. She's nothing but a whore. You honestly believe that I care about what you do to a common prostitute?"

"Very well, Niko."

From behind the tall bushes, two more men in black suits appeared with a blonde woman. Her curly hair cascaded down to shoulders exposed by the white-and-black polka-dotted dress she wore. The woman was blindfolded and had a gag in her mouth. She tried to scream as the men ushered over to the edge of the cliff, but the handkerchief did its job keeping her voice silent.

The men stopped at the precipice and awaited their employer's orders. Gikas looked over at the woman then back down at the fat man on his knees by the fire pit. "Are you sure you don't want to save her, Niko? She's quite breathtaking."

Teridis's eyes remained slits, unyielding to the test. His silence said enough.

Gikas gave a quick nod and one of his guards yanked down the gag, letting it dangle around the woman's lithe neck. "Niko!" she screamed. "Please, just give them whatever they want." Her begging did little to change the mind of the hardened man. "I'll do anything. Please, just don't kill me."

"You think you can play games with me, Dimitris?" Teridis gazed up at his captor. "I know full well that you will kill us all anyway. So go ahead; do your worst. I will give you nothing."

Gikas let out a sick laugh. "I thought you might say that. Very well, say goodbye to your wife...or whore, rather." He gave another nod to one of the guards, who shoved the woman in the back, sending her over the ledge. Her screams faded as she fell the several hundred feet to the waves and rocks below. Gikas turned back to his prisoner. "Too late." He put his hand to his chin. "Now, I wonder who else I have to kill to get you to sign that paper." He waited for a moment to add dramatic effect. "Ah, yes. Your little boy. That might do the trick."

Teridis was already horrified that he'd just witnessed the murder of his wife. Now, Gikas was threatening to take the life of his only son, the heir to everything he'd built. Teridis had been a ruthless businessman, a tyrant of industry. He'd had men killed before, and done far worse than that, but in his heart, he had a soft place for his son. Niki was to be the heir to the Teridis empire. Even though the boy was only seven years old, he'd shown his father's tenacity early on.

Gikas knew all of this, and it was time to apply pressure on the place it would hurt Niko Teridis the most.

The prisoner looked up into Gikas's eyes. For the first time, there was desperation on the fat man's face. "No," he said, shaking his head. "Not my son."

"It doesn't have to be this way, Niko. You can still save your son's life." Gikas displayed a small, yet insincere expression of compassion.

Another guard who had been hiding behind the bushes stepped out holding a young boy. The brown-haired child was dressed in a T-shirt and cargo shorts. He too wore a blindfold and had a handkerchief strapped across his mouth.

"Niki!" Teridis cried out and attempted to push himself off the ground. One of the guards quickly shoved him back down on his face. Tears began to stream from the prisoner's eyes.

The guard holding the boy removed one hand from the child's shoulder and pulled the gag down. "Papa!" he screamed as soon as the rag was removed. "Papa, what's happening?"

"Nothing, Niki," Teridis answered between sobs. "Everything is going to be fine. Papa just has to do some business with these men first."

"I'm scared."

Teridis shook his head. "You don't have to be afraid, my son. Everything is going to be all right."

Gikas glanced at his captive with a questioning look. "So we have a deal?"

The portly man was broken. The sight of his son being held hostage was more than he could bear. It was the only point of humanity he had left in a world of cruelty and desensitized emotion. Teridis could not let his son die. He knew that Gikas would kill him. It was too late to save himself. Now his concern was that Niki's safety would be guaranteed.

"I will sign the papers," Tiridus said, choking back the tears. "But only if you guarantee not to harm my son. If you swear to me that my son will be safe, I will give you everything."

A gust of wind passed over the group as Gikas soaked in the moment of triumph. "That's better, Niko." He took the papers and set them down on a stone bench next to where Teridis knelt. One of his guards placed a pen on top of the small stack. "I swear, I will not harm your son. Now sign the documents before I change my mind."

Teridis crawled over to the bench and picked up the pen. He didn't even bother to read what he was signing. His thick fingers hurriedly scrawled his signature on the lines at the bottom of each page until he had signed them all. Then, he defiantly slammed the pen down on the top page. "Now let my son go."

Gikas snatched up the papers and pored through them in seconds, checking to make sure each one had been signed. Satisfied they met his requirements, he passed them back to the guard. He turned his head back to the guard holding the boy and motioned back in the direction of the bushes. "Put him with the girl in the basement."

"What?" Teridis asked, rage and confusion mingling in his voice. "You promised you would let him go! We had a deal, Dimitris!"

Gikas had kept his calm long enough. He turned around slowly and stared down at his portly rival. "The deal, Niko, was that I would not harm your child, which I will honor. Letting your son go free, however, was never part of the arrangement."

Fury blazed in Teridis's eyes amid tears and sweat. "You lying, low life, crooked..."

"Monster?" Gikas interrupted. "You know, Niko, it doesn't matter how many words you try to use to describe me. I gave you a chance to join me, and you refused. The first duty of any good king is to eliminate his rivals. Since you turned away my generosity, you must be taken care of."

Teridis stared up into his captor's eyes. He wouldn't beg for mercy, though Gikas wouldn't bet against it. The man had been a coward in his business dealings. Why would anything change now?

"Well, my old friend, I suppose this is goodbye," Gikas said and turned away, nodding to his guards. "Time for you to join your wife."

"No." Teridis shook his head rapidly back and forth. "No. Please, Dimitris. You don't have to do this. You have everything I own. It's all yours now. Send me to exile. Please, I'm no threat to you now." The pleas for mercy would do him no good, and Gikas kept his back turned to the man.

The two guards behind the prisoner stepped forward and grabbed the desperate man under his armpits, lifting him off the ground surprisingly easily for a man of his girth. He struggled for a moment until one of the muscular guards twisted his arm in an awkward angle. Teridis let out an agonized howl and immediately ceased his struggle as the guards dragged him toward the cliff.

"Dimitris! You coward! You won't even look me in the face while your goons do your dirty work for you. I'll see you in Hades, Dimitris!"

Gikas put his head down for a moment as his guards stopped at the ledge with the captive. He turned and gazed across the short span into the questioning, horrified eyes of the man. The sound of the waves crashing below reached a crescendo. "For old times' sake, I'm going to do my own dirty work this once, Niko." He took a rapid step toward the men by the ledge and brought his right leg up. The Italian shoe Niko had spit on struck him hard in the chest, and the force of the blow sent him reeling over the edge. His screams faded much like his wife's as Gikas watched the blubbery body drop to the jagged rocks below. The foamy water splashed over the body a second later, and pulled it out to sea. Gikas spun around and began walking back down the path to his home.

Now no one would stand in his way.

15

ROME, ITALY

The three men burst through the metal door to a surprisingly quiet alley. Sean could hear the perpetual whine of the sirens echoing down the narrow side street, but no emergency units had arrived in the back, not yet anyway. Their car, however, was waiting by the sidewalk as Sean had requested.

"You know something, Wyatt?" Yarbrough said, still grimacing from the bullet wound. "I think these guys may have underestimated you."

"I get that a lot," Sean said in a fake smug tone. "The underestimating thing, I mean. I think it might be the hair." He cast a wayward eye up, pretending to glance at the messy blond strands.

Yarbrough laughed, followed by short and painful cough.

"Take it easy there, big guy. We'll have you to the hospital in no time," Sean said in a calm voice as he opened the back door of the sedan.

"Get us to the closest hospital," Sean ordered urgently.

Carl nodded and stepped on the gas as soon as the men had closed the doors. A moment later the car was winding and jerking its way through the streets of Rome. Chaos had fallen on the square, which made Sean glad it was in the rear window and disappearing fast. Fire trucks, police cars, and other emergency vehicles had arrived on the scene faster than Sean had expected.

The driver whipped the vehicle sharply to the right and down another side street, smack into the middle of a town market. The sidewalks were lined with awnings and tents, full of produce, meats, breads, and trinkets. Throngs of pedestrians flooded the road, blocking the thoroughfare completely. The driver slammed on the brakes, and the car came to a screeching halt, throwing everyone forward in their seats.

Agent Yarbrough winced and grunted. "You might need to pick a different street," he said, trying to remain calm.

"My mistake, guys," Carl said in a frustrated tone. He threw the car into reverse and backed it onto the previous street.

"Looks like I may have to sit this one out on the sidelines," Yarbrough said, disappointment apparent in his voice. "Is your next move to head to the train station and see what Ms. Villa hid in that locker?"

"That's the plan."

"Good," Yarbrough said and closed his eyes slowly for a second. Sean could tell the man was desperately trying to fight off the pain. "You're the only one that can get her back. The president is stuck between a rock and a hard place. We can't just go in with guns blazing like we did with bin Laden. There's a lot more at stake here."

"I understand." Sean wasn't lying. He understood how the politics of the world worked, and how the bureaucracies were limited in what they could do, especially when the country was an ally.

Greece had been a friend of the United States for a long time, never having any reason to be at odds with one another. If the president sent in a special forces unit on a rescue mission, that could lead to trouble on a massive scale. Other countries would begin to distrust their allies and wonder how much of that sort of thing would go on in their own backyards. Other American presidents had ordered these kinds of missions, but it wasn't a precedent President Dawkins wanted to continue. Sean was the only person capable of doing what was needed. It just so happened that what he wanted and what the president needed were in line.

The car veered to the left and then back to the right, merging into a huge roundabout packed with trucks, motorcycles, and passenger vehicles. The cluster of machines seemed to have no order, people zipping in and out of lanes without so much as a wave of the hand, much less a turn signal.

Their driver seemed adept at moving Roman traffic puzzle, deftly weaving in and out of tight spots until he reached the outlet he was looking for. The car dove out of the circle and down another road, heading for a tall, gray building straight ahead.

"The hospital is there," he said, pointing at the facility. "Do you want me to pull around back or..."

"We'll take him to the front," Sean interrupted. "No need for secrecy now. He's lost a lot of blood and needs to get that wound closed up."

"Sean," Yarbrough interrupted. "Leave me at the hospital. I can have backup there in five minutes. I'll be okay."

Tommy cast a worrisome glance at his friend, then back to the wounded agent. "That's not really our style."

Yarbrough shook his head and put on his sternest expression. "You and I both know you may not have a lot of time. Villa may not have much time, and we believe Gikas is going to make his move in the next few days. The only way to save her is to find out what it is that man is looking for."

Sean thought about it for a moment as the driver of the vehicle steered the car into the hospital's driveway and up to the front door. "You're sure you'll be okay?" He sought Yarbrough's eyes for an honest answer.

"No organ damage. Though I might not be able to throw a baseball again for a while." He forced a fake grin onto his face.

"All right," Sean nodded.

Tommy got out of the car first and ran around to open the door for Yarbrough. Sean dashed inside, and then reappeared through the door pushing a wheelchair. He rolled the chair around to the other side of the car where he and Tommy helped ease the injured man into the seat.

Sean took him to the door where Yarbrough stopped him. "Go on," he ordered, looking up with a stoic glare. "I can take it from here. Go find your girl and bring her back safe."

Sean didn't need to say anything. His quick nod told the man he understood. There was an additional message that Yarbrough passed through the air between them. It was unspoken, but Sean heard it nonetheless.

He left Yarbrough at the threshold of the hospital and ran back to the car. Tommy had already gotten back inside when he slid into the front passenger's seat.

"You sure he's going to be all right?" Carl cast a wary eye over at Sean.

"I've seen worse, but I don't like to leave a man behind. He'll survive." Sean thought for a second and peeked back at the doorway. A triage nurse had taken the handles of the wheelchair and was pushing Yarbrough away, most likely to the emergency room. "We need to get to the train station," he said after watching the Secret Service man disappear.

"Train station? You taking a trip somewhere?" Carl raised an eyebrow.

"I guess that depends."

"On what?"

Sean stared ahead through the windshield. "On what we find there. I have a feeling that whatever it is, we aren't going to get a chance to do any sightseeing in Rome."

16

ROME, ITALY

Thanos tried to hold back his anger, when all he wanted to do was unleash all that inner fury and kill something, or in this case, someone. He stared hard into the green eyes of his sniper. The man wearing a black combat vest still had the high-caliber rifle slung over his shoulder.

"You're sure that you hit one of them?"

"Yes, sir," the man with a flat top haircut said. "I believe in the chest or shoulder."

"That actually makes a huge difference, you idiot." Thanos paused for a minute, frantically attempting to figure out his next move. "What did the target look like?"

A confused look passed over the man's face. "He was tall. Looked fairly strong. And he was black."

Thanos's eyes grew wider. That last revelation was not good. He knew that Sean and his friend Tommy were in the room with a Secret Service agent. If the sniper had put a bullet in the agent, that could be big trouble for Thanos's employer, unless of course there was no way to trace the incident back to Gikas. An old familiar urge was creeping its way into Thanos's mind. His thick muscles tightened, and he could feel the vein on top of his head pumping hard.

"You've been watching that room for the last week, correct?" he asked in a calm voice.

"Yes, sir." The mercenary's voice trembled somewhat. His accent was distinctly Bosnian. The man had served in some harsh conditions during the war in Kosovo, so Thanos knew what he was capable of, and his limitations.

"You followed the woman to and from the room, yes?"

The sniper answered with a nod.

"Where was the last place you saw her other than getting food?"

The man's eyes lowered for a moment, searching the carpet for the answer. Then it dawned on him. His head lifted and an epiphany shone on his face. "The train station. I lost her in the locker room for a few minutes, but found her as she came out one of the exits."

Thanos scowled. "And you didn't think that was important enough to report to me?"

"It was only a minute, two at the most. She still had her bag when she left the area. If she had left something there, I would have noticed."

The defense was weak, and the mercenary knew that Thanos saw right through it. "You idiot! She left it there! Whatever Villa was trying to hide was in her bag when she went in. Obviously it didn't look like she was missing an item because you couldn't see in the bag."

He turned to one of the other men in the room. "You all checked the room after you took her?" He received a nod from all three men at once. "And you found no trace of what she had discovered? Not even the key to the locker? Surely she must have had a key if she had a storage box at the train station?"

"Sir, I assure you, we searched the entire room and found nothing," the sniper insisted, still standing behind Thanos.

The broad-shouldered Greek had heard enough. He spun around and simultaneously pulled out a Glock with a sound suppressor attached to the end. He squeezed the trigger four times, sending all four rounds into the chest of the Bosnian before the man could even blink, much less defend himself. The force sent the man reeling backward, stumbling over a chair and landing on his back. His long rifle dropped to the floor next to him. A thin river of blood trickled from the corner of his mouth. His body shivered, then was still.

Thanos put his gun back in his jacket and turned around to face the last two. They clearly had no intention of dying like the other guy, no matter who their boss was. They each took a few steps back and put their hands on their weapons inside their holsters. Thanos smiled and put his hands up. "Relax, men. You two are safe. He made a mistake and had to be punished. You both will split his share."

The words seemed to please the two men, who eased their positions to a more relaxed stance. They both kept a safe distance, however, just in case.

The phone in Thanos's pocket began to ring, cutting the silent tension in the room. He slid the device out of his pocket and put it to his ear.

"What's your status?" Gikas asked through the earpiece.

"We hit a minor snag, but everything will be back on track within the next few hours." It wasn't a lie, but it wasn't exactly the truth either. Thanos had learned that when one was working for ruthless men, one had to be wise as to the information that was divulged, and the manner it was delivered.

There was a pause before Gikas continued. "Do you have Wyatt?"

"Not yet," Thanos answered unapologetically. "But we know where he is headed. We believe the woman may have hidden something at the central train station here in Rome. It is likely the clue to what we're looking for."

He was making up the details now. For all he knew, Villa could have dropped off a makeup kit in the locker, and without the key they wouldn't know which locker to look for. The only thing Thanos and his men could do was show up at the station and watch for Wyatt. If Villa's boyfriend had somehow procured the key to the locker, he would lead Thanos right to it.

"Good. See to it this is taken care of before sunset tonight. Things will be put into motion in two days, and I need the mechanism to know exactly what to do."

"You will have it. You can always count on me."

The call ended, and Thanos put the phone back in his pocket. He turned his attention back to the other men in the room and thought for a second before speaking. He didn't mind being the lapdog for Dimitris Gikas. A well-paid lapdog could live like a king, after all.

He peered at one man and then the other. "Now, do you two know what locker area he was talking about in the train station?"

Both men nodded rapidly. One answered, "Yes. We can lead you there, but we do not know which locker was hers."

Thanos's eyes narrowed again. "Do you think you could figure that part out if Wyatt doesn't lead us to it?" His tone carried a warning; one that indicated the sniper's fate would become theirs if Thanos wasn't given what he wanted.

The men glanced at each other questioningly for a second before giving another quick nod.

"Good. Take me there."

17

CORFU, GREECE

The little boy sat on the cold, hard floor across from Adriana. He'd cried for at least thirty minutes when the guards first brought him to the damp cellar. Now he sat quietly, staring at the wall.

She'd tried to comfort him when he'd been dropped off, but the child would not respond to any of her questions. Eventually, Adriana decided the best course of action was to let his emotions run their course. She hadn't had much experience with children. The few friends she kept in contact with from her time at the university had already gotten married and had kids of their own. Adriana had decided to take a different path for her life. She had no time for children, and no desire to make that time. Things were hectic in her world. Exhibit A was the cellar in which she lay at the present moment. Having a family of any kind would be nearly impossible. It would imprison her like a wild animal that desperately wants to roam free.

Still, she did like young people. She admired their lack of understanding about the world and their surroundings. Rules didn't apply to them in many ways. Children were dreamers and still believed that anything was possible. They were innocent, for the most part. That innocence was what pulled her to continue reaching out to the young boy with her in the cellar.

"What is your name?" she asked in a kind voice, pressing him gently to open up.

He hesitated, uncertain if he could trust the strange woman across the room. He eyed the bonds around her hands and feet suspiciously.

"It's okay, she insisted. My name is Adriana. They've kept me in this place for two days now. I was just hoping to make a new friend." She smiled cutely at him as she finished the sentence.

Her grin broke through the ice of his gloom, and his lips parted ever so slightly. "My name is Niki," he said, timidly. He didn't move, though, keeping the distance between them.

Adriana forced herself to continue smiling, even though she was extremely uncomfortable. "And what is your last name, Niki?"

The child hesitated again for a moment before answering. "Teridis." He looked down at the floor once more after saying the name.

The boy's answer stunned Adriana for a second. She immediately recognized the last name. The Teridis family was extremely wealthy, second only to the man who held her prisoner. Adriana also knew about the stories of shady dealings involving the Teridises' businesses. Niko had a reputation for killing first and acquiring second. If this was Niko's boy, that could mean only one thing, Gikas was making a power play for the Teridises' holdings. Acquiring businesses of that magnitude would represent a significant increase to the Gikas empire.

"Niki?" She said after thinking for a few seconds. "I need your help with something. Would you like to help me?" She spoke like she'd heard other people talk to children in the past.

"I want my mama," the boy said in a whiny voice. He was on the verge of tears again, something Adriana desperately wanted to avoid.

She hoped a little sympathy would help move past the issue. "I'm sure you do, Niki, but right now your mama isn't here."

"She was near me in the bushes," Niki said, choking back the sobs. "Then she wasn't there anymore. She told me everything would be okay. Where is she?"

The parents were *here*? "In the bushes? What bushes?" Adriana was curious about what the boy had seen.

"The men who took my mama and me made us stand in the bushes near the sea. I could hear the waves. They told me to be quiet because we were hiding from someone."

They'd been near the cliffs on the edge of the property. Not a good sign. Gikas must have taken Niki's parents there to get rid of them. Adriana had seen the cliffs before. They were a perfect place to dispose of a body, or in this case, two. The rocks would cut up the flesh, and the tide would pull the corpses out to seas. They would disappear within hours, consumed by carnivorous sea life. The fact that the boy was still alive proved Gikas wasn't a total monster, but he wasn't exactly a saint either. She pondered what unscrupulous future the Greek man had in mind for the young heir to the Teridis fortune. What was Gikas's motivation for keeping the boy around? She assumed the man would pawn him off to some orphanage sooner or later, unwilling to kill a young innocent.

Then again, if the boy had seen her face and was kept alive, Gikas might be inclined to kill him too. The thought was disturbing, but one she needed to face as a real possibility. Adriana needed to escape, but more than that she needed to get the child to safety. The problem was that the Gikas property was several miles away from town, and even if the kid reached the city, it wouldn't necessarily be the safest place for him. Gikas owned the local authorities, and purportedly had eyes everywhere. The only chance young Niki had to survive was to stick close to her, at least for as long as they let her live.

"Are you cold?" she asked with genuine concern.

Niki didn't say anything for a minute, and then nodded slowly. He pulled his knees up under his chin and folded his arms across them, burying his face in his forearms.

"You should go sit in the sunlight that's coming through that little window over there. It isn't much, but it will keep you warm during the day." Adriana nodded to the narrow beam of light pouring into the room. She'd found a little solace in the dank room by wiggling her way over to the light, just to keep her sanity for the last few days. The sun didn't shine through the window but for a few hours, so she wanted the young boy to take advantage of it while he could.

He didn't respond at first, but after a minute or two, began slowly inching his way toward the light playing across the floor. After a long couple of minutes, he finally arrived in the warm afternoon glow and stretched out a little. He lifted his face and let the warmth of the sun soak into his skin.

"Does that feel a little better?" Adriana asked.

The boy nodded.

"Good. Go lie down and get some rest while it's still warm. Tonight, you may find it hard to sleep. It can get chilly down here in this cellar after the sun goes down."

Niki obeyed and stretched out on the floor, resting his head on his left bicep. He closed his eyes and after a few minutes began breathing in a regular rhythm.

Adriana sighed. She needed to find a way out of this place.

18

ROME, ITALY

Sean knew that the Stazione Termini, the main train station in Rome, was one of the busiest places in the city. Fortunately, he and Tommy arrived at a moment when there seemed to be a lull between arrivals and departures. A lull, however, was a relative term in the crowded city. There were still thousands of people hustling to and from different train platforms, but the two friends had both seen worse. The room had been well designed to hold throngs of travelers, with wide and long expanses allowing for freedom of movement. The undulating ceiling soared overhead, giving the main entrance an even more open feel.

Sean scanned a few of the information signs before finding the one that directed the way to the locker area. Out of habit, he took a quick look around, making sure they hadn't been followed. As before, he had requested that the driver hang around outside in case they needed to leave in a hurry. He pointed at the sign and started in the direction the arrows suggested. Tommy stayed close behind him, cautiously holding his back pocket with one hand.

When he noticed the odd behavior, Sean had to ask. "Not sure I want to know the answer to this. Why do you have your hand on your butt?"

Tommy cast him a chiding glance. "Rome is notorious for pick-pockets, man. All it takes is bumping into one random thief, and your cards, identification, everything are gone. I'd watch your wallet if I were you."

Sean smoothly fished out a money clip from his front pocket and held it over his shoulder for Tommy to see. "Grandpa always said to keep your pictures of Andrew Jackson in your front pocket."

Tommy shook his head slowly and smiled. "I guess that's one way of handling it."

Sean put the money clip back in his pocket and turned to the left, continuing to follow the signs to the locker area. They strode quickly through the main terminal's access corridors and finally arrived at the entrance to a vast room, full of gray lockers. Yellow paint marked the numbers over top of the storage units that were stacked two high, up to the low ceiling.

"I guess lockers have changed since the last time I had to use one," Tommy said. "These things are a lot bigger and more secure looking than I remember."

"And they take credit or debit cards, too," Sean added, pointing at the card slot and keypad. "We need to find locker number fifty-seven."

He followed the numbers, all of which were in the hundreds, until he noticed the descending order. The two traced their way around the room until they reached the back wall. The huge storage units lined the back wall for at least sixty feet, giving it the feel of a minimum-security bank.

"Here it is," Tommy said, stopping at the locker on the second level marked with the number fifty-seven.

Sean halted next to him and gave another paranoid glance in both directions. The locker area was vacant, and much quieter than the rest of the train station. Other than a security camera at one end, they were alone in a major metropolitan train station.

Tommy stared vapidly at the gray box. "I wonder what's in there," he said in an absent tone.

Something was bothering Sean about the storage area, and he

wanted to get what they came for and figure out what it was later. He took the key and shoved it into the keyhole, and then twisted it hard. The door swung open, and the two men stared inside. What they found astounded and confounded both of them. They stared for several seconds in disbelief. Sean reached into the locker and pulled out a paper bag from a fast food chain. He frowned, wondering what it meant. What was Adriana up to?

"What is it?" Tommy asked, trying to look into the bag as Sean opened it up.

Sean couldn't help but smile as he stared into the bag. It was completely empty. "Nothing," he said and showed Tommy the contents.

Tommy's eyebrows stitched together. "I don't understand."

It was perplexing on several levels for Sean. If there was nothing in the bag, he would have no way of finding what it was that Gikas wanted. Without that, he had no leverage.

A strange idea occurred to him as Tommy bent over and examined the empty locker. Sean turned over the bag and found something written in pencil on the bottom. The faint, barely noticeable words spelled out someone's first and last name.

Vincenzo Cagliari.

"Clever," Sean said just above a whisper.

Tommy stood up straight again and looked back at his friend. "What?" he asked.

Sean didn't get a chance to answer. A voice from the other end hall broke their silence.

"Both of you stand perfectly still." The words came from a stocky, bald man with a scar across one cheekbone. Two other men, both muscular and carrying weapons aimed straight in Tommy and Sean's direction, escorted him. The way the men moved, Sean knew immediately they were mercenaries. He'd seen the type before. Unfortunately for him, he'd seen the type recently.

"Do you want me to raise my hands or just keep them down?" Sean asked in a smart aleck tone. "Most of the time when someone gets the drop on me, they ask me to put my hands up."

"From what I know about you, Mr. Wyatt, very few people catch you by surprise." The hulky man's remark meant he had either been watching Sean for a while, or simply done a little research.

"You must feel pretty special then." The snide comment did little to change the men's stone-cold demeanor.

"What is in the bag, Mr. Wyatt?"

A quick snort escaped Sean's nostrils, and despite having guns aimed at him, he kept a grin on his face. "There's a camera behind you boys. I'd say you have about ninety seconds to put those weapons away and get out of here before security arrives."

The man, who was apparently in charge of the other two, never flinched. "I'm aware of the cameras," he said, stepping confidently toward where Tommy and Sean were standing. "I'll ask again. What is in the bag?"

"You wouldn't believe me if I told you." The men hadn't seen him examine the bottom of the bag. He was willing to bet they wouldn't think to do the same.

The three men were only fifteen feet away now and closing. "Fine. Set the bag down and step back."

"All right," Sean said and did as instructed. Tommy followed by his side, stepping away from the spot as Sean set it on the floor. "Just take it easy. You guys don't want to fire those weapons in here. And we don't want to get shot. So relax, come get the bag, and we will all be on our way."

The bald man shook his head slowly, never breaking his poker face. "Regardless of what is in the bag, Mr. Wyatt, you will be coming with us."

"Well, there is where you're going to have a problem," Sean said, keeping his hands out to his sides as he continued to retreat from the paper bag. "It's going to be difficult for you to transport two hostages through the multitude of people out there. All it takes is one hysterical woman to see those guns, and it will become chaos."

Scarface reached the bag and stopped. "Don't move any farther," he ordered, bending one knee and reaching down at the same time to grab the object.

As he did, Sean twisted slightly and slipped something out of his belt with his right hand in a subtle movement. The three henchmen didn't notice.

"I'm telling you," Sean said, "you're going to be disappointed. Pretty sure that bag was left here as a decoy."

The permanent scowl on bald man's face deepened as he opened the top of the bag and realized what Sean was talking about. "Is this some kind of joke? What did you do with it?"

"Do with what?" Sean asked as honestly as he possibly could.

"It was empty when we found it." Tommy corroborated the story.

"You think me a fool? I am going to ask you one last time. What was in the bag? I have no problem killing you and taking it from you." The bald man was nearly yelling now. His irritation had reached boiling point.

The tension between the men was as thick as mud. Sean knew the man wasn't bluffing, even with the watchful eyes of the camera behind them. "Okay. Okay. Take it easy," Sean said finally. "Here," he held out his hand and produced a small, metallic disc, slightly larger than a watch battery. "I don't even know what it is."

"Set it on the floor and back away," the bald man ordered, wagging his gun in the process.

The other two men behind him were clearly jumpy. The slightest provocation would cause them to open fire so Sean moved carefully and did as he was told, setting the disc on the ground.

"Close your eyes," he whispered to Tommy as the man reached down to grab the shiny object.

Tommy was confused but did as directed.

A second before the stranger grasped the disc, a blinding flash of white light erupted from it. Sean had closed his eyes just a moment before the mini-flashbang went off and now opened them as the men in the room began to scream. One of the weapons fired, sending a bullet bouncing off the floor and lockers.

"Go!" Sean snapped at Tommy.

The two Americans turned to their right and sprinted out of the corridor toward the exit. They reached the entrance to the locker room and turned back the way they'd come, heading toward the main lobby of the Stazione Termini. Ahead of them, hundreds of people began pouring onto the floor, exiting a train that had just arrived.

"Head into the crowd," Sean ordered, pointing at the throng of people. A few seconds later, they blended into the mob of travelers in the vast terminal.

"Where are we going?" Tommy asked as they slowed their movements to better blend in with the crowd.

"Not sure yet. But we know who we need to meet."

19

ROME, ITALY

Sean and Tommy's driver was waiting within view of the exit when they left the building. So far, the guy was two for two with his timing. Sean hoped Carl didn't have to bat again. In his previous line of work, he knew it was far better to handle things himself rather than rely on other people. Too many cooks in the kitchen led to mistakes. Mistakes led to big problems.

The two friends slid into the vehicle, and Carl pounded the gas, zipping the car back into traffic before thinking about where they were headed. Sean liked the guy's style.

"Any trouble getting what you were looking for?" the man behind the wheel asked.

"A little," Sean said, watching the lines of people and cars flash by in a blur. "Nothing we couldn't handle."

"Yeah," Tommy interjected. "Where did you get that thing, anyway?"

Sean smiled mischievously and gave his old friend a wink. "A buddy of mine from DARPA sent that over a while back. Thought I would think they were cool." He produced another metallic disc from a modified notch on the inside of his belt and handed it to Tommy.

Tommy palmed the device and eyed it carefully. "How does

it work?"

"You press it like a button. It can be timed up to six seconds. Press it once for every second." Sean continued to stare out the window. "I didn't think I'd ever need to use them in the field, but when Yarbrough told me who he was and who he worked for, I thought I might bring a few with me just in case."

Tommy passed the disc back to his friend after another minute of curious examination. "Well, it's a good thing you did. Handy little diversions, those things. Couldn't your buddy with DARPA get in big trouble for passing out government-funded toys like that?"

Sean nodded. "Probably. But it's more like field research for him. Little things like that won't send up a bunch of red flags if they go missing. Besides, he probably built them in his own workshop or somewhere off the clock."

Something occurred to Sean as the car weaved through the busy city streets, zooming by pedestrians and other vehicles. They didn't know where they were going. He pulled out his phone, opened the Google Maps app, and typed in the name he'd seen on the bottom of the bag. Sean's memory was something that had served him well over the years. It wasn't quite to the level of most who had an eidetic ability, but it was close. After a few seconds, the server brought back several search results, more than Sean had expected. He scanned through a few before deciding there would be a faster way to get the man's address.

He closed the application and pulled up the text messaging app and then typed a short message to Emily. Finding someone's address online could be easy or difficult. They didn't have time to drive around Rome on a wild goose chase to figure out where Vincenzo Cagliari lived.

Sean looked back through the rear window. No suspicious vehicles were in pursuit. He took a deep breath and calmed his nerves for a second. "Just keep driving away from the station," he said to the driver, doing his best to keep the tension out of his voice.

"Who were those tree trunks back in the locker area?"

For a second, Sean didn't answer. His thoughts were on Adriana.

He knew they had probably been the men who had taken her. The thought sent a chill down his spine and raised the hairs on his arms. "I'm guessing they work for the man who has Adriana."

Tommy didn't respond for a moment. "Dimitris Gikas?"

Sean nodded but remained silent. He didn't want to talk about that stuff right now. At the moment, all that matter was finding the relic the Greek wanted so badly. Then Sean would consider that situation.

The driver carefully guided the car through the mayhem of Roman traffic and the haze of exhaust that lingered over the streets. In a matter of a few minutes, the mobs of people and vehicles began to thin as the driver pushed farther away from the train station. Outside, the Basilica di Santa Maria Maggiore passed by. Its matching blue domes and the crucifix-topped obelisk made it an easily recognizable historical landmark. Sean knew the Diocletian Baths were nearby as well, another ancient place of significance. The thoughts on local history distracted him until his phone vibrated.

He saw Emily's name appear on the screen and quickly entered the lock code to access the text. She had not only given him the location he needed, but a short history on the name of the man they were looking for.

"Head toward Piazza Navona," Sean said to the driver.

Tommy gave a quizzical look. "You wanting to see the Pantheon?"

"That's where Cagliari lives."

"Must have a lot of money, that guy," the driver commented as he turned the car down a side street. "Navona is an expensive place to live."

Sean scanned over the text from Emily again to make sure he got all the details right. "Vincenzo Cagliari was a professor at the world renowned Sapienza University of Rome. Seems he is one of the foremost experts on Julius Caesar."

Tommy's face wrinkled. "You said he *was* a professor. Not anymore?"

"He retired. The guy is in his seventies. I'd say after a lifetime of working in the field he probably deserves a little rest and relaxation."

Tommy laughed louder than he'd intended and shook his head. "Well, if rest and relaxation was what he wanted, he's sure as heck not going to want to meet us."

Sean's eyes squinted slightly as he nodded. "Good point," he said, acknowledging his friend's funny quip. "Still, we're going to have to risk ruining the old guy's retirement, at least for a day. If Adriana wrote his name on that bag in hopes we'd find him, it must mean that he knows something we need to know."

"Or maybe she left something with him," the driver interjected. The two passengers looked at him then back at each other. For a second Carl felt like he'd overstepped his bounds.

"Exactly," Sean agreed, easing the man's nerves. "Let's just hope the men from the train station don't figure out where we're headed."

"They didn't strike me as the clever type," Tommy noted.

Sean peered straight ahead. "Don't be too quick to judge. Those men were good enough to figure out where we were headed and when we would be there. If they can do that, they might be able to figure out our next move."

"So what do we do? Try to throw them off the trail? Go to some decoy spots?"

"We don't have time for that kind of stuff, although I do like the idea." Sean thought about it for a few seconds. "No, we just have to move faster and stay one step ahead of them."

Carl swerved the vehicle past a fruit truck and back into the lane, narrowly missing an oncoming Fiat. "And what if they do figure out where we're going?" Tommy asked, grabbing onto the hand grip above the window to brace himself.

"I don't know. I guess we'll just have to figure out a plan when we get there."

Tommy laughed and shook his head. "You know, in the short time you've been gone from the agency, I'd forgotten how much of this stuff you just make up as you go along."

Sean raised an eyebrow. "It gets the job done, doesn't it?"

Tommy took in a long breath. "Usually. Let's just hope the time never comes when it doesn't."

20

ROME, ITALY

Thanos rubbed his eyes as tears rolled down his cheeks. It had been five minutes since Sean Wyatt had detonated some kind of improvised flashbang device, and his eyes still burned from the searing white light. He and his men pushed their way through the crowd, hurrying desperately to figure out which way Wyatt and his friend had gone. It was too late, though. Their quarry had disappeared into the waves of tourists and commuters like a thief in the night. In between rapid blinks, his eyes darted left and right, scouring the crowded lobby for any sign of the Americans.

"No sign of them," one of the henchmen said, returning from a fruitless search to the eastern side of the station. Thanos already knew they'd be long gone.

The problem now was figuring out where they'd headed. Thanos had checked the paper bag as soon as his eyes had re-acclimated to their surroundings following the bright flash from Wyatt's little trick, but it had been empty. He'd thrown it aside and hastily stormed out of the locker area.

"Should we go back and check out the locker, sir?" the other grunt asked.

Thanos nodded, saying nothing.

The three made their way back to the locker area, rudely shoving people out of their path as they moved through the outer edge of the lobby and into the corridor. Walking eased dramatically upon getting back to the locker area, and they hurriedly made their way to where Wyatt had detonated the small explosive. When they reached the spot, the three were greeted by an unexpected surprise. Two security guards were inspecting the black burn marks left on the floor by the tiny flashbang. One was down on a knee, running his finger along the streaks. They were speaking in Italian, saying something about how the flash had shorted out the camera in the corner. One of them held the paper bag in his hand. He was looking at the bottom of it with a curious expression. Thanos held up his hand for the men behind him to wait a moment. They were hidden from view by a perpendicular wall of lockers. This meant he and his men still had the element of surprise with the two guards.

Thanos took a step back and listened carefully, knowing the guards had not seen or heard him since their backs were facing him.

"What does this mean?" the man with the bag asked in rushed Italian. "Vincenzo Cagliari?"

Vincenzo Cagliari? Had he heard correctly? Thanos leaned farther around the corner, listening closer.

"Throw that trash away," the other guard said in a reprimanding tone. "We have work to do."

"Why would someone write that on the bottom of a paper bag?"

Thanos was grateful he spoke fluent Italian. It had been an easy enough language to acquire after years of speaking Spanish and French. There were enough similarities among the foundations of each language that he'd learned it in a matter of less than two months. He continued to listen patiently to the conversation going on between the two guards to see if he could glean any more information.

The security man on one knee stood up and grabbed the bag from the other, tossing it at a trashcan right next to the corner where Thanos was standing. As soon as the bag hit the rim of the can and fell in, the guard saw Thanos leaning around the corner and immediately produced his sidearm. He pointed the barrel at Thanos's head with a nervous finger on the trigger.

"You there," he shouted in Italian. "Stay where you are!"

Thanos didn't move, but he could sense the men behind him slinking away. He slowly put his right hand up in the air and his left around his back, quickly motioning for his men to go around behind the security personnel.

"I'm sorry," he said in an accent that very nearly sounded American. "I don't speak Italian. I'm here on vacation, and I lost my wife."

The two men exchanged a suspicious glance before the one on the right spoke up. "He's the one from the camera footage we saw earlier. Call for backup." The one in charge then turned his commands to Thanos, speaking in rough English. "Keep your hands up and do not move."

"Very well," Thanos said, again in English. He stood perfectly still as the man began taking cautious steps toward him.

The subordinate security guard started to move his left hand toward the radio attached to his shoulder to call for reinforcements when Thanos saw his men slip up behind the two uniformed rent-a-cops with knives drawn. Their movement was stealthy and swift as they simultaneously stepped toward their targets. The subordinate officer was nabbed first, Thanos's man drawing the shiny blade across the throat of the unsuspecting guard. He gurgled slightly for a second and dropped to the ground just as the other guard was snatched by the second henchman, who jammed the tip of his blade through the back of the man's neck and out the front of his throat. He collapsed a moment later, next to his partner.

The victims' bodies shook violently on the floor, resisting death for a few short moments before stiffening.

Thanos took a step away from the scene, making sure he stayed clear of the camera's view.

"Do you need the bag, sir?" one of his men asked, about to bend down and pick it up.

"No. We have everything we need."

The three men made their way back out of the locker area and into the throng of people once more. Thanos gave a quick check around to make sure they hadn't drawn the attention of any additional security personnel. A few police were making their way toward the locker room from the far side of the train station. As soon as the authorities discovered the two bodies, the entire place would be locked down. Getting to the car was imperative.

Thanos moved fast, weaving his way through the flood of people, knocking over an elderly woman as he did. His two men followed close behind, sensing their boss's urgency. The doors were only forty feet away, but it seemed like two miles. The crowd had thinned out a little, making their escape quicker, but Thanos couldn't help but feel like the police were watching their every movement. He took a quick look up at one corner of the room where three cameras were mounted together, watching the entire lobby of the station. He knew they'd been seen at some point. And even though no one realized what was going on at the moment, they would be easily traced later on.

His men were known mercenaries, hit men hired by the highest bidder. No doubt Interpol would have little trouble figuring out who they were. His identity, however, was kept immaculately anonymous. He'd spent untold amounts of time and money keeping it that way. The less anyone knew about him the better. The only soul on the planet who knew Thanos's true identity was his employer, Dimitris Gikas, the only man he ever trusted. Still, all anyone needed was a picture to post anywhere, and his anonymity would quickly evaporate. With social media swarming everyone's lives, his name would be irrelevant. People would recognize the face. A face was all one needed to get arrested.

Twenty feet from the exit, Thanos believed they had made it. He could smell the outside air coming through the doors, sensing their escape had been made. His relief, however, was short lived. Two uniformed police officers appeared in the doorway directly in front of Thanos and his men. The police stepped through the portal and strode purposely in Thanos's direction. The officers' eyes locked on the three men as they moved cautiously toward the killers. One of the policemen touched his shoulder radio and said something quietly into the microphone.

Thanos couldn't make out what he'd said above the noise in the crowded station, but he kept walking toward the exit, moving deliberately now so as not to spook the officers. He wasn't a man to be made nervous easily, but in this instance he knew that being arrested wasn't an option. He and his men could kill the police, but it would be in a room full of witnesses and cameras. Knowing the latter, he would have to rest his hopes on the diplomatic reach of his employer to get them out of trouble. Thanos hated having to do that. He'd only used Gikas's influence one other time, when he'd killed a prostitute in Budapest. He feared he might have to make that phone call again tonight.

Less than ten feet away, the two policemen split apart and circled around the three men. Thanos watched, somewhat disbelieving, as the two uniformed policemen disappeared into the mass of people. He spun around and picked up the pace again with his two assistants in tow. They needed to get to the car and figure out just who this Vincenzo Cagliari was, and why Adriana Villa had thought him so important.

21

CORFU, GREECE

The door to the cellar burst open, flooding a small area of the stone floor with light from a staircase. Dimitris Gikas stood on the threshold, staring in at the scene. The light silhouetted his figure. Niki scooted toward the back wall. Adriana returned his stare with fierce eyes.

"What is so important about Cagliari?" Gikas asked bluntly. He took a few steps into the cellar, clicking the hard bottoms of his Italian leather shoes with each one.

For a split second, Adriana's eyes twitched. She instantly regained her composure, not wanting to give away the secret she held in her mind. "I do not know who that is," she lied.

Gikas's lips pouted mockingly and his eyebrows lifted. "Oh. So, you do not know the man whose name you wrote on the bottom of a bag and left in a locker in a train station? It seems highly probable that you do indeed know who Vincenzo Cagliari is."

She shook her head, this time keeping her lips pursed tightly.

"Well," Gikas put his hands behind his back and walked a little farther into the room. "That is a shame. Because right now I have three of my men en route to Cagliari's home." Gikas stopped a few feet away from Adriana. She glared up at him from the floor like an angry cat that had been declawed. "You see, my men found what you left in the train station in Rome. They are going to ask Signor Cagliari a few questions. Then, they are going to kill him. I figured since you knew him, I might tell my men to be merciful, perhaps execute him quickly. Since you do not know him, you would have no problem with my drawing out the old man's death."

Adriana fought to keep her breathing calm. If Gikas was telling the truth, her old friend would be in grave danger. Other thoughts mingled with the concern. How had his men found the key? They must have returned to the hotel room and discovered it on the floor near the entrance. She wished there was a way to reach out to Cagliari, but there was nothing she could do. Another thing occurred to her, something that brought a terrible sense of doom to her. Sean hadn't found the key. That meant he was not on his way to save her. If she was going to get out of this alive, she would have to do it on her own.

"Nothing to say about that?" Gikas interrupted her thoughts. "Very well. I will tell my men to do their worst on the good professor."

He swiveled on one foot and started to leave the room when Adriana stopped him. "Wait!" she shouted, freezing him just before he reached the entrance. He spun around, eager to hear what she would say.

"Please. Just wait." She hesitated for a moment, not sure what to tell the evil man standing before her. "I have known Signor Cagliari most of my life. He was like an uncle to me. Please, I beg you. Do not harm him."

A curious look washed over Gikas's face. "Now that depends on what you are going to tell me. Doesn't it?"

"What do you want to know?" she stalled, still formulating a story. She had to think fast. Gikas would easily smell a lie. Whatever she came up with had to be convincing.

He walked back to where she sat on the floor and leaned over her, bending down at the knees. "Cagliari either knows something, or you gave him something, or both. What is it? If you tell me what it is he's hiding for you, I may consider letting the old man live. But if I find out you're lying to me, or have misled me in any way, I will cut out your tongue, and Cagliari will suffer an excruciating death."

Adriana swallowed hard, peering through narrow slits at the man standing over her. He was almost close enough to strike in the groin with her boot, but it would be a fruitless maneuver that would only bring worse consequences down on her, and possibly the young boy cowering in the corner. The latter concerned her more than her own safety.

She drew in a deep breath and waited before answering his request. "Let the boy go, and I will tell you what you want to know."

A snort escaped Gikas's nostrils. Something about the request must have amused him. "You are in no position to negotiate, young lady."

Her steeled expression never faltered. "If I'm in no position to negotiate, then why are you here?"

He stood erect and thought for a few seconds. "Very well. I will have the boy taken to an orphanage in the city. He will be well looked after there. In return, you need to tell me what Cagliari is hiding." Gikas raised his finger in warning. "But do not lie to me. If you do, I will know it. And if that is what happens, you and your friend will suffer greatly."

"Call your men first."

Gikas leaned back and tilted his head up as he laughed at the request. His voice bounced off the stone walls around them. "You are a bold little girl. I'll give you that. You certainly have no fears."

Adriana stared hard at him. Her hair had been pulled back tight in a ponytail, but one strand had slipped and was cascading down her face, past her cheek. "We all have fears, Dimitris. Even you."

His curiosity aroused, he pushed the conversation further. "And what is it you believe I fear, Ms. Villa?"

When she answered, she didn't flinch. "You fear losing. And you fear anyone who can make that happen."

"Ah. That is what you believe? That I'm afraid to lose?" Adriana's nostrils flared, but she didn't answer. "You are mistaken. I am not afraid of losing because I never lose."

"You will someday."

"Perhaps. But it will not be today. Now, if you don't mind, I would appreciate it if you would quit delaying and tell me what it is I want to know. My men will be at Cagliari's within the next twenty minutes, so your friend is running out of time."

Adriana let out a long sigh. "I gave him a map," she said suddenly.

Gikas raised a wary eyebrow. "What kind of map? And what is so special about it?"

She swallowed, formulating what to say. "It is written on an ancient scroll. There were only three of its kind. The other two have been lost to history. They were created by order of Julius Caesar himself."

Gikas listened intently, his eyes widening with every word. "And what is on this map?"

Adriana looked up into the man's eyes. "It shows the way to the last Antikythera Mechanism."

22

ROME, ITALY

C arl parked the car next to the sidewalk on the outskirts of the Piazza Navona. "You'll have to go on foot from here," he explained. "No cars allowed where you're heading." Both of the friends gave a thankful nod for the information.

A few minutes later, Tommy and Sean were making their way through the maze of old homes, shops, and cafes. They pushed quickly through the heavy visitor traffic at the Fontana del Moro, a fountain many believed to be a tribute to the ancient god Neptune. Its rose-colored marble base and dramatic sculptures drew the imagination and admiration of many a tourist.

The little streets teemed with people, many busily striding from one place to the next, others strolling casually through. Sean looked at his phone a few times to make sure they were walking in the right direction. He'd entered the address Emily sent to his Google Map application. Based on the blinking blue dot on the screen, they appeared to be only a block away from Cagliari's home.

They hurried by a coffee shop, its patrons sitting out on the patio enjoying conversation. The rich smells of Italian coffee hung in the air as the men passed by. Sean and Tommy both loved good coffee, and they exchanged a longing glance as they left the shop behind.

"Next time," Sean said, knowing what his friend was thinking.

"I do love coffee the way the Italians make it."

Up ahead, the narrow thoroughfare twisted to the right, angling its way slightly up a small hill. Just around the bend in the alley, Sean stopped at a red door and double-checked the number attached to the side of the sill. "This is it," he said after confirming the text from Emily.

The door was set in a three-story, beige stucco building. The adjacent structure was of the same build and design, save for brighter burnt-yellow paint. Many of the buildings in the Piazza Navona featured similar architectural and design expression.

Sean rapped firmly on the entrance and took a step back. He glanced down one direction of the alley and then the other, an old paranoid habit he'd kept for nearly a decade. An elderly couple walked slowly down the other side of the narrow road. A man in a business suit walked by, talking on his cell phone in Italian and clearly in a hurry to get somewhere. A few tourists lumbered by, speaking in an English accent, talking about a place where they'd like to eat later.

The door creaked open slowly, allowing only a slim space to see inside. A pair of old, gray eyes stared out from the opening. The orbs were set deep in a pair of recessed sockets and placed underneath a wrinkled, pale forehead. The man's white hair and sagging skin below his jaw emphasized his age.

"Signor Cagliari?" Sean asked in as respectful a tone as possible.

"Si. Sean Wyatt?" The question caught Sean off guard. How did he know?

Sean nodded. "Yes, sir. I'm Sean Wyatt, and this is my friend Tommy Schultz. Would it be all right if we came inside?"

"Of course, Sean," the man answered in strong voice. "I have been waiting for you. Please, come in quickly." Cagliari opened the door wider and beckoned the two visitors to enter.

The two looked at each other curiously, and then did as told. Once inside, the old man looked down both stretches of the street before closing the door and locking it.

Inside the apartment was like stepping out of a time machine and into a world that had long since been left behind. The high ceilings were accented by ancient timbers, running from one side of the great room to the next. The kitchen to the left had been modeled in the Tuscan design, and featured exquisite tiled floors and backsplashes, complementing the pale stone countertops. On the far wall of the great room, a floor-to-ceiling bookshelf stretched high and wide, burdened with hundreds of books on every single level.

"Please," the host said, showing the way to a plush, navy blue couch, "sit down. I am sure you have many questions."

The men accepted the offer and sat down on the surprisingly soft cushions.

"Can I offer you a glass of wine or perhaps some coffee?" Cagliari asked, shuffling toward the kitchen.

Tommy remembered the smell of the coffee from the street and was about to accept when Sean gave him the silent shake of his head. "We're in a hurry," he mouthed.

"No thank you, sir. I do appreciate the offer," Tommy said, full of resignation.

"No worries. I am just finishing my daily glass. I hope you don't mind." The old man scooped up a thin, long-stemmed glass with a small amount of deep-red liquid still in the bottom.

"Not at all, signore. It's your house," Sean smiled at the man as he returned to the great room.

Cagliari padded over to a leather club seat and eased into it, sighing as if he'd just run ten miles to get there. He took a long sip from the glass before setting it on top of a small, glass top end table.

"So, you have come for the scroll." Cagliari spoke in a casual, matter-of-fact tone.

Tommy and Sean glanced at each other, not sure what to say. Sean spoke up first with a bewildered expression. "We aren't really sure what we are here for, signore. We were hoping you could help us with that. All Adriana left us was your name. She left you a scroll?"

The old man had lifted the wine glass to his mouth once more and took another draught. He shook his head fervently at the question. "No, my friend. She did not leave the scroll with me. You are looking for the scroll. It is not in this place."

Tommy seemed more befuddled. "What scroll, signore?"

"Now that is the question." He set the glass down again and folded his hands over the tops of his legs. "The scroll is hidden. I have searched much of my life to find another Eye of Zeus, but it has eluded me. If you can find the scroll, you can find the missing device."

Sean jumped back into the conversation. "So it's a map?"

"Possibly," Cagliari said, putting his hands out with palms up. "No one really knows for certain. The common theory is that, yes, the scroll is a map."

"I'm sorry, signore," Sean put a hand up and stopped the man. "I feel like there is a backstory we are missing. Would you mind filling us in on where the scroll came from, and why we are looking for it?"

"Certainly," the man said with a wide smile. His teeth were in remarkable shape, clean and bright. "I began my career as a young student of archaeology, much like yourself, Mr. Wyatt." He jabbed a crooked finger in Sean's direction. "When I was thirty years of age, I stumbled upon a story about an ancient mechanism that could forecast future events. This is the relic known as the Antikythera Mechanism, or in some circles, the Eye of Zeus."

"Wait," Tommy interrupted. "People believed this thing could tell the future?"

"Yeah," Sean answered for Cagliari, "I forgot to tell you about that. Just let him finish, and I'll fill you in later." Then he switched his attention back to the old man. "Please, professor, continue." Tommy held his tongue incredulously.

Cagliari nodded and smiled before he went on. "At first," he laughed, "I thought much like you did. The ancients had many strange superstitious beliefs. Some seemed downright outlandish. However, when I discovered that Julius Caesar had a keen interest in the Eye of Zeus, my disposition changed immediately.

"Gaius Julius Caesar was not a man with whom to be trifled. His command was law, and only his ambition for the Roman nation

trumped that. He knew that with great plans come great consequences, both within circles, and without." Sean nodded. He knew
what Cagliari was referring to: Caesar's betrayal by those who were
closest to him. "Caesar knew that he could never let those who would
betray him take hold of the Eye of Zeus. It would mean the collapse
of everything he'd worked so hard to establish."

Outside the great room's window, children laughed and squealed
as they ran by, probably playing some game. Sean's mind was on full
alert, and every sudden noise jerked at his attention.

Sean finished Cagliari's story. "So he hid it."

"That is correct."

"Where?" Tommy asked.

Cagliari's smile broadened and he took another sip of wine.
"That, my friend, is a question that had occupied my mind for nearly
three decades." He stared down at the floor for a minute. His smile
never faded, but Sean could tell he was thinking about something
jarring, regret perhaps. "All the time I spent working on that project
never came to fruition. Of course, I was working at the university
most of the time so my work on the Eye of Zeus came out of my
personal time. Sad to say, I gave up a few good relationships as a
result. Still, I never found the thing. That was, until I met your
friend."

"Adriana." Sean said reverently. His heart thumped again in his
chest. He rarely worried about people. Worrying never helped
anything. It was like experiencing failure in advance, but rarely did it
help someone prepare for it, much less help the situation.

"Yes," Cagliari said proudly. "She's a remarkable woman. Adriana
was able to figure out an ancient mystery that had remained hidden
for centuries, and to these old eyes for many years. The solution was
so simple. It was hidden right under my nose the whole time." He
laughed again at the thought.

The old man stared at the floor for a few seconds before realizing
his guests were waiting for more answers. He looked up and began
speaking again.

"For years, I pored through the secret writings of Julius Caesar. I was granted access to the archives within the Vatican, a privilege that few ever attain. I found hundreds of texts concerning battles, planning, and even some things on civic responsibilities such as sanitation, water, and crime. When I finally found an entry regarding the Eye of Zeus, its meaning escaped me. I spent almost a year of my life desperately trying to unravel the last thread of the mystery."

"What thread was that?" Tommy asked like a boy hearing a ghost story around a campfire. He leaned forward in his seat, on the edge of the cushion.

Cagliari stood up and padded over to a humble wooden desk in the corner of the room. The little workstation was only three feet wide and made from maple worn by time. The man picked up a copy of something sitting on the right side of the desk and brought it back over to his guests. He handed it to Sean and returned to his seat.

Tommy stood up and anxiously stepped over to Sean's side to look over his shoulder. The sheet of paper was a copy of a document that must have been thousands of years old.

"I found that in the Vatican archives a few years ago," Cagliari interrupted the silence. "I suppose it took a pair of young eyes to understand its meaning, though. It seems that is life's way. The older, more educated of us are too set in our ways to be open to new ideas."

Sean read the words, written in Latin. "These were written by the hand of Julius Caesar?" Even though what he had in his hands was just a copy, Sean still appreciated the gravity of the document.

The old Italian nodded silently, beaming with pride.

Sean and Tommy both did the translation in their head as they stared at the sheet, puzzled by the riddle.

The key to the Eye of Zeus is in the mouth of the great god.

23

ROME, ITALY

"That's a strange riddle," Sean said flatly.

Tommy echoed his friend's sentiment by repeating part of the phrase. "The eye is in the mouth? No offense, signore, but I can see why that had you stumped for so long."

"None taken, Thomas." The man grinned. "I must say it was a relief that someone actually figured it out. I would have gone to my grave entirely frustrated if your friend had not come along and saved me."

Sean didn't want to be rude, but he knew that time could be running out for Adriana. "What was her solution to the riddle, signore?" he asked as politely as possible.

Cagliari sensed Sean's urgency and happily obliged. "The life blood of the city of Rome is its river, the Tiber. It has always been the source of vitality for Romans, dating back to its earliest settlers. In the beginning, the first people here believed that the river was a gift from their gods, a blessing that would help them build a great society. They were not wrong about that part." Cagliari winked then went on. "The name Tiber was bestowed upon the river as a tribute to the ancient king Tibernius, who drowned in its waters.

"According to the Roman legend, Jupiter made the king a god and tasked him with guarding the people of Rome from his river throne. In the lore, the river flowed from the god's hair and beard to the people."

Now Sean understood the riddle. The Tiber River was the great god. That meant the key to the Eye of Zeus would be somewhere near its mouth. Sean frowned.

"The mouth of the great god? So we are supposed to search the mouth of the river? That covers a huge surface area where the river meets the sea. How would you know where to start?" A sickening feeling crept into Sean's stomach. They didn't have time to do a full-on excavation at the mouth of the Tiber.

Cagliari's eyes gleamed like someone who kept a grand secret. "You are correct, Sean. If we were looking for the mouth of the river, that would be a problem. Fortunately, it is not the mouth of the river you seek, but the mouth of the god himself."

The answer struck Tommy first. "The river's source. It would have to be a spring or something small. Right?"

Their host nodded. "Correct." He drew the last remnants of wine into his mouth and continued. "You can find the source of the Tiber in the Apennine Mountain Range, on Mount Fumaiolo. It is a few hours north of here, but it is a well-known location. Italians consider it a historic landmark. Benito Mussolini put a plaque there to commemorate it. The river begins as a spring flowing from a small opening in the mountain. According to the answer your friend, Ms. Villa, provided, it is there you will find the key to the Eye of Zeus."

The last sentence brought up another question in Sean's mind. "You said we will find the key. What does that mean? The relic isn't there?"

Cagliari's mouth creased to one side. "No. You will not find the last Antikythera Mechanism at the source of the Tiber. That would have been too simple for anyone living in Caesar's time, or so he thought. The key is like a map. It should tell you the location of the Eye of Zeus, but beware: It is likely that Caesar made the key difficult to decipher. If I were to guess, he probably called upon his years at sea to create the last piece of the puzzle."

"What makes you think that?" Tommy asked, returning to his seat.

The old man glanced down at his empty glass with a longing expression, and then leaned back in his chair. "Julius Caesar loved his time with the Roman navy. He reflected back on it throughout many of his journals as some of his favorite years. The time he spent upon Roman vessels shaped who he was as a man. It hardened him, focused him, and educated him in ways he would not have imagined before. It would make sense that his riddle would have something nautical in it."

Sean absorbed the information quietly. Inside his head, the gears were turning. They needed to get to Mount Fumaiolo fast. "Will you be going with us to the mountain?" he asked respectfully.

"I appreciate the sentiment," Cagliari said with a smile. "It would be a great honor. Alas, I am too old to be running off on such adventures, Mr. Wyatt. It is time for me to pass the quest for the Antikythera Mechanism to someone a bit younger than I with the energy to see it through."

"Are you sure?" Tommy pressed, probably just being polite.

"I am quite sure. I would only slow you down, and as I can see, you are in something of a hurry."

"Thank you for your help," Sean said. "I hope I can repay you someday."

Cagliari raised a dismissive hand. "No repayment necessary. Now, you should get going. It's a few hours' drive from here, and you need to get to the mountaintop before dark."

Sean and Tommy stood simultaneously, followed by their host. The three men started to head to the door when their goodbyes were suddenly interrupted by five vigorous knocks. The three froze in place at the edge of the living room.

"You expecting company?" Sean asked, just above a whisper.

Cagliari said nothing at first, but shook his head slowly. He pointed to the back of the great room to a dark doorway. "Quickly," he said in a hushed voice.

The old man moved fast toward the back of the house. Sean was surprised at his speed. Cagliari led them through the short archway and to the left where a set of stairs descended into the basement of the home. The three men hurried down the steps and through another door. They were greeted by a vast wine cellar with racks of bottles lining the walls.

"Where are you taking us?" Tommy asked, wondering if they weren't being put in a corner with no escape.

Their host flashed another mischievous grin. "Some of these old buildings have secret passages built in. It was one of the reasons I bought this home. I couldn't help myself. I love mysterious things." He stepped over to a narrow wine rack that stretched up to the low ceiling. Cagliari reached out his hand and pulled on the third bottle from the top of the far right row. The entire wine rack swung slowly away from the wall like a giant door, revealing an opening behind it.

"Quickly, gentlemen."

Cagliari removed a cell phone from his pocket and tapped on the screen a few times until the light on the back side of the device came on, illuminating a dark, musty passageway behind the wine rack. He disappeared behind the rows of bottles, still moving faster than Sean thought possible.

"I guess this is our way out," Tommy said.

"I guess so."

The two followed the old man into the entry of the secret passage and pulled out their phones, turning on their lights the same way Cagliari had.

The Italian stepped over to a handle on the wall and pulled it down gently. A second later, the wine rack swung closed, immersing the three men in the darkness of the corridor, save for the light their phones provided.

"Where does this lead?" Sean asked as Cagliari began to make his way forward.

"Ironically, it leads to the river."

24

ROME, ITALY

T hanos banged on the door one last time. "Signor Cagliari!" he shouted in Italian. "This is the police."

A few tourists passed by and stared at the three men hovering around the red door. Thanos's two assistants made sure to look as menacing as possible to avert further intrusion by curious eyes. His driver had just parked the car outside the Piazza Navona near one of the grand, domed cathedrals situated on the edge of the square. On the walk over, they kept their eyes straight ahead, hidden by sunglasses to further protect their identities.

The door remained shut, which either meant Cagliari wasn't home or he wasn't answering. There was another possibility as well. Sean Wyatt could be inside. "Be ready," he said to the other two. "Be careful, though. If you fire your weapons, do not hit the map."

Thanos had just gotten off the phone with Dimitris. Apparently, Adriana had given up the information they needed. Thanos hoped that she hadn't been roughed up too badly. He wanted to have that pleasure all to himself.

"Once we are inside, if there is no one here, search everywhere you can. The map is probably a parchment scroll. It will look very old. Understand?" The other two nodded.

Thanos took a quick look down both sides of the street. Satisfied the coast was clear, he stepped toward the door and slammed his heavy 'foot into the middle of it. The door gave way easier than he thought, bursting open and swinging hard into the doorstop. With guns drawn, his two mercenaries entered the living quarters first. One made sure the right was clear; the other took the left. Thanos went in directly behind them with his gun held in front of his chest.

The inside of the home was deathly quiet; too quiet for the burly, bald man. Thanos scanned everything rapidly, and then silently motioned for the guy on the right to go to the back of the home. He'd walked into more than a few ambushes before. From his experience, before the storm things were always calmest. He pointed for the other one to check out the upstairs area.

The men obeyed and disappeared to their assigned locations. Thanos lowered his weapon, keeping it at the ready, and closed the door behind him. No need to leave it open for the wandering eyes of the city's visitors.

While his men were searching the house, Thanos stepped into the great room and surveyed the space. He made a note of the sofas and chairs, the coffee table and other furniture. The decorations weren't to his taste, but then again he preferred to keep things mini-malist. Furniture and interior decoration was for function only. His eyes stopped on an object that appeared out of place in an otherwise clean room. An empty wine glass rested atop the end table next to one of the chairs. Thanos picked up the container and inspected it closely. It was hard to tell how long it had been sitting there, but the mere fact that it was not put away contrasted the otherwise orderly apartment.

That meant Cagliari had either left in a hurry, or absently forgotten the glass. Something told Thanos it was the former. The glass was still slightly warm to the touch. His eyes darted around suspiciously. If Cagliari had left recently, he wouldn't be far away. He set the object back on the nightstand and purposefully made his way over to the little workstation in the corner. There was a series of envelopes, letters, and sticky notes atop the desk. The three shelves attached to the desk and flush to the wall held more envelopes and letters. One particular envelope caught his attention over all the others. It had the name *Adriana Villa* on the bottom left corner.

Thanos picked it up carefully and took a quick look around to make certain no one was sneaking up on him. Paranoia from years in the field taught him never to let his guard down. He slid a fingernail underneath the seal and ripped it open, then pulled back the edges and peered into the envelope. A folded piece of paper was cradled inside. Thanos pulled out the sheet and unfolded it. His eyes widened as they scanned the content of the letter. He could hear his man's footsteps upstairs as he moved through the home, probably sifting through drawers and cabinets. The man Thanos had sent to the back of the house returned to the great room and found his employer staring at a sheet of paper.

"What is it?" the mercenary asked.

"It's what we were looking for," Thanos answered.

His assistant appeared dubious. "I thought you said it would be on an old piece of parchment or something."

"The original probably is. This is a copy. Cagliari must have duplicated it and brought it here."

The younger man squinted. "Then where is the original?"

Thanos shrugged. "Doesn't matter. We have what we need. Now we can get the boss what he wants." He knew that Gikas would be pleased with such a quick end to the search. The wealthy man would likely reward Thanos with some kind of a bonus. Gikas had been generous with his money before. This time, Thanos hoped that would be the case again. And there was the issue of what to do with the Spanish woman. His employer had made mention of her before. Just thinking about the wicked things he would do to her made Thanos's skin flush. Quickly, he refocused his attention to the current situation.

The mercenary still looked curious. "So where to next?"

"Ostia," he tapped on the paper, showing it to his subordinate. "The mouth of the Tiber River."

25

ROME, ITALY

Vincenzo Cagliari led the way through the secret passage as if he'd done it a hundred times before. Something told Sean that the old man probably used the corridor more frequently than necessary simply because he liked it.

"I have a question," Tommy said as the group reached a curve in the path. "If this device really could predict the future, why didn't Julius Caesar just use it to evade his enemies or to tell him how to take them all out?"

"A good question," Cagliari answered. "And one that I have asked myself many times. It wasn't until I began looking into the strange world of quantum possibilities that I realized the answer."

"Quantum possibilities?"

Sean kept his mouth shut, knowing the answer but deciding to let the old professor do the talking.

"Yes," Cagliari said, continuing down the passageway. The path started to angle downhill ever so slightly. "Quantum mechanics tells us that in the universe there are limitless possibilities to everything. As it applies to our lives, that brings an entirely new meaning. Many people believe that our lives are on a linear path, like a train on its tracks. Try as we might, we are not permitted to leave that track; at least, that is what many people think. Quantum mechanics tells us that not only are we on that track, but that there are trillions of other tracks running alongside us, and at any time we can choose to jump to another set. The catch is that when we switch to a new path for our life, there will be a different set of outcomes in response to that jump."

Tommy processed the information for a moment. "Sounds like the old television show *Quantum Leap*."

"It is very much like that show. I discovered it when I was doing my research." Cagliari looked back over his shoulder with a wink and a wry smile. "Essentially, the Eye of Zeus calculates possibilities based on decisions, locations, and people involved. Caesar initially believed that it was a gift from the gods. With the power of the Antikythera Mechanism, he was able to win major battles and claim the largest empire for Rome in its history up to that point. But the Eye of Zeus also came with a curse.

"Caesar became obsessed with it. The more he studied the outcomes the relic predicted, the more it began to occupy his every thought. He lived in constant fear, and no matter how many calculations he ran with the device, the ending always came out the same for him. Caesar realized that he could avoid death for a time, but eventually it would catch up to him. So he hid the Eye of Zeus until such a time when a worthy person could find it."

"Are we worthy?" Sean asked in a somewhat sarcastic tone.

"In my opinion, at this point, whoever finds it is worthy," Cagliari quipped. "It has been hidden for so long, a person who finds it would certainly qualify as that." His laughter echoed through the corridor.

"I don't understand," Tommy said. "I mean, if he didn't want anyone else to be able to use it, why not just destroy it? Then no one would ever be able to use it again."

Sean had wondered the same thing but had refrained from asking the question.

Cagliari stopped and swiveled around to face the other two. "You have to remember that even though the great leaders of the past were very intelligent, logical men, they also held a great deal of respect for their deities. While Zeus was not the god Caesar worshipped, he was still a deity to be respected by all, if for no other reason than to play it safe."

The explanation made sense and seemed to satisfy Tommy's curiosity. Cagliari spun back around and took off again, plunging forward into the darkness.

After another ten minutes of vigorous walking, the passage straightened out and the three men could see a faint light coming from a point in the distance. The musty, dank air dissipated, mixing with the typical smells of the city. Fifty feet later, the light took the shape of an arched doorway, protected by a metal gate. Cagliari lifted an old latch and flung the gate open. He stepped out of the tunnel onto a narrow landing and into the warm sunlight. The Tiber River flowed by, just beyond the embankment beneath their feet. The noise of cars, people, and other reminders of the bustling city resumed in their ears.

"I'll need to call our driver and tell him where we are," Sean said, turning off the flashlight on his phone and pulling up the keypad.

Cagliari walked over to a steep set of concrete stairs and ascended toward the street. Tommy and Sean did the same while Sean looked up the number of their driver. When they reached the top of the steps, they found Cagliari standing face to face with a police officer. The policeman had a surprised look on his face and seemed more confused by Sean and Tommy's arrival.

He began speaking in rapid Italian, too fast for Sean to understand. The officer's hand gestured toward the river and a sign that obviously warned people that the area was restricted.

Cagliari began speaking in a calm tone, trying to explain that the three had gotten lost and ended up down in the sewer. Sean hoped the policeman was buying it, but from the suspicious look on his face, he wasn't.

Suddenly, the officer's eyes widened as they came to rest on

Tommy's jacket. He reached up to the radio on his shoulder and said a few words in muffled Italian. They were spoken slowly enough that Sean could understand them, which was a blessing and a curse.

The cop was calling for backup, for two armed Americans.

26

ROME, ITALY

"We have the map," Thanos said proudly into his cell phone. He and the other two marched hurriedly back to their car on the other side of the Piazza Navona.

He wanted to call Gikas as soon as possible, but knew once they re-entered the throngs of people in the plaza, it would be difficult to hear.

"Outstanding work, my old friend," Gikas replied. "You have done well. There will be a special treat waiting for you in the cellar when you arrive."

Thanos tried not to let carnal thoughts take over what needed to be done. The Eye of Zeus wasn't in their hands just yet.

"Where does the map indicate the relic can be found?" Gikas asked, getting the conversation back on track.

"Ostia," Thanos answered. "The clue is written in Latin, and the image displays the mouth of the river. Cagliari must have been working with Villa. I found the map in a letter addressed to her."

"Excellent." Gikas paused for a second before asking, "What did you do with the good professor?"

It was Thanos's turn to wait for a moment before answering. "He was not home. We left the apartment as soon as we found the map. I would rather not leave too many loose ends lying around. I assumed you would agree. Cagliari will have no idea who stole the map. And without it, he will be lost."

Gikas had become accustomed to the high body count his right-hand man tended to leave in his wake. Leaving Cagliari alive was an odd move, but one that Gikas agreed with. Time was of the essence. Things were becoming more and more unstable with the Greek government. He was scheduled to give a speech at a rally in two hours. Now that the Eye of Zeus was within his grasp, he could relax and prepare to rally the nation to his cause.

"Let me know how things are progressing in Ostia."

"Of course."

Gikas ended the call, and Thanos slipped the device back into his front pocket. The three men reached the parked car and slid into the hot, leather seats. A few minutes later, they were back in traffic, winding through the busy streets of Rome.

The Tiber River meandered through the city off to their left like a giant anaconda. Ahead on the left, Thanos noticed three police cars on the side of the road, with half a dozen police officers surrounding the area. Thanos narrowed his eyes as he peered through the wind-shield. The driver brought the car to a near standstill as the commotion with the authorities slowed traffic.

His eyes grew wide as Thanos realized who was being arrested. "No. We could not possibly be that lucky."

The driver glanced out the window in the direction his boss was looking. "What? What are you talking about?"

Thanos pulled out his phone and quickly dialed Gikas.

"Something wrong?" the man's voice asked through the earpiece. "I just got off the phone with you."

"It's Sean Wyatt, sir."

"What about him?"

"Looks like he's being apprehended by the local authorities."

"What?" Gikas had to ask again to make sure he'd heard correctly.

"Sean Wyatt and his friend are being put in the back of two police cars here in Rome. They're in handcuffs." Thanos explained what he was seeing as plainly as possible.

Citizens and tourists had begun to gather around the odd sight, as people tend to do when there is something unfortunate happening to someone else. Several were taking pictures or video with their phones. Some just stood with mouths agape.

"Any idea why he's being arrested?" Gikas asked with new energy in his voice.

"No. But from what I can tell, it looks like they are in major trouble."

The cars in front of them began to pull away. Thanos's driver hesitated for a second, waiting for orders. Thanos wanted to know what his employer thought as well. "Want us to stop and see what's going on?" he asked into the phone.

Gikas thought for a moment. "No. I'll see to it that Sean Wyatt is taken care of. We have what we need. Proceed to the location in Ostia and let me know when you have a progress update."

"Will do." Thanos slid the phone back into his pocket as the driver stepped on the gas, leaving Wyatt and his friend to the police.

Thanos looked back one last time in the rearview mirror and noticed the police car pulling out onto the street in the other direction. He didn't smile often. It was part of being the bad guy who always got things done. On this occasion, however, Thanos allowed himself to smile. Just a little.

27

ROME, ITALY

T he cell door slammed shut without Sean saying so much as a word in protest. The polizia had detained him and Tommy on illegal possession of firearms, something that could cause them no end of trouble in a European country. They were in someone else's territory now, which meant that the president would likely not be of any help. As he'd insinuated before, if another government got wind that President Dawkins was behind Wyatt's investigation, it could mean big trouble both at home, and abroad.

Fortunately, the Italian police had let Cagliari go free. He had no weapons on him, and because the man was old the authorities had decided not to charge him with trespassing. The last thing Sean had done before being detained was to tell Cagliari to find Emily Starks and tell her what happened.

He hoped the man could deliver, but there was really no telling at this point. Tommy was in the cell next to him, demanding to speak to an attorney. He'd issued verbal threats and angry insults the entire ride from the river to the police station. While Tommy did have a substantial financial fortune behind him, at the moment he was just another prisoner.

"I'm an American citizen!" he shouted at the two guards who had deposited him in the cell next to Wyatt's. "I have rights. I want to call my attorney."

The two guards disappeared around the corner, ignoring the requests. Tommy languished for a second at the barred wall before slumping down on a metal bench.

"Don't think it works that way here, buddy," Sean consoled.

"It's a democracy, isn't it? It should work the same."

Sean didn't answer immediately. He had other things on his mind. If Gikas somehow found out that they'd been arrested, the Greek might try to make some kind of a play to have them both killed. The Italian government had dealt with its fair share of corruption in the past. Made sense there were still plenty of people who would be more than happy to do a few bad deeds for profit.

"Just try to relax," he said to Tommy. "Emily will get us out of here."

"You think Cagliari can find her? She works for a government agency, Sean. She's not supposed to be easy to find. It's not like the old guy can just pull up Google and do a quick Internet search for Emily Starks's phone number."

Tommy wasn't saying anything Sean didn't already know. That didn't make it any less true, though. Something else was bothering Sean. One of the guards had been eyeing them since they'd arrived. He doubted it was because the guy didn't like Americans. The policeman appeared to be waiting for something. But what? Being on foreign soil many times in the past, Sean had seen a number of things happen that got swept under the rug. He wouldn't be surprised if someone tried to kill both him and Tommy, thinking that no one would notice. If Sean had to bet on it, that guard would be his first suspect for the job. He hoped he was just being paranoid again, but like he'd learned so many times before, better to be over prepared than not at all.

"Seriously," Tommy was still ranting about being arrested, "how can they keep us here like this? Has the whole world gone insane?"

"Tommy," Sean finally said, tired of hearing the complaining. "We were caught with weapons we aren't allowed to have here. Whether you like it or not, we broke the law. Just try to relax, man."

Tommy was speechless for the first time in the hour since they'd been marched into the police station. Sean figured his friend hadn't had a lot of experience with being kept behind bars. Sean, on the other hand, had been in plenty of situations like this. He remembered the worst being just outside Moscow. In post-communist Russia, anything went. At least the Soviets had standards, albeit minimalist at best. He'd been found snooping around some of the old KGB archives and taken in for questioning. The escape had been easier than expected, something that would not have been true had the Soviets still been in charge. But the prison itself was one of the foulest, dirtiest places Sean had ever had the misfortune of being stuck in. It made the current situation seem like the Ritz.

He took a look outside the cell and through the square window at the top of the door that led into the main area of the station. He could still see the man who'd been watching them the whole time, and now the guy was talking to another officer. Sean put his head back down and stared at the floor when the suspicious-looking guy pointed in his direction. Sean wondered if the officer had noticed him looking at him, not that it mattered. Now Sean was fairly certain the man in the uniform was working for someone else. Gikas? No way of knowing at the moment, and it didn't really matter who he was working for.

Sean had seen that look a dozen times; it was a face that killers wore. They probably didn't realize they were wearing it. For Sean, however, it was a dead giveaway.

The door to the holding area suddenly opened, and a portly man in a tie and police hat wobbled in. He had a thick mustache and a fleshy face that seemed to fit with his rotund body. When he spoke, his baritone Italian voice boomed throughout the cinder block room.

"So, gentlemen. It seems we have a bit of a situation here." He carried a clipboard in his hand and glanced down at it for a second before resuming. "Sean Wyatt?"

"Si," Sean answered with the Italian form of the word *yes*.

"Your friend with the United States government called. You and your friend are going to be released immediately."

"Thank you, signore," Sean said respectfully as he stood.

"Of course, your weapons will remain here. Foreigners are not permitted to carry guns, Mr. Wyatt. Please remember to abide by the laws. If you are arrested again, I may not be able to help you. At that point, it will go over my head."

Sean gave an appreciative nod. "Thank you, sir. We will be sure to stay clear of trouble from here on out."

The policeman unlocked the two cells and lumbered back toward the door. "Please, follow me. You will need to sign a few papers before you are released." He stopped and spun around, eyeing both of the Americans. "Also, you have a friend here. Signor Cagliari is a well-respected man in this city. See to it that you do not get him mixed up in anything criminal."

"We definitely won't," Sean answered.

Tommy remained silent on the matter until they cleared the front desk of the police station. Cagliari sat alone on a bench against the far wall of the lobby, a surprisingly cheerful look decorating his face. He had picked up a magazine somewhere and was scanning through it when the two Americans approached.

"Ah, good. I'm glad your friend was able to get you out so quickly," Cagliari said with a twinkle in his eye. "That's a good connection, that Starks lady. Useful to have someone like that in your life, no?"

"I've bailed her out of plenty of sticky spots too," Sean said defensively.

Tommy snorted. "Pretty sure you owe her right now."

Sean's head snapped to the side, surprised by his friend's joking insult. "Didn't realize you were keeping score. Last I checked I got you out of some tight spots too." He smiled as he made the statement.

"Yeah, but this little trip is putting us closer to even, I think," Tommy replied with a crooked grin of his own.

"Fine," Sean said, giving up, realizing the conversation wasn't going to get them anywhere.

They went around to the front of the receptionist's desk, which was protected by a bulletproof glass window. The woman in uniform had already processed their information and had their identification and phones ready to be returned.

"Grazie," Sean said, scooping up his belongings and sifting through his credit cards to make sure everything was in order. Slightly relieved to see nothing had been lost, he put his cards and identification back in his money clip and slid it into his pocket.

He turned his attention to their new Italian friend as they descended a set of stone steps and exited the building. "Signore, are you sure you don't want to go to Mount Fumaiolo with us?"

"I'm quite sure. I do appreciate your entertaining the idea of having an old man like me along on your quest, but I believe my race is run in regards to field work." Cagliari stopped on the sidewalk and spun around to face Tommy and Sean. "You will be able to move faster without me tagging along. All I ask is that when you discover the relic, I be invited to be one of the first to examine it."

Sean smiled and extended his hand. "Done." Cagliari grasped his hand and shook it firmly. "Thanks again for all you've done, Signor Cagliari. I can't tell you how much I appreciate it."

He pulled Sean close as if he were about to share a great secret. He spoke in a hushed, just-between-us-guys tone. "You better take care of that woman of yours when you get her back. She is one in a billion."

"I intend to."

The older man let go of Sean's hand and reached out to take Tommy's, shaking it in the same, strong manner as before.

"Like Sean said, sir, thank you for your help. We will be in touch as soon as we have the device in our possession."

Cagliari gave a quick nod. "I know you will."

He turned and walked down the sidewalk toward one of the many cathedrals dotting the Roman landscape. After twenty seconds, he had disappeared into the throng of people bustling about their day.

The sun was still high over the horizon. Sean looked down at his phone to check the local time. It was getting late in the afternoon.

The little delay of getting arrested had taken up more than two hours of their time. They were lucky it hadn't been more, and Sean knew it.

Tommy checked his phone too and realized how late it was. "What are we going to do?"

Sean already had a plan. "First, we get our car."

"Obviously."

Ignoring Tommy's comment, Sean kept talking. "We need weapons and flashlights."

"Flashlights we can get in a grocery store," Tommy said, and then paused as he thought about the other item on the list. "The guns might be a problem."

Sean shook his head. "I know someone who can help us with that."

He had worked with a low-level arms dealer out of the Czech Republic during his days with Axis. The guy was smart about his business, never getting too over his head when it came to inventory or the types of weapons he dealt. Sean didn't mind bending rules, so he forged a relationship with the guy. It had turned out to be an extremely beneficial one for Sean. The arms dealer had intel on everything that happened on the black market, as well as some of the inner workings of local and regional governments.

Last he'd heard, the guy had moved his base of operations to Rome. From what Sean had heard, it was because of his Italian wife.

Tommy looked skeptical. "Someone from your days with Axis?"

A coarse grin crept to one side of Sean's face as he started to dial their driver. "Don't worry about it. He's a good guy...for an arms dealer."

28

C orfu, Greece

ADRIANA HEARD the helicopter leave over an hour ago. More time than that may have passed, but without access to any kind of clock she really had no idea. For all she knew, Gikas could have left three hours ago. The only information she had was that the man was going to speak somewhere. To whom, and where, was a mystery. In the far reaches of the northwestern part of Greece, Corfu was more of a remote outpost than anything. Its vineyards and beach towns were sparse at best. The nearest city with a significant population would be at least an hour's flight by helicopter.

That meant if Gikas had a thirty- to forty-five minute speech, he wouldn't be returning for another hour...maybe. With the head man gone, she reasoned that some of the security forces he employed would have gone with him. Maybe only a few of them, but that was better than none. It would mean fewer men to deal with on the grounds, and any edge she could get she would take.

She'd spent the better part of the last thirty minutes trying to grind away the ropes that bound her hands behind her back. After a tireless effort, and rubbing her wrists raw, she was finally able to get the bonds loose enough to wriggle free.

Niki had watched her from the corner. He remained quiet, and far away from her as Adriana struggled to free herself. She thought about asking the boy to help her, but decided against it. He was already afraid enough. More than that, if one of the guards did a random pop in to check on the prisoners and caught the boy helping her, the punishment could be severe. That was a risk she wasn't willing to take.

She shook her arms and hands, letting the blood flow back into her fingers. The ropes had been so tight; relief flooded her to have them finally removed. A few times she'd lost feeling in her fingertips from the constriction.

Niki still sat in the corner, watching her warily as she tugged at the rope around her feet. It took a considerable effort to loosen it, despite having the use of her hands, but after a few minutes her legs were free as well.

Adriana stood up and wobbled for a second, not having been on her feet for some time. She moved cautiously to where the frightened boy crouched in the shadows. "Niki, are you okay?" she asked quietly, just barely audible.

He shook his head.

"Are you afraid of what those men might do to you?"

He gave a shy nod.

"That's okay," she smiled at him reassuringly. "It's okay to be afraid, but I need you to answer me honestly. This is an important question. Can you handle it?"

"I guess so," he volunteered.

"Good. I think you can. I need to know, are you a fast runner?"

The boy seemed to cheer up slightly, and answered her query with a dramatic nod.

"Are you faster than most of the boys in your school?" she asked, pressing the line of questioning.

He gave the same response.

"Good," she said, "because I'm going to need you to run very, very fast. Do you think you can do that?"

"Yes," he said, still nodding.

"Now, we are going to play a little game with these men. It's called escape from Alcatraz."

Niki giggled a little at the last word.

"I know, Alcatraz is a funny word, isn't it?"

He gave two huge nods.

"Well, today we are going to play that game, and if you can get to the church in the little town down the road, you will be the winner. Do you want to play?"

"Yes," Niki answered.

"Now if the men catch me, you have to promise me that you will keep going. After all, you want to win the game, right?"

"Okay," he said with a final nod. "I promise."

"Good." She ran her hand on his soft, young cheek. "I'm going to lure one of the guards in here to start the game. I'm going to pretend to knock him out, but he is just pretending to be asleep. It's all part of the game, but you must not say anything to the guards. No matter what, stay close behind me, and when we reach the road start running and never look back."

Adriana stood up and grabbed a small wooden step from the base of one of the wine racks. She positioned it directly under the narrow window in the corner and put one of her feet on it to boost herself up. She stretched as far as she could to reach the latch on the window, and was relieved to find that it opened easily.

"Are we going through that window?" Niki asked?

She smiled down at him as she stepped off the stool. "No. But we want to make it look like we did."

She moved quickly back to the wine rack and grabbed one of the bottles. "Come over here, and remember to stay perfectly still when the guard comes in." Adriana grabbed Niki's hand and pulled him over to the interior wall, near the doorway.

"Are you ready to start the game?" she asked, looking at the boy to make sure he was still composed. Surprisingly, he appeared to be fine, and was smiling at the proposition of doing something fun for a change.

"Good," she said. "Here we go."

Adriana stepped forward and fired the wine bottle toward the wall near the window. She grabbed another two and chucked them in quick succession into the same area, spilling dark-red liquid all over the floor and wall as the glass shattered on stone.

The guard's reaction was faster than she anticipated. The sound of a key being inserted into the door lock clinked throughout the room. A few seconds later, the door swung open, and one of the guards stepped in, holding a gun in his hand. He looked around for a second, and then noticed the open window on the other side of the room.

As soon as he saw it, his suspicion kicked in. He touched an earpiece that dangled from his right ear and spoke into a concealed microphone. "We have a problem," the man said in a heavy Greek accent. "The prisoners have escaped through the window. Everyone be on the lookout for the woman and boy."

He took a few more steps toward the corner where the gentle sea breeze rolled up the hill and down through the little window. The sound of the waves crashing against the shore accompanied the fresh air. Adriana put her finger on the boy's mouth, her last warning for him to stay quiet as she stepped lightly from the shadows. She tiptoed across the hard floor, careful to step as stealthily as possible.

The guard had reached the window and was inspecting the broken glass and spilled wine. He never saw or heard Adriana take the final step between them before she wrapped her hands around his head and snapped it to the left, breaking his neck in one quick movement. The body collapsed to the floor amid the shards of splintered glass. Adriana wasted no time, taking the man's handgun and the extra clip he had attached to his belt.

She spun around to make sure Niki was still there. The frightened boy stood with mouth and eyes wide as Adriana returned to his side with the weapon in hand. "He'll be okay, Niki. He's just pretending.

Remember, stay behind me until we get to the road. Then you run as fast as you can toward the town. Where are you going when you get to the village?"

The boy hesitated for a second, reluctant to speak. Finally he said, "The church."

Adriana rubbed his head, tousling his hair, and smiled proudly at him. "That's right. You head for the church. Now, stay close. These men may shoot at us, but they aren't real bullets. They're just bb's. If I hit one of the guards with it, they have to fall down and pretend to be dead. That's part of the game. Understand?"

Niki nodded eagerly.

"Good. Let's go."

She stepped into the open doorway with the weapon drawn in front of her. The staircase was clear. She grabbed the boy's hand and led him up, careful not to pull on his arm too hard. They reached the top of the stairs, and she let go of his hand and motioned for him to wait for a moment. Adriana peeked around the corner of the doorsill and found a large, empty kitchen. She started to step out of the stairwell when she heard footsteps coming from the left. Instinctively, she retreated into the shadows for a moment to wait. With the weapon she'd taken from the guard downstairs, shooting the current threat would be no problem. She had the element of surprise, but firing the gun would draw too much attention. If at all possible, Adriana needed to wait to shoot the gun as an absolute last resort, at least until the boy was out of harm's way.

A set of kitchen knives on top of the kitchen's island caught her eye. As a child, her father had let Adriana play with dangerous things most parents would never dream of allowing their child to even touch. Throwing knives at the oak trees on her family's estate had been one of her favorite activities. She remembered the warm summer days out in the yard with her father as he went through the correct motion of how to throw a knife with deadly accuracy. At the time, Adriana never imagined she would need to use that skill for any real-world applications. Since becoming a reclamation thief, she'd made use of the ability more times than she could count.

The guard seemed on edge, and walked over to one of the far windows in a hexagonal dining area. He pulled down one of the blinds to take a look outside. It was the moment Adriana needed. She moved quickly over to the island and withdrew one of the large blades from its sheath. She gripped the tip of it in a sleight of hand motion and flung it at the unsuspecting guard. The sharp edge struck deep into the base of his neck. He started to collapse, but managed to turn around just in time to see Adriana leaping toward him. Her knee caught him square in the jaw, rendering him unconscious. The man slumped over onto his side. She yanked the blade out of the bloody wound and returned to the island to grab two more like it.

Niki was peeking out from the staircase with apprehension. She called to him, "It's okay, Niki. Come on. We have to go."

The boy reached out his hand for Adriana. She smiled weakly at him and clasped it tight. "I promise, everything is going to be all right."

29

OSTIA, ITALY

T hanos's driver parked the car outside a small cafe on one of the quieter streets of Ostia. The coastal Italian town was known as one of Italy's favorite vacations spots. Being a borough of Rome made it extremely appealing for Romans who needed to get away from the craziness of the city. The only problem was that so many of them seemed to have the same idea.

On the journey there, Thanos allowed himself a few moments to enjoy the view of the rolling countryside. He watched farms, trees, homes, and occasional remnants of the Roman Empire blur by. Thanos was always on the clock, always working, constantly considering his next move; a mindset that had kept him alive during times when others would likely have faltered. He took the map out of his pocket several times and looked over it to make sure that they were heading in the right direction. Based on the location indicated by the document, they would find the relic somewhere on the coast. He assumed there would be a cave, or rocky cliff there. Such an area would have fewer visitors and lend itself to a more private search. The last thing they needed was some idiot with a metal detector snooping around.

That thought brought up another potential problem. What if they needed tools to perform an excavation? He'd never been a part of anything like that before and was unfamiliar with the process. He would figure it out. How hard could it be? A few shovels, maybe a pick, and they'd be good to go. They could purchase those things at a local hardware store if need be.

His mind drifted to the future. He'd made his bed with Dimitris Gikas because Thanos was all about putting himself in the best position to succeed. He knew what Gikas had been planning and had wanted in from the start. The way Thanos saw it, he was betting on the best horse in the race. And his employer had rewarded him substantially. He was completely satisfied with being the right-hand man. It was all about survival. Well, survival and the occasional carnal pleasures that he so enjoyed. Thinking about it brought back the possibilities with the Spaniard being held captive back in Gikas's island compound. He forced himself to suppress his excitement. It had been quite a while since he'd been afforded a little private time. The last was a young Asian girl he'd left under a pier in Taipei. While he was there to procure investments for his employer, Thanos had taken a few hours to walk the streets one night. The prostitute had been exactly what he needed. When he was done with her, he squeezed the life out of her and dumped the body. The memory caused his heart to start pumping hard again, and he pulled out the map once more to take his mind off the distracting thoughts. Fortunately, they arrived at their destination a few minutes later and he could refocus his energy.

Thanos got out of the car and scanned the area. Hotels, shops, cafes, bars, and restaurants abounded. Holidaygoers laughed happily as they walked by on the sidewalk. Thanos ignored all the revelry and pulled a sheet of paper out of his pocket. It was the map he'd retrieved from Cagliari's home. He looked closely at it, comparing it to a map of Ostia he'd procured on his smart phone. According to the analysis, they were close to the spot marked on Cagliari's map. Something, however, didn't add up.

Ostia is historically famous for its ancient Roman ruins, gardens, and a world-renowned Roman theater. While many Italian citizens visit for the beaches, the town thrived on the backs of international tourists. Foreign money brought in tens of millions every year. Rome would always be the most popular tourist destination for people anxious to see into the history of the long-lost empire, but Ostia was for those who wanted to get a little off the beaten path and get a more personal, up-close glimpse into this growing borough.

When Thanos had realized where Cagliari's map pointed, it made perfect sense. Julius Caesar had been a sailor at heart. It would make sense that the emperor would hide his most prized possession next to the thing he loved the most, the sea. Ostia also seemed like the right location due to the amount of history surrounding the area. Sure, it had become a modern town like anywhere else, but with so many millennia-old cemeteries and buildings, Thanos had been certain the seaside town was the final resting place for the Eye of Zeus.

Now, he wasn't so sure.

The other two men got out of the car while the driver remained behind the wheel. "Stay here," Thanos ordered. "You two come with me."

The driver nodded and kept his eyes forward while the other two subordinates fell in line behind the bald man.

Something wasn't right. His pace quickened as he strode down the sidewalk, staring at the sheet of paper and comparing it to the image on his phone screen. His shoulder plowed into a young man in a blue tank top and Wayfarer glasses, but he kept going, leaving the drunken beachgoer swearing something at him in Italian.

Thanos turned right at a breach between two buildings and headed through the shaded alley. On the other side there was another small piazza, featuring a huge fountain in the middle of a pedestrian roundabout. The fountain's sculpture of a man holding a spear and shield represented a great Roman soldier, perhaps someone the city revered. Thanos didn't care. He needed to get to the spot on the map.

He led his men around the fountain and through the square, heading toward the sea, as far as he could tell. Through the crevasses between the smaller buildings ahead he could see that his assumption was correct. Beach umbrellas came into view, along with thousands of beachgoing tourists in bathing suits, bikinis, and sundresses, all soaking up the rays of sunshine from the cloudless sky. The sounds of the people were drowned out by the waves crashing on the edge of the sand.

Thanos slowed his steps. A terrible feeling crept into his mind. He glanced down at the map again, though this time he didn't need to. He walked through another shorter alleyway and onto the sandy beach. The hot sun beat down on him in his black suit jacket, making the irritation inside him swell to boiling point. His right hand involuntarily crumpled up the sheet of paper and dropped it on the ground.

"What is the problem, sir? Where does the map say to go?" one of his assistants asked.

The bald man didn't say a word for a moment. He simply stood there, taking in the scene. All of the people going about their day, enjoying the sunshine and the water, had no idea what was going on. He let a few seconds slip by before turning around and heading back the way they came.

The two subordinates looked at each other with a worried glance. One shrugged at the other and mouthed, "I don't know."

"Sir," the shorter one said, catching up to his boss who continued walking without turning around. "Where are we going? Didn't the map say this was the spot?"

"Yes. It did," he answered, keeping his face forward and his stride long.

The answer did nothing to satisfy the underling's curiosity. "So, why are we leaving?"

Thanos stopped in the middle of the piazza, near the fountain they'd walked by a few moments before. A vein on the side of his head pulsed visibly in the late afternoon sun. A bead of sweat formed on his forehead and rolled down his face, past his eye and off his cheek. "The old man tricked us."

30

ROME, ITALY

"I still can't believe we are going to see an arms dealer," Tommy said in a derisive tone. "You know what? I can't believe you even know an arms dealer. You used to work for the United States government, Sean. Aren't the arms dealers the bad guys?"

Sean laughed as he pulled the car into an empty parking space. The two had dropped off their driver at the hotel, deciding it might be better if they go the rest of the journey alone. Sean reasoned that he would rather not make his shady friend nervous. The driver was more than happy to take the rest of the day off. He was getting paid no matter what. After a day full of high-intensity intrigue, the guy probably needed a break anyway.

"Marek is not a bad guy. It's not like he deals with nuclear weapons or nerve gas. He mostly peddles small arms." Sean could tell his explanation did little to calm Tommy's nerves.

"So you're on a first name basis with this goon? Oh, so what, he's a black market weapons dealer with a conscience?"

Sean took a deep breath and removed the keys from the ignition. "Look, we need guns. Marek has them. Don't make this weird. Okay?"

Tommy's eyes nearly popped out of his head at the last comment.

"Weird? Do you know what's weird, Sean? That we are buying guns illegally, in a foreign country, from an underground dealer!"

Sean opened the door and exited the vehicle. "Try to keep your voice down. This is a suburban neighborhood. I don't think Marek wants the residents' association knowing his vocation."

"Oh, you think?"

Once they'd dropped off their driver at the hotel, the drive to the Balduina section of Rome had only taken twenty minutes. It was one of the quieter neighborhoods in the city, home to many expats and those looking to be close to the culture of Rome but not always in the middle of it. Sean had been somewhat surprised to find that Marek had relocated to Balduina. When the two initially met, Marek was an avid clubgoer and in constant party mode. The suburban residence community was a far cry from the club scene in Prague.

Apparently, the Czech had become somewhat reclusive.

Sean scanned the area for a moment, taking in the modern homes and apartments that contrasted the more historic parts of the city. Some of the houses even had large terraces, and he imagined the views must have been impressive since Balduina sits atop one of Rome's many hills. The Vatican wasn't far from their current location. Sean figured getting there on foot wouldn't take long, and many of the rooftop patios almost certainly had a clear line of sight to the famed dome of St. Peter's Basilica.

There was a significant decrease in foot traffic in the area, too, probably a result of it being almost purely residential. Unlike in the center of the city, the sidewalks lacked the shops, cafes, and bars that drew so many cars and pedestrians. The more Sean thought about it, the more he realized that Balduina would probably be where he would settle down if he lived in Rome.

It actually made perfect sense that Marek lived there now. Who would suspect an arms dealer living in a quiet little neighborhood like this? It was unlikely that any of the retired Americans or local families even gave the Czech a second glance. To them, he was probably just another foreigner who had fallen in love with Rome but wanted to have a little quiet distance between himself and all the activity of the busy town center.

Tommy must have been thinking something along the same lines. "What kind of arms dealer lives in an area like this?"

"Exactly," Sean said, effectively ending the discussion and leaving Tommy befuddled.

He led the way, walking across the street into a small commons area filled with green shrubs, decorative trees, and a palm tree standing in the center. The brick sidewalks wound their way through the space, leading to the six or seven homes wrapped around it. Sean and Tommy passed the first two, both cream-colored, Mediterranean-style houses, and stopped at the third, a modern three-story building painted a burnt yellow. Sean could see a railing on the top floor, indicating that the home had a deck. He was usually afraid of heights, but a few stories never bothered him much.

"And you're sure this guy is expecting us?" Tommy interrupted his thoughts, staring at the door with a nervousness about him.

"Yes, he's expecting us. Are you sure you're okay?" Sean stared at his friend as if he had eyeballs growing out of his arms. "You can wait in the car if you want."

Tommy forced himself to settle down and took a long, deep breath. "I'm fine. Just not used to associating with criminals."

The door opened just as he was finishing the sentence. Inside, the pale man with cropped brown hair raised an eyebrow. "Criminal?" he said in a mild, Eastern European accent.

"Marek," Sean interjected, "it's good to see you again, my old friend. How have you been?"

For a second, Marek stared at Tommy as if he were about to answer the question, but once Sean stepped in the way he forgot all about the comment.

"Where have you been, Sean? I don't hear from you for years except the occasional text message you send me on my birthday." The Czech reached out with both arms and wrapped them around Sean in a big hug.

Marek had clearly been in better shape during the earlier part of his life. His arms wore signs of once being strong and lean. Now they had softened over time, along with his midsection. Still, Tommy figured the man was no one to mess with in a fight. Marek's stubbly beard was still dark, which belied his age as still being somewhere under forty.

Sean let go of his old acquaintance and introduced his companion. "Marek, this is Tommy Schultz. You two play nice," he joked. "Tommy is one of my oldest friends. And I trust him with my life."

Marek's suspicions eased visibly. "Very well. Any friend of Sean's is welcome in my home."

"Thank you," Tommy offered. "It's just that...well, I've never met an arms dealer before. Especially not at his home."

A thunderous laugh erupted from Marek's mouth. He leaned back and slapped his knee as the laughter kept coming for a good twenty seconds. Sean chuckled a few times, uncertain if he should be laughing or not.

"Tommy, I assure you, my home is completely safe. I mostly deal with police, former military, teachers, those kinds of people. I don't sell guns to drug dealers or terrorists...not that I know of." He gave a quick wink to Sean and started laughing all over again. Tommy joined in the laughter this time, though hesitantly. "Please, come in. Let's have a drink to old times."

Sean held up a dismissive hand. "Maybe some other time, my friend. We are kind of in a hurry, and time is running out. We need to get a couple of guns from you and be on our way."

Marek didn't attempt to mask his disappointment. "That is unfortunate. I was hoping we could talk for a while. Are you in some kind of trouble?"

"Not at the moment," Sean said, glancing around to make sure no one was nearby. "A friend of mine is, though. She needs our help."

"A woman? Sounds like you have a soft spot for her, old friend."

"I do. Can you help us?"

Marek's face beamed with pride. "Of course I can help you. Please, come in."

Inside, the home was much neater than Tommy would have

expected. Everything was in perfect order and immaculately clean. A wide, flatscreen television hung over a gas fireplace on the far side of the living room. Dark ceramic tiles covered the floor, balanced by deep, hunter-green walls. There were a few pieces of furniture: a sofa with tan fabric, a few leather seats, and a pale wooden coffee table. A picture on a glass end table featured a picture of Marek and his wife, a woman with remarkable almond skin, curly dark hair, and brown eyes the color of coffee.

Sean pointed to the picture frame with his thumb. "She the reason you left Prague?" he asked cordially.

Marek had stepped into the kitchen for a moment. The sound of hands rustling through papers and miscellaneous drawer objects echoed through the huge home. "My wife?" he asked from out of sight. "She was certainly a big part of why I came here."

"What was the other part?" Sean asked, meandering over to the television. He peeked out of the nearest window through one of the blinds. There was no activity outside, for which he allowed himself a moment of gratitude.

The noises in the kitchen ceased, and a second later Marek reappeared in the archway between the two rooms. "Let's just say things were getting a little too crazy back home."

Tommy entered the conversation by asking, "Crazy?"

Marek shrugged. "People I didn't trust started asking for favors. Random customers were showing up at my door at all hours of the day." He held up a finger to emphasize his point. "I don't sell to people I don't trust. And I don't trust random customers."

"Marek's business is 100 percent referral," Sean explained.

"That's right," their host agreed. "But when the referrals start making referrals, things get a little shady."

Tommy resisted the temptation to point out that the man's profession was shady, for which Sean silently commended him.

"I would rather make less money and have less trouble than have a pile of cash and a pile of problems," Marek finished making his point.

"Makes sense," Tommy nodded.

The Czech smiled. "So you need guns? Right this way."

Sean and Tommy followed the arms dealer down a wide hallway and into a study. The room was only a few hundred square feet and looked like it had been decorated exclusively from the IKEA catalogue. Everything had been designed to maximize space and functionality.

Next to the door, a closet with wooden folding doors spanned eight feet from the corner of the entryway to the exterior wall. Marek pulled back one of the doors and reached into the closet. The sound of an electric motor suddenly whirred to life beneath the small computer workstation. Something was coming up out of the floor. Sean watched with a wide grin as the secret compartment continued to rise in front of the bookshelf. The six-foot long cabinet had been topped with tiles to match the floor so that any casual observer wouldn't even think there was anything underneath. It had worked, since neither Sean nor Tommy had noticed it.

The machine stopped its task, leaving the showcase on full display for the three men. Attached to it were over twenty different handguns, and two HK-5 submachine guns.

"Now," Marek said, stepping in front of the two guests, "as I recall, you were a Ruger man the last time I saw you. Right?" He ran his finger along the second row until it stopped on a brand new Ruger .40 caliber.

"I was," Sean corrected him. "I've been liking the Springfield lately. Bought an XD not long ago. It's a great piece."

Marek raised an eyebrow. "Croatian guns, huh? Well, I have to admit, they do make a fine weapon. And I just happen to have one right here." He reached over to the third row from the top and pulled out the black weapon. "Like this?" he asked and handed it to Sean.

"That's the one," Sean said, smiling. He pulled the slide back and checked the chamber to make sure it wasn't loaded.

"Magazines are on the back side of this display. I only have two for that gun. Hopefully you won't need more than that. If you do, you're in a war that would require more than one gun anyway." Sean chuckled at the comment.

The Czech turned his attention to Tommy. "What about you, my good man? Any preferences?"

"That Sig 9 will work," Tommy answered confidently.

"Ah, that is a fine weapon," Marek said, removing the gun from its holster on the wall. He passed it gently over to Tommy, who copied Sean's habit of checking the chamber.

"How much do you want for them?" Sean asked after looking over the weapon more thoroughly.

"Please." Marek put his hands out in a gesture that suggested Sean's question was ridiculous. "You take these guns and go help your girl. Don't worry about paying me for them. I have plenty of money." He motioned to the home by waving a hand around. "Does it look like I'm hurting here?"

Sean insisted. "You have to make money on these. You're running a business."

Marek put both hands up, ending the conversation. "Please, it is my pleasure to help you out, Sean. I won't take your money. You helped me out when I needed it the most. You were the only person that offered. I will never forget that."

Sean took a deep breath, knowing that there was no way he was going to end up being able to pay anything for the guns. "Fine. I'll take them. I won't forget this, though," Sean pointed at him, sending a fake warning with his eyes.

"I'm glad I can repay you, my friend," Marek said. "Are you sure you can't stay for one drink?"

Sean glanced out the window at the sun sinking farther into the afternoon sky. "Afraid we have to decline for now. It's going to be dark when we get up in the mountains, which is going to make things difficult enough." Then Sean had another thought. "You wouldn't happen to have any flashlights would you?"

Marek grinned again. "Of course. But you'll have to pay for those." He winked and began booming with laughter again. "I kid. I think I have a few you can take." The Czech stepped over to a bureau and pulled open the second drawer. He produced a few aluminum-cased flashlights and placed them in the palms of the two Americans.

"These are top of the line, very bright. You should do fine with these." He paused for a moment, seemingly pondering something. "If you don't mind me asking, Sean, what kind of trouble is your girl in?"

Sean sighed before speaking. "I wish I knew. We think a man named Dimitris Gikas took her. He's from Northern Greece, near the border of Albania. Have you heard of him?"

Marek's expression changed instantly, becoming one of deep concern. "Yes. I have heard of him. He is one of the most powerful men in Greece, very wealthy, very ambitious. One of his men contacted me several months ago, a man I had done business with in the past. He asked me if I could connect him to a volume dealer. Said he had a big order to fill. I guess he thought I would know someone because of my business. To be honest, I try to keep out of the underground these days. Every now and then I hear something, though."

"And what have you heard lately?"

Their host glanced around as if to make sure no one else was listening. "Dimtris Gikas is planning something big."

"Like a government takeover?" Tommy asked.

Something clearly wasn't right. Sean could see it in the big Czech's face.

"Bigger," he said. "I don't have as many ears as I used to, but the ones I do have are hearing that Gikas has big aspirations."

Sean and Tommy waited with heightened anticipation.

"He wants to establish a new Greek empire. Gikas believes he is some kind of great leader like Alexander the Great, and that he will return Greece to its former might."

Eyebrows on both the Americans furrowed.

"You mean he plans to invade other countries?" Tommy asked, still trying to wrap his head around it.

"I'm not sure," Marek answered, crossing his arms. "But it certainly sounds like he intends to overthrow the current government, which in its current state, would not be a difficult thing to do if someone had the resources."

"And with a powerful device like the Antikythera Mechanism, he could foresee every move an enemy would make. He would know everything before it happened."

Marek's face curled in confusion. "An...ti...ky...what?"

Sean turned to leave. "I'll tell you all about it some other time, my friend. We have to go."

31

CORFU, GREECE

Adriana peeked around the corner of the kitchen and into the wide-open living room area. Several sofas and seats had been placed in the thousand-square-foot room. She slid two of the knives into her belt, one on each hip, and kept the third in her left hand, the gun in her right. She and the boy moved stealthily across the span of the giant living space, reaching the front door within a few seconds. Just outside the front door, two guards stood on the landing, staring out at the grounds. They seemed to be on alert, no doubt from the information relayed by the guard she'd killed in the cellar.

She pulled Niki close and glanced at the other side of the room. A pair of French doors led out onto a deck overlooking the sea. She could see there was a guard out there as well, but only one. Those odds were a little more in her favor. Careful not to make a sound, she made her way back around the room, staying close to the wall to keep out of sight in case one of the men on the front porch happened to look back into the mansion. She reached the back of the house and stopped at the door. The guard still had his back to them, but as soon as she turned the latch he would look back to see who was coming out. There would be only a split second to make her move and take the man down.

A plan quickly formulated in her head. She would open the door, leap at the guy and shove the knife into his chest, letting her momentum knock him over the railing to the ground below. The fall was only a few feet and wouldn't kill him, but the tip of the knife in his heart would.

She reached out, clasped the handle, and started to pull it when a voice from across the room stopped her cold. "Don't move!"

Adriana froze in place and risked a glance out of the corner of her eye. A guard had entered the room from a hallway near the front of the house, on the other side of the living room. He must have been walking around to check the place. Stupid luck had led him to catching the escapees.

"Put the gun down," he ordered, aiming his own weapon at her.

"Okay," she said. "Please, just don't hurt the boy. This was my decision. It isn't his fault."

"Shut up!" the man shouted. He reached up to his earpiece and spoke into his radio. "I found them. They're in the house, in the great room. She has the boy with her."

The man on the back porch turned around. Shock washed over his face as he realized how close he was to being killed.

"Put the gun down, or I will shoot the boy," the guard said from across the room.

"I'm putting it down. Please, just relax. See? I'm putting it down?" She bent over and started to lay the gun on the floor. As she did, her head disappeared from the man's view behind the sofa closest to her position. She turned her head to Niki and whispered, "Get on your belly."

The door opened behind her, disrupting the silence as the guard from the back porch entered the room.

"Now," she ordered Niki. The boy obeyed and dropped to his stomach in a quick move.

Adriana reached up and grabbed the guard's hand from the door latch. She twisted it to an unnatural position and used the man's weight to spin him around in front of her as a human shield. The other guard opened fire, squeezing off four rounds, all thudding into her captive's chest. The man struggled for a moment, and then began to go limp as the bullets found vital organs.

"Cover your ears, Niki!" she shouted. The boy had already done so as the sound of the initial gunfire rang out through the room, louder than anything he'd ever heard before.

She poked her gun around her human shield and unleashed a volley of six shots. Two pinged off a stone column near her target; two others went through the window. One found the man in the gut and the other in his shoulder, sufficiently removing him as a threat.

Adriana dropped the dying man and reached down for Niki's hand. "Come on! We have to go!" He shook his head in defiance, with his hands still covering his ears. "Niki, please," she pleaded with him. "You want to win the game, don't you? You're a fast runner, right?" The boy nodded and seemed he might be willing to get up.

Suddenly, the front door to the mansion opened and one of the two guards on the front landing opened fire. She dropped behind the sofa as bullets zipped through the air over her head, shattering the windows behind her while others thudded into the doorframe.

She pulled herself along the hard floor to the other side of the sofa and slid around the corner. Her hands guided the sights of the weapon directly at the man's chest. She forced herself to breathe slowly, calmly, and pulled the trigger twice. The two rounds sunk into the guard's chest and knocked him back through the door. She crawled back over to where the frightened boy still lay on his belly with his hands on his ears.

"Time to go, Niki. Stay low and follow me. When you get to the road, remember: keep running as fast as you can."

The boy nodded reluctantly. There was no more time for her to coddle him. She reached down and grabbed him with one hand and the dead man's gun with the other. That should give her a further twelve shots. The remaining guard on the front porch was speaking frantically into his radio, calling for backup. She fired another shot in his direction, narrowly missing his neck. The guard ducked out of sight below one of the large windowpanes. She fired two more shots through the glass to keep him down and then darted through the back door and onto the deck.

Dragging the young boy along like a ball and chain, Adriana made her way down the south side of the deck. The porch ended at a small embankment, filled with landscaping grass, flowers, and various shrubs. Just beyond it, she made out the pool area and patio where Gikas had entertained her on a previous night.

She looked around the corner of the house and saw two men rushing toward the front porch. Hopefully they would assume she and the boy were still tucked behind the sofa. As soon as the men disappeared from view, she hopped over the railing and grabbed Niki under his armpits.

"We're almost there, okay? We just need to go around this little mound and you'll be on the road. Remember, you have to beat me to the church in town. I will be chasing you," she made herself smile to keep the boy calm.

He nodded and smiled back at her.

She led him around the mound and stopped on the other side. Adriana stared at the front of the house. Three men were on the porch. One of them stepped into the doorway and fired three shots, then quickly ducked back behind the wall in case of return fire. Good, she thought. They still believed the two escapees were inside the house.

Niki let out a sudden yelp, and Adriana whirled around to find a guard holding the boy by the back of the neck. The guard's strong, broad face showed no intention of mercy. His physique bulged through the tight clothes, neck muscles like a rugby player.

Adriana waited for a second, not sure what to do.

"Put the gun down, or I will break the boy's neck," the guard said. He shook Niki hard to emphasize his point. She leaned over to do as she was told, setting the weapon on the ground next to the guard's feet.

He let go of the boy and pushed him aside, taking a cautious step toward the dangerous Spaniard. She still held the knife in her hand, something the guard had already noticed. He motioned to the blade by waving the barrel of his gun. "Drop the knife as well."

She hesitated for a second.

"Do it, or I will shoot the boy in the gut."

The man suddenly yelled out in pain. His arm lurched back, pointing the gun into the air as he leaned back in a quick, jerky motion. Adriana saw Niki on all fours behind the big guard, sinking his teeth hard into the guy's calf. It was all she needed.

Adriana took the knife and slashed out with it, jerking the sharp edge across the man's throat and then kicking him in the chest. The giant stumbled back, grabbing in vain at the gaping wound on his neck. She swiveled back around and crouched down in a quick movement. Her hand grabbed the gun from the ground and brought it up instantly, ticking off three shots at the guard. Two of the bullets found nothing but air, the other plunged into the man's head, toppling him into the weeds just off the path.

She smiled down at the boy and reached out her hand. "Good job, Niki. Quickly. You have to run now."

The two took off down the driveway. The three remaining men on the porch had heard the shot from the side of the mansion and were closing in. Adriana fired a few warning shots at them, effectively halting their advance and sending them sprawling for cover. The boy sprinted down the gravel driveway, running as fast as his little legs would carry him. She stopped and kept her eyes on the men on the porch. Her finger pulled the trigger again, sending another volley of rounds harmlessly into the side of the house, but effectively keeping the men down. One of them tried to hide behind a post and fired blindly into the air, using a spray-and-pray method.

Adriana turned her head and looked down the road. The boy had covered sixty yards and was almost out of sight. They were going to make it.

Then something struck her hard in the middle of her back, sending a crunching, dull pain through her body. The momentum of whatever had hit her carried her to the ground, smashing her face onto the gravel. Two giant arms wrapped around her for a second, then let go as a guard she'd not seen stood over her. The world spun around in her eyes as she tried desperately to regain her bearings. The silhouette of the big man was outlined by the waning afternoon sunlight. He was raising one of his arms in the direction Niki ran. She made out the image of a gun in his hand and realized what he was about to do.

Adriana kicked out with all her might, sending her heel into the side of the man's knee. Ligaments and cartilage gave way behind the force of her attack, and the guard screamed out in agony. He stumbled for a moment but never fell. She looked down the road, her vision still blurred from hitting the ground. Niki disappeared around the bend behind a thick stand of trees. Adriana smiled feebly, knowing that the boy had made it. The smile was wiped away as the guard brought the tip of his boot into her ribs. The power of the kick sent her rolling onto her other side. He kicked her again and again, finally grabbing her by the shirt and lifting her off the ground.

She coughed violently but stared defiantly into the man's cold eyes. His head was shaved, and he had a full goatee of black facial hair. Anger flamed in the man's eyes, no doubt from the injury she'd inflicted on his knee. Adriana quivered as the man stared into her eyes and drew back his massive fist. It was the last thing she saw before everything went black.

32

APENNINE MOUNTAINS, CENTRAL ITALY

D arkness had fallen across the Apennine Mountains by the time Sean and Tommy reached the park area at Mount Fumaiolo. The drive had taken close to three hours, a little longer than Sean had been led to believe. A few last dying rays of sunlight peeked over the horizon far to the west, casting a pale-orange glow across the sky until it met with the coming darkness.

Along the way, Tommy had interrogated Sean about the back-story with Marek. "So what's the deal with that guy giving us these guns for nothing? What did you do for him?"

Sean laughed at the reminder. He'd not thought about the sequence of events for a long time. Truthfully, he rarely thought about it. Marek had been going through some tough times. He owed the wrong people a ton of money from a gambling debt. Sean had gone to Marek's place to ask some questions about a potentially huge arms deal that he'd gotten wind of. From what he'd heard, some Russian mobsters were trying to ship a load of military-grade weapons to a terrorist camp just inside the Pakistani border.

He hoped Marek knew where the deal was going down and who the major players were. When he'd arrived, however, Sean found

Marek in a bit of a pickle. The Czech had been tied to a chair, and his home had been doused in gasoline.

"Fortunately," Sean explained, "I was able to take the men out before they set the whole place on fire. It was pure luck that I arrived when I did. Marek believes that it was some kind of divine providence or something."

"Well, that explains why he treats you like his own personal savior," Tommy said.

"I guess," Sean let out an uncomfortable chuckle.

Tommy tried not to get into the details of Sean's previous life when he worked for Axis. His friend didn't talk about those days much, and the last thing Tommy wanted to do was pry. But in this case, he let his curiosity get the better of him. "I assume you stopped the weapons deal?"

"I'm sorry, buddy. That is classified information." Sean left him hanging for a minute as he steered the car through the tightening curves of the mountains. "But yeah," he glanced to the side for a brief second, "we definitely took them down. Marek happened to know someone who was directly involved with the operation. He was more than happy to fill me in on the details. We had an international all-star team there waiting to take down the whole thing."

"Sounds exciting."

"It was for about thirty seconds. Then the rest of it was just a ton of paperwork. Fortunately, we Axis guys are usually just shipped somewhere else and the paperwork is taken care of back home at HQ."

The rest of the trip had been mostly quiet. Sean tried to distract his mind from thoughts of Adriana. He didn't want to worry, but bad men sometimes did horrible things to women. He pushed the thought as far out of his brain as he could, instead focusing on the road ahead. At one point, Sean gave his phone to Tommy and asked that he text Emily, thanking her for getting them out of trouble earlier. He knew that she wouldn't hold it against him. Emily wanted Sean back in Axis in a bad way. He had been her top agent. Truthfully, he could have been the heir to the director's position when their former boss had stepped down. She'd believed that Sean would get the job, and was surprised when the Secretary of State called her to make the announcement. What Emily didn't know was that Sean had recommended her for the position. He was never much of a desk jockey. His soul called him to be active, doing things, not just filling out paperwork. One of the reasons he'd taken the job at the IAA was because Tommy promised him all the field work he could handle. The job certainly had delivered that, but no matter what he did Sean couldn't seem to get away from international intrigue. He was beginning to resign himself to the fact that he was good at it and that was why he seemed to keep being brought back in to things like the current situation.

Sean shook his head, trying to refocus. This situation was different. Some wealthy Greek businessman had kidnapped Adriana to find some ancient relic. The guy was clearly insane, or at the very least some kind of high-level narcissist. Sean wished he could just be back at his beach shop, soaking up some sun and watching the waves crash in on the sand. He'd saved up a ton of money over the years to set up his little business. And his cabin in the mountains provided an excellent retreat from the crazy world. No matter where he went, though, it seemed like he would never be able to escape those who wanted or needed to find him.

Upon arriving at the top of Mount Fumaiolo, Sean found a designated parking area and pulled the car into a space near a wooden fence. A sign next to the trailhead indicated that the park was closed after dark. Fortunately for the two Americans, there was no sign of a park ranger to tell them to leave. Sean assumed whoever had been working the park earlier had probably left right after sunset. He wondered how many people came to the historic site on a daily basis. The isolated location made for a long drive from most Italian cities. He and Tommy had been fortunate and had not hit much traffic on the way out of Rome. Although not hitting traffic was a relative term. There always seemed to be a ton of traffic in the old city. Spending much of their lives in Atlanta, Sean and Tommy were both familiar with what huge traffic problems looked like.

A cool breeze blew through the trees as the men exited the car. Tommy shivered for a second and zipped up the jacket he'd thrown on earlier. "Glad I brought this," he said.

The temperature on the mountain's peak was at least twelve degrees cooler than down in the valley. Fortunately, the two friends knew that ahead of time and had planned accordingly.

"Kind of eerie up here with no one around," Tommy added, moving toward the trail beyond the wooden railing.

Sean looked around in the darkness for a moment. He agreed internally. It was kind of creepy. He tried to imagine what kind of people had come to this place throughout history. Knowing that Julius Caesar had come here to hide a precious clue was a sobering thought. "Just keep an eye out," he said. "I don't know much about this area. There could be gypsies or something hanging around."

Tommy raised an eyebrow and snorted. "Gypsies?" He laughed out loud a second time.

"Just be on your toes. You never know." Sean gripped the gun Marek had given him. He'd seen too many things, been caught off guard enough to know that just when things seemed the least threatening they could get bad fast.

The two pulled their flashlights out of jacket pockets and flipped them on. A bright, nearly full moon cast a ghostly glow through the perfectly clear sky. On the drive up the mountain there had been several pull offs that provided outstanding views of the countryside below. It was yet another place Sean wished he could come visit again when his life wasn't in turmoil. The moon's light shone through openings in the forest canopy, giving a little illumination to scattered areas in the woods.

Their flashlights were still a necessity, though, as darkness permeated the majority of the area. Neither man wanted to trip over an unseen rock, or worse, twist an ankle. A severe sprain sounded like nothing serious, except for the fact that it would slow them down immensely. Fortunately, the path had been well maintained by the Italian parks service, and there were only a few big roots jutting out of the ground here and there. The path itself rose steeply at first, winding its way through the woods. A sign on a tree told the Americans that they were headed in the right direction, and that the source of the river was just up ahead, only a few hundred meters away.

Tommy spoke up, apparently never comfortable with silence. Maybe the strange feeling in the air made him want to strike up a conversation. "We miss having you around, Sean," he said, his voice cutting through the trees. "Not the same without you."

Sean smiled, keeping his eyes on the trail in front of them. "I miss working with you too, buddy. But you know I had to do it."

"I know." Tommy kept his eyes ahead as well. "I know. But I also know a part of you misses it. The thrill of discovery, adventure, unraveling a piece of history with every artifact we find, you have to admit it is a pretty good gig."

He was right about that part. Sean had loved his job, until it started to feel more like his work for the government than as an artifact recovery agent. "I haven't really had a chance to miss it yet, buddy. I just got my shop going a few weeks ago. I'm sure that when things die down I'll think about some of the good times we had, but for right now I'm good. Well, except for the fact that my girlfriend has been kidnapped by an insane person who may or may not have intentions of overthrowing a major European government."

Tommy laughed at the last comment, though there was a sense of worry buried within his friend's sarcasm.

Both of them had been avid campers throughout their friendship, having spent many a weekend in the mountains of eastern Tennessee and western North Carolina. Despite the extensive amount of time they spent in the woods, there was something different about being in a foreign country, stalking through a forest at night.

"It's creepy out here," Tommy said, changing the subject of the conversation. "I never did like being in the woods at night. Just something about it that unnerves me."

"I'm the same way. I never liked being in the woods after dark. Especially alone." He didn't say anything for a few seconds as they continued up the trail. "I am glad you're here, though. Not sure if I ever told you, but you really had me worried after that bombing in Cairo. I didn't know if you were going to make it or not."

Tommy smiled in the darkness. "Yeah, well, I don't really remember much about it. I just remember waking up in a hospital in Athens. But thanks for worrying about me. It's kind of strange that if we find this Antikythera Mechanism thing that I'll be headed back to Greece. I've only been there a few times, now twice in a couple of months."

The trail began to level off and bent to the left around a thick clump of trees. The sound of trickling water began to fill the air. They followed the path to where the mountain began to rise again, its shadow jutting into the sky and blocking out a giant section of the starry blanket to the north. Sean flashed his beam in the direction he thought the sound was coming from and saw a wooden railing much like the one near where they'd parked. Just beyond the fence, a spring flowed from an opening in the mountain. Two flat stones on either side, and one on top, surrounded the water's source. They were so strategically placed that Sean assumed they were put there by human hands. Whichever way the heavy rocks had arrived in the location, they'd certainly been there for several centuries. An opening in the forest canopy allowed the moon's pale light to illuminate the area, as if the heavens themselves were honoring the ancient site.

"Looks like that's our spot," Tommy said, overstating the obvious. "Strange to think that this is the start of one of the most famous and historic rivers on the planet."

"Yeah, it's funny to think of it that way, but you're right. That river has played a key role in the development of civilizations, waging wars, and the rise and fall of kingdoms. And it all starts right here with this little spring."

The two paused for a minute to contemplate the significance of where they were standing before Tommy spoke up again. "So what are you thinking? The riddle says that this thing will be in the mouth of the river, right?"

Sean nodded. "That's what it says. I assume that means in the hole where the water is coming out. That's the literal mouth, I suppose."

"Makes sense."

They turned their flashlight beams to the shallow pool of water that collected around the spring's source. The water brimmed at a point before beginning its long descent down the mountain. The two noticed several stepping stones in the pool, large enough for a person to stand on comfortably with both feet. The flat rocks appeared to lead all the way from the bank to where the water trickled out of the hole in the earth.

Sean stepped over to the embankment and reached out his right foot. Placing it on the first stone, he tested its stability, pressing his weight upon it and trying to move the object around. The rock didn't budge, and he brought his other foot over to join the first. He took another step to the next rock, testing it out as he had the first. Sean wasn't worried about the water's depth; it was only six to ten inches at best. The temperature, however, was another issue. The last thing he wanted to do was drive back to Rome with wet socks, or bare feet, as the case would probably be if he fell in.

After a slow few minutes of carefully making his way across the stepping stones, Sean finally reached the river's source. He crouched down on one knee next to where the water splashed into the pool.

"See anything?" Tommy asked loudly. His voice carried through the shadowy tree trunks of the forest, sending back a strange echo.

"Not yet," Sean answered, shining his light around in the crevasse. He bent over a little farther, trying to get a better view into the dark recess. With his left hand, he braced himself against one of the stones and stuck the light into the hole, just above where the water streamed out. "Looks like there's some kind of lip inside here."

He took the flashlight and jammed the end of it into his mouth, clutching it with his teeth so that he could use both hands to investigate further. Sean reached his right hand into the cavity, tilting his head to the side to make sure the light was where he needed it. "I hope there aren't any snakes in this thing," he yelled back to his friend on the bank.

Tommy was leaning over the top railing of the fence, eagerly watching his friend's progress. He looked like a kid at a toy store. "It should be okay. I don't think there are any snakes at this elevation. And if there are, they'll be pretty dormant in these cool temperatures."

"Good point," Sean said, still hoping his friend's rationale was sound.

His right hand came to rest on a wide, stone shelf on the upper left side of the hole's interior. Sean felt around for a few seconds, a sense of panic beginning to set in. "I found a shelf, but it's empty." He reached deeper into the cavity, nearly all the way to his shoulder, his face pressed against the steep embankment.

Sean was about to give up, resigned to the fact that someone had probably come along and taken whatever it was that would have been hidden inside. For the briefest of moments, it made him think about how the pyramids and so many other historic locations had been pilfered by the greedy. He took a deep breath and stretched his arm in just a little farther, pressing his shoulder fully into the hole. Unable to avoid it anymore, the frigid, flowing water ran down his shirt from his armpit to his belt. He ignored the cold liquid, desperate to find the item that could possibly save Adriana. A second later, his middle finger touched something on the shelf. It was cold and dry to the touch. With every ounce of energy he could muster, Sean extended his fingers another inch deeper into the crack. Three of his fingers found the top of something that felt like a stone cylinder. He pulled the object along the shelf toward where he was crouched. It rolled easily, confirming its wheel-like shape.

"Did you find something?" Tommy shouted across the water.

The sudden noise of his friend's voice startled Sean. His arm jerked to the right, nearly knocking the precious object into the water flow. He let out a long breath and ignored Tommy for a moment. More cautious and deliberate, Sean continued to roll the cylinder along the shelf until his elbow was nearly in the clear again. His fingers wrapped around the little tube and he pulled it free of its ancient resting place.

For a second, he stared down at the strange piece. It was carved from white marble and only seven inches long, perhaps two inches in diameter. Sean tried to remember if he'd seen anything like it on his previous journeys, but he couldn't recall ever finding such an artifact.

"What is it?" Tommy asked impatiently. He'd climbed over the fence and was standing next to the water.

Sean didn't answer immediately. He continued to examine the cylinder, rolling it over in his fingers. The open end had been sealed with a deep, crimson wax. As he turned the object, he found an image engraved into one side. The profile of a man with a wreath atop his ears and wrapping around his head, stared off to the right. Sean recognized the Latin words immediately. It was the royal seal of Julius Caesar.

33

CORFU, GREECE

A blurry light seared through the cracks of Adriana's eyes as she gradually awakened. The haze slowly began to fade, giving way to her surroundings. She was back on the floor of the cellar. The light emanated from a solitary light bulb overhead. The back of her skull ached, sending throbbing pain signals through her brain every second. Instinctively, she tried to reach up and massage the spot that seemed to hurt the most, but immediately realized her hands were bound tightly behind her back. Her neck was sore from lying on her side, though for how long she didn't know. Her ankles had also been tied up, preventing her from any movement other than wriggling like a worm on the floor. There was a sharp pain coming from her side, though she didn't know why. It felt like one of her ribs was badly bruised, maybe broken.

Adriana tried to collect her thoughts amid the pain and confusion. What happened? She remembered running down a gravel road amid tall stands of grass and trees. There was a boy running ahead of her. Who was he?

Then the story began to come back to her. Niki. The boy's name was Niki. He'd been imprisoned with her in the cellar. They'd tried to escape. She'd taken out several guards, but something had happened.

Someone tackled her from a blind side. She hadn't seen it coming. Adriana winced. The pain in her ribs stabbed at her with every breath. The man who had tackled her had also kicked her in the side. The awkward position in which she lay wasn't helping the pain. She needed to roll over to her other side to take a little pressure off the injury. It took a minute, but after rocking back and forth she was able to roll over onto her other side. The movement had increased the agony during the process, but now at least her ribs weren't killing her.

The whole room was still somewhat blurry, despite her regaining consciousness. She'd hit her head pretty hard on the gravel road. Adriana took a long, deep breath and sighed. She needed to focus. Another realization hit her: Niki was gone. Had the boy made it to the town? She'd told him to go to a church, but she wasn't really sure if the kid would be able to find his way. Children frightened easily. If he had gotten lost, he could be in worse trouble than he would have been in the cellar with her.

Adriana shook her head. No, Niki had made it. Kids were resilient. She remembered playing in her father's vineyard outside of Madrid. Their family's land holdings were vast, and extended for hundreds of acres across the countryside. She'd gotten lost in the rows of grape vines when she was only five. She'd been running through the fields with a paper kite flying a few feet above her. Before she realized it, Adriana had lost track of where she was. She had never been to the far reaches of her father's land before. There were tall trees protecting the boundary of the vineyards, trees she'd never really seen before. The curious part of her had wondered what lurked beyond the tree line, in the dark shadows of the forest. The other part of her had a healthy fear of the unknown, and had steered her back toward the house.

After a few hours of wandering through the seemingly endless rows of vines, she began to worry. The day was getting late, and she'd not had anything to drink since lunch. Her parched throat begged for water or something cool to drink. Eventually, Adriana calmed herself enough to plop down on the ground and think. She looked up at the sun and remembered where the sun always set in relation to her home. *West*, she thought. She stood back up and looked in the direction of the dropping sun, then spun around and headed in the opposite direction, resolved to keep walking until she found her way home. And find her way she did. Her father had been looking all over for her and had gathered the field workers to help with the search. She remembered how he hugged her when she arrived at the house. He'd picked her up and squeezed her so tight she'd squirmed a little, telling him she was going to pop. He kissed her forehead and cheeks, relieved that she'd come back safely.

"Promise me you won't run away like that again," he'd said.

"I didn't run away, Papa," Adriana had answered with childlike innocence. "I was just on an adventure."

Even now, with the throbbing pain and the dire situation facing her, she smiled at the memory. She wished her father could be there to pick her up and take her back into his home, clean her up and take care of her. Adriana had been independent since that day in the vineyard. She hoped Niki had the same spirit, the same sensibility that had led her home. The boy would be fine, she told herself.

A loud thud followed by a crash sounded from behind her. Someone had kicked open the door, spilling a little more light into the room. The loud noise hadn't helped her headache, but the more pressing concern was who had entered the room. A second later, she got her answer.

"It seems you were unhappy with your accommodations," the oddly familiar voice said. Dimitris Gikas stepped around into her field of vision and stood over her for a moment. He wore a navy blue suit with a blue-and-white striped tie. Even from her spot on the floor, he stank of expensive cologne, obviously one of those people who always put on too much. He crossed his arms and stared down at her with an angry expression. "Where is the boy?" he asked.

"I don't know." It wasn't a lie. She truly had no idea where Niki was at the moment. She hoped he was in the safety of a sanctuary somewhere, but Gikas would never get that information from her.

"I see." He took a few steps to the side and then returned. "You killed a few of my men, you know. That is something I cannot let go unpunished."

"I don't care. Anyone who works for you deserves to die."

Gikas jerked his head back and frowned. "Anyone? Even the secretaries for my companies? The people I provide jobs for in the cities, on my farms? You seem to think of me as some kind of monster. When the reality is I am more likened to a savior."

"What kind of savior imprisons innocent children and murders people in cold blood?" She found speaking only served to increase the pain in her head, but she had to keep the conversation going. It was the only thing keeping her from losing consciousness again.

"Innocent?" he shrugged to the side. "In the history of this world, many innocent people have had to die to create a greater future; it is part of the grand drama that plays out. The role of the innocent is to provide purpose for the rest of us, a rallying cry for those who would revolt, or a footstool for others to reach greater heights."

"Is that all they are to you? A footstool?"

Gikas's face radiated with vanity. "Of course. The greatest leaders the world has ever known were always aware of this. Do not get me wrong, each person has their purpose. Some purposes are grander than others."

Adriana flashed an expression of disgust. "And what is your grand purpose, Señor Gikas?" She let her Spanish roots come out with the last part of the sentence.

He raised an eyebrow. When he spoke, he didn't answer the question right away. "Democracy is dead, Miss Villa. It has failed miserably. All over the world, the experiment with republics and democracies is collapsing before our eyes. Democracy is a temporary form of government, Miss Villa. The Scottish historian Alexander Tytler said that. He knew that when people realized they couldn't simply vote for their best interests when bribery and corruption would rule in reality, that the government would collapse. And we are seeing it happen right now."

She struggled in vain against the bonds on her ankles and wrists, not to get free, simply to find a less uncomfortable position. "So what would you do? Bring anarchy to the governments of the world; throw them all into chaos so you can do as you please?"

Gikas tilted his head back and let out a laugh. "Oh, certainly not, my dear. Quite the opposite, in fact." He waited for her to ask, almost begging her to. When she didn't, he went on. "People are meant to be ruled. They say that they want freedom and other nonsense, but the truth is human beings want boundaries, rules, restrictions. They crave it deep within their subconscious. It is in their nature to be subservient. The greatest empires the world has ever known weren't under the rule of democracies or republics. They were led by one man."

Adriana's eyes widened at the realization. "You would be emperor?"

He rolled his shoulders. "King. Emperor. Consul of the state, you may call it anything you wish. But yes, I believe that the only truly functional form of government is a monarchy. One person must make the decisions for the good of the people."

"For the good of the people?"

His lips creased to one side of his face. "Of course. When there is order, crime is lower, the economy thrives, and people have purpose. Unemployment will drop. The military will be strong again. Our country will return to its former glory."

"And none of this has anything to do with your ego," she spat in a dubious tone.

He raised an eyebrow. "Ego? Perhaps I am ambitious, but someone must lead, and who better than I?" She didn't offer a response to the question.

Instead, she asked a question of her own. "And how will you convince the people to allow this? They will not stand for it. Your countrymen have a long history of believing in democracy. Do you think they will just forget it and let you have your way?"

He took a step away from her and folded his hands behind his back. When he reached the window in the corner, he stopped and gazed out at the starry sky. "Of course, the masses will need some kind of reason for things to change. As it is, they will simply replace the current government with a replica. If that happens, the entire fiasco will start all over again. If we are to initiate real change, we must completely eradicate the old system."

Adriana's eyes narrowed. She didn't like where this was going.

"Earlier you mentioned chaos. While I do not believe in an anarchist society, I do feel strongly that there must be a little chaos for order to prevail. In the case of my beloved country, it will require only a little push. And when it all comes crashing down, I will be there to save them."

"And what kind of push are you talking about? Killing your fellow countrymen?"

He paced back over to where Adriana lay on the floor, stopping short in case she got the guts to try to kick him in the shins. Despite her bonds, Gikas knew she was like a coiled snake, always looking for a way to strike. "No," he answered, looking down at her. "Although there will likely be much death in the wake of the government's collapse. No, my push is a simple one. I will starve the people into submission."

Adriana's face twisted in confusion. "What do you mean, starve them? How could one person starve an entire country?"

"Ah," he smiled at the question. "It's actually quite simple. All it really takes is the purchase of most of the country's food suppliers. For the last several years, I have been buying farms, distributors, and producers in nearly every corner of the country. The orders for food are all automated now, all delivered digitally by computer. It is easy enough to begin restricting orders. When a grocery store asks for a hundred units of something, we simply tell them we only have twenty."

She tried to process what he was saying, but it still seemed implausible. "There is no way you could own that many companies to make such an impact."

His eyebrows raised in contention. "Really? You are seeing this sort of thing happening all over the world. Facebook has bought numerous companies. Twitter has as well. YouTube was purchased for nearly two billion dollars. Why not in the food production industry? Over the last decade, I have bought up 40 percent of Greece's food producers. When I begin to cut back what we send out, the other companies will not be able to fill the void."

Gikas's voice took on a dark, sinister tone. "Nothing drives people to madness like hunger, Miss Villa. They will do anything to feed themselves or their children. And when their government fails to aid them, the people will be ripe for revolution. Who better to lead them than the one who feeds them?"

"You will lose hundreds of millions with this scheme. It cannot work," Adriana said, though her words lacked true conviction.

He put his hands behind his back again. "The money I lose will pale in comparison to what I will make in the long run. Besides, money is nothing without power. Greece will kneel before me as their savior, their king. After that, the possibilities are endless."

She had one last question but wasn't sure if he would answer it or not. He'd been in such an informative mood, Adriana needed to know. "Why do you need the Antikythera Mechanism so badly? What does that have to do with your Grecian manifesto?"

He spoke frankly. "Surely you know, Miss Villa. The Eye of Zeus can foretell the future. Once I have it, I will be able to snuff out my enemies before they rise up. I will be able to forecast the maneuvers of any military on the planet and move my forces accordingly. Even the military might of the United States will not be able to stop me."

"So what, you want to take over the world? Good luck with that."

He started for the door and stopped at the threshold. "No, Miss Villa. I do not wish to take over the world. It is far too large, with too many people. I simply state that no military will be able to intervene in what will happen here. The meddlesome Americans always try to police the activities of the world, and their friends, the British, usually come along. In this case, they will be powerless to do anything to stop me. Besides, those countries only get involved when there is money to be made. It's in their capitalist nature. If they don't see a financial opportunity here, they will not come. I will be elected as the new ruler of Greece, and when I am, I will make every country in the European Union pay for turning their backs on us."

Before she could ask anything else, Gikas disappeared into the doorway and slammed it shut.

Adriana took a slow breath, grimacing at the pain each time she took in air. Right now her primary concern wasn't her own health. This madman had something big planned, and she needed to figure out how to stop him.

34

APENNINE MOUNTAINS, CENTRAL ITALY

S ean considered breaking the wax seal right away, but he feared that the cold, moist air on the mountain might not be the best environment to expose a potentially delicate and vital piece. His curiosity desperately wanted to know what was inside, but it would have to wait until they got back to the hotel where they had a few things that could aid in the preservation of the tube's contents.

"It's a marble cylinder," Sean said loudly to Tommy. "There's an image of Julius Caesar on one side."

"What do you think is in it?" Tommy asked, ready to explode from excitement.

Sean carefully made his way back across the stepping stones, much faster than he did the first time. When he reached the embankment, he placed the cylinder in Tommy's hand. "Not sure, but it's probably the map we're looking for. We should take it back to the hotel and open it in a safe environment in case it's written on some kind of paper."

"Good idea," Tommy agreed as he examined the object with a sense of reverence and jubilation.

He had always been like that when the two discovered something out in the field. Ancient artifacts were a link to people from the past, real lives that had walked the same earth, breathed the same air. What Tommy held in his hand right now was a direct connection to one of the most influential and famous people in the entire world's history. Julius Caesar had held that very cylinder in his hands. The thought overwhelmed him for a moment.

"Pretty cool, huh?" Sean said, observing his friend's reaction to the piece.

"It's always awesome when we find something like this," Tommy said, his voice still distant.

Sean put a hand on his friend's shoulder. "I know, buddy, but we can admire it later. We have to get this back to the hotel and get it open. Right now, it's the only thing that can give us an in with the man who took Adriana."

Tommy nodded and handed the cylinder back to Sean, who gripped it tightly. The two friends climbed back over the fence and started to head down the trail toward the parking area when they simultaneously froze in their tracks. Something flashed in the darkness about a hundred yards down from where they stood. It was only for a second, but both of them saw it. Someone was coming up the path, trying to conceal their lights.

Instinctively, Sean grabbed Tommy and pulled him off the trail and behind the wide trunk of an oak. He watched from around the back of the tree, seeing the faint light flash again. Whoever was trying to shade the flashlight was doing a poor job of it.

"You think it's a park ranger or something?" Tommy whispered, hopeful with the question.

Sean shook his head and responded in an even quieter tone. "A ranger wouldn't be trying to sneak up on us. And there are two of them."

"Gypsies?"

"Doubtful." Sean gave a quick twist of his head, along with a derisive glance. He put his finger to his lips, motioning for Tommy to stop talking.

Sean pulled out his gun and held it close to his face. Tommy copied the gesture.

The two figures continued to sneak up the trail toward the spring. When they reached the crest of the hill and left the shadows of the forest, Sean realized who the men were. Standing in the moonlight on the edge of the clearing, the Roman police officers looked around confusedly. They ceased their efforts of trying to hide their flashlight beams and began flashing them around, searching desperately for their quarry.

The skinny officer, who Sean had noticed was staring at him at the jail, was saying something in Italian. He was a little too far away to understand everything, but it sounded like he was giving orders. Sure enough, the thicker cop started to fan out, walking around the fence, searching the area. The one in charge went around to the right, following the path in a direction that wound its way uphill.

Tommy glanced at Sean as if to ask what he should do. Sean held up a finger and motioned for his friend to follow around the broad tree trunk. As the man in uniform neared their line of sight, Sean and Tommy shifted to the right, keeping their position behind the tree. Sean took a quick look across the clearing at the other officer. He was at least sixty yards away at that point, and moving cautiously up the hill, shining his light into the woods. Satisfied the leader was far enough away to make his move, Sean stepped out from his hiding place and back onto the trail's soft dirt. He moved quickly on the balls of his feet, careful not to step on a twig that would snap and draw his target's attention. He held his weapon level, belt high, aiming it straight at the back of the chubby policeman.

Sean was only a few feet away from the man when something rustled in the woods off to his left. He didn't know if it was a squirrel, a chipmunk, or something bigger. It didn't matter what it was, because the cop spun around at that noise, waving both his flashlight and his gun as he turned. His eyes grew wide when he realized one of the men he was searching for was right behind him. He tried to raise his gun to fire, but Sean was on him before he could make the move. Sean leapt at him and lashed out with his right foot in a flying sidekick. The force of the blow struck the man's hand hard enough to knock the weapon to the ground. The cop's next move was an attempt to call his partner for help, but Sean nipped that as well, striking the man across the jaw with a dramatic upper cut. The stunned Italian policeman staggered backward before falling flat on his back.

Sean wasted no time rolling the man over and finding a pair of handcuffs on the left side of his belt. He slipped them out of the holster and cuffed the cop's hands behind his back, leaving him lying face down in the dirt.

Tommy shook his head in mock condemnation from his hiding place behind the tree. Sean deftly returned to the spot next to his friend, his breathing slightly elevated from the brief encounter.

"Good job," Tommy said, admiring the handiwork. "But what are we gonna do about that one?"

Sean stared up the hill. The other cop was nearly a hundred yards away, his flashlight weaving back and forth as he scanned the woods. "When he comes back down the hill, we flank him just as we did with his partner."

Tommy nodded his approval.

Sean glanced down at the ground and found a medium-sized rock, about the size of his palm. He handed it to his friend who took it with a confused look on his face. "When I tell you to, throw that into the water over there. It will get the other cop's attention and he'll come back down to check it out. When he does, I'll be waiting for him over there behind that other tree." Sean pointed to a similar oak about twenty yards away on the edge of the trail.

"You don't think I could take him?" Tommy asked, feigning insult.

Sean raised an eyebrow. "Please, be my guest. I'll throw the rock if you'd prefer."

Tommy pulled the stone away, shielding it from his friend. "No, it's cool. Go ahead. I'll do it next time."

Sean grinned and passed his friend a suspicious glance. He gave a single nod and took off toward the other tree, staying low as he moved. Tommy watched as Sean worked his way through the shrubs and undergrowth until he reached his destination. Sean stood up behind the tree and held up his hand, motioning for Tommy to wait.

Tommy shrugged, wondering what he needed to wait for, but obeyed nonetheless. A second later, Sean made a throwing motion with his hand, giving the signal for Tommy to do his thing.

He stepped back to toss the rock, but slipped on some loose leaves. The slip caused his balance to shift and the trajectory of the rock to change dramatically. Tommy chucked the stone high through the air and over the water, landing it on the hill above the mouth of the spring.

The noise startled the police officer who'd been searching off to the right of the trail. He swiveled around instantly, shining his flashlight to his left, where the rock had landed among some leaves and sticks. Tommy glanced over at Sean, who was glaring at him with a disapproving and questioning expression.

Up on the hill, the skinny officer had left the trail and was checking around the area where the stone had landed. Tommy was frustrated with himself for screwing up, a feeling that compounded as the policeman noticed his partner lying on the ground in the moonlight.

The cop instantly turned paranoid and started waving his gun around in every direction. He flashed the beam of his light into the woods, desperately trying to find the men who'd attacked his fleshy partner. After a few moments of uncertainty, he made his way down to the other side of the spring and back onto the trail. The officer reached his partner, who was beginning to regain consciousness, signaled by his moaning.

"Giovanni," Tommy heard the leader say. "What happened?"

All he received was another aching groan.

Tommy looked down and saw another rock at his feet. It was slightly larger than the one he'd just thrown. He eased his way down to one knee and picked up the stone, casting a glance back at Sean as he stood up.

In the shadows, he could see Sean mouth a sentence. "What are you doing?" He received no response.

Tommy ignored him, turned back toward the two Italian police-men, and cocked his arm. He had played baseball most of his life until his parents' death. He'd even had some major league teams scouting him when he was in high school. Tommy had shown a great deal of promise as a pitcher, but when he'd had rotator cuff surgery it took a few too many miles per hour off his fastball. He tried to reha-bilitate the arm and get it back to where it was, but things were never the same. His fastest pitch could only reach into the low eighties, which might not have been a problem for some teams. However, the issue of him being damaged goods at such a young age scared away any of those teams that had an interest in Tommy Schultz.

He spent a few months trying to reinvent himself as an outfielder. His arm was still good enough to play left or right field. One tryout with the Cleveland Indians had gone particularly well, and he made it down to the final cut, only to be told he wasn't fast enough. Running speed wasn't an issue with pitchers, which made it a perfect place for Tommy. After the Cleveland tryout, he resigned himself to playing recreationally in town and pretty much gave up his dream.

Now he had a chance to put all those years of hard work to good use. He twisted his body and stepped forward, firing the rock at the Italian policeman who was busy trying to uncuff his partner. The projectile covered the distance in less than a second, striking the skinny cop on the bridge of his nose. The blow sent him toppling over, dropping his flashlight and keys in the process. Blood gushed from his nasal passages and oozed from a cut between his closed eyes. Tommy's throw was a perfect strike, and knocked the guy out cold.

Tommy rushed out from his hiding place, sprinting across the span in a few seconds. He skidded to a stop, grabbed the lead cop's cuffs out of their holster, and quickly bound his hands. Sean ran out from his position, unable to hide his surprise at the result of his friend's plan.

"I guess you still got it," he said with his hands on his hips.

"They said my fastball didn't have enough on it."

"Looks like they were wrong."

Tommy stared down at the two men piled on top of each other. The fat one continued to moan and he was starting to roll around a little.

"What should we do with them?" Tommy asked.

Sean bent down and took both sets of keys from the men. "Let the park ranger deal with them in the morning."

35

ROME, ITALY

During the few hours' drive back to Rome, Sean and Tommy did everything they could to stay awake. They'd been up for more hours than they could count, and their energy had been depleted both by travel and by the exertion of their activities. Sean had never been a good night driver, so Tommy had elected to take the wheel, thinking he would be the safer option. At first, they'd tried to find something to listen to on the radio. That had been a fruitless endeavor, however, as they quickly learned that the local taste in music contrasted theirs remarkably. After searching the channels in vain, Tommy elected the silence of the road over the bad music options.

The two tried to keep up conversation to make staying awake a little easier. Sean recounted a number of times where he'd actually fallen asleep at the wheel, but been fortunate enough to snap awake before his car went off the road.

That part of the conversation had been less than comforting for Tommy, who, while a better driver in the late hours, was still battling with heavy eyes. He redirected the conversation back to the stone cylinder. "It's amazing that you are holding something that was last seen in this world over two thousand years ago, and the last eyes that saw it likely belonged to Julius Caesar."

"It is pretty remarkable," Sean agreed, taking a closer examination of the tube. The Latin engraved on the side had suffered almost no erosion, and was just as clear as it must have been two millennia before when it had been created.

Tommy glanced at it out of the corner of his eye and then quickly put his focus back on the road. "I've never seen anything like that before. Do you remember finding a cylinder like that on any of your IAA missions?"

Sean shook his head. "No. I didn't." He turned the object over, reading the inscription again. He'd read it a dozen times already, trying to figure out what it meant.

Both men could read Latin. Being the foundation of several world languages, knowing Latin was how Tommy and Sean were able to speak multiple languages. The meaning of the words wasn't the problem. Interpreting them had been easy enough. The problem was the message itself.

The light that brings darkness.

Sean traced the outline of the letters with the tip of his finger. "The light that brings darkness," he said quietly.

"That's an odd thing to inscribe on an old piece of rock," Tommy said, casually. "Still no thoughts on what it means?"

Sean put the object back in the front pouch of his book bag and zipped it closed. "It sounds like a warning to me. But to someone with an evil mind and even darker aspirations, it could be exactly what they're looking for."

"Gikas?"

"Bingo. And if he gets his hands on the Eye of Zeus, it could potentially be catastrophic." Sean let the words hang in the air.

Their car approached another car in the right lane, driving much too slowly. Tommy steered into the left lane and passed the slow moving minivan. When they were clear of the other vehicle, he returned their car back over to the right. They hadn't seen many cars on the lonely highway, which was most likely because they were out in the middle of nowhere between Rome and the mountains.

Tommy had another thought. "What if this Eye of Zeus doesn't do anything? What if it's just an ancient artifact used to navigate the seas?"

"Well," Sean shrugged, "I don't know what to believe about the device. What I do know is that the guy who wants it is also the guy holding Adriana against her will. I could take or leave the ancient relic, but if finding it means finding her and getting her to safety, then I will do everything in my power to do that."

The mood shifted for a moment. Tommy guided the conversation back to the issue of the warning on the stone tube. "I mean, is it really possible that the ancient Greeks found a way to tap into quantum fields around us?"

An exit sign passed by. Just beyond it, another sign told them how many kilometers until they reached Rome.

"History never fails to surprise me," Sean answered the question after a minute of thought. "Just when we think we've got it all figured out, there's a new discovery that changes our perceptions of the ancient world. We still don't know how the people of the past created the pyramids, Machu Picchu, moved the giant stones in Cuzco, or any number of other things we can't seem to explain."

He stopped for a moment, thinking quietly to himself. "Anything is possible. That's one thing the quantum universe has taught us. Literally, anything could be possible. So can I rule out the notion that an ancient computer made from brass is capable of telling the future? No, even though it sounds a little hokey."

The mood settled into the silent whine of the engine and the constant swoosh of the wind passing over the side mirrors. Off in the distance, the faint glow of the city on seven hills arose from the darkness.

"I guess after all we've seen I can pretty much believe anything," Tommy said, voluntarily breaking the silence.

"When we find it, we'll see what it's all about," Sean said wearily. He yawned after speaking.

"Almost home, buddy. We'll get a good night's rest and figure out what's inside that thing in the morning."

Sean was thinking differently. "There's no way I'll be able to sleep tonight if we don't open this first. I have to know what's inside it."

Tommy glanced at him out of the corner of his eye again. "Are you sure? I mean, we've been at it all day. We need to get some shut-eye."

"What if there's nothing inside it? I have to know." He stared straight ahead at the long stretch of highway.

"Okay. We can do that. But once we've opened it, we are going to get some sleep. Okay?"

Sean twisted his head to the side and smirked at his friend. "Of course."

Something about Sean's mischievous tone didn't do much to convince Tommy, but it was all he would get for now.

36

CORFU, GREECE

T he javelin zipped through the air in a perfect line, arching high through the sky and striking the target almost dead center. Dimitris stood in a field of tall, golden grass. The coastal breeze waved the blades back and forth in constant motion. The effect the wind had on Gikas's throw was minimal.

He'd taken to throwing javelins two decades before. While he didn't have the strength to compete at an international level, his accuracy was second to none. The target, a hay bale with a four-foot diameter, was nearly thirty yards away, a distance that would challenge the accuracy of the best of throwers.

"Do you know why I enjoy the javelin?" Gikas asked, turning to Thanos.

"No," his trusted assistant said. He didn't seem to care what the answer was. The sun had only been up for half an hour. For as long as he'd worked for Gikas, he never did understand the man's early morning rituals. Today was the first time he'd witnessed the javelin target practice.

Thanos and his men had been called back to Corfu upon giving Gikas the news that the map leading them to Ostia had been a ruse. They had returned to the home of Vincenzo Cagliari, but the place was swarming with police. Why, Thanos couldn't be certain, but there was no way they could get inside. Had the old man contacted the authorities? Didn't matter. There wasn't time to sit around and lay siege to the retired professor's home, waiting for the police to leave. Instead, they'd taken Gikas's plane back to Greece that night.

Gikas strode back to a rack where several other javelins hung in place. "I love the javelin throw for a few reasons. One, it is a direct lineage to my country's heritage. We invented the sport. It's been a part of the Olympic Games since they began."

"The other?" Thanos asked with an air of disinterest.

"It's precise. Granted, in the Olympics, you are trying for distance over hitting a target, like the one out there," he said, pointing to the bale of hay. "But even with the distance event, the thrower must be perfectly balanced. They must keep the shaft of the javelin at just the right angle. Their approach must be light, yet swift. The body becomes a symphony in motion before launching the spear into flight."

"I suppose so."

Gikas turned to one of Thanos's men, named Teo Bourdon. "What about you, Teo? Have you ever tried javelin?"

Bourdon had been a soldier in Bosnia during the war that had ravaged the Balkans after the fall of communism. When the war ended, his exploits and reputation had travelled far. When Thanos had heard about him, he knew Bourdon would make an excellent addition to his unit under the service of Dimitris.

Teo had made more money than he could have hoped to in the mercenary free market, which was a considerable amount. Warriors like him went for a premium, often serving private security companies in hostile areas. The Middle East bloomed with such killers. He'd decided to join up with Thanos, having heard of the bald man's seedy reputation from a few odd jobs he picked up along the way. One thing Teo had always appreciated was knowing a situation before going into it. With the current arrangement, he knew he most definitely could not trust a single person who worked for Dimitris, including Gikas himself. That fact gave Bourdon a little comfort in that it kept him constantly focused, ever aware that one of the people nearest him could turn their back on him without provocation. Even now he watched Gikas closely as his primary employer circled the rack of javelins like a hawk circling an unsuspecting rabbit.

"No, sir," Bourdon answered. "I have not, but I am always willing to learn new things."

Gikas stared at him for a moment, impressed with the man's demeanor and level of respect. "I like that answer. We are constantly learning new things in this world. Those who are unwilling to adapt and change will be left in the dust, crushed by the whims of fate."

"Indeed."

He motioned for Bourdon to follow him. "May I have a moment with your assistant?" Gikas asked Thanos.

"He works for you."

Gikas gave a quick nod and a smile. "Come, Teo. You would be surprised at how far the javelin penetrates into the target," he said as the two walked away from the throwing area. "The tip is very sharp, and when thrown properly carries a great deal of force with it."

The two men reached the target, and Gikas bent down to show Bourdon how far the spear's point had stuck into the hay bale. "Imagine what it would do to a human," he said nonchalantly.

"One of those to the chest or stomach would mean almost certain death."

"Essentially." Gikas stood up straight again and put his hands on his hips. He gazed out across the field, surveying his property. His eyes passed over Thanos, who stood with his back to them. He held a cell phone to his ear, busily talking to someone. Gikas reached down and yanked the javelin out of the target. He stared at the shiny object for a moment, admiring the fine craftsmanship that had gone into its creation.

"It really is an elegant weapon, don't you think?"

"That's a good way of putting it," Bourdon agreed.

Gikas set the base of the shaft on the ground for a moment, holding it upright next to him. "Sometimes, it's good to hold on to the old ways. Like with this javelin. It's important to remember that old things can still be of service to us."

Bourdon nodded, though he hid his confusion. He wasn't sure where the wealthy Greek was going with his line of thought.

"Of course, sometimes we have to let old things go, especially when they have worn out their usefulness. You won't find a rotary telephone outside of a museum. When a new television comes out, you get rid of the old and replace it with the new one." Gikas waited for a moment. "It's particularly crucial to get rid of things when they no longer work. If you had an old television set that stopped working, you would need to get a new one whether you wanted to or not."

"I suppose so."

Gikas nodded, looking in the direction of his head man. In a quick movement, he jerked up the javelin and turned his body toward Thanos. In three short steps, the shaft soared through the air. It only took a second to reach its target. The tip of the javelin sunk deep into Thanos's back and ripped through his ribcage, protruding out of his chest. For a second, the bald man wavered. The cell phone fell from his hand onto the ground as he reached down with both hands to clasp the spear. He staggered around for a few seconds, spinning in a circle. His face was awash with confusion and anguish as he peered into his boss's eyes one last time. Then Thanos slumped over in the grass, his body concealed from view by the tall, waving blades.

Teo said nothing, nor did he appear shocked by the sudden murder of the man who'd brought him onboard with the Gikas operation. He simply stared stoically at the spot where Thanos had collapsed.

"He served me well for many years, Teo. But even someone who has been loyal to me as long as Thanos has can wear out their usefulness. Just like the television that doesn't work anymore, he had to be replaced." Gikas turned back to the mercenary. "You're in charge now, Teo. I do not want you to live in fear that any failure will result in your death. Failing is how we learn, it's how we grow and adapt to the things that life throws at us."

Bourdon lowered his eyebrows. "This isn't about losing Wyatt and any connection to the map?"

Gikas waved a finger in the air. "Oh, it most certainly is about that. Failure can be acceptable. But when the failure is so huge that it is difficult to repair, that becomes a different issue completely."

"I see."

"So, do not fail me the way Thanos did, and you will be fine." He put his hand on Teo's shoulder.

"Understood, sir. Failure is never an option for me. Especially big failures." Teo's face hardened with determination. "What would you have me do first?"

"Have the men toss Thanos into the sea. After that, get something to eat. I understand I brought the two of you out here before you had a chance to get breakfast." The stark contrast between the cold murderer and the caring, sympathetic man speaking at the moment wasn't lost on Teo. He kept his observations to himself, however. "When you've finished eating, come to my study. We will need to find a way to learn of Sean Wyatt's whereabouts and track him down before it is too late."

Teo's mind ran with questions. He asked the first one that came to mind. "What would Wyatt want with the device you seek?"

Gikas threw his hands up in the air. "I'm not sure. He's a treasure hunter. For several years he worked for the International Archaeological Agency, which is really just a front for pilfering the treasures of the ancient world."

"I'd think you would admire that part," Bourdon tested his boss's demeanor.

For a second, Gikas thought about the comment, and then let out a thunderous laugh. "You're right. I do admire them for that!" His voice continued to boom across the meadow for half a minute. When he finally let the moment pass, Gikas continued speaking. "I have to assume that he is trying to find the Eye of Zeus because he believes if he finds it he will find his woman, the Spaniard."

"Ah," Bourdon gave a nod. "That makes sense."

"But Wyatt is not one with whom you should meddle. He is quite dangerous." Gikas held up a warning finger.

Bourdon crossed his arms, contemplating what his employer had said. "I know about Wyatt. In his previous life he worked for a United States government agency called Axis. I read his dossier after being brought on the job by Thanos. His exploits are fairly remarkable, but I am confident he is more lucky than anything else."

"Oh?"

"Wyatt finds himself in sticky situations quite often. I personally observed his escape from the train station. In any other spot, we would have had the drop on him and killed him before he could do anything. Unfortunately, we were in a train station. Next time, he won't be so lucky."

Gikas nodded. "Good. I like your optimism. See to it that he is not."

"As to our meeting and determining what we should do next, sir, I have a man in Rome that can be at Wyatt's hotel room within the next thirty minutes. Wyatt and his companion left most of their belongings in that room. At some point they will have to return to get them."

"They will be wary of watchful eyes, Teo," Gikas said, doubtful.

"Certainly they will. But my man will remain unseen, and he is an expert at surveillance. Wherever Wyatt goes, we will know."

"Excellent," Gikas said patting the younger man on the back again. "I already can see I have made a good choice with you."

37

ROME, ITALY

Paulino pressed the end button on his cell phone. His highest-paying client had just called him from somewhere on the Greek island of Corfu. Teo hadn't needed to tell him where he was. Paulino knew within twenty seconds of receiving the call. The homemade tracing software had been downloaded onto his mobile device so he could use it from anywhere in the world that had a cell or Wi-Fi signal. At some point, he planned to link the phone to a network of satellites, thus creating a more powerful platform to find anyone who called him, from anywhere, regardless of signal strength. He sat back in his black mesh desk chair and put his hands behind his neck, stretching out his muscles. He needed a break after staring at his four computer screens for the last nine hours. His machines had been running hard all day, downloading information at an incredible rate and maxing out the bandwidth normally available to an entire city block. A wry grin snuck onto his stubbled, muscular face as Paulino considered all the angry people in his building, frustrated by the fact that they couldn't get on their beloved social media networks.

It had been a simple enough trick to build the bypass into the system and redirect the bandwidth directly to his apartment. He'd cleverly made the setup impossible to track, sending a fake signal through the fiber optic network all over the city. At the moment, the decoy signals were telling the local Internet providers that someone in the Vatican was using up the bandwidth. It was one of his prouder ruses. Paulino doubted the Internet company would even make the phone call to question as to why it was happening. Eventually they would, but by then he'd have already set up another decoy.

The first time Paulino had tried the trick, the authorities nearly nabbed him, figuring out that there was no way an orphanage was using the Internet that much. The nuns must have been beyond confused at the accusations. Paulino allowed himself a short laugh at the thought.

Most of the time, his software hacked its way through people's accounts, bringing in a whopping quarter million in euros every single year. He stole enough to live comfortably, but never so much that he would get caught. Of course, like any intelligent businessman, he liked to diversify his sources of income. Black market surveillance with a sprinkle of murder always paid well. On top of that, it kept him from getting bored. Sitting in front of the computer for hours on end took its toll on his interest level. Getting out and killing someone every now and then did wonders for his energy.

The call from one of his regulars had been an extremely profitable one. Over the course of the next few hours, he was going to make a lot of money, more than he would make in the next three months combined.

Teo had always been generous with his payments. As a result, their relationship had been a good one. Bourdon paid; Paulino delivered. It was simple enough. And Bourdon never asked what Paulino's last name was, or even if it was his real name. He didn't care as long as the job was done, which it always was.

"So you want me to kill them both?" he'd asked Bourdon during the phone conversation.

"No. Not this time. I need them alive. They have something my employer wants very badly. You have to make certain that this piece is not damaged in any way."

Based on the previous assignments Bourdon had given, it was an odd request, but no killing might make it easier this time around, though less interesting. "What does this object look like?"

"We don't know."

Paulino let out a short laugh. He crossed one leg over the other and rested his elbow on top of his knee. "Then how will I know what not to damage?"

"Just follow them, Paulino. This is a watch-and-follow job. You won't need to do anything except tell us where the marks are going. We will take care of the rest."

That did sound boring.

Before the Italian could protest, Bourdon added another bit of information. "You may have to sneak onto their private plane. It's parked at the airport right now, but if they decide to go somewhere, you'll need to go as well."

The last part caused Paulino to frown. "That could add significantly to my costs. What happens if these marks fly to India or South America?"

"They won't. Our hunch is that they will stay in the Mediterranean area."

"And what gives you that hunch?" Paulino asked suspiciously.

"Because the artifact they are looking for is hidden somewhere in that vicinity."

Paulino had thought silently for a few seconds before making an offer. "I'll do it for twenty-five thousand, but it's only that much because I could end up in the middle of nowhere."

Bourdon didn't respond immediately to the proposal. The Italian thought that maybe the amount had come off as greedy. With all the different unknowns in play, though, he considered it a fair amount. If his client wanted to pay less, he would simply turn it down.

"Sorry, old friend. I don't think you understand who I am working with." Before Paulino could decline the job, Bourdon continued talking. "You'll receive a hundred for this one."

The Italian's eyes grew wide. Had he heard right? A hundred thousand euros for a watch-and-follow job? "When do I start?"

"Right now. The two men are staying at a hotel in the city. They'll be heading back there now. Their names are Thomas Schultz and Sean Wyatt. Wyatt is a former American agent, so he will be on the lookout for anyone suspicious. We received word this morning that two of my employer's paid associates were found handcuffed and beaten in a park in the mountains."

Paulino nodded. "Understood. Blend in. Stay back..." He stopped and thought for a moment. "Wait, how am I supposed to get on a private plane with these guys if I have to keep my distance?"

"That's why I pay you. I'm sending you the address right now, along with some images of the marks. I expect to hear from you soon."

The text message had come through almost immediately after Bourdon had ended the conversation. Paulino intensely examined the images of the two men. They would be easy enough to find. He looked at the address and the name of the hotel. Bourdon had even provided the room numbers. He could be there in under twenty minutes, depending on the traffic.

Paulino checked his watch. It seemed like most people didn't wear watches anymore, electing instead to simply check the time on their phones or tablets. It was one of the few old-fashioned things he clung to in a life that had become deeply embedded in the digital age. Local time was still early. Even though he'd been working through the dark hours of the morning, Paulino wasn't about to let a hundred grand get away from him. He got up out of his chair and wandered through the clutter to the refrigerator, tucked away in the corner of his tiny kitchen. It contained only a carton of milk, a few bottles of Peroni beer, a box of takeout from two days ago, and ten energy drinks. He pulled out one of the cans and popped it open, guzzling half of the contents in a matter of seconds. He lowered the can and sighed with relief.

The men he was to follow would probably be getting up soon. He would need to hurry.

Paulino stepped over to the round nook table at the edge of his kitchen. It was littered with wires, motherboards, compact discs, papers, and a cigar box. He picked up the box and set it closer to where he was standing. Opening it, he fingered through several passports, driver's licenses, and six thick stacks of euros. In his business, having other identities was of the utmost importance. While most people working in the underworld had a fake ID or two, few of them went the extra mile to create backstories for each one.

He selected a passport from Slovenia, flipped it open, and stared at the image. For this one he'd decided to be an advertising agent. He had business cards to go with the name and had even created a website, social media profiles, and outsourced online content to make his identity seem more like a real person. If any security pulled him in for questioning, say, in an airport, he could prove who he was and what he did beyond simply providing them with a fake passport.

Details were high on Paulino's priority list. It was how he'd evaded trouble with the authorities all along.

He slid the passport into his back pocket and a wad of the money into a front pocket. If he was going to play the part of a high-end executive, he'd need to put on a different shirt, probably something with a tie.

A few minutes later, Paulino looked like a completely different person. He'd thrown on a white button-up shirt with a black tie and matching black jacket that went with his designer jeans. The fake, wire-frame glasses added to the imagery of a young, wealthy executive. On his way out the door, he picked up the Walther .22 pistol off the table, along with the sound suppressor lying next to it. Even though it was an observational mission, Paulino preferred to always be prepared.

38

ROME, ITALY

A thin line of sunlight poured across Sean's face from the window on the other side of the room. He groaned at the brightness filling his eyes.

The night before, he and Tommy had spent over an hour carefully opening the stone cylinder. They'd been surprised at how well the wax had sealed the cap into place, especially after such a long time and what had to be extreme conditions on the mountain. Temperatures would drop to well below freezing during the winter, and the summers could get fairly hot. Tommy reasoned that inside the miniature cave of the spring, temperatures would stay more consistent, and thus not damage the object or its contents.

With white gloves and special tools, the two managed to remove the cap and open the ancient tube. Sean held the cylinder up to the light and looked inside. The hollowed out space was about half an inch in diameter, only big enough to hold a small piece of paper, or in this case, a tiny scroll. Sean reached in with a pair of tweezers and ever so gently removed the roll of animal skin.

After twenty minutes of cautiously rolling the scroll out a few millimeters at a time, the two men stared down at what appeared to be a map of ancient Greece. The detail was remarkable, even given the abilities ancient cartographers displayed in many instances. Whoever had drawn it had taken into account most of the surrounding islands, along with providing their names.

Tommy's wonder at the aged document rapidly turned to confusion. "I don't understand. This is just an old map of Greece. I expected there to be an X or something marking the spot."

Sean would normally have laughed at his friend's comment; instead, his irritation had overridden his sense of humor. "Why would Caesar go to all that trouble to leave a map with no directions on it?"

"It doesn't make sense," Tommy agreed.

Sean removed the white gloves and rested both palms flat on the work table, leaning over it and scanning the map slowly, taking in every single detail. "We have Corfu right here," he said, pointing at the map. He moved his finger to a place where another city had been labeled. "Thessaloniki is here." Then he waved the finger around at all the islands on the bottom of the scroll. "He even made sure to detail the names of all these islands. But why?"

Sean lay in the soft bed, staring at the window with a dazed consciousness. They'd gone to bed, unable to figure out what the meaning of the map could be. What good was a map that didn't tell the reader where to go? Sean had sealed the map in a large plastic bag to preserve it and left it on the desk. Both men were exhausted and decided that maybe a fresh pair of eyes would help them see things a little more clearly in the morning.

Outside his hotel room window, Sean could hear the streets of Rome beginning their morning activities. He rolled over and stared at the ceiling for a second before a deep voice nearly startled him right out of the bed.

"Good morning. Sleep well?"

Sean quickly flipped over, grabbing the gun from under the pillow next to the one he'd used. He let go of the weapon when his eyes adjusted to see who had spoken to him. Agent Yarbrough sat in the corner near the closet with one leg crossed over his knee. His right arm was in a sling, but he was dressed in his usual secret service attire as if he were going back to work that same day.

"Jeez, Yarbrough. You scared the crap out of me. You're lucky I didn't shoot you." Sean swung his legs over the edge of the bed and planted his feet on the thinly carpeted floor. He always slept in a T-shirt and boxers. His left hand reached out and grabbed the khakis from the back of a nearby chair. He stood up, slid the pants on, and stared curiously over at the agent. "What are you doing here? I thought you'd be in the hospital."

"I was...for a few hours," he answered with a sly grin. "Gonna take more than a sniper bullet to keep me down. I was lucky. Whoever the shooter was didn't use a big round." He glanced down at the sling. "It'll be a while before I throw a baseball again, but I'm okay."

"I'm glad you're okay," Sean said as he zipped up his pants. "But that still doesn't answer the question as to why you're here."

"Always direct, huh?"

"Usually. I don't like to beat around the bush."

Yarbrough smiled. "I like that. I'm sure the president would too." The agent paused for a second and then went on. "He wants an update on your progress."

"The president?"

Yarbrough nodded. "According to our sources, Gikas has been buying up companies left and right in Greece."

"Yeah, you guys mentioned that before."

"It would seem he is becoming more aggressive now. One of Gikas's main rivals has disappeared, along with his wife. They have a young boy named Niki who has also disappeared."

Sean's eyebrows furrowed. "You think Gikas killed them?"

"We don't know for sure," Yarbrough shrugged. "But it's only a matter of time until he makes a power play to take over the Greek government."

Sean shook his head and made his way over to the workstation where the map still lay on the surface, shrouded in clear plastic. "So what?" he asked and turned back around to face Yarbrough. "If the people want a new leader, isn't it their right to choose who that leader is? If they don't want Gikas they can pick someone else."

"Sure," Yarbrough said with a slow nod. "But not if he begins to starve his people into submission."

The dubious look on Sean's face transitioned to concern. "Starve?"

"Our intel on the Greek situation is that Gikas controls a significant percentage of food distribution companies all across the country. Right now, those channels are only running at 70 percent capacity, down 20 percent from two weeks ago."

"He's closing the supply chains," Sean realized out loud. "When too many people begin to starve, they'll riot in the streets. Government officials will be publicly executed."

"And they will be all too happy to vote for someone who can feed them," Yarbrough finished Sean's thought.

Sean considered the theory. Would Gikas really starve tens of thousands of his fellow countrymen? If he did, chaos would certainly ensue. "A lot of people will die," he said finally.

"Yep. And we have a feeling that would only be the tip of the iceberg."

Sean pulled a chair over and sat in it backward, resting his arms on the top of its back. "Why do I feel like you're about to tell me why the president wanted me involved from the beginning?"

Yarbrough held up a hand. "It's not like that, Sean. We didn't have enough information to be sure at first. Now it looks like our suspicions were right all along." He swallowed hard and then started speaking again. "We believe that Gikas is going to try to crash the European stock market."

The absurd-sounding sentence hung in the air for a moment as Sean took in the information. His eyes narrowed. "How would he do that, with a computer virus? The world's stock exchanges are the most secure computer systems around. The best hackers on the planet wouldn't dare touch them with a ten-foot fiber optic pole."

The joke was lost on Yarbrough. Instead, he stayed locked in on

Sean's eyes. "He isn't going to use a virus. He's going to use the Eye of Zeus."

Things quickly began to add up in Sean's mind. "If the device really can tell the future, Gikas could make every correct move on the stock market. He could buy and sell at just the right times. He'd make billions in a matter of weeks."

"And worse," Yarbrough added. "He could destroy companies if he wanted. In a position of power, where money doesn't matter, Gikas would be able to inflate the value of his holdings. He could send prices of everything from corn to toilet paper through the roof. If he had access to what the markets were going to do, he could become the most powerful man in Europe in less than a month. And he would have the power to bring much of the continent to its knees."

Sean stared at the floor for a moment, dazed by the information. "That's too much power for any one man to have," he said after a minute of thought. "That's why Julius Caesar hid the thing."

"Precisely. And that is why we cannot let it fall into the wrong hands. The Antikythera Mechanism has to be found and destroyed."

Sean wasn't so quick to agree with the last statement, but Yarbrough was right, at least if what they believed about the device was correct. "You're certain that this thing can tell the future?" Sean still needed convincing.

Yarbrough took a deep breath, wincing as he did. Apparently, the bullet wound in his arm was still tender. "Because of the damage done to the original, all we have is speculation, well-researched theories. But from all we have learned about the device, it does seem like that's what it was used for."

Sean let out a long sigh. "Well, I guess that changes things a bit."

A knock at the door interrupted the conversation.

"It's probably Tommy. I assume you have a guy at the door," Sean said with fake derision. He got up, stalked over to the entry, and peeked through the eyehole. Tommy was outside, glancing nervously down both sides of the hallway.

Sean opened the door and his friend stepped in, surprised to see

Yarbrough sitting in the corner. Tommy's face curled, confused as to what was going on. "What's he doing here?"

"It's good to see you too, Tommy," the agent said sarcastically.

Tommy felt guilty for two seconds. "Sorry. You know what I mean. How long have you been in here? Did he come in here last night?" he asked, raising an eyebrow.

"Very funny," Sean said, closing the door after giving a quick look around outside. "Agent Yarbrough was just giving me the lowdown on what they think Gikas has planned."

"Basically," Yarbrough cut in, "we believe he is going to try to starve the people of Greece into submission by cutting off supply lines for food."

Tommy shook his head. "The people would kill him for that."

"The people," Sean corrected, "won't know it's him. They are already suspicious of their inept government. If something like this happens, there's only one place the blame will get directed."

"I hadn't thought about it that way."

"I'll fill you in on all the other stuff later. It goes way bigger than just Greece." Sean moved back over to the map on the desk. "We can't let him get to the Antikythera Mechanism. It's a key piece to his plan."

Tommy joined him at the workstation. "Yeah, but how do we know where it is? There's nothing on this map that suggests the location."

"That is the map to the Eye of Zeus?" Yarbrough asked, cutting into the conversation again.

Both men turned back to him and nodded. "Yeah," Sean said. "We found it last night in the mountains at the source of the Tiber. Ran into a few crooked cops. Although they probably had a worse night than us." He passed Tommy a knowing, just-us-guys glance and smirked.

Yarbrough ignored the last part. "Guys, if this is the only map leading to the Eye of Zeus, why not just destroy it? Then Gikas will have no way of finding it."

Tommy and Sean were appalled at the idea. "First of all, with all due respect," Sean began, "that thing deserves to be researched and analyzed. It could change the future of technology if what we have learned is true. Second, just because we destroy the map right now doesn't mean the thing won't be found someday. And we will have no idea who that person is or what they might do with it. Better to have it in the right hands than no hands at all."

Yarbrough considered Sean's rationale. "You really believe that's what's best?"

Sean's face remained stern. "You know as well as I know the other reason I can't trash this," he tapped on the plastic protecting the map. "It's the only bargaining chip I have to get Adriana back."

"You might as well forget about that idea," Tommy added. "There's no way he's going to let anything happen to the device."

An uncomfortable silence fell on the room for a moment. Yarbrough stared at the two friends with a hint of disbelief. Finally, he said, "I understand. If I were in your shoes I would do the same thing."

"Right," Sean said and turned his attention back to the map. "The problem is we don't know where to look for it."

His eyes pored over the old piece of animal skin, desperate to find the solution to the riddle. They'd stayed up late the night before, hoping to find a clue, but none was had. They decided fresh eyes would help their plight, but as they peered at the document nothing stood out.

Yarbrough stood up and walked over to the other side of the desk. He was out of his league when it came to that sort of thing, but he was still curious. "What are we looking at?" he asked, trying to help despite doubting he could.

Sean gave a quick explanation, walking Yarbrough through the ancient map of Greece and the names of all the cities and islands. The agent paid close attention to what Sean was saying, and when he was done speaking asked, "So, I don't mean to ask a dumb question, but these names are all in Latin?"

Sean smiled. "Yes. They're all in Latin, the language of ancient Rome."

"I see. So what do these names mean?"

Tommy cut in, explaining the meaning of a few names on the map. When he reached one of the islands to the west of Greece, he paused for a second with his finger resting on top of the outline.

"What is it?" Yarbrough asked. "Don't know what that one means?"

Tommy didn't respond to his question. Instead, he directed his attention to Sean. "Do you see the name of this island?"

Sean leaned over for a closer look. There was one word written below it. *Inferus.*

His eyes grew wide. "Wow. How did we miss that last night?"

"Miss what?" Yarbrough became more confused than he had been previously.

Sean pointed at the word that had caught their attention. "Inferus. It means under in Latin."

The blank stare on Yarbrough's face told the other two that he had no idea why that meant anything. "So?"

"Inferus," Tommy explained, "is not the name of an island. It's not a name for anything. It's a description. Caesar is saying that the Eye of Zeus is under the island."

The agent thought for a moment before speaking up again. "I still don't understand. How could something be under an island?"

Sean and Tommy both had to admit that was a good question. What had Caesar meant when he put the Latin word for under on the scroll? How could something be under a land mass?

They'd hit another wall, or so it seemed. For the next few minutes, no one said anything, each man trying to explain the strange message left on the animal skin two thousand years ago. It was Sean who spoke up first. "An underwater cave," he said. "That has to be it."

Tommy perked up. "Of course. There must be some sort of entrance under the water. We will need to find this island on a current map."

"Way ahead of you," Sean said, pulling his laptop out of a black book bag on the floor next to the desk.

He opened the silver MacBook Pro, bringing the screen to life instantly. A few keystrokes later, he was on his favorite search engine, typing in the words that would bring up a map of Greece. The Internet in Rome had been surprisingly fast, much quicker than Sean had expected upon arriving. Where he was from in the United States, fast Internet was something many people took for granted until they traveled to a country that either had no Internet, or where service was terribly slow. The hotel where he and Tommy were staying didn't have that problem. Thankfully.

Sean clicked on the top link from the search results, and a second later the requested map appeared. He zoomed out at first, trying to get a better overall view of the country's layout. He scrolled around until he found a group of islands that appeared to be similar to those on Caesar's map. A few clicks of the mouse zoomed the overhead view in a little closer. Sean's eyes went back and forth between the animal skin on the desk and his computer screen, comparing the outline of the islands from both until he finally found what he was looking for.

"There." He pointed at the screen to a small island. It looked almost identical to the one drawn two millennia ago. The other two looked over Sean's shoulders, virtually standing on top of him as he zoomed in for a little closer look at the island's topography.

"Doesn't look like anyone lives there," Tommy said, observing the steep, rocky cliffs and the rugged terrain.

"It doesn't look like it's very big," Yarbrough said, squinting to get a clear view.

"Perfect place to hide something important. No one would even notice this island," Sean said. He stood up straight. "We're going to need a boat and possibly some scuba gear. Can you make that happen?" He directed the question at Tommy.

Tommy thought for a second. "Should be able to. I can call around and see what we can dig up. It shouldn't be a problem."

"Good." Sean turned his attention to Yarbrough. "You coming with us on this one?"

The agent shook his head and lifted the sling slightly. "I better not. I've probably done enough damage for one trip."

"We'll bring you back some gyros," Sean said jokingly.

The two friends said their goodbyes to Agent Yarbrough, promising they would update him as soon as they had secured the artifact and rescued Adriana. Tommy returned to his room and grabbed his things. Sean packed up the small amount of stuff he'd brought to Italy, along with Caesar's map. Now that they knew exactly where they were going, he didn't need it, but he figured it would make a nice addition to one of the museums in Rome or at the historical center in Atlanta.

Ten minutes later, Sean and Tommy were on their way to the airport with an air of determination and uncertainty looming over them.

While Tommy was preoccupied with the Eye of Zeus, Sean's mind was somewhere else, on a woman from Madrid, a woman he needed to save.

39

ROME, ITALY

P aulino sped through Rome's busy streets in his red Alfa Romeo. The car was one of the luxuries he'd afforded himself as a result of his work from the last few years. While he kept a small, minimal apartment, Paulino had always had a penchant for fine Italian automobiles.

At the moment, he was in a hurry to reach the airport. He had called Teo and informed him that Wyatt was heading to Greece, information he'd gathered using a special listening device that could zero in on very specific targets.

The conversation among the three men in the hotel room had been short, but Paulino got what he needed. He was glad he'd left his apartment when he did. If he'd delayed at all, he might have missed the details of Wyatt's plan.

There were still a few things up in the air, some of which Paulino could handle. He knew that Wyatt and Schultz were going to Greece, and he'd heard them speaking of an island where the artifact was hidden. The men had also mentioned a boat and scuba gear, which meant they were going to be looking for whatever the object was, under water. His problem, however, was that he didn't know which island they were going to search. Hundreds of islands surrounded the

Greek coastline. Guessing the correct one would be nearly impossible. Since they would be on open water, it would be difficult to follow the treasure hunters without being spotted, and as soon as he was seen things could get dicey.

An idea popped into Paulino's head: He could put a homing device on Wyatt's boat. He would need to find out which port they would be leaving from, however, a trick that could also be formidable.

The gears turned rapidly in his mind as he tried to come up with a solution. First, he needed to call the pilot Bourdon had provided. His employer's boss had given him a private jet for the mission and told him to take the plane wherever necessary. The pilot, however, would need to file a flight plan, as would Wyatt's. Wherever Wyatt was going in Greece, that's where Paulino would go as well. A plan began to formulate in Paulino's mind. It was brilliant in its simplicity. Now all he had to do was make it happen. He called the pilot of his private jet and requested the captain determine which private planes had filed a plan with Greece as the final destination.

The rest of the drive to the airport couldn't go fast enough. Paulino couldn't squelch the feeling that he was in a race against time. Every red light he encountered built up the tension inside him. At a particularly busy intersection, he started to lose his patience with the other drivers, but didn't honk his horn no matter how tempted. The last thing he needed was to draw attention to himself or get into trouble with the polizia. When the light turned green, he pounded the gas, zipping through the intersection and down the crowded street. Paulino had seen movies and television shows where people were able to hack into the traffic grid and control the flow of traffic. He wished desperately that he had access to that kind of virus, but he knew that stuff was fantasy. Still, it would be nice.

He reached the airport in good time, though he would have preferred faster, and steered his car toward the private terminal. After a quick check through security, he made his way to the hangar where his jet awaited. The big doors had been rolled back, and a ground crew busily made the final preparations for the plane's departure.

Paulino parked his car inside the hangar, off to the right, and stepped out, carrying nothing but a black Swiss Army book bag. He preferred to travel light. All he really needed was his laptop and a few hygiene necessities. Clothing was something he could buy if he needed a change of clothes beyond the T-shirt and shorts he'd packed in the bag.

As Paulino approached the plane, the captain stepped out onto the landing and came down the stairs. The uniformed pilot smiled and briefly shook his guest's hand.

Paulino dispensed with the pleasantries. "Did you find out where they were going?"

The man appeared puzzled for a moment, but answered the question without delay. "Yes," he said in a cheerful Italian accent. "It was strange, though. There were three flights going to Corfu within the next hour. One of the planes belongs to the United States government."

Paulino raised a suspicious eyebrow. "What about the other two?"

"A surgeon taking his family on vacation, and the other was for a CEO of a major media company based in Florence."

The revelation was cause for concern. Paulino wondered if his employer knew that the United States government was involved in what they were doing. It didn't change his plan, but it might be something Bourdon would be interested in. "Let's load up and get to Corfu then," he said to the pilot. "We do not have much time."

The pilot's face expressed concern. "Is the American plane the one you are looking for?" His question was innocent enough, but he clearly didn't want to cause any trouble with the American government.

"It seems that way," Paulino answered. "Don't worry. They will not cause you any trouble. Besides, we are leaving before them. Right?"

The man nodded. "Yes. They are not scheduled to take off for another forty-five minutes."

"Perfect," Paulino said. "Then we will reach Corfu first."

40

CORFU, GREECE

"They are on their way here," Bourdon informed his employer.

Gikas remained stoically calm. "Here?" he asked, uncertain he had heard correctly. "They are coming to Corfu?"

"Yes."

The wealthy Greek wasn't sure how to react. His surprise was evident, washing away the normally unemotional expression on his face. He had long suspected that his home was close to where Caesar had left the Eye of Zeus, but Gikas didn't dare let himself get his hopes up. It was folly to dream wistfully that the thing he coveted most in the world would be right under his nose. That seemed to be exactly the case.

"There is a problem, however," Bourdon added.

"Problem?" Gikas didn't like the sound of that. Problems were something his hired hands dealt with. Whatever it was Bourdon was about to tell him, he hoped the mercenary would be able to handle it. Otherwise, Gikas would begin to question his decision about bringing the man onboard.

"The plane they are tracking is an American government plane."

"Yes, I am aware of the Americans' involvement. It seems their president would like to intervene in our affairs. Unfortunately for him, they are too late."

The two men sat in the dimly lit study, located in the east wing of Gikas's coastal mansion. The room's bookshelves overflowed with hardbacks on topics ranging from ancient history to modern fiction. Despite barely having enough time to breathe while running his various operations, Gikas still tried to make time for reading; it was one of the few guiltless pleasures he permitted himself.

The study had been wrapped in rich mahogany paneling, accented with iron candle sconces and a matching mini chandelier overhead. His opulent desk featured hand-engraved pillars for legs, a tribute to the ancient architects of the mighty Grecian temples.

Gikas sat behind the desk, staring at his computer screen. He'd been waiting to initiate his plan until the right moment. He could delay no longer. While he wasn't exactly concerned about the American government meddling with his plans, he couldn't afford to sit around and see what happened.

His fingers flew across the keyboard as he typed out a quick sequence of characters. He hit the enter key, and the screen changed back to the desktop.

"What was that?" Bourdon asked. He didn't care about whether or not he was prying. When he wanted information, he asked for it.

"I just initiated the plan. In the next few hours, all my distribution centers will reduce their shipments by 50 percent. By the end of the day, people will already begin to feel the effects of it. Of course, I will leak reports of huge production shortfalls. The media will tell the public that the crop output was far lower than originally thought. A story about a meat shortage will also go through the various media channels, many of which I am a primary shareholder. The people will not stand for it. They will ask the government for help, and their government will not have the means to help them."

"It sounds like a good plan."

"Thank you," Gikas smiled proudly at the compliment. "I believe so as well."

"Will the government not ask you to assist them?"

Gikas shrugged. "How can I help them? As far as they know, I am taking a huge loss with my holdings right now."

Bourdon nodded. "Clever."

"Yes. And once I have the Eye of Zeus and am the new king of Greece, I will be able to topple every nation without so much as firing a single bullet."

Gikas had ambition. Bourdon had to admit that. As long as the paychecks kept coming in, he didn't care how the money was made. His own ambitions crept up in the back of his mind as well. It would be nice to be the right hand of the most powerful man in Europe. If he was right about this Eye of Zeus thing, he would be the most powerful man in the world. Another thought occurred to Bourdon, one that he kept to himself. If this ancient relic really could tell the future, what was to stop him from taking it as his own? Deep inside his heart, he began to conceive a treacherous plan. For now, he needed only to serve his master. He would do as he was told. Let Gikas have the device and test it out. No point in betraying the man if the relic turned out to be useless. But if it worked, the possibilities were limitless.

"Like I said, sir, an excellent plan," he changed the subject. "What should we do about Wyatt? And what about the girl?"

"I have a yacht waiting in the marina. Have your man stay onboard with Wyatt and his friend. He will need to let us know exactly where they are going. We will follow from a distance and overtake them. If it is out at sea, there is nothing they can do to stop us." Gikas sounded excited for the first time since Bourdon had met him.

"His plan is to put a homing beacon on their boat. He will relay the signal to me and I will be able to track it."

"Good. Grab the girl and take her to the boat. If there is any trouble with Wyatt, I want her there as a bargaining chip."

41

THE NORTHERN MEDITERRANEAN

"Reports are coming in that there will be a huge production shortfall this year from many of the region's farmers. They are saying that the shortage is a direct result of the erratic weather patterns that have impacted the area over the past ten months." The reporter from the BBC news network presented the breaking news in an emotionless tone.

Sean and Tommy stared at the screen from their tan leather chairs inside the plane. On the way to the airport, Sean had sent Emily a message relaying their theory on Gikas's plan. She'd responded like she always did when Sean needed something: by getting right on it.

When the news report came out, Emily sent him a quick message. *Looks like you were right. Turn on BBC news.*

The blonde reporter continued talking on the screen. "This, amid growing concerns over the Greek economy, will surely serve to add fuel to the fire for those wishing for a change in government. The economic distress Greece has been under for the better part of a decade has been widely publicized. With tensions growing, many pundits wonder if this will be the straw the breaks the camel's back."

Sean and Tommy's mouths were gaping as they watched footage

of people standing in line at supermarkets in Athens and Thessaloniki. Everything seemed orderly for the moment, but that could change quickly. If the food supply was cut off, people would only stay calm for so long. Hunger made humans do crazy things. Sean had seen it firsthand on a mission in Nigeria. He shook his head at the memories.

"At present, it seems order is being maintained by most of the public."

Tommy muted the television as the screen cut away to an on-the-street interview with a consumer in a supermarket line.

"I can't believe how fast this happened," he said, staring at the screen for a few more seconds.

Sean stood up, walked over to a small refrigerator on the other side of the plane, and took out a bottle of water. He twisted off the lid and took a few sips, then put the cap back in its place. "It's just like when the weatherman predicts a snowstorm in the South. Remember back home in the winter? All it takes is predicting that there will be an inch of snow, and everyone goes crazy. The grocery stores get packed with people trying to buy eggs, milk, and bread. Gas stations fill up too, with people trying to make sure they have full tanks in case they can't get to a fuel source during the storm."

Tommy nodded. "Yeah, people do go a little crazy back in the South when there's a hint of snow in the forecast. A few of my friends who go a tad overboard with conspiracy theories believe that the grocery stores are in cahoots with the local news stations. They say the stores pay the stations to forecast snow to drive up sales."

Sean chuckled at the idea. "I've heard some people say that too." He turned his attention back to the issue at hand and pointed at the screen. "This is just the beginning. All Gikas has done so far is send out a message saying that there's going to be less food than they expected. At the moment, there's not even a real shortage."

"I guess you're right back in the thick of it again, huh?" Tommy asked as he watched Sean go through his routine.

"Seems that way." Sean clicked the magazine back into place and put the gun back on the coffee table in front of him.

"I'm sorry for that. I know you've been trying to get out of these kinds of situations for a while. Seems as if no matter what you do, you always get pulled back in."

A reluctant smile crept onto Sean's face. "I've made my peace with it," he said, staring at the television screen. The BBC was showing images of protestors outside the Greek parliament, carrying signs and shouting angrily at the building. Police with riot gear were standing off to the side at a safe distance, not yet engaging with the protestors.

Tommy hesitated to say anything, but he was never one to keep his thoughts to himself. "Unfortunately, you're good at this sort of stuff, Sean. I mean, I've never seen anyone able to think and act as quickly as you do in some of the situations you've been in. It's one of the things you're good at."

Sean snorted. "Yeah, well, maybe the universe is trying to tell me something."

"I'm not saying that," Tommy said defensively.

"I know, but it's true. Maybe the universe really is trying to tell me something. People say that you should do what you are. It could be that this is who and what I am. That doesn't mean I'm going to stop trying." He smiled at his friend and leaned his head back against the headrest.

Tommy's phone dinged, interrupting the quiet whine of the jet engines. He checked the screen and entered his security code. His fingers swiped the screen as he read an e-mail. "Looks like we have a rental boat and all the dive equipment we need. Our driver will pick us up at the airport and take us straight to the marina on the coast of Corfu."

"That was fast," Sean said, impressed.

"Hey, it's what I do," Tommy pointed a thumb at his chest and grinned proudly.

"When this thing goes down," Sean said suddenly, "I don't want you to get too involved. This is my fight, not yours. I don't want you to be in harm's way. Okay?"

"Ha! Sorry, buddy, but I'm in this with you. I'm always in this with you. That's what brothers do. And since I didn't have a brother growing up, you'll have to do. Besides, you know I can take care of myself."

"Yes, you can."

The flight attendant appeared from behind a curtain at the front of the plane and strolled down the aisle toward the two men. Her fiery-red hair was tucked up in a bun. Green eyes twinkled in the middle of a perfectly chiseled face of creamy skin. Her pouty lips turned up in a smile as she neared the two passengers. "Can I get you gentlemen anything before we begin our descent?"

"No, ma'am," Tommy answered. "I'm good."

Sean waved a hand dismissively. "No thanks. I appreciate it."

She gave a pleasant nod, turned and walked away.

When she was gone, Sean tilted his head toward his friend. "She's cute."

"Yeah she is. The government sure knows how to pick 'em."

"For sure." Sean thought for a second and then grinned mischievously. "You gonna ask her out?"

Tommy just shook his head and turned his attention to the tablet he removed from his book bag. "No. I'm not going to ask her out."

"Why not?" Sean protested. "Did you see the way she smiled at you?"

"She didn't smile at me any way."

"Whatever, man."

Sean had known for years that Tommy wouldn't know a girl was flirting with him if she slapped him on the side of the head. He'd seen it all the time when they were younger. Tommy had always dressed a little differently, more like a college professor than a high school kid. He liked looking sophisticated, which really worked to his favor even though Tommy thought it to be to the contrary.

"Women like that aren't into guys like me."

"Women like that? You mean attractive, friendly women?"

He shrugged but said nothing, instead choosing to tap on his tablet screen and begin perusing some research on ancient Chinese structures.

"Well, whether you believe it or not, women like that do find you attractive. One of these days, you're just going to have to accept that." Sean ended the conversation and checked his phone. No new messages appeared on the screen.

He was going to have to buy Emily dinner when he got back to Atlanta for getting them out jail back in Rome. He, no doubt, would also have to endure another round of her attempts to recruit him back to work for Axis. She'd recently moved the entire operation to Sean's backyard in Atlanta after a sequence of events with the location in Washington, D.C., made her realize it was time for a change of venue.

Axis worked as a part of the Department of Justice, but with such a small scope that they were able to maintain a low profile. At any given time, Axis only employed twelve field agents to handle the delicate missions handed down from the feds. Keeping such a small, tight-knit group made administration much simpler, and it kept the possibility of a leak pretty much at zero.

The plane bounced a few times, jostling its occupants. Despite being terrified of heights, Sean loved flying. It was a good thing he did since global travel usually required a flight of some kind. He'd seen turbulence turn full-grown men into squirming little children. A few bumps thirty thousand feet in the air never bothered him. For some reason, being fifty feet up on a scaffold did. He smiled as the plane hit another batch of aerial potholes. Tommy found the turbulence less amusing and remained focused on his tablet.

Sean glanced over his friend's arm at the screen. "Boat shopping?" he half joked.

"I'm checking out the boat we're taking out to the island. Pretty nice, actually."

"Forty-three foot, Princess V39? Little fancy for what we need isn't it?"

"It will get us where we need to be. And fast," Tommy said.

The captain's voice came over the intercom. "We will begin our descent in a few minutes and should be on the ground in Corfu within the next thirty. Please fasten your seat belts. And I apologize for the turbulence. It's a little bumpier than we expected. Nothing to worry about, though. Again, we should be on the ground in Corfu within a half hour."

"Never understood the thing about seat belts in an airplane," Tommy commented as he buckled the strap across his waist. "We're traveling at several hundred miles an hour. If something goes wrong, what's the seat belt going to do?"

The plane hit another huge air pocket that sent Sean's water bottle two feet into the air. He quickly snatched it before it hit the ground and secured it next to his hip, between the armrest and his leg. "It's so that if the landing is a little rough, or we hit big bumps like that, you don't crack your thick skull on the ceiling," Sean said dryly, casting his friend a derisive glance.

"Good point."

The rest of the flight went uneventfully. It always impressed Sean when a landing went so smoothly. He'd experienced his fair share of terrifying ones, the worst of which had been at the Seattle airport. When his plane landed there, it jerked to one side and then the other, causing everyone onboard to move over nearly one full seat position. He'd wondered how it hadn't flipped over onto its side. Then again, Sean didn't claim to understand all the mechanics and physics behind aviation. He convinced himself he was being irrational about the whole thing. That didn't change the fact that he still thought about it. Fortunately, the pilot of their flight to Corfu had kept the landing uneventful.

After a few minutes of waiting on the tarmac for the other planes to get out of the way, the private jet taxied its way over to an empty area where a tractor waited with a set of stairs, ready to dock with the plane.

Once the plane came to a full stop, the men grabbed their backpacks and walked down the aisle toward the cockpit and the exit. The redhead stood by the door with a broad smile on her face, showing off her almost perfectly white teeth. "Good luck," she said to them both, though she gave an extra long look at Tommy.

"Thanks," Sean said. "I'll let the pilot know when we need to leave." She nodded pleasantly at his comment.

Sean quickly made his exit, leaving Tommy awkwardly alone with the flight attendant. "Thank you," he said in an uncomfortable tone. "I noticed that you weren't the flight attendant that was with us on the way over from the United States."

"True," she said, still grinning. "We sometimes change over at different locations."

"Ah. Well, are you going to be taking us back to the States, or will we have someone else on the way home?" He hoped his question didn't sound too creepy.

She seemed taken aback by the question, but maintained her friendly demeanor. "Actually, I will be. We don't have anyone here on this island. It is kind of remote, after all."

"Right," he said blushing. "Good point." Tommy started for the exit and stopped. He turned around and stared at her for a second. "What's your name? I didn't get it on the way here."

It was her turn to blush. "My name is Amanda," she answered, never losing the bright smile.

"My name is Tommy. It's nice to meet you, Amanda." He tipped his head to her and pivoted around.

He saw Sean standing halfway down the stairs, waiting for him. "Good job, Captain Awkward." He shook his head and laughed as Tommy lumbered down the steps toward him.

"She's definitely not into me," Tommy said with a disappointed pout.

"You have so much to learn about women."

The two friends hit the tarmac and walked toward a door in the middle of the building directly in front of them.

"Isn't that all men?" Tommy asked, half joking.

Sean simply raised an eyebrow, as if to say, "touché."

A security guard waited just outside the entrance to the building. When the two men approached, he opened the door for them and gave a quick explanation of where they needed to go to get through customs.

Sean thanked him and led the way through the door into the private terminal. Corfu's airport seemed somewhat small by American standards but was still large enough to boast the title of International Airport. Although to be fair, the large island was situated above Greece's northern border. It was actually parallel to the Albanian coast, northeast of the Greek mainland. The island's airport claimed to be the third busiest in the country. After flying out of Hartsfield International Airport in Atlanta, Tommy and Sean were delighted to find such a *busy* airport nearly vacant by comparison.

Inside the building, a single worker sat on a high stool, surrounded by a four-foot-high counter. A sign on the desk's surface indicated it was where travelers would gain admittance into the country. The squatty, dark-haired man behind the desk busily thumbed his way through a magazine.

"How many people do you think he has to process in a given day at this airport?" Tommy asked in a whisper as the two approached the checkpoint.

"We might be the first people he's seen all day," Sean answered.

The man noticed them coming and put down the magazine in an attempt to look professional. Sean and Tommy decided to let him believe he succeeded.

"Welcome to Corfu, gentlemen," he said in perfect English. "Here for a bit of leisure?"

Sean and Tommy glanced at each other questioningly. Sean turned to the man and answered. "Actually, we are here on business. But if we get time we might get in a little leisure as well."

"Well, we have a beautiful countryside here and many quiet beaches where you can relax. Corfu is one of the best-kept secrets of the Mediterranean."

The two exchanged a few more pleasantries with the security worker. Sean remembered the good old days when he didn't have to fill out forms or go through security checkpoints. As an operative for Axis, he'd been allowed special privileges. Waiting in line was almost never a requirement. At times, getting through customs only required the wave of a badge.

When the two completed their check-in, they gathered their things and went through a set of glass double doors. A long corridor extended a few hundred yards to the main terminal, where the majority of visitors could claim their baggage and find transportation. Sean led the way, stepping onto one of the people movers to quicken the pace as they walked. They reached the other end of the passage and found the main terminal. A steady but small stream of tourists meandered through the facility, seemingly not in a hurry to get anywhere.

The terminal's interior design starkly contrasted with its bland, utilitarian exterior. Huge cylindrical steel beams jutted up at sharp angles, supporting a gently sloping, curved ceiling. The entire place had a futuristic appearance, with sleek metal facades, railings, ceiling panels, and girders. It somehow reminded Sean of his childhood visits to Space Mountain in Disney World.

"You got us a driver, right?" Sean asked.

"You heard me make the phone call, remember? You were right next to me on the plane." Tommy glared at him as if Sean's head was on fire.

"Right. Sorry. I just want to make sure we have everything covered." Sean said apologetically.

Tommy smiled at his friend. "It's okay, man. I know you're worried about her. It's going to be fine. We'll get her back." His face took on a serious expression. "And we're going to make the guy that took her pay."

Sean nodded. He appreciated his friend's confidence. Deep down inside, however, he wasn't entirely convinced.

42

CORFU, GREECE

P aulino stood waiting for his marks to arrive in the terminal. He held a cardboard sign in front of his chest that had the names *Wyatt* and *Schultz* written on it with a black Sharpie. He found the sign in the passenger's side of the car the men had arranged for as their transportation on the island. Along with it, he discovered the orders for the boat rental, a picture of the boat, the address of the marina, and some other miscellaneous paperwork.

It was almost too easy.

Killing the driver had been simple enough. He'd waited outside the terminal for almost half an hour, watching the pickup area for Wyatt's driver to arrive. A few drivers had come through, each of whom he questioned briefly by asking if they were there to pick up Sean Wyatt. The first three said no. The last one's yes was also his death sentence.

Paulino explained that he was a liaison for Wyatt and Schultz and that their flight had been delayed due to a small storm hovering over Rome. He told the driver that the two men should arrive in the next hour, and that he was to wait in the parking area. The driver thanked him for the information, which led Paulino to requesting a seat in the car. The day's temperature had already warmed to the low eighties, and since they were both working for the same people the driver had no problem allowing Paulino to sit and wait for their clients to arrive.

A few minutes later, the driver eased the car into a parking space near some shady trees on the far side of the lot. Paulino meticulously surveilled their surroundings, gratefully noting the absence of any security cameras in the area. The driver put the car in park and left it running to keep the interior cool with air conditioning. Paulino made polite conversation for a few minutes, asking the man how long he'd been driving, which company he worked for, if he liked his job, and other random crap like that. Socializing for the sake of socializing was one of the things Paulino detested the most. The man's responses actually made the desire to kill him that much stronger.

The driver talked about how he had dropped out of high school and never attended college. He'd been driving for the last fifteen years of his life. His wife had left him because she said he drank too much, which made him drink more. By the end of the conversation, Paulino felt more like a psychologist than a contract killer.

Still, he remained in character, acting sympathetic to the man's woeful existence. When the driver finished, Paulino asked if he'd be interested in smoking a cigarette. The man accepted, and the two got out of the car and stepped around to the front near the fence where the row of trees blocked the view to the road twenty yards beyond. Paulino removed a pack of cigarettes from his jacket pocket and offered one to the driver, who took it graciously.

Paulino took a step forward to light the cigarette for the man, and as he reached up to flick the lighter, withdrew a small pistol from his jacket. The silencer on the end of the barrel allowed only a few clicking sounds to escape the weapon. The puffs of smoke wafted away in mere seconds. The driver's horrified face grimaced in questioning pain as he fell to the ground in a heap. Blood began to course through his white dress shirt as he gurgled his last few labored breaths. Paulino looked around casually as if nothing had happened, and then proceeded to light his own cigarette. He leaned against the car for a moment, watching the area with cautious eyes, making absolutely sure no one had seen his deed. About half way through the smoke, he flicked it to the ground and mashed it with his shoe, twisting the heel to make sure the fire was out. After taking another quick look around, he stepped over to the body and grabbed it by the wrists. He pulled it over to the car in the adjacent parking space and tucked it neatly under the front bumper. Satisfied that the corpse was out of plain sight, he slid into the driver's side of the still-running car and pulled out of the spot.

Now, standing in the main terminal, Paulino waited patiently for his marks at the end of a long corridor that he'd been told connected to the private port of entry. He hoped the real driver's ridiculously long conversation hadn't caused him to miss the two Americans, but he doubted it had. Paulino had left Italy with a decent head start, and the flight had been a short one. The man his employer worked for definitely had style, and money. The plane had been one of the most opulent modes of transport he'd ever seen. Paulino hoped whoever was supplying Bourdon with money would be interested in hiring him on again in the future.

Two men came into view, walking toward him on one of the people movers. They matched the images Paulino had pulled up on the Internet: a shaggy blond haired guy about six feet tall, and a slightly shorter one with darker hair and broad shoulders. It had to be them.

As they approached, Paulino put a welcoming smile on his face and displayed the cardboard sign proudly. "Mr. Wyatt, Mr. Schultz?" he asked, effortlessly losing his Italian accent and mimicking the way he'd heard Greeks speak on previous occasions.

"That's us," the blond man answered. "I'm Sean Wyatt, and this is my lovely assistant, Tommy Schultz."

The one named Tommy shook his head and rolled his eyes. He offered his hand, which Paulino took and shook firmly, but gently enough to appear subservient. He played the role to perfection.

"It's a pleasure to meet you both. I understand I am driving you to the marina. Correct?"

"That's right," Sean said. "We appreciate you doing this on such short notice."

"Not a problem," Paulino said with a smile. "I know a quick route to get you on the water as fast as possible. Would you like me to take your bags?" He was surprised to see how light the men were traveling, merely carrying one backpack each.

Tommy waved off the offer. "No thank you. We got it."

"Very well, sir. If you will follow me, I'll take you to the car, and we can be on our way."

The three men made their way through the terminal toward the entrance. As they walked, Sean asked if it was a busy time of year for the airport.

Paulino made up a convincing enough answer, explaining that many people tried to get out of the cities and come to Corfu when the weather got warmer. Since it was still only spring, things were still a little slow in the area, but he expected it to pick up in the summer months. The Americans seemed satisfied with the answer and didn't say anything else. Paulino led the way to a black Mercedes Benz near the front of the airport parking area, and popped the trunk open with a remote key.

"I'll put your bags in the trunk, if that is all right with you," he said, reaching out both hands.

Sean and Tommy nodded and handed the driver their backpacks. Tommy walked around and got in the car behind the driver's seat, while Sean entered the other side. When both men were in the car, Paulino carefully packed the bags into the trunk. He looked up over the brim of his eyes to make sure the men in the back of the car couldn't see him, and then unzipped the front pouch of one of the backpacks. It was empty, which meant the owner probably wouldn't check it: a perfect place for the homing beacon. He reached into his pocket and produced the tiny metal disc, slipped it into the backpack's pouch, then zipped it closed and stood back up. He gently closed the trunk and walked around to the front door, giving one last look around before getting behind the wheel.

He steered the car into the traffic lane and followed the line of other vehicles out of the airport pickup and drop-off area. Once they were on the main road, Paulino continued to play his role by striking up a conversation. He hoped the two Americans wouldn't drone on like the real driver. Not that it mattered; he wasn't really going to listen to anything they said. He knew exactly how to play people in social settings. He'd make it look like what they were saying was fascinating or compelling. His body language would say all the right things, along with a few robotic responses he'd put together. To the talker, it seemed like he was paying attention, but the fact was, he hardly ever did.

"So, are you two here for a little excursion around the island?"

Sean was staring out the window. He'd never been to Corfu before, and whenever he visited a new place he always liked to observe his surroundings, the people, and the culture. "We're not exactly here on vacation," he answered cryptically.

"Oh?" Paulino answered. "You're here on business? A boat like the one you rented is an odd place to take care of business." He hoped he hadn't pushed the line of questioning too far, but it seemed like the natural progression for the conversation.

"We're researchers," Tommy explained shortly.

"Researchers? So you're scientists? What is your field of expertise? Marine biology?"

Sean was more than happy to let Tommy handle the questions from the friendly driver. "We're archaeologists here on a special assignment."

Paulino raised his eyebrows. "Sounds exciting. How long are you here for?"

"Not long, hopefully. We're here to investigate a site and then head back home."

"That sounds like a long way to come from America just to check out a location."

Sean finally decided to pop in and try to end the conversation about their project. "Our job is to map the area. Once that's done, the rest of our team can come in and take care of the rest. It's how our organization works."

Paulino accepted the explanation, not wishing to push the issue further. He didn't need to know why the men were there. He had essentially taken care of his end of Bourdon's assignment. The homing beacon was already in place. Bourdon had already deposited half of the hundred thousand into Paulino's account via electronic transfer. After dropping off the two Americans at their boat, he was to meet Bourdon on the other side of the marina. He would then receive the rest of the money. It was almost too easy.

The forty-minute drive to the harbor in Agios Stefanos on the other side of the island turned out to be visually stunning. High vistas and rolling hills filled with trees and set into rocky cliffs were a treat for the eyes. Sean suspected the drive to reach the marina would have been even shorter if not for traffic lights and the slow speed of the island's drivers. Although being a tourist destination probably added to the lack of urgency from most of the vehicles. Most tourists were not likely in a hurry, as he'd already witnessed in the airport.

Corfu struck Sean as a strange place. Geographically north of mainland Greece, it was more like a Mediterranean version of Alaska in the United States. Contained in the island's two hundred and thirty square miles were farms, vineyards, a few thriving cities, and an abundance of coastline. The city of Corfu, which served as the hub of the island, was a tightly packed town of colorful buildings, homes, and businesses. Sean wondered how a man like Gikas could have attained so much power on the mainland from a remote place like this. Then again, maybe that was the man's secret to success. Staying removed from all the political and economic turmoil going on several hours away in Athens gave him anonymity, which he would use right up until the point when everyone needed him the most. Then it would seem he appeared as if from nowhere, a savior on a white horse to help the Greek nation and lead it to prosperity once more.

After thirty minutes of relative silence, the harbor appeared in front of them as the car rounded a rocky bend in the road. The horse-shoe-shaped bay housed a gigantic marina, filled with hundreds of sailboats, yachts, and cabin cruisers, all floating on an aqua-blue sea that stretched out to the horizon. Sean remembered his little shop back in Destin, thinking about the beautiful waters of the Florida

Panhandle. Even on its best of days, the waters of the Gulf of Mexico were no comparison to what his eyes gazed upon now.

"That water is absolutely perfect," Tommy commented, leaning over the seat in front of him to get a better view as the car wound its way down the gradual slope toward the sea.

"It certainly is," Paulino agreed, acting as though he'd beheld the sight a thousand times. "The locals here are very proud of this location. Even though many visitors come to Corfu throughout the year, the citizens of this area prefer not to let the secret out."

"I can see why," Tommy said. His eyes still gaped at the vision.

The driver steered the car through a few stop signs and into a parking lot adjacent to the marina. He parked the car after passing through an open gate, then switched off the vehicle and hurriedly got out of the car to get the luggage from the trunk for his passengers. Paulino set the backpacks on the ground and double-checked one of the forms he'd found in the front of the car before killing the real driver.

"I believe your boat is over here," he pointed to one of the nearby docks.

Tall white masts bobbed and wavered as the boats they were connected to shifted in the sea's rippling waves. The sound of ropes banging against the metal filled the air with each ship's movement.

Sean took in a long, deep breath, letting the fresh sea air fill his nostrils. One of his favorite things about the sea was how the air seemed to be able to cure any nasal-related problems such as allergies, a common nuisance that came with living in the southeastern United States. Whenever Sean had visited the salt water in the past, his sinuses cleared almost as soon as he reached the sandy shores.

Now, he couldn't enjoy it as much as usual. Someone he cared for deeply was in trouble, if she was still alive. He snapped his head, shaking off the thought. She was still alive. Gikas needed her alive. Sean had seen this kind of thing play out dozens of times. Gikas would keep his prisoner alive until he had what he wanted. Then either he would try to kill everyone, which was the likely outcome, or he would make the trade and send Sean and his friends on their way.

The possibility of the latter was slim to none. Knowing this, Sean had a backup plan. He preferred never to have to use contingency plans, but with his experience he knew they were a necessity.

Paulino led the men down the gangway and onto the dock. Tommy and Sean preferred to carry their own bags, which was fine with the Italian. Just because he was making a hundred thousand euros didn't mean he was going to be anyone's slave. They passed several boats before coming to the one Tommy had booked on the plane. It looked like it had barely been used.

"I believe this is your boat, gentlemen," Paulino said, motioning with his hand in an inviting manner.

"Very nice, Tommy," Sean said with his hands on his hips as he admired the gleaming white vessel. "Well done." He slapped his friend on the back and stepped aboard into the aft part of the boat.

"You will find the keys tucked away in the side panel near the steering wheel," Paulino said.

Sean moved up to the console and lifted the lid of a small glove box. He removed the keys and held them up so the other two could see. "Got 'em."

Tommy turned to the driver and offered his hand. "Thank you so much for doing this, again on such short notice."

Paulino took his hand firmly and realized there were some folded bills in Tommy's palm. He looked down and smiled. "Oh, sir, you don't have to do that."

"Please, take it. It's the least I can do for your trouble."

"Thank you, sir. I do appreciate it. And it was no trouble at all." He motioned to the cabin cruiser bobbing gently in the boat slip. "I do hope you two get to enjoy this fine vessel for a little while, at least. Thank you again." He turned and walked steadily down the dock's walkway while Tommy spun around and climbed aboard.

As they prepared to take the boat out to sea, they didn't see Paulino turn down a different direction than they'd come.

When he was out of sight, he looked down at the money Tommy had given him. Two hundred euros was a hefty tip for an ordinary driver. To him, it was chump change. In a few minutes, he would be collecting another fifty thousand. He considered wadding up the cash and tossing it into the water out of spite, but he decided against it. Money was money. He could buy a few drinks with it at least. He stuffed the folded bills into his front pocket and continued marching toward the rendezvous point.

43

NORTHWESTERN GREECE

T ommy and Sean sifted through the storage crate on the back of the boat. It had been delivered before they arrived and contained all the scuba gear they'd requested: tanks, regulators, masks, fins, and a few other miscellaneous things. Untying the ropes and getting the boat out of the slip only took a few minutes. Both of them had grown up with friends who had similar vessels, so they had spent a great deal of time on the lakes surrounding their hometown. The biggest difference between the cabin cruiser they were driving now and those back home was that most of the lake boats weren't seaworthy. Their hulls and motors weren't designed to take the rigors of the open sea and salt water, something Sean had enquired about at one point during one of their fresh water voyages.

Tommy stood behind the wheel, keeping the speed down as they maneuvered their way through the no-wake area of the harbor. Sean told him to drive since Tommy had more experience with boats in sea conditions. Most of Sean's time driving a boat had been on a lake, which was a totally different thing altogether. Out beyond the last dock, a rock formation broke the waves from coming into the bay. It appeared to be man-made, a common construction for places where people wanted to build marinas but couldn't due to the damage done by unchecked tides.

After a few minutes of trolling through the marina's tight channels, they reached the more open area of the bay and increased speed slightly. Tommy still kept it low because of the warning signs. The last thing they needed was to tick off any of the local authorities when they were so close to their goal.

Sean busily looked over the map on his phone screen. He'd been sure to charge the device on the plane so he would have plenty of battery life during their search for the mysterious island. He compared the image on the screen to a map he'd dug out of another storage box in the cabin of the boat. Spreading it out on a small table behind the driver's console, he was able to analyze the two maps at the same time, verifying the direction they would need to go once they reached the open sea. While Sean had never had any real experience in nautical navigation, he could read a map and use a compass. As long as they had those two things, reaching their destination shouldn't be a problem. The boat, like most Sean had been on, had a compass built in to the dashboard, so he had everything he needed.

The day turned out to be a good one for cruising on the sea. The sun shone brightly in the pale blue Mediterranean sky. An occasional fluffy cloud or two drifted by, doing nothing to take away from the perfection of the day. The sea's white caps drew closer as the boat neared the harbor's entry. Tommy kept a watchful eye on the depth finder to make sure he was staying safely in the channel. The last thing they needed was to run aground before even getting out to sea.

His diligence paid off, and a few minutes later they were plowing ahead at nearly full speed into the crashing waves. The bow of the ship rose and dipped dramatically with each wave they encountered. Sean had to look up from the map to keep from getting queasy. He didn't usually get sea sick, but it had been a while since he'd been on water like this. Up ahead, the waves began to diminish as they got farther out from the shore.

"Am I going the right way?" Tommy asked loudly, almost shouting above the noise of the water and the boat's engine.

Sean checked the compass and the map. He'd drawn a line on the paper to chart the direction they needed to go. "Yeah. Keep heading west. When we reach Mathraki, we will have to alter course slightly and go southwest."

Tommy acknowledge the information with a nod and double-checked the compass to make sure he was staying on course. Up ahead, he noticed a land mass jutting up from the sea on the right.

"Is that the one?" he asked, thinking they hadn't gone the requisite distance yet.

"No," Sean said shaking his head. "That's Diaplo. It's the one right in front of you."

Out in the open water, the ride was much smoother, though still nothing like the lakes back home in Tennessee and Georgia. With the ride becoming less bumpy, Sean was able to return his attention to the map, taking a long inventory of the island's terrain they'd be visiting.

Six miles off the northeastern coast of Corfu, the island of Mathraki jutted up out of the Ionian Sea. Sean took a second to admire the surrounding view. He glanced back at the island of Corfu, growing smaller as they got farther away, its mountains rising majestically in the distance. The Ionian Sea boasted unique geography, with several rocky islands dotting the blue waters. Most of them seemed to be inhabited; even the smaller ones had fishing villages planted firmly along the shores. A ferry lumbered through the water on their left. Its deck was loaded with people, many of whom were taking pictures and staring out at the scenery. More tourists, Sean thought.

Ten minutes passed, and Mathraki loomed larger and larger in front of them. Off the port bow, Sean noticed a small land mass rising up out of the sea. He took a quick glance down at the map to recheck his bearings.

"You're going to want to bear south toward that island over there," Sean said, pointing at the giant tree-topped rock about a mile away on their left.

Tommy nodded and steered the boat in a sweeping turn, leaving Mathraki on the starboard side and lining up the bow with the small land mass Sean pointed out. He moved the throttle forward a little and increased their speed. Being out of the choppy part of the water, Tommy felt more comfortable going a little faster.

They reached the crystal-blue waters surrounding the small island in less than four minutes. Tommy throttled down the engine and let it coast toward the sandy shore. He continued to watch the depth gauge to make sure they didn't hit a reef as he guided the vessel slowly into a small cove. The island couldn't have been more than a square mile or two in size. It featured a white sandy beach wrapped by steep, rocky cliffs. Off to the left, the horseshoe-shaped cove straightened out to a flatter beach with a thicket of trees, thick brush, and grass. In the middle of the island, a short plateau rose above the sea, giving the top of the land mass what was sure to be an enviable view of the surrounding area.

Sean stared at the sight with wide eyes, steadying his balance with a hand on one of the nearby rails. "This part of the world is so awesome," he said, almost to himself. "If we read that map from the mountain correctly, Julius Caesar was here a few thousand years ago, looking at this very sight."

"It is pretty incredible," Tommy agreed as he adjusted the wheel back and forth, keeping the boat on a firm course. "I think we should probably weigh anchor over there in that cove. From there we can swim over to the beach and check out the island by foot."

"Sounds good," Sean said with a nod. He moved across the deck to the back where they'd stowed the cargo bin containing the scuba gear.

He opened the hatch and removed two pairs of fins, then laid them on the deck before closing the lid. They wouldn't need the dive gear just yet. First, they would need to scope out the terrain and find the point of entry for the underwater cavern.

Tommy turned off the main engine and hit a switch on the dashboard that triggered the anchor on the starboard side of the bow. The heavy metal object descended rapidly into the water, plunking into the liquid with a small splash. When the chain went slack, Tommy halted the anchor motor and retracted it a few inches.

"Okay," he said, "we should be good here."

He put his hands on his hips and took a second to gaze out at the view. The mountains of Corfu appeared much larger from the sea. A large, white yacht was motoring slowly out of the harbor where they'd been less than half an hour ago. The ship was enormous, though he couldn't guess its length from so far away. The fact that Tommy was able to see it from such a distance underscored the vessel's mass.

"I wonder who owns that thing," he said as he stared at the opulent yacht.

Sean had removed his pants and replaced them with swimming trunks. He was sitting on one of the aft seats and attaching one of the fins when Tommy mentioned the white ship. He glanced up and scanned the distant coast for a second before catching a glimpse of what his friend was talking about. "I don't know, but whoever it is has money, that's for sure. More money than they know what to do with."

Tommy snorted a short laugh. "Looks to me like they know exactly what to do with it. Buy a ridiculously large boat."

Sean grinned at his friend's comment. "Fair enough."

Tommy stood by the seat across from Sean and quickly changed into his swimming suit. "I figure we'll start on that beach over there," he said and pointed to the flat area on the left side of the island. "Then we can work our way up and over the plateau and down the other side."

"Sounds good."

"Any idea what we might be looking for?"

Sean peered at the island. From fifty yards out, he couldn't see anything of significance. The small piece of land didn't look like much. Maybe an interesting place to hang out for a day to get away from other people, but other than that, it couldn't have appeared less consequential. He studied the rocky facade, scanning from one end to another, still finding nothing of note.

"Not a clue," Sean said after another minute of looking. "If we can't find anything on land, we might have to take the boat around to the other side, maybe check it out from the water."

"Good idea."

The island wouldn't take long to circle with the boat, but would take a considerable amount of time for swimmers to get around, especially in the Ionian Sea.

Sean noticed his friend eyeing the water suspiciously. "What's up? What are you lookin' for?"

"Oh," Tommy said, returning his attention to the flippers on the floor. He slid one foot into one of the fins and then the other. "I was just wondering if there were sharks in these waters."

Sean tightened the last strap on his flipper and smiled. "Yeah, there are a lot of different species of sharks in this area. But most of the time they don't bother people."

Tommy looked up in surprise. "Wait, what? There really are sharks here?"

Sean laughed. "Yeah. I mean, there are sharks in a lot of places. But there are a lot of them in the Mediterranean. Trust me, though, they aren't going to bother you."

Tommy wasn't convinced. "How do you know that?" There was a hint of panic in his voice. Where Sean was terrified of heights, Tommy had a healthy fear of sharks, however irrational it likely was. Sean was certain his friend had watched the *Jaws* movies too many times.

"They talked about it on *Shark Week*. Less than half a percent of shark attacks on humans annually in this part of the world. It's actually really low, though scientists aren't sure why considering there are so many people here."

Tommy's incredulity was written all over his face. His mouth dropped wide open in disbelief. "*Shark Week*?"

"Yeah, you know, on television."

"I know what *Shark Week* is. Just not sure I believe everything on television."

"It's going to be fine, buddy. There probably aren't any in this shallow water." Sean stood up and moved over to the edge of the boat, then leaned over and hung his feet off the side. "Come on," he said, motioning with his hand.

Tommy looked doubtful for a minute, but finally got up and stepped over to the starboard side of the boat. Sean dropped into the water and started kicking his legs to maintain his position while he waited on his hesitant friend.

"The water feels great," he said and started swimming toward the island. The fins on his feet propelled him forward like a human torpedo.

Tommy scanned the rippling surface of the water one last time as he hung his legs over the edge and paused. He shook his head. "*Shark Week?*" he said to himself, and then dropped into the warm water. He trusted Sean, but he paddled and kicked hard so he could reach the shore in less time, just in case.

44

NORTHWESTERN GREECE

The giant yacht cut easily through the Ionian waters as it motored away from the island of Corfu and into the open sea. The ship's hydrodynamic shape and powerful engines made sailing aboard the vessel extremely smooth. Unless conditions were somewhat extreme (like massive waves), the occupants aboard the yacht experienced a comfortable journey.

Paulino stood on the starboard side of the ship with one hand on a chrome railing. He stared out across the water at some of the surrounding islands and back at Corfu's mountain range still high in the distance. He'd just made a lot of money, which made him extremely happy. When he left Wyatt and Schultz with their boat, Paulino had swiftly made his way over to the other side of the marina where he met up with his employer, Teo. Along the way, Paulino had been extremely cautious, wary that one of the Americans might see him heading in an odd direction and become suspicious. They hadn't seen him, though, and now Paulino was a special guest aboard the yacht of Dimitris Gikas, the man who had apparently bankrolled his little mission.

When he arrived at the huge boat, Paulino expected the exchange to be simple. He would give Bourdon the tracking monitor, and then the remainder of his fee would be wired to one of his secure bank accounts. He'd been surprised when Bourdon invited him aboard the ship for a drink.

"Come, you have traveled far and I just made you a lot of money. The least you can do is have a drink with me," Bourdon had said.

Paulino wasn't one to turn down a drink, and his employer was right: Paulino had traveled a great distance. Maybe a little boat ride and a drink would be a nice diversion before he headed back to Rome, on Gikas's private plane, he hoped.

He took a drink from the tumbler Bourdon's bartender had offered. Paulino's drink of choice had always been gin. Apparently, Gikas was a man of good taste. The bartender had a full bottle of Hendrick's Gin behind the bar and poured a generous serving on ice for the ship's special guest.

Paulino savored the piney flavor of the alcohol as he swallowed another sip, gazing out across the sun-drenched waters. He'd worked hard for this. He deserved it.

"How's the drink?" Bourdon's voice startled him from behind.

Paulino spun around, nearly spilling some of the clear liquid as he did so. He recovered quickly and took another sip. "Outstanding," he said with a grin. "Your friend certainly has good taste in alcohol, and in boats." He motioned to the luxurious vessel with his free hand. "This ship is amazing."

"Only the best," Bourdon said with a sly grin.

"So," Paulino said with a curious expression on his face, "when do I get to meet this mysterious friend of yours? I don't believe I have ever seen Dimitris Gikas before."

"He should be out on deck soon. He's taking care of some business inside the ship. I believe he is acquiring a small pharmaceutical company. That's just between you and me, though." Bourdon gave a quick wink.

Paulino gave an understanding nod. "I will be sure not to mention it. He must be a very powerful man."

"He is, and you have done him a great service. We are tracking

Wyatt and his friend and will have them in our custody within the hour."

Paulino was in the middle of taking another drink when he heard Bourdon's comment. He nearly spit some of the gin back into the glass, but managed to keep it in his mouth and swallow. "In your custody? I thought you just wanted to watch them."

Bourdon shrugged and shook his head slowly. "No, we needed you for that so we could find exactly where they were going and apprehend them. You don't have a problem with that, do you?"

Paulino was quick to shake his head defensively. "Not at all. What you do with them is your business and no concern of mine. I just didn't know what you wanted with them. You can kill the Americans for all I care." He hurriedly put the tumbler to his mouth again and pulled in another draw of the cool liquid.

Bourdon looked back at the big island and then out at the smattering of smaller ones. "Do you know why we want those two Americans?"

The Italian puckered his lips and shook his head. "No. Should I?"

"Do you know who they are?"

"I found some information about Schultz online. Wyatt was a little more difficult to gather any intel on, but I found a few things, along with the dossier you gave me. They sound like a couple of treasure hunters if you ask me."

Bourdon took in a deep breath and let it out slowly as if savoring the fresh air. "Wyatt is extremely dangerous. He is a former agent of the United States government. His friend, though slightly less deadly, is still not one to be trifled with. They have something that my employer, Mr. Gikas, would very much like to have."

"Oh? What would that be?"

Bourdon put both hands on the railing and leaned over, contemplating the answer. "A map."

"A map?" Paulino echoed. "What kind of map?"

"Mr. Gikas is a collector of ancient Greek relics and pieces of historical value. He has an extremely strong connection to the past in this way. The map that the Americans possess leads to one of the most important artifacts in Greek culture. That object would be the culminating piece in his collection. He simply must have it, and will not stand for the Americans to steal it out from under his nose."

Paulino frowned. "Must be a pretty important piece for him to go to so much trouble and spend so much money to acquire it."

"It is," Bourdon said with a slow nod. "He will stop at nothing to obtain it. That's why we are going after the Americans right now."

The Italian's frown deepened. "I don't understand. Why did you want me along for the ride if you were going after them? I doubt I would be much help in a fight." He glanced down disappointedly at his drink, which was now nearly empty.

"Oh, we don't need your help with detaining the Americans," Bourdon corrected. "We have enough trained men onboard for that."

"I noticed," Paulino motioned to two of the men in tight, black short-sleeved shirts and sunglasses. Their muscles bulged through the thin material. Each man wore the same, emotionless, stern expression. "You could probably take over a small town with these guys."

"Indeed," Bourdon said, agreeing with the sentiment. "They are some of the best mercenaries money can buy. Mr. Gikas takes his private security very seriously."

The boat began to steer to port as it neared a fairly large island straight ahead. Paulino held his empty glass and watched as the island off to the starboard side disappeared behind the cabin of the yacht. The boat's engine quieted dramatically and the vessel slowed down to an idling speed. "I don't understand. If you have all these guys, why did you want me along for the ride?"

"Mr. Gikas requested it."

"And he always gets what he wants, eh?"

"Correct." Bourdon stood up straight again. He was wearing a light windbreaker in spite of the warm spring air.

Paulino thought for a moment then asked, "Would it be all right if I got another drink?" He held out the glass and raised his eyebrows.

"Certainly," Bourdon said with an overly polite smile. He took the glass and started for the rear of the cabin, and then turned around. "Gin on the rocks, right?"

Paulino nodded his confirmation. "With a splash of soda water, if you don't mind."

"Of course."

Bourdon disappeared around the corner, leaving Paulino alone by the railing. He leaned over, resting his elbows on the shiny metal as the boat coasted slowly through the clear water. Tiny ripples of waves slapped against the hull, providing a peaceful accompaniment to the trolling engines and the sea breeze that blew across the deck.

A few minutes passed before Bourdon returned with a half-full glass in his hand. "Here you go, old friend."

Paulino reached out his hand eagerly. "Many thanks," he said and grabbed the cold tumbler.

He put the rim to his mouth and started to take a drink when suddenly a gloved hand wrapped around his face and yanked his head back. Another hand grabbed his arm, causing Paulino's hand to loosen and drop the glass overboard. He struggled for a few seconds, attempting to scream through his covered mouth. Bourdon watched with a fervent curiosity as his employee resisted the much stronger man who had surprised him from behind. After a moment of letting Paulino struggle, he nodded to the henchman who twisted the Italian around, facing him out to sea. Bourdon removed a subcompact 9 mm from inside his windbreaker and pressed the sound-suppressed barrel to Paulino's back.

"We do appreciate your service, Paulino. But like you said, there is nothing more you can do for us."

The Italian squealed through the gloved fingers, jerking back and forth in a vain attempt to get free. Bourdon squeezed the trigger five successive times, sending a spray of blood out into the azure Ionian Sea. Paulino's body shuddered for a moment and then relaxed. Bourdon then placed the barrel to the back of Paulino's skull and pulled the trigger one more time, sending a round through the front of the Italian's head. The body went completely limp, most of its weight slumping over the boat railing.

Bourdon's security man hefted Paulino up by the legs, dumping him overboard into the rippling water. The bloody body floated face down for a few moments before gradually sinking into the abyss.

"The sharks will like easy meat," Bourdon said casually. The mercenary didn't say anything. He just watched over the side of the boat as the body disappeared. "Tell our employer that Paulino has been taken care of and we are ready to proceed."

The muscular guard nodded and headed back around to the side door he'd come out of a few moments before.

Bourdon looked out across the sea and took in another deep breath. Soon, Gikas would be one of the most powerful men in all of Europe. And Bourdon would be the second in command.

45

NORTHWESTERN GREECE

S ean reached the white sands of the little island's beach just a few yards ahead of his friend. Driven by fear, Tommy had swum faster than Sean believed possible. Scattered bits of seaweed, empty shells, and a few rocks cluttered the shoreline. The two men found a clean place to sit down on the sand and remove their fins.

"Shoulda brought some sandals with us to walk around on those rocks up there." Sean motioned toward the plateau above the cliffs. "I hope the surface isn't too sharp. Sometimes there can be a lot of jagged spots on rocks like those."

"Well, it's too late to go back," Tommy said, still huffing from the physical exertion of the swim. "We'll just have to try it and see." He yanked off a flipper and laid it next to the other one.

Sean shook his head while staring at his friend with a look of amusement. "You really are terrified of those sharks, aren't you?"

"Better safe than sorry, my friend."

"I guess," Sean said and pushed up from the ground. He looked around at the terrain for a second, trying to figure out where they should begin their search. "Let's start over there at the base of the cliffs on the other side and see if we can find anything, then work our way around."

"Sounds good."

Tommy stood up and followed Sean as he carefully maneuvered his way across the sand toward the far corner of the beach. The farther they went ashore, the more dead tree branches and large rocks they had to avoid. After a few minutes of strategic movement, they reached the other side of the flat beach where it rose sharply thirty feet into a jagged stone cliff. The sand dropped off steeply into the light-blue water at the edge. Sean could see a few small fish swimming around in seemingly random directions, darting back and forth. He grabbed onto a piece of the cliff that jutted out and tested his weight on it. Satisfied it could hold him, he leaned out around the corner of the rocky face and surveyed the area.

"See anything?" Tommy asked, standing behind his friend, peeking over his shoulder.

Sean shook his head. "Nothing over here. Looks like the water gets pretty deep around this bend in the rocks, but no sign of anything unusual." He pointed back to the middle of the shore where a steep slope led down to the sand. "Head over that way and let's walk up top to see what's up there."

Tommy nodded and led the way, again stepping cautiously through the brush, sticks, and rocks on the sand. Halfway to their destination, they passed a small fire circle with some charred wood in the center. "Looks like a few people have been camping out here," Tommy said, glancing at the fire pit as he walked by.

"Nothing new under the sun, I suppose. Seems like every piece of remote land has been touched by human feet at one point or another."

"Yep," Tommy agreed. He stopped suddenly and held up his right hand. Sean knew why his friend had halted. He'd noticed the same thing out in the water, creeping in their direction.

"Who do you think that boat belongs to?" Sean asked.

"I was just about to ask you the same thing. It's the one we saw before."

Sean twisted his neck to the side to loosen his nerves. "Yeah. It seems an awful lot like they followed us over here."

"Coincidence?" Tommy twisted his head around and raised an eyebrow as he looked at Sean.

"I really wish I could believe in those," Sean said. "Unfortunately, I've seen too much to the contrary in my life so far. I don't believe in coincidences."

"You think they're authorities?"

"No," Sean said definitively. "Not on a boat like that." His voice picked up a little urgency. "Come on, let's get to the top of the ridge and see if we can get a better look."

Sean stepped in front of his friend and stayed low, using the island's thick brush for cover as he moved toward the steep path leading to the top of the plateau. He kept his eyes on the approaching vessel as well as on the trail. The cliff closest to where they'd weighed anchor wrapped around the route to the top, providing a little extra cover. It took less than a minute for the two men to reach the grassy plateau. Once on the ridge, they crouched even lower, careful to stay hidden among the tall blades of grass. The breeze from the sea caused continuous movement from the vegetation, another thing Sean counted on to conceal their presence. Just because their boat was anchored in the cove didn't mean he wanted whoever was approaching to know where they were. He preferred to find out who was encroaching first.

The two Americans reached the edge of the cliff and peeked through the last stands of broad grass, using their hands to keep some of it clear to give them a good view of the yacht's passengers. They thought the boat was big from a distance, but up close they realized how truly impressive it really was.

It featured two floors above the deck, and one below. The windows were difficult to see through due to the dark tinting, but Sean assumed the top floor was where the captain drove the behemoth. The front of the vessel featured sharp-angled design, from the fiberglass wall up to the windshield. It had to be at least eighty feet long, if not a little more.

"I wonder how much gas it took just drive that thing over here from the marina," Tommy said in a hushed tone as the two stared at the yacht.

Sean kept his eyes on the ship. "There's no telling. But I'm guessing the guy that owns it isn't worried about gas mileage. He's probably got a Bugatti in his garage too." He squinted in the sunlight and was able to make out a man in a windbreaker standing on the main deck, leaning casually over the railing.

Tommy saw the man as well and wondered who it was. "You think that's the owner of the boat?"

"Maybe. That's definitely not Dimitris Gikas, though."

"How do you know?"

Sean glanced at his friend out of the corner of his eye as if Tommy had a tree growing out of his face. "Because I always do my research on the enemy."

Tommy realized it had been a stupid question. Sean had always been thorough. When someone was able to catch him off guard, they'd really accomplished something. That's how well prepared he was for everything. Back in the days when he'd worked for the IAA, the other employees used to say that Sean Wyatt always had a plan for everything. While not entirely true, it was pretty close.

"What do you want to do?" Tommy asked, trying to get a better view through the weeds and grass.

"Well, whoever it is, they know we're here. No point in trying to change that. If that guy on the deck is the owner of the ship, then it's probably just a local land owner or something."

"He looks like he's pretty relaxed, like he's just out to enjoy a day cruising around the islands." Tommy's observation made sense, especially to the casual observer, but Sean was no casual observer.

"Something isn't right," Sean said after a moment of thought.

"What do you mean?"

"It's too quiet. A guy like that, with enough money to buy a ship like that, doesn't go out to sea to cruise around alone. Where is the crew? And usually men with that kind of dough have two or three female companions sunning on the platform across the bow."

Tommy frowned. His friend was right. It did seem odd. "Maybe he's here with his wife," he said, offering an unlikely yet plausible scenario.

"Doubtful. That doesn't look like a guy who would be anywhere except a fundraiser with his wife, if he's married at all."

"Ever heard of not reading a book by its cover?"

"Well," Sean angled his head a little, still staring at the yacht, "in my line of work, you gotta go with what you have."

"You mean your former line of work."

Sean's eyes went sideways for a moment at his friend's comment. "Touché."

The man on the boat's deck straightened up and leisurely made his way around the side of the boat to the bow where a doorway led into the cabin. He disappeared inside, closing the door behind him.

"Doesn't seem to be in a hurry of any kind, does he?" Tommy asked.

"No," Sean shook his head. "But something isn't right. It's almost like he wanted us to see him standing there, looking like he wasn't up to anything."

"You really can't switch off the paranoia, can you?"

"Nope. It's kept me alive this long. Stands to reason I shouldn't quit now."

Tommy scooted back a little from the cliff's edge and turned over onto his side so he could face Sean. "Well, what do you want to do? Sit here until they leave?"

Sean wormed his way back away from the ledge, staying on his stomach. He shook his head. "No. They already know we're here. If it's someone harmless, they will see us walking around and not think anything of it. If they aren't harmless, they'll be looking for us soon anyway."

"Is it possible we could search the island and then sneak back onto our boat?"

Sean had to consider it for a minute. They needed to find the cave where Caesar had hidden the Antikythera Mechanism, but doing so would require them to scour the rest of the terrain, and not all of it would be able to keep them hidden from view. If they couldn't locate the Antikythera Mechanism, Adriana could die. Getting back to the boat wouldn't be easy either, but he figured they could stay low in the water and reach their boat without being spotted. Maybe. That would require getting in the water on the other side of the island where they'd just been, and swimming all the way around. Wading back in from the sandy beach would put them in wide-open view.

"For now, let's do as much as we can to stay out of sight and search the rest of the island. We have to find that artifact. There's no going back without it."

Tommy saw the resolve in Sean's eyes. He knew what was at stake, and he knew that they couldn't leave unless they had Caesar's device in their possession. "Okay, buddy. Let's do it."

The two stayed low on all fours, crawling backward away from the cliff until they had reached far enough inland that they could get to a crouching position without being seen. They remained in a low stance as they moved farther across the plateau. When they reached the middle of the island and could no longer see the yacht in the cove, they stood up and stretched their legs for a second. The rocky ground had scuffed their elbows and knees but hadn't been as jagged as it appeared from the water. Most of the surface was sandy dirt, and the bits of rock that shone through the loam had been worn smooth by time and weather.

Sean took the lead and headed in the direction of the far corner of the plateau above where he'd been looking around the corner just a few minutes before. His reasoning being that searching the part of the island that was out of sight first would be their best strategy. If they found anything out of the ordinary, then they could set about trying to sneak back onto their boat.

The two made their way along the far ledge, scouring the surface for any clues as to where the relic might be hidden. Minutes passed as the Americans inched their way around the edge of the plateau. Sean was especially cautious as he leaned over the ledge to examine the water below. His fear of heights was something he'd battled since he was a young boy. He never really knew why high places terrified him so much, and his parents were equally as baffled. In the current situation, he wasn't as fearful as he would be on a tall building or some other man-made structure, but it was still uncomfortable. The fact that there was water at the bottom of the cliff might have made things a little better, except that Sean had experienced a terrifying moment when he was cliff jumping with some friends in high school.

The cliff had not been quite as high as the one he stood on now, and when he jumped, he plunged deep into the water, all the way to the bottom. When his feet hit the lake's floor, he pushed hard and paddled toward the surface. He hadn't realized how deep the water would be or how far down his momentum would carry him. He'd taken a long breath just before hitting the liquid surface, but it very nearly wasn't enough. Sean was so close to daylight, but his lungs screamed out for air as he kicked harder and faster with his feet. Finally, after almost giving in to the urge to open his mouth and inhale, his hand broke through to open air. He took in oxygen in huge gasps as he dog paddled in the water for a minute. Relief had washed over him, and he took a moment just to feel grateful he was still alive.

Over on the boat, his friends hadn't even noticed. They were busy laughing, joking around, and getting ready to climb back up to the top of the cliff for another round of jumping. Sean swam back to the boat and struggled up the ladder. He sat on one of the cushioned benches for a minute, contemplating how close he'd come to death. He never jumped off a cliff again.

Remembering that experience, Sean hoped he wouldn't have to take the leap off the cliff he was now peering over. He would if he had to, but his preference would be an easy entry into the water from the shore.

The two friends gazed into the deep water below, noting the stark contrast between the light-blue shallow water and the darker, almost foreboding depths..

"You were right about it getting much deeper down there," Tommy said, pointing a finger at the area in question. "What do you think that gets to, twenty to thirty feet deep?"

"At least," Sean nodded. "You can see the bottom easily over there at the corner, but in a matter of ten feet it just drops off."

They examined the area for another few seconds before Sean spoke up again. "Come on, we need to keep searching. Even if those people are just touring around on their yacht, I don't feel like dealing with their questions about who we are and what we're doing here."

"Good call," Tommy agreed.

The two got moving again, checking the ground with every step they took to find any signs of a Roman or Greek presence on the little piece of land. For the next forty-five minutes, Tommy and Sean crept along the south side of the island. After they reached the western edge, they moved twenty feet into the middle and backtracked the way they'd come. They repeated this process until they had finally come back to the point where they could make out the top of the giant yacht in the harbor. The sun sat high in the sky, shining warm rays of light down onto the island.

Tommy stood with his hands on his hips as he glanced up at the almost cloudless sky. "What do we do now?" he asked. Both of them had been on searches like this a dozen times before with the IAA. They knew that patience was an essential part of any good archaeologist's repertoire. At the moment, however, time wasn't on their side.

"This side of the island is in plain view of the other boat," Sean said, waving his hand to the area in question. "If we go looking around over there, whoever is on the boat will see us."

"So what do we do?"

Sean thought about it for a moment, and then shook his head. "We aren't going to find anything up here."

"What do you mean?" Tommy asked, puzzled by his friend's sudden willingness to give up.

Sean frowned as he surveyed the terrain. "Caesar's clue was whatever place held the Eye of Zeus was under this island. If we are looking for a way in, it won't be up here. And I doubt there would be an arrow or anything pointing the way in plain sight."

"Okay then. So we get back in the water and swim around the back side of the island and see what we can find."

"It's our only option."

Tommy didn't like the idea. He'd forgotten about the sharks while they were walking around on land, but now the irrational fear began to creep its way back into his head. "You're sure that's the only thing we can do?"

Sean rolled his eyes. "Tommy, enough with the sharks already. I'm telling you, you're not in a *Jaws* movie here. These species almost never attack people."

"Almost," Tommy countered.

"Fine, they never attack people."

"You said almost. That means it happens every now and then. I don't want to be the one that accounts for the almost." He was being defiant, but he knew there was no other choice. They were going to have to swim around the island. "Let's make it quick."

Sean smiled. "Don't worry, if a shark comes near I'll punch him in the nose."

His words comforted Tommy for a second, then, "Aw, crap!"

"What's the problem now?"

Tommy's face was forlorn. "We left our flippers on the beach. No way can we get them without being seen."

Sean let out a sigh. "I guess that means we'll have to do it the hard way."

"I was hoping you wouldn't say that."

46

NORTHWESTERN GREECE

B ourdon stepped into the enormous living room on the main floor of Gikas's yacht. Four men with thick muscles stood guard, one in every corner. Gikas sat alone on a plush suede couch, watching a flatscreen, high definition television on the wall opposite. A beautiful brunette reporter in a blue dress sat behind a desk talking about the escalating problems in Greece.

"More than three thousand people gathered outside the Hellenic Parliament building to protest the government's inability to address the food shortages," she reported. "It is expected that the number of protesters will continue to grow as the state of civil unrest nears boiling point. It was announced just yesterday that food production in the entire country is going to be only half the national average. The report stimulated a severe escalation in food prices all over the country.

"In Athens, police were called in to put down a few riots at local markets and grocers. Thessaloniki also experienced similar, minor criminal outbreaks. While the incidents have been small thus far, local authorities are concerned that unless something is done soon, hunger will drive people to do irrational and dangerous things."

The screen switched and displayed a balding man with a thick mustache. The remnants of hair on his head and the facial hair were streaked with gray. "I implore the people of Greece to please be civil and patient. We are still investigating the report that was released concerning our food supply, and while our fears may be true there are contingency plans in place for this sort of thing. We must remain united as a country and a people."

The man disappeared as the camera shot changed to one of the protesters. Their voice was translated to English by a female voice. "This government has done nothing to help its people. The economy here has been bad for years. The jobless rate is too high. And now they are telling us that our farmers and production facilities couldn't get enough food for everyone? It is time for a change. We need new leadership."

Gikas chuckled as he leaned back in the soft couch, his arms splayed out to both sides. He turned the hand holding the remote toward the television and hit a button. The screen went black, and he set the remote down on the cushion next to him.

"So, Teo, what do you have for me?" he asked, turning his attention to his new head of security.

Bourdon walked around the edge of a matching suede chair and helped himself to a seat. "I took care of Paulino. No loose ends there, just like you requested."

"Good," Gikas nodded. "I always prefer to keep things as simple as possible."

"Of course. I do as well."

"What of Wyatt and Schultz? I noticed we have already slowed down."

Bourdon nodded. "They made anchor in a cove not far from the island."

"Any sign of them?"

"No," Bourdon shook his head. "There has been no movement on the boat, and I'm pretty sure I saw someone moving in the grass on the upper part of the island. I'm certain they are wandering around, probably searching for the artifact."

Gikas's eyebrows lifted. "Aren't you going to stop them?" He seemed surprised that his new apprentice would be so lackadaisical.

Bourdon crossed his arms and smiled. "I thought you had more faith in me than that. I sent three men over to their boat. They swam over to the near side of their craft as I was out on the deck. If Wyatt and his friend were watching me, it was unlikely they saw the three men as they approached Wyatt's craft. They waited, shielded from sight by the boat's hull until I came inside. Whoever may have been watching would have lost interest within a minute or two. Our men are climbing aboard Wyatt's vessel as we speak, and when the Americans return with the relic they will be shot on sight and the object will be yours." He leaned back proudly as he finished the description of his plan.

Gikas was impressed, but there was still something bothering him. "What if they don't have the Eye of Zeus in their possession?"

"My men were instructed to kill Wyatt and his friend only if they had the device with them. If there is no sign of it, the men are to bring the Americans back to this ship where we can interrogate them ourselves."

Silence pervaded the room after Bourdon finished his explanation. A few moments later, Gikas began clapping. The four guards in the room eyed each other suspiciously, unaccustomed to seeing their employer express himself in such a manner. "Impressive, Teo," he said after ending his applause. "An excellent plan. So, all we have to do is sit and wait for Wyatt and his friend to fall right into our trap."

"Precisely. Have your ship's captain steer us out of the cove and out to open water. It will appear that we are simply out for a leisurely boat tour and have continued on our way. When our men have commandeered their boat and taken them prisoner, they will radio us, and we will meet them back at this spot."

"I like it," Gikas said as he crossed his arms. "Mikel," he called to one of the other guards in the room. "Have Serge take us out of this little bay and back out to the open sea between the islands. Have him sit there and wait for further instructions."

The guard stepped forward and gave a quick nod before striding over to a door at the other end of the cabin and disappearing through it.

Gikas stood up and made his way over to a bar in the corner near the television. He picked up a decanter half-full of clear liquid and removed the crystal cap. He glanced back at Bourdon and motioned with the bottle, "Would you like a drink?"

"No, thank you," Bourdon said. "I never drink when I'm working. And I am almost always working. I find that in my line of employment, it is essential to keep one's wits as sharp as possible."

Gikas flicked his eyebrows and gave a nod. "I can appreciate that. And I agree. You should most certainly keep your wits about you." He poured a few ounces of the alcohol into a tumbler and set the decanter down, replacing the lid as he did so. He lifted the glass and sniffed the drink with a long inhalation. "You know, most Greeks prefer ouzo. It's the drink of our homeland."

"Not you, though, eh?"

Gikas shook his head. "No, I have always had a preference for good vodka. And this is the best money can buy. Perhaps when this little matter regarding Wyatt and Schultz is done, you will have one with me."

"It would be my pleasure."

The boat's engines grumbled deep from the aft of the yacht, and the huge vessel began to move again. Its weight and size made the interior of the boat extremely stable, and its occupants barely had to brace themselves as the ship's captain steered the yacht out of the cove and back into open waters.

Gikas took a sip of the vodka and clicked his tongue, then let out a sigh as the warm sensation trickled down his throat. "Go downstairs with two of the men and bring up the woman. I want her on deck when we apprehend Wyatt and his friend. If he won't tell us what we want to know, maybe the sight of her in pain will change his mind a little."

"Of course," Bourdon nodded. He motioned for the two closest guards to follow him. Then he walked to the front of the cabin and descended the stairs to retrieve Adriana.

A smile eased onto Gikas's face. Everything was going according to plan. Wyatt had led him straight to what he wanted.

47

NORTHWESTERN GREECE

S wimming without the aid of fins made for a much more difficult task than Sean had anticipated when he made the suggestion. The water fought against their progress with every stroke and kick. For a moment, Sean wished they had gone back to the beach and risked being seen in order to get the flippers, but he knew their current plan was the only way. It gave them an element of surprise and might just get them the upper hand in whatever showdown was about to occur.

Tommy breathed heavily as he chopped wildly through the water. He tried desperately to keep up with Sean, but didn't have nearly as much experience swimming in the sea. Sean wondered if his friend had much swimming experience at all, based on the unorthodox technique Tommy was using. He looked more like an octopus flailing arms and legs around everywhere as he fought to keep going forward. It would have been worse had they been farther out from the island. Fortunately, where they were, the water wasn't as rough as it would be fifty yards away.

Sean took a second to dog paddle and look back at where they'd started. He frowned. They'd only gone thirty yards, and already his friend was gasping for breath. He continued to hover in place to let Tommy take a minute to rest.

"I'm...not used to...swimming in this kind...of water," Tommy said, stopping his reckless movement, taking a moment to rest like Sean was doing.

"Yeah, it's a lot different than swimming in a pool."

"I don't understand how you do it," Tommy said, spitting out a little water through his lips. "You make it seem so easy."

Sean kept his hands out wide, maintaining his position. "Just used to it, I guess." He turned his attention from his friend back to the rocky face of the island.

The stone cliff rose high above them to the plateau where they'd been just a few minutes before. Sean had noticed how much deeper the water was where they now floated from his view up on the island. Swimming in it now, he was intrigued by the odd drop on the sea floor. Usually, the area surrounding an island had a more gradual decline until it reached an underwater shelf, which would dramatically fall into the depths of the sea. Sean surveyed the jagged rock, searching it for a telling sign of what they had come to find.

"I'm going to get a little closer," he said and took a few strokes toward the island.

"That's fine," Tommy said, still trying to catch his breath. "I'll just wait here for the heart attack to kick in."

"If you didn't struggle so much and relaxed your swimming strokes, you would spend less energy and go a lot faster."

Sean stopped about ten feet short of the rocks. His eyes scanned the surface again, studying it carefully. This had to be the place. He knew it. He just needed some kind of confirmation. Suddenly, his gaze froze on something that seemed out of place on such a rugged facade. He'd not noticed it before, but now that he was closer he could see it plain as day. The lettering had been carved into the stone to appear almost invisible, as if it were part of the natural formation of the island. Seeing it now, he realized how the word had been camouflaged. It couldn't be seen from a distance much greater than twenty feet. He let out a grin as he stared at the word.

Inferus.

"Hey, Tommy," he shouted back at his friend. "I think we found it."

"What?" Tommy's face curled into a frown as he desperately tried to stay afloat. "What do you mean we found it?"

Sean pointed up at the word chiseled into the stone. "This is the spot." He looked down into the water where his feet were kicking at a smooth, constant pace. "I knew there was something funny about this spot. It has to be an underwater entrance cut into the base of the island."

"Great!" Tommy said in mocking excitement. "Tell you what. Why don't you go down and check it out, and I'll stay here and wait."

"Okay," Sean said. He somersaulted over and disappeared head first, diving into the water.

When his feet disappeared, Tommy shook his head. "I was kidding," he said to himself.

Thirty seconds went by, and he started to worry about Sean being down for so long. He watched as his friend maneuvered through the clear water, but it was difficult to see with the constant ripple of the sea. All he could make out was his friend's blurry image below.

Ten seconds later, Sean reappeared on the surface and took in a huge gasp of air. He wiped away the water from his head and eyes and allowed a smile to pass over his face. "There's a cave entrance down there," he said proudly. "And the symbol of Julius Caesar is carved over top of it."

"Are you serious?" Tommy asked excitedly. He'd forgotten his exhaustion and replaced it with enthusiasm. "I really wasn't sure we would find anything."

Sean cast a disappointed glance at his friend. "Haven't you learned never to doubt me?"

"Not yet," Tommy winked.

A low rumble from around the edge of the island caught their attention. They both shared a moment of concern. Sean paddled a few strokes out away from the island to get a better view of what was happening. The white yacht was trolling away from the small land mass. "Looks like whoever is in that yacht has seen enough. They're leaving."

"Probably just out for a little midday tour of the islands," Tommy added.

"The good news for you is that we don't have to go all the way around the island without our fins. Now we can go back and get them."

Tommy squinted his eyes disapprovingly at Sean's little barb. "You know what? That is good news. And if you don't mind, I'm going to head back that way right now. You just hang out here with the sharks while I go back to the beach." He started his wild flailing again as soon as he finished the sentence.

Sean laughed, though he wasn't sure which was funnier, the sight of his friend swimming or the fact that he knew he was terrible at it. Not wanting to make Tommy feel worse about his technique than he already did, Sean waited for a few minutes before swimming toward the shore.

Several minutes later, the two had their fins attached and were stepping back into the water of the cove, heading for their boat.

"Will we be able to get into the cave with our scuba gear on?" Tommy asked, wading into the water with his fins.

"Yeah," Sean nodded, walking awkwardly beside him. "It looks plenty big enough. We shouldn't have any problems."

Once they were in deep enough water, the two began paddling back in the direction of their boat, which was anchored in the peaceful waters of the cove. Tommy moved much faster now that he had his flippers on, letting his legs do most of the work. The two arrived at the back of their craft and pulled themselves up onto the back landing.

Sean removed the flippers and twisted his head to see where the yacht had gone. It had disappeared from view, leaving them alone in the cove, which was exactly what he preferred. The fewer eyes watching what they were doing, the better.

"I'll pull up the anchor, and we can take the boat around to the other side. We can park it there and get our dive gear ready."

Tommy finished taking off his watery footwear and stood up. "Good. I'm tired of all this swimming," he said and then froze in place as if he'd seen a snake. He slowly raised his hands to shoulder height.

"What is it?" Sean asked, as he dropped his fins onto the aft deck. He didn't need his friend to answer. His eyes followed Tommy's to the cabin of the boat where three men had appeared from inside. Each one held a gun, aiming straight in the two Americans' direction. "Or we could just do whatever these guys want."

48

NORTHWESTERN GREECE

"Y ou cannot do this, Dimitris. People will starve to death in the streets. There will be anarchy. Please, I beg of you, do not do this."

The man's voice on the phone sounded like a hungry cat crying for a scrap of food at the end of a long day. Hardly becoming for a man of his position. The man on the other line was Petra Samaris, the prime minister of Greece. He'd been appointed by the president, whose role in government affairs was considered mostly ceremonial. It was Samaris who had led the charge during the economic downturn. He'd promised the people that he would lead them back to prosperity if given the time. Much like any other politician, it seemed Samaris was full of empty promises.

Now he had no other cards to play. He'd put everything out on the line and lost. Dimitris Gikas held all the power, and there wasn't anything Samaris could do about it, a fact the prime minister was apparently aware of.

"Thousands of your fellow countrymen will die, Dimitris. How can you just sit by and let that happen while your stores are full of the food that can save them?" Samaris was near the point of sobbing. He must have known that if the people revolted, he would be the first to hang from the gallows' noose.

Gikas had let the man talk for the last few minutes. He had but a moment to spare with the desperate leader. Ten minutes before, his men had informed Bourdon that they had taken control of Wyatt's boat and were bringing it back to rendezvous with the yacht. Everything was going according to plan. Sure, there'd been a few kinks along the way, but that's the way complex plans went. One had to be always willing to adjust, be flexible to anything that came along. Adaptation was one of Dimitris Gikas's finest attributes.

When he spoke, his voice carried an air of disregard and complete lack of sympathy. "Mr. Prime Minister, I apologize, but I will not be able to respond to your request. I'm out at sea at the moment, and I simply cannot reach my distribution facilities until the end of the week."

Samaris's tone turned threatening. "You release the food, Dimitris, or I will send the army to release it for you."

Gikas allowed himself a short laugh. "Do you really think that wise, Petra?" He said the name with disdain. It was disrespectful to call the prime minister by his first name, a fact Gikas knew Samaris took seriously. "Send the army to my facilities, and I will burn them all to the ground. It would be a shame if there were several explosions at the distribution centers right when your soldiers showed up. Of course, there would be many innocent people working there that would die, a fact that the news reports would claim was your fault, along with the deaths of many soldiers."

"You're bluffing." Samaris sounded hopeful.

"Am I? Do you honestly think that I don't have a backup plan for every possible contingency you have thought of or will think of? I have no problem destroying my own plants. They are insured well beyond what they are worth. I will make more money while your little reign at the helm continues to unravel."

Silence pervaded for a moment before Samaris spoke again. "What is it you want, Dimitris?"

Gikas paced over to the little bar on the side of his yacht's living room. Two guards stood next to Adriana Villa, her hands and ankles bound in thick rope. Her mouth had been gagged with a hand towel from one of the bathrooms so she wouldn't say anything during the phone call that would give away their position. Even though Gikas was in a position of absolute strength at the moment, one well-placed cruise missile would wipe him off the planet.

"What do I want?" he asked as he poured himself a short refill of vodka. He set the decanter back on the bar and took a quick sip, savoring the warm feel of the liquid. "There is nothing you have that I need, Petra. You should have planned better. Your administration has squandered any little bit of money the government had left, and you have betrayed the people." Gikas's tone turned sour. "If any Greek people die as a result of this famine then their blood is on your hands, not mine. Justice will be done, Petra, of that you can be sure. Now if you will excuse me, I have some business to tend to."

"Dimitris! Don't you hang up the..."

Gikas hit the end button on his phone's touch screen and tossed the device on the couch. He turned his attention to the Spaniard tied up in the seat across from him. "Now," he motioned with the wave of a hand, telling the nearest guard to unbind the gag from his prisoner's mouth. "I'm terribly sorry I had to do that. Couldn't have you yelling out our position or something crazy like that while I was on the phone with the man I'm unseating."

"Your plan will fail," Adriana spat. Fire burned in her eyes like an angry tiger, ready to pounce on its prey.

He shrugged and pouted his lips. "Possibly. But highly unlikely. Your boyfriend and his companion are on their way to this yacht as we speak. It seems they did not find the relic, but they did find where it is. The Eye of Zeus will be mine soon enough, and then, not a single soul on this planet will be able to stop me."

The door on the other side of the room swung open, startling everyone inside. Bourdon pulled his weapon, but lowered it immediately upon seeing it was his men with the two new prisoners. One of them kicked Wyatt in the kidneys, sending him to the floor just inside the living room. His hands were tied behind his back, though his feet were free. Wyatt's face bore a cut on one cheek and a swollen left eye.

"I see you roughed him up a little," Bourdon commented casually.

One of the muscle-bound guards rolled his shoulders. "I didn't want him to get any ideas."

"Now, now," Gikas interrupted as he stepped over to Wyatt, putting his feet right in front of the American's face. "Is that any way to treat our guests?"

Tommy stood in the doorway with one of the other guards directly behind him, watching his every move. "We don't have the Antikythera Mechanism, Gikas. So you may as well just let us go." Tommy's offer seemed to have no effect on the rich man.

Though Sean did admire him for the effort, he knew there was no getting out of this. He cursed himself for not being more aware to the possibility that someone could be on their boat. He wondered if the men had stowed away onboard before they even left the marina, but he doubted it. They'd gone through the cabin to check on the supplies they had ordered. There weren't that many places to hide on the small boat. A thought flashed through his mind. "The driver worked for you, huh," he said, more as a statement than a question.

Gikas gave an impressed nod and a quick flick of the eyebrows, or maybe he was just mocking the former agent. "Yes. Your driver was one of my employees."

"Was?" Tommy asked.

"Well, you know how things can get sometimes. He was more of a temporary worker. My associate here had to let him go." Gikas motioned at Bourdon by waving his nearly empty tumbler in the air. He knelt down beside Sean and stared into his eyes with a firm glare. "Now, you are going to tell me where the device is, and you are going to retrieve it for me, or I will kill your friend and let my men have their way with your woman. Is that clear enough for you, Sean Wyatt?"

Sean fought to keep his anger at bay, but his temper raged inside like a caged lion. "You don't need them," he said, his jaw clenched tight. "Let them go, and I'll get you the Eye of Zeus."

Gikas clicked his tongue a few times, chastising Sean for even considering such a counter offer. "You are in no position to make proposals, Sean. I am in total control right now. So you can do as I say, and bring me the relic, or I start making things very bad for your friends." He paused for a moment, and then stood up. He walked over to Adriana and put his hand behind the back of her head, grabbing her hair hard. Gikas yanked on it, causing a short squeak to come from her mouth. "Women, you see, are so easy to manipulate. You can force them to make whatever sounds you wish. I wonder, Sean, have you ever heard a woman screaming for help, struggling against a man? How long do you think she would be able to struggle against one of my men here?" He pointed at the guards in the room.

Sean's inclination was to say something about how she could hold her own and those men might be the ones not lasting very long, but he didn't want to provoke the madman. If he said anything remotely reckless, Gikas might hold true to his word. That was something Sean could not allow.

"No comment?" Gikas asked. He wandered over to the door where Tommy stood. Anger seeped through Tommy's pores as the man came close. "I'm certain your friend here would not make a peep, right up to the moment I put a bullet through his brain."

"Enough," Sean said confidently. "I'll get you the device. But you have to give me your word that these two will not be harmed."

Gikas smiled for a moment, and then flashed a perplexed look at Sean. "Usually, men in your position would think that someone like me is a madman. Would you take a madman's word for anything?"

"Like you said before, it doesn't seem like I have much of a choice. Just promise me you'll let them go, and I'll get you what you want." Sean was still on the floor, but he sat up just enough to stare Gikas in the eye.

The Greek came close and leaned over. Sean could smell the man's breath on him along with the expensive, yet overpowering cologne on his neck. "Good. You will take Teo and two others with you. If you try anything funny, you know what will happen."

Sean never flinched. A thin trickle of blood ran down his cheek. "I need them to help me get the Antikythera Mechanism," he said, motioning with his head toward Adriana.

Gikas put his hands behind his back and shook his head. "No, I do not think so. You may try to escape. And while I trust my capable assistants here, I don't want to tilt the odds in your favor in any way."

"Fine," Sean relinquished. "I know you won't let me take her. To you, she's too valuable of a bargaining chip." Gikas nodded at the assessment. "But I do need my friend. There could be a riddle or an ancient language down there that I may not understand. He's an expert at those things. Let him go with me, and I promise we will bring the Eye of Zeus back to you safely. When it's in your possession, you let them go."

Gikas leaned his head back and stared at the ceiling while taking in a long deep breath. He seemed to consider Sean's offer for a moment before answering. "Very well, Sean. Take your little friend with you."

"We'll need our scuba gear," Sean said almost as Gikas was ending his sentence. "And if your men are coming with us, they will need some too."

"Not a problem. Our ship has enough diving equipment for several people. Since I'm letting you have your friend along, I'm going to time you. If you aren't back within two hours, I will start cutting off your girlfriend's toes, one for every ten minutes you are delayed. Once I'm done with those, I will go to fingers. After that, well, let's say I won't be doing any more cutting. I will just let my men do whatever they want. Understood?"

Sean thought about it for a second. When he responded, there was a sharp edge to his voice. "Yeah. I understand."

49

NORTHWESTERN GREECE

The guards hurriedly loaded the scuba gear and other necessities onto the boat Sean and Tommy had rented. They'd earlier tied the cabin cruiser to the yacht to keep the two boats together, so untying the ropes was the last thing the guards needed to do before setting off. When everything was ready to go, Tommy and Sean were placed in the back seat on the aft deck and watched carefully by two guards armed with submachine guns. Bourdon stood next to the guard who drove the boat, directing him which way to go as the man pulled the craft away from Gikas's yacht.

In the pale-blue sky, a few white clouds danced along in front of the sun, blocking out the warm rays of light for a few minutes. The sea had whipped up considerably, creating deeper swells to the waves that had previously been mere ripples.

It was getting late in the afternoon. Sean glanced down at his watch to check the time. It was definitely getting late for a dive. The last thing he wanted was to be stuck in an underwater cave at night. He'd been taken on just such an expedition during his dive certification. Their class was required to do a cave dive at night. He assumed it was so they would become accustomed to losing their bearings and having no surface light to guide them. It was one of those rare occasions when he'd felt extremely uncomfortable. Sean remembered how difficult it had been to know when they had entered the cave; first realizing they were no longer in open water when the roof of the underwater cavern scraped against the tank on his back. It had been a startling experience, but thanks to the class instructor, everyone did fine and received their certification.

Sean never thought he would actually have to use that part of his learning in the real world. Now he was glad he'd done it. The gears in his mind turned with ideas, some fanciful, others somewhat more practical. He was always looking for an edge in a situation like this. At present, there were two men with guns aimed at him and Tommy, plus two others backup thugs. A direct assault on the first two would end badly. His imagination played out the scenario in a matter of seconds. One move toward the men, and they would cut him down.

He hoped the driver of the boat would hit a wave awkwardly, one that would jostle everyone from their positions and give him a tiny window of opportunity. Unfortunately, even though the seas had picked up slightly, it was still relatively smooth sailing. Sean's thoughts went to a more plausible scenario. When they arrived at the location at the rear of the island, one of the men would stay behind to watch the boat. That would level the playing field somewhat, making it three on two. If there was a way to get the odds even, Sean knew he and Tommy had a chance.

"What happens if we get there and the artifact is gone, or the cave is closed off inside?" Tommy's question interrupted Sean's thoughts.

Sean hadn't realized it, but he'd been staring through the men, toward the island ahead. "I'm sorry?" he said, angling his head a little toward his friend. His movement was subtle, so as not to make the jumpy guards do anything stupid, like squeeze a trigger.

"The Antikythera Mechanism device. What if it isn't there?" Tommy repeated his question. "I mean, we may not be the first people to find this place. If someone got there before us, we're screwed."

Sean took in a deep breath and let out a long sigh. "I hadn't thought about that." He shook off the thought. "No, it's still there."

"How do you know?" Tommy's eyebrows stitched together.

"Not sure," Sean shrugged. "I just do."

Bourdon stepped between the two armed guards and cut into their conversation. "Hey! Show us where we need to go." The order came with the brandishing of his own weapon, a black Beretta .40 caliber. "And no funny business."

Sean held up both hands to show his intentions were purely obedient, and then he pointed a finger toward the approaching shoreline. "You'll need to go around behind that beach right there. We believe the entrance to the cave is on the other side."

Bourdon pivoted around and gave the instructions to the driver. The man at the control console spun the wheel to the left, and the boat veered slightly, splashing water and mist into the air, a little of it over the side of the boat. After the driver guided the boat around the sandy beach and to the side of the island that was out of the yacht's line of sight, he throttled down the engine, slowing the cruiser to an idle.

"Pull it over a little closer to that cliff right there," Sean said, motioning with his hand to the place he and Tommy had found an hour or so ago.

Again, Bourdon relayed the message, and the driver eased the boat to a place in the water about twenty yards from the island wall.

"This is close enough," Sean said. "You'll want to drop anchor here. We'll have to swim the rest of the way."

Bourdon said some things in a foreign language. Tommy and Sean glanced at each other for a brief moment, looking for the answer to each other's question. How were they going to get out of this?

"He will stay with the boat," Bourdon said, snapping at the two Americans. "We will accompany you on the dive. I don't think I have to remind you that these weapons are still lethal underwater. So if you try anything stupid you can expect to never see the surface again. Understood?"

The two captives nodded.

"Good. Now suit up." Bourdon stole a quick glance at the waning sunlight. "I don't wish to be underwater after dark. And do not forget, Sean Wyatt, you are on the clock."

Sean didn't need the reminder. He knew he had less than a hundred and five minutes to get back to the yacht with what Gikas wanted. Had the Greek been bluffing? He doubted it. Dimitris Gikas didn't seem like the type. He struck Sean as the kind of guy who would do everything he said. It was a rare case where being a man of one's word was a bad thing.

Bourdon slid the tanks, masks, regulators, and other items over to Sean and Tommy, keeping his weapon trained on the two as if they were coiled snakes, ready to strike.

Ten minutes later, all the men had put on their gear and were hanging over the edge of the boat. Bourdon had been the last to suit up, but he did so rapidly, causing Sean to think this wouldn't be the man's first time on a dive.

"When we get in the water, we will head down to the base of the island. You'll see an opening with a mark over it. That's where we go in." Sean made sure to speak slowly and clearly. For the moment, he needed to play nice. "Stay close to me on the way down. Don't want any of you getting lost."

Bourdon's eyes narrowed at the comment. He slid the scuba mask over his eyes and fell backward into the sea. A second later, he popped up with his weapon pointed at the Americans. One of the other guards motioned for Tommy to get in the water. Tommy obeyed and splashed in, holding his mask to his face. One of the other guards entered right behind him, and swam over to make sure he didn't swim off. Sean and the last guard followed, leaving the driver alone with the boat.

Under the surface of the sea, Sean pointed down toward the island's foundation and motioned for the others to follow. It was much easier to see with the mask on than when he'd explored the area before. Having access to air was also a huge relief. Holding his breath for long periods was not one of his strong suits, despite being in good physical condition.

The five men kicked their legs, sending them down into the

shadowy depths. A school of *Diplodus* fish scurried by, the entire group moving as one shimmering unit. Their jerky motion startled one of the guards, who eyed the fish suspiciously.

In less than a minute, Sean reached the underwater face of the wall where a cavity opened up. The hole stood at around six feet high and four feet wide, plenty big enough for the men to get through with their gear, but not more than one at a time. Over the arching entrance, Sean pointed to a circle that had been cut into the stone. Engraved in the center was an algae-covered image of Julius Caesar.

Bourdon motioned with his hand for Sean to go in first. Bourdon would follow, then a guard, then Tommy, then the last of his mercenaries would bring up the rear. Clearly, Bourdon didn't want to leave the fate of this mission in anyone else's hands but his own.

Sean gave a quick nod amid the bubbles escaping from his mask and turned to enter the cave. The men simultaneously turned their lights on as they began to traverse the darkness. The last guard to enter the cave twisted his head around warily, looking out into the deep sea before following the others.

The light from Sean's mask pointed the pale beams straight ahead, into the clear water. The light in his hand flashed off the sides of the corridor. He marveled at the passageway, wondering if it was created by human hands or by nature. It would have been an incredible feat for it to have been done by people. The ancients didn't have access to dive equipment like he and the others were using. To accomplish such a construction project would have required the sea level to be forty feet below where it was now. The sides of the wall, however, were hewn smooth, as if cut intentionally. The width of the corridor also remained consistent, which was something Sean had rarely seen in caves created by time and the elements. The submerged passage came to a sharp ninety-degree turn then continued for ten feet before turning sharply back to the left.

Sean continued flicking his fins, cruising through the underwater labyrinth until he reached a sloping wall directly ahead. The stone angled up at a gradual angle, much like a ramp. He aimed his flashlight up, surveying the area to make sure it was clear of any surprises.

Julius Caesar was clever if not cunning. Sean had a feeling that there would be one more trial before the ancient Roman emperor would give up his most prized possession. He turned around and motioned to Bourdon, pointing back at the ramp. The man nodded and followed closely as Sean paddled up through the shaft.

Sean's head broke the surface first, followed closely by Bourdon. The two men looked around to gather in their surroundings as they planted their feet on the stone. The underwater shaft had opened into a small pool, housed in a circular chamber cut into the island's rock. As Sean stepped forward awkwardly in his fins, Tommy and the other two remaining men broke through the surface. Their lights played along the walls as the men glanced around at the scene.

It wasn't until after he removed his dive mask that Sean truly realized the gravity of where they'd arrived. His eyes scanned the perfectly cut, circular room. Above, a domed ceiling had been carved into the rock. He marveled at how anyone had been able to accomplish such a task, and with such precision. The dome's smooth surface must have taken years to complete with the tools available during the Roman Empire.

Tommy and the other guards arrived next to Bourdon and Sean, who were now completely out of the water and standing on a stone platform, masks dangling in their hands. Bourdon still gripped his dripping weapon, aimed at Sean's abdomen. As incredible as the scene was, he wasn't about to let Wyatt catch him napping.

Tommy took off his mask and spun slowly around in a circle. He pointed at the objects lining the walls all the way around the room. "I don't understand," he said in a beleaguered tone. "Wasn't Caesar a follower of the Roman gods?"

Every eight feet or so, a stone likeness of every major deity from ancient Greece stood silently against the wall, all of them staring with lifeless eyes toward one side of the room where the ramp flattened out and led to an archway. Just beyond the opening was another, smaller chamber.

"Yep," Sean nodded slowly. "But the Antikythera Mechanism was believed to be a gift from the Greek god, Zeus. It would make sense that Caesar would pay homage to the one he believed created it, even if he worshipped other gods."

"Well, I don't know that I buy the idea that it was created by Zeus."

"Gentlemen," Bourdon interrupted the discussion that was quickly derailing the speed of their mission. "Where is the device?"

Sean looked around at the sculptures and noticed that the head of each was turned to face the arched entryway at the top of the ramp. "There's only one deity that's missing in this room. My guess is; he's the one guarding the relic that's named after him."

"Zeus," Bourdon said, realizing what Sean meant. "Move, up the ramp. Now."

Tommy and Sean removed their flippers under the watchful gaze of their wardens. The guards removed theirs one at a time so that two guns were aimed at the Americans at all times. When everyone's feet were bare, Bourdon motioned for the captives to lead the way.

The two friends walked cautiously up the stone slope, their eyes scanning the walls for any sign of danger. When they reached the top of the ramp, they stopped and stared upon a message carved into the stone over the arch.

"What does that say?" Bourdon asked.

"It's Latin," Sean answered. "You don't speak Latin?" He fired a diminishing glance at the man.

Bourdon's eyes narrowed to slits. "Tell me what it says, or I will cut out your tongue."

Sean rolled his eyes. "That's a bit ironic, don't you think?" He spun around and gazed at the phrase.

Tommy spoke first. "The worthy shall release their burdens and tread carefully."

Sean frowned. He knew there would be some kind of final test. In this instance, however, he had no idea what it meant. The other problem was that time wasn't exactly on his side. He needed to get the device and take it back to Gikas before he harmed Adriana.

Tommy shined his flashlight into the next room. It was a smaller, cube-shaped chamber. Bourdon motioned for the two Americans to move forward. As the five lights illuminated the darkness, a giant figure revealed itself in the shadows along the far wall. A massive sculpture of Zeus sitting on a golden throne towered all the way to the ceiling, nearly fifteen feet high. The statue held a lightning bolt in one hand and a scepter in the other. A long flowing robe draped over the figure's shoulder and down past his waist, to his sandaled feet. His thick hair and beard were meticulously detailed, as were the statue's abdominal muscles, biceps, and pectorals. The face of Zeus stared straight ahead, as if guarding the doorway with his stern expression.

"You don't think..." Tommy started to ask, his voice echoing in the still silence of the chamber.

"No. It can't be," Sean said.

"Are you sure?"

"The fabled statue of Zeus by Phidias was much larger than this one, and the records of it say that it was still in Greece long after Julius Caesar died."

"Oh yeah. I guess I didn't think about that."

"Silence!" Bourdon ordered. "Men, shine your light over there, to the right of the statue."

The other four did as ordered and redirected their flashlight beams to their right. Just in front of the sculpture's throne, a marble cube sat on the floor. On its top, a shiny, almost gold-like object reflected some of the light back to the men.

It was the Eye of Zeus.

"That's it," Sean said with more than a hint of relief. He started to inch his way forward when Bourdon's voice stopped him again.

"I think you've gone far enough, Mr. Wyatt. You and your friend step over to the side right there." He waved his gun barrel in the direction he wanted the Americans to go. When they had done what he requested, he spoke again. "Good. I can't have you doing something foolish like trying to destroy the device, now can I?"

"If we don't get that thing back to your boss, he's going to kill Adriana," Sean protested angrily. "So if you're going to grab it, hurry. We are running out of time." He had glanced at his watch again, seeing that he still had a good fifty minutes until his time was up.

"That seems to be your problem, not mine," Bourdon said snidely. He switched his attention to the closest guard and motioned toward the device with his free hand. "Lars, bring me the relic. We'll be taking that back to Mr. Gikas."

The one named Lars did as instructed and walked the remainder of the stone pathway to the foot of the giant statue.

Bourdon watched out of the corner of his eye as his subordinate carried out his command. "As for the two of you," he said to Sean and Tommy, "I believe my employer will no longer require your services."

"Gikas said that he would let Tommy and Adriana go if I led you to the device. He gave his word." Sean's argument bounced off the hard walls.

Bourdon shook his head. "True, but I never gave mine. Goodbye, Mr. Wyatt." He aimed the weapon at Sean's head and started to squeeze the trigger.

A sudden movement over by the statue grabbed Bourdon's attention, and he held back from firing for a split second. The guard he had sent to grab the Eye of Zeus disappeared with a short scream, followed by a splash. The sound of arms thrashing wildly in the water resounded throughout the room. Suddenly, the man screamed out in profane agony before it muted to a gurgle and then silence.

50

NORTHWESTERN GREECE

I n the confusion of the startling event, Sean had finally gotten the window he needed. He leapt hard at Bourdon, sinking his bare heel squarely into the man's chest. The force of the blow sent him crashing to the floor. His gun clanked loudly on the hard surface a few feet from his hand.

Sean's attack happened so fast that the other guard didn't have a chance to stop it, but now he had spun around and was bearing down on the American with his gun. A second before he could pull the trigger, Tommy launched an attack of his own. His fist snapped a few inches behind where the man's jaw was, sending him staggering backward. While he lost his balance, the guard never lost his gun, and as he regained his senses he began to raise it in Tommy's direction. Tommy didn't stop with one punch, however. He brought his foot through the man's wrist in a roundhouse kick, sending the gun flying across the room into the shadows.

Fifteen feet away, Bourdon had scrambled off the floor, a snarled look on his face. "You should not have done that," he said threateningly to Sean.

"Oh, I'm sorry. I should have let you just shoot me in the face, then?"

Bourdon pulled a knife out of his utility belt and brandished it menacingly. "It would have been an easier death than what you will receive now."

"I've never done things the easy way."

Bourdon growled and lunged at Sean with the tip of the knife, swinging it down across his body and then back up. Each time he stabbed and swiped with the sharp edge, Sean dodged it. One strike came particularly close to his stomach, causing him to arch his body like a cat to miss the blade. Bourdon's reaction was just as quick, slicing through the air as he spun around trying to catch Sean across the neck, the target rolling across the floor just clear of the attack.

Meanwhile, Tommy was in mid-dance with the guard. The two men circled each other, around and around, neither one willing to commit immediately to an assault. The guard had at least a twenty-pound advantage over Tommy, and was clearly much stronger, but what the man possessed in bulk, Tommy had in agility.

When the hulk of a man finally stepped in to throw a jab, Tommy easily sidestepped it while grabbing the man's elbow and using his momentum against him. Falling forward, the man's face ran smack into Tommy's elbow, instantly breaking his nose. It was a wound that would have dropped a normal man. Unfortunately, the guard was no typical combatant. He swung around angrily in a blood-infused rage and brought his fist across Tommy's face. The power of the round-house punch sent Tommy to the floor in a haze of pain. He winced at his throbbing cheek but forced himself to stand back up. Before he could manage it, the guard's huge foot whipped up from the floor and through Tommy's chin. He nearly flipped over backward from the energy of the strike, landing face down on the hard stone.

Sean saw his friend go down out of the corner of his eye, but he couldn't help him immediately. Bourdon lashed out again with the knife, this time overcommitting his body in the lunge. Sean used it against him and grabbed the man's wrist that held the knife. He twisted the arm around behind Bourdon's back and yanked it up, nearly breaking the bone. The knife dropped to the floor, but Bourdon deftly shifted his stance and used Sean's back as leverage to jump and roll behind him. Suddenly, Sean was on the defensive with the enemy's forearm wrapped around his neck. Bourdon squeezed hard, closing off his opponent's airway. Sean struggled, pulling at the muscular arm, desperately trying to free his throat to draw in another breath. He attempted to drop to his knee to throw Bourdon over his back, but the move only tightened the man's grip. Sean's face reddened, swelling with the strain. He only had another ten seconds or so before he would black out. With the last ounce of strength he possessed, Sean reached back with his hands and felt for the killer's eyes. Bourdon twisted his face around violently, resisting the move, but one thumb caught him right in the soft eye tissue. The moment Sean felt it, he shoved his thumb deep into the man's socket.

Bourdon let out a howling scream, and both his arms let go of their death grip, moving his hands to the now-bloody eye. Sean fell forward onto the floor, landing close to Tommy, who struggled to grasp for consciousness. Sean gasped for air on his hands and knees, trying to regain his bearings.

The guard had left Tommy on the floor and walked over to the corner to retrieve his gun. Blood oozed freely from the man's nose as he bent down and picked it up. Bourdon recovered as well, and stumbled over to where his own pistol lay on the stone surface. Sean noticed all four of the men's flashlights sat in a heap between him and Tommy. His friend groaned and clutched at the floor, slowly coming out of the haze.

"Tommy," Sean hissed.

"Yeah?"

"Cut the lights."

"What?"

"Hurry. Cut the lights."

Then Sean's odd request made sense. Tommy quickly grabbed at two of the nearby flashlights as Sean did the same. The guard in the corner had his weapon in hand and was stalking back to his victims. Bourdon had likewise repossessed his gun and spun around as the Americans simultaneously hit the switches on the lights.

The room was instantly cast into pitch darkness. A shot rang out from where the guard had been standing, sending the metal round pinging off the stone walls in a deadly ricochet.

"Don't fire, you fool!" Bourdon yelled in darkness. "You could kill both of us."

The villains swiveled around in one direction and then the other, trying to get any sort of bearing on their prey. Sean flashed his light rapidly one time, momentarily giving away his position, but the blink of light was so fast it did more to disorient the killers than anything else. Bourdon and the guard both spun in the direction of the light, but they were too slow. The guard scuffed one of his feet, again giving away where he stood. Even a quiet sound like skin on stone echoed in the cube room.

While Sean maneuvered silently around behind where Bourdon stood, Tommy felt along the floor with his fingertips. He'd seen the knife when Sean strobed his light. If he could get the blade, it would give him a weapon at the very least.

Sean hit the switch on his flashlight again, this time twice to amplify the strobe effect. Tommy saw the direction his friend was moving. Sean was flanking the man in charge of the operation. Tommy also saw something else in the momentary burst of light. The knife was only a few inches away.

He carefully reached out his hand and grasped the weapon, cautious not to let it make a noise that would give away his position. He pushed himself up off the ground gradually, still wary that the slightest sound could mean his end. Like a cat, Tommy padded toward the last place he'd seen the guard standing with his gun. He hoped he remembered correctly. The absolute darkness made moving around almost like playing roulette.

Fortunately for Tommy, the guard made a fatal mistake. Letting his fear get the better of him, he shouted out a challenge to the elusive Americans. "Come out of the dark and fight like men!" he shouted. "What kind of cowards hide like rats in the sewers?"

Bourdon wanted to yell at the man to shut up, but he would have given away where he was standing. He knew exactly the game the two Americans were playing, and he wasn't about to let them sneak up on him from behind. Inch by inch, he moved toward the last place he'd seen in the light, over by the statue. The gentle splashing of water from the hole his man had fallen into helped guide the way. No one could sneak up behind him if he stood with the water to his back. If he played his cards right, he could use the momentum from an attack against one of the two men and send them into the water as well. Then the odds would be in his favor again.

Tommy could hear the guard's panicked breaths as he closed in on the terrified man. He could even hear the guard moving the gun around from left to right, just above the quiet swishing of the water fifteen feet away. Tommy deftly tiptoed around behind the man, with the blade in hand, and closed the gap swiftly.

The guard never saw the attack coming. Tommy pounced on the man from behind, wrapping his forearm around the man's jaw and quickly drawing the sharp edge of the knife across his neck. Tommy made sure the blade sunk deep into the skin, cutting off the vital lines that carried blood to the brain and heart.

The man gasped for a moment, then gurgled loudly before firing off two shots with his gun. The bullets ricocheted around the room, sending sparks off every wall. Tommy kicked the man in the lower back, sending him toppling over onto his face. The dying guard's mouth could only let out a few more gulps of noise before he went completely silent.

Bourdon knew the guard had made a fatal mistake. He did not intend to do the same. After thirty seconds of careful movement, he found himself with his heels on the edge of the water. The Eye of Zeus would be right behind him, but without light he wouldn't be able to find a way to reach it. Just the same, now he was a badger in a corner. He ducked down behind a column that marked the short path to the Antikythera Mechanism and held his weapon in front of his chest. If anyone made a wrong move and got too close, he wouldn't miss from short range.

Sean heard Tommy take down the other guard. For a high-end mercenary, the man clearly didn't realize he was making too much noise, although that was often the case with big men. Moving around the position Bourdon had been in, Sean refocused his thoughts on the last man standing. If he was Gikas's righthand man, he probably had a great deal of experience in all kinds of situations. Sean doubted the man would be stupid enough to stand around and wait to be killed. He knew it was a gambler's spot; that he would have to risk moving through the darkness and bumping into someone instead of staying put.

Sean reached the place where he'd last seen his quarry, or at least close to it, and found that his assumptions had been correct. Gikas's man had moved somewhere else. But where? Sean's mind rapidly ran through the possibilities. He would need to get somewhere he could protect himself and not be flanked from behind. That meant either a corner, or maybe by the water where the other guard had fallen in. Sean doubted the man had found his way to the exit. If that were the case, there would likely have been a splash of some kind as the man's feet hit the water. No, he was still in the cubed chamber. Sean considered the options. He wished he could communicate with Tommy, but that was out of the question. That brought up another dangerous possibility. He and Tommy could take each other out with friendly fire. Sean winced at the thought. His cheek still hurt from the fight, but it was the least of his concerns. He had to find Gikas's lead man.

He wouldn't be in a corner, Sean decided. It would be too obvious. Sean put himself in Bourdon's shoes. If it were him, he'd go to the least likely place an attacker would think he'd be. Over by the water, near the Eye of Zeus, was a perfect place to hide and an excellent place to take out an assailant attacking from the front. Sean pictured the man hiding behind a short stone column, waiting with his gun at the ready. To make absolutely sure, he flashed his light one more time.

No one was in the corners, but in the instant the light burst through the room, he could see Tommy standing in the center over the dead guard. A second of relief pulsed through him, though he'd figured his friend had come out ahead. More importantly, he knew where Bourdon was hiding.

"Tommy," he said into the dark. "You okay?"

"Yeah," Tommy answered reluctantly. For a split second, he wondered why Sean would risk giving away his position to the enemy. Another split second brought about a higher knowledge of how his friend operated. Sean wouldn't have done it without a plan. "I'm good. Though I can't say the same for the guard."

"I didn't see the other guy," Sean said in a whisper, projecting his voice toward the far wall near the entrance. "Let's check out the main chamber. He may have gone back in there to grab his tank and goggles for an escape."

"Good call," Tommy said in a hushed tone.

Sean had no intention of going back into the other room. He shifted stealthily around to the column, using his toes to feel his way around on the floor and one hand in front of his body to find what he was looking for. When his fingers touched the smooth stone pillar, he froze in place. If he had guessed correctly, Bourdon would be hiding just on the other side, waiting to fire his weapon.

Bourdon crouched on the floor, ready to kill whoever risked coming too close. He'd never been nervous about anything in his life. His military training in the Balkans had eradicated any sense of anxiety he had left from childhood. Now, however, there was a hesitancy in his throat as he swallowed, keeping his breathing even and low so as not to alert the Americans of his position.

The conversation between the two friends may have been a decoy to try to draw him out. Bourdon was no fool. Even if the Americans made their way back to the water in the other room, he was going to stay put.

His finger tensed on the trigger as he drew in another slow breath.

Something crashed hard into his jaw, sending him tumbling head over heels backward. He fired off a desperate shot, but the bullet pinged harmlessly off the ceiling and floor. The ground gave way to a brief moment of air before he felt the water smack against his back. Bourdon kicked his feet hard and swung his arms violently, forsaking his weapon in the process of trying to stay afloat in the death trap. He felt something rub against his foot for a second. It was smooth and rubbery. Next, it rubbed against the calf of his other leg. A terrible feeling of dread filled Bourdon's heart just before he felt the first teeth sink deep into his thigh.

He let out a scream of agony, still thrashing around in the darkness. The sound was brief, though, as another of the sea's killing machines tore into his torso and pulled Bourdon under the water.

Sean had calculated his swing perfectly. He'd climbed up onto the pedestal and risked kicking the invisible target. His foot swung low, increasing the likelihood of making contact. From the feel of it, he was fairly certain he'd hit the killer squarely under his chin.

He turned on his light, and Tommy followed suit, bringing the room back into pale illumination once more. Sean got down from his perch and shined his light into the trap. The seawater was stained red with blood.

Tommy stepped close and looked down into the cavity. "I thought you said the sharks in these parts never attacked humans. They just killed two people!"

Sean shrugged. "Yeah, but they were bad people."

Tommy just shook his head.

The two shifted their gaze to the Antikythera Mechanism sitting on the cubed plinth. Along the edge of the deadly trapdoor, two lips stood out from either side of the floor.

"Here," Sean said, handing his flashlight to Tommy. "Hold this."

Tommy did as he was told and kept both lights shining in front of Sean as he carefully put the outer edge of both feet on the lips of the crevasse. He inched his way forward, legs spread apart in an upside down V-shape as he shimmied his way toward the shining metal object. It was a slow process with a horrifying death waiting below, but Sean made it safely to the other side of the trapdoor and planted both feet on the square surface surrounding the marble altar. He stared at the object for a moment, praying silently that Caesar had left no other traps to be triggered. Sean's fingers touched the cold, metal surface. He gazed at the intricate inner workings of gears and arms, not unlike the innards of a clock. Odd symbols were etched into three wheels that stood out from the rest of the device. He remembered what the president had said about those characters. The meaning of them had never been released to the public.

As his hands wrapped around the Antikythera Mechanism, his mind started wondering if he should indeed give it to Gikas. Up until now, he'd been making it up as he went along. The curious part of him wondered how the thing worked. The archaeologist in him wanted to turn one of the wheels and change the alignment of the symbols to see what would happen, but he didn't have time. An idea sparked in his mind. Perhaps he and Tommy wouldn't have to hand over the Eye of Zeus after all.

He picked up the bronze object, surprised at how light it felt in his hands, and tucked it under one arm like a football.

"Is it heavy?" Tommy asked, concerned that Sean would drop it or not be able to make it back across the span.

"No, I got it," Sean said.

"It's a shame we have to give it to that madman. But there isn't any other way, I suppose."

Sean shook his head as he began to slide his feet back onto the two lips of stone and work his way across the watery hole. "No, there is another way."

51

NORTHWESTERN GREECE

"It might work," Tommy said with a hint of doubt in his voice.

The two friends stood on the deck of the rental boat with their scuba gear still attached. Swimming out of the underwater cavern had been easy enough, only taking them a few minutes to get back up to the surface.

On the horizon, the sun eased its way toward the sea. Sunset was coming soon. Sean wished they could wait to implement his plan under the cover of darkness, adding stealth to the element of surprise.

"It has to work," Sean said.

"Look." Tommy pointed around the edge of the island. "Just like you said. The yacht's turning around and coming this way."

"Why wouldn't they?" Sean asked. "Makes no sense to stay parked out there when they could sit next to our boat and wait for their prize to come to them."

"I hadn't thought about that."

The white yacht gradually came about and pointed its nose right at the Americans' position.

"You don't think they saw us, do you?" Tommy sounded slightly worried.

"Not yet, but we need to get back in the water before they do."

Tommy didn't wait for the order. He slipped his mask back on and switched on the air for his tank. Sean did the same and slung a black satchel over his shoulder. The two dropped back in the water and disappeared from view.

Ten minutes later, the larger boat eased next to the cabin cruiser. The yacht's captain didn't lower the anchor, instead electing to keep the ship under his direct control. On the starboard deck, two guards with sunglasses and submachine guns paced in opposite directions, keeping ever-watchful eyes on the sea.

They never expected two men to emerge from the water onto the rear of the boat. Sean and Tommy quietly pulled themselves onto the narrow swim deck attached the hull. Careful not to make too much noise, they slipped out of their dive gear and peeked over the edge of the aft railing. One guard stood alone, staring off at the other island a mile or so away. Taking the knife Tommy had kept from the dead guard in the cavern, Sean slid over the railing and onto the aft deck. He felt an old energy creeping into his body. It was the same thing he'd felt on countless Axis missions all over the world. The sensation had kept him alert and quick, two things that were absolute essentials for a field agent. Fortunately for him, the guard wasn't nearly as alert.

Sean grabbed the man's mouth and jabbed the tip of the blade through the back of his neck. The guard's struggle weakened almost instantly. Sean lowered the body to the deck slowly so as not to draw any unwanted attention.

Tommy joined him onboard, holding a Berretta in one hand. Sean slid the knife back into the sheath he'd confiscated earlier and brandishing the newly dead guard's weapon in its place. A pop startled the two men, and a piece of the wooden railing exploded into splinters. Tommy and Sean both ducked instinctively, but they were in the open with no cover in sight.

The gun fired again, and Sean rolled to the starboard side, spotting where the shots were coming from. He squeezed the trigger four times. Two bullets plunked into the back part of the cabin, one went into the horizon, and another landed at the feet of the guard he was targeting.

The guard fired again, causing Sean to roll back to his left, where Tommy was scrambling to get up. More shots came from the port side of the boat, ripping the deck and railing to shreds. The only thing saving the Americans was the fact that the boat continued to rock back and forth, making accuracy with a firearm a huge problem.

"Follow me," Sean said and dove toward the cabin, closing the gap between him and the attacker.

The yacht suddenly lurched forward, throwing the Americans off balance for a moment.

"You aren't going at them?" Tommy shouted, but it was too late. His friend was already making his move. He had no choice but to follow. "This is a bad idea!" he yelled, tucking in close behind Sean.

"No choice now. Gikas knows we're on board."

The two dived and rolled into the back of the cabin, which provided them with a moment of cover from the barrage of bullets. The moment ended quickly, though, as guards stepped around both sides with weapons drawn. Both men fired simultaneously at the sight of one another, sending multiple rounds into each man's chest. They realized too late that they were firing on their own men. One of the guards collapsed to the deck, while the other stumbled backward and flipped over the railing into the sea.

Sean and Tommy exchanged a shrug.

"There's no way you planned that," Tommy said insistently. He shook his head in haughty derision.

"Not exactly like that, no."

"You didn't plan it at all," Tommy pushed.

"Can we please talk about this later? We have to find Gikas."

Footsteps pounded the deck as more men ran down the aisle toward the back of the yacht. Sean reached up and grabbed the handle of a door. It wouldn't budge.

"Okay," he said, glancing at his weapon. "Like I always say, the best defense is a good offense."

Tommy's eyebrows lowered, knowing what his friend had in mind.

Sean popped up and spun around the corner of the cabin, gun extended in front of him. He fired repeatedly at the row of guards rushing too quickly toward him. They never had a chance, one dropping, then the next, until there was a pile of three bodies heaped onto the walkway. Sean tossed the gun into the water and grabbed two from the dead hands of the mercenaries. Securing the satchel around his shoulder, he pushed on.

As Sean continued rapidly but cautiously down the walkway, a door on the side of the cabin suddenly opened. A hand holding a black pistol stuck through the opening, but Sean's reaction was too fast. He grabbed the wrist attached to the hand with the gun and yanked it hard. Caught off guard, the armed attacker flew out the door, slamming into the railing. The gun fired, punching a splintery hole in the wooden deck. Sean twisted the man's arm around and then brought it forward over his own and pulled down. The appendage snapped, causing the henchman to scream in pain. Tommy lunged at him and punched the guy in the neck with his elbow. The yelling came to an abrupt halt once the man's throat was crushed. He clutched at it with his only remaining good hand as he stumbled clumsily over the railing and into the sea.

Tommy shook his head and hurried after his friend. "So, your plan was charge?" he said as the two moved up the gangway.

Another man in black appeared on the roof just above them, taking aim at the two intruders. However, Tommy was quicker and unleashed a volley of three bullets, two of which struck the villain in the center of his torso. The man clutched his shirt as he fell over the upper railing and splashed into the water below.

"Seems to be working just fine, thank you," Sean said in a tone smacking with contempt.

Something creaked suddenly above and behind where Tommy was standing. He didn't have time to react as another guard dropped down from the roof on top of him. Sean pointed the barrel at the attacker and squeezed the trigger as he pinned Tommy to the deck, but the weapon clicked. He was out of bullets.

The guard and Tommy rolled a few feet toward the aft deck, locked in a deadly struggle. Sean took a step to aid his friend when another guard swooped in from above, crashing into him from behind. The guard's elbow dug deep into Sean's collarbone on impact, sending a surge of new pain through his body as he collapsed to the floor. Unlike Tommy's assailant, the one coming after Sean wasn't able to grab onto anything, keeping the two separate for a moment.

It was only the briefest of moments, however, as the man in the black outfit came barreling at Sean, readying to strike him in the face with a heavy boot. Sean rolled out of the way with the narrowest of margins, bumping to a stop against Tommy's side.

Sean didn't have time to ask how his friend was fairing in his fight, but in the two-second glance he'd taken it appeared that the two were locked in a grappling stalemate. Pushing himself up from the deck, Sean slid to the left as his attacker swung his foot again. This time when he missed, he struck the man on top of Tommy squarely in the ribs. The man grunted at the blow, and his arms weakened for a split second, giving Tommy the momentary advantage he needed to break the deadlock. He rolled the man over, straddling his torso with a constricting leg grip.

Tommy unleashed a flurry of punches, landing punishing strikes across the man's jaw with his fists. The muscular guard put up his elbows to block the attack and managed to use his weight to roll over again, tumbling Tommy back to the corner of the main cabin.

Sean steadied himself for another advance from his henchman. The man whipped out a knife from his belt and held it at length, brandishing it menacingly. It wasn't the first time Sean had been in a knife fight without a knife. His years of training and experience taught him one important thing when it came to that kind of situation: Always let the man with the weapon make the first move. He'd seen some of his colleagues make the mistake of going on the offensive when they were unarmed in hand-to-hand combat. The reasoning behind letting the armed opponent take the offensive was that momentum could be used as a weapon against them. Knowing this, Sean waited patiently, faking a move to the left, then back to the right, leading the dance but letting the guard think he was in control. Even thought the thickly muscled attacker had the advantage, a look of doubt revealed itself behind his focused, snarling face.

He didn't let the man realize it, but as they continued their dance, Sean made sure to keep the distance exactly where he wanted it, close enough to tempt an attack, but far enough away to stay safe. Sean watched his opponent's eyes closely for the tell that would signal the man's intent. It was just like playing poker, something in which Sean was also extremely proficient. The guard's cheek twitched ever so slightly, signaling his intentions. It was followed by a fierce lunge and swipe of the blade at Sean's chest. He deftly took a short step back and grabbed the man's wrist. As planned, he pulled the guard toward him, using the man's forward momentum to reel him in like a hooked fish. The next move happened so fast the guard didn't have half a second to react. Sean pressed his left elbow into the crook of the attacker's arm, and the other elbow against his forearm. The combination caused the strong man's arm to bend backward instantly, sending the tip of his blade deep into the base of his own neck. He gasped at the sudden pain of the mortal blow and immediately attempted to retract the knife from his body. Sean released the man, letting his momentum carry him to the railing. Just as the guard jerked the weapon from his throat, Sean jumped into the air and sent his heel into the middle of the man's back with a flying sidekick. The body flipped over the railing and into the sea with a splash. Sean only glanced at the water for a second before turning his attention back to Tommy in time to see his friend's opponent charging wildly across the deck, intent on planting a broad shoulder into his target's midsection.

Tommy staggered for a second, but steadied himself in time to take a quick sidestep and shove the guard headfirst into a metal container near the railing. The man's progress halted with a heavy thud, and he collapsed to the deck. Sean hurried over to where

Tommy stood and looked down at the unconscious guard. He glanced up at his friend, who nodded. The two men grabbed the guard by his feet and ankles and tossed him into the sea. The body disappeared into the foamy white wake behind the yacht.

Sean led the way back toward the front of the boat, reaching down to grab his gun from the deck as they moved along the narrow walkway.

They reached the front of the cabin and the door to where Gikas had brought them before. Sean was about to open the portal when a familiar voice halted them in their tracks.

"Stop right there, gentlemen. I think you've gone far enough."

The sound sent chills through the Americans' spines, and the hair raised on their necks. Sean and Tommy turned their heads cautiously to see the silhouette of Dimitris Gikas standing on the bow of the ship. The gun in his hand pressed hard into the side of Adriana's head. Her hands and feet were still bound together. Gikas's free hand was wrapped around her shoulder, holding her tight.

"I have to admit, Sean, taking out all my guards like that, pretty impressive."

Sean ignored the comment. "Let her go, Gikas."

"Give me the device, and I will let her go. It really is that simple. Or do not, and I will splatter her brains across the Ionian Sea."

"You kill her, I kill you," Sean said menacingly. He extended his weapon, pointing the barrel straight at the Greek's head.

"Which is why I do not want to kill her," Gikas said in an ironic tone. "I assume the device is in that bag you have there?"

"That's right."

"Good. Now, what did you do with Teo and his men? I assume they are dead?"

"You're two for two."

Gikas shrugged. "Well, I can always find more mercenaries. Thanks to the wars you Americans wage, there are highly trained soldiers for hire all over the world. Now," he waved his free hand at Sean, "put the bag down, and I will let your woman go."

Tommy kept his gun trained on the Greek, staring at him through narrow slits. "No funny business, Gikas. We will blow you to kingdom come."

"You have my word, gentlemen. All I want is the device. Now please, put it on the deck over there."

Sean lowered his weapon slowly. "If he tries anything, kill him," he said to Tommy.

"I got him."

Sean stuffed the gun into his belt and took a step over to the center of the bow where Gikas had instructed. He removed the bag from his shoulder and set it down before unzipping it.

"Good," Gikas said. "Show it to me."

Sean did as he was told, pulling the bronze piece out of the satchel. The glimmering metal flashed in the waning rays of sunlight. A look of relief washed over Gikas as he realized the future of his kingdom was finally at hand.

"It's beautiful," he said, staring at the object. "Now leave it there and step back over to your friend with the itchy finger."

Again, Sean obeyed and returned to Tommy's side. "I held up my end of the bargain, Gikas. Now it's your turn."

The man paused for a moment, leaving a few seconds of uncertainty that made Sean queasy, like he'd just been had.

"Yes. It is my turn. And I am a man of my word." Gikas shuffled a few feet to the starboard side of the bow, keeping Adriana close. "I will let the girl go."

Gikas moved suddenly, shoving Adriana over the railing and into the water. Before Tommy realized what had happened, the Greek dove for cover behind a bulkhead.

Sean's reaction was instant. He dove headfirst into the choppy waters, desperate to save her, knowing that with her hands and feet bound, she would sink like a rock.

Tommy fired a few shots with his gun and then followed his friend into the water, leaping over the edge to help save Adriana.

In the darkening water, visibility narrowed by the second. Sean's panicked eyes darted back and forth, scouring the depths for a sign of her. He heard Tommy hit the water nearby just as he saw her figure several yards away, sinking fast. Sean swam toward her, harder than he'd ever done in his life, kicking with every ounce of his energy. Adriana tried to kick her legs together to maintain some kind of upward momentum, but it was a vain effort.

Bubbles began to trickle out of her mouth as Sean reached out to grab her. His fingers wrapped around the rope on her wrists, and he pulled hard toward a surface that seemed so far away. He couldn't believe how a woman in such good shape could be so heavy. They were still fifteen feet from the surface, and Sean didn't know how much longer she could last.

Suddenly, the burden lightened, and Sean realized that Tommy had grabbed on to Adriana's belt and was helping to pull her upward. With his friend's assistance, they breached the surface of the water in five seconds, careful to make sure Adriana could breathe first. At first, she coughed, then gasped in huge gulps of air, panting loudly. Sean took a breath of air and pulled the knife out of its sheath, making quick work of the ropes on her wrists, and then submerging once more to saw through those on her feet. Tommy kept his arm around her chest, holding her afloat until Sean was done. When he resurfaced, Adriana was kicking on her own, but clearly struggling.

"Can you swim?" he asked her, not thinking of anything else except getting her back to the safety of the rental boat.

"I...I can swim. Just not very fast."

Sean smiled at her and grabbed her, pressing his lips against hers. He let go after a few seconds and looked her in the eyes. Her wet hair streamed across her forehead in a tangled mess. "I thought I'd lost you," he said, the tears in his eyes masked by the seawater.

She smiled at him, though clearly in pain. "I knew you would come for me."

"Hey, I came for you too," Tommy said from behind her.

She twisted her head slightly to look over her shoulder at him. "Yes, you did," she said, still trying to smile.

Tommy returned the grin as he clumsily attempted to maintain his buoyancy. His expression turned sour, and he pointed back to where the yacht had been. "Gikas is getting away with the artifact."

Sean's determination flamed through his eyes as he stared after the boat. "We can still catch him if we hurry."

The three swam as fast as they could, back toward the rental boat. The going was slow, however, and reaching the back deck of the cruiser took them nearly twenty minutes, despite their close proximity. The three had to stop several times to rest. Adriana had a particularly difficult time. She didn't seem able to do much more than kick her feet. Whenever she tried to paddle with her arms, she winced in pain and was resigned to using a meager breast stroke. When they arrived at their boat, Sean climbed aboard then reached down and pulled Adriana up next to him. Tommy grabbed on to a handhold and yanked himself up onto the aft deck.

"Can you catch up to him?" Sean asked as he tended to Adriana and helped her lie down on the back seat of the boat. He noticed she had a severe bruise on the right side of her ribcage, no doubt the reason her swimming ability had been hampered.

Tommy glanced back at the giant yacht. The white ship grew smaller and smaller in the distance as it neared the main island of Corfu. A foamy wake trailed off and disappeared behind it. Daylight was nearly gone.

"Absolutely," Tommy said confidently.

Sean didn't have a plan of attack. He just knew they had to get to Gikas before he escaped. If the Greek reached land, he could go almost anywhere in the world in a matter of hours, and no one would be able to find him.

Tommy stepped around to the console of the boat and started to turn the key in the ignition when a thunderous explosion in the distance stopped him cold. He spun around and saw the giant yacht engulfed in a ball of fire and black smoke. The sudden blast and searing orange flash startled Sean, and he turned around in a snap to see what had happened. As he stared at the fiery destruction, Sean's jaw dropped. Someone had destroyed Gikas's vessel. But who?

Adriana lifted her head up and craned her neck just enough to see over the back of the seat. "Did you two do that?" she asked, eyeing the scene in disbelief.

"Wasn't us," Sean said, slowly shaking his head from left to right. He gazed with wide eyes at the flaming wreckage.

The luxurious yacht burned brightly on the water, pouring billows of dark smoke into the clear, twilight sky.

"Yeah, but who?" Tommy asked. "And how?" His face twisted, perplexed. Whoever it was sure used a lot of explosives."

"Or a small amount of high-grade stuff," Sean suggested. There were only a few people in the world who had access to the more advanced explosive materials. The United States military did, in the special ops divisions. He was sure some of Great Britain's military branches could get it as well. Sean doubted it was them. They were unlikely to be involved with Gikas. There was no reason.

"You think it could have been a rival? Someone he pissed off?" Tommy asked.

Sean was paralyzed, still looking on at the blazing ship. Most of the hull had already burned, and the fire inched its way toward the water's surface.

"Maybe," Sean said.

"You think we should check it out? What if whoever did this is still hanging around and comes after us next?"

"Good point. Take us over there nice and slow, and keep an eye out for anything unusual."

Adriana put her head back down on the cushion, but the two men kept staring at the fiery remains of Gikas's yacht. As they watched, they noticed some movement along the water just beyond the bow of the yacht. The object had a low profile and sped quickly away from the burning boat.

"Is that...?" Tommy started to ask.

"Navy SEALs." Sean answered the question before his friend could finish. "You can see four of them crouched low in the raft."

Tommy took on a bewildered look. "What are they doing here?"

Sean reached into his pocket and pulled out a tiny metal, pill-shaped object.

"Is that what I think it is?"

"Yep. Homing beacon. I gave Yarbrough the signal before we left.

Although, I didn't know they were so nearby. They cut it awfully close."

Tommy shook his head. "Sometimes you still surprise me."

"Excuse me," Adriana cut into their moment. "If it's all right with you two, I'd like to go to a hospital now." She rolled her head over to gaze into Sean's eyes as she still winced against the pain.

"Yeah," he said with a huge grin on his face as he looked down at her. "We can do that."

52

WASHINGTON, D.C

"The world owes you a debt of gratitude, gentlemen." John Dawkins sat in his high back leather chair with hands folded atop the Resolute Desk. His face expressed approval and appreciation.

It was the first time Tommy and Sean had ever seen the inside of the Oval Office in person. Most Americans had seen it in pictures, but very few people were ever allowed to actually go in. Emily Starks stood off to the side of the desk with a proud smile on her face, wearing her usual gray business suit. The president had requested her presence to join the two friends at the White House. Agent Yarbrough stood on the other side of the desk with his arm still in a sling.

"Glad we were able to help, sir." Sean gave a nod, keeping his hands folded behind his back.

"You two saved a lot of lives. Of course, the Greek prime minister can never know what happened."

"Of course."

"I wish we could have retained the Antikythera Mechanism," Tommy said with regret. "Such a shame."

The president's tone turned grave. "I think that artifact is better left at the bottom of the Mediterranean, Tommy."

"Still, would have been cool to see how it works."

"Well," Dawkins said in a mysterious tone, "I guess we'll never know."

There was something in the way he said it that caused Tommy and Sean to wonder if the president was telling them everything. Neither of them pushed the issue. They'd done what was needed, saved a lot of lives, and more importantly to Sean, saved Adriana.

The thought of her reminded him of his next appointment. "Mr. President, I don't mean to be rude, but I have a date I really want to get to."

Dawkins raised his eyebrows, amused that someone would blow off the leader of the free world. He smiled and nodded slowly. "I understand, Sean. Go meet that lovely Spanish lady. You've earned it."

"Thank you, sir." Sean started for the door with Tommy in tow.

As one of the assistants in the room turned the knob for him, Dawkins stopped them. "I'll be in touch again."

Sean paused for a moment, looking down at the floor. He smiled and disappeared out into the maze of desks beyond. One of the interns with a badge politely ushered the two men through the passageways of the famous mansion and out to the side door where they could go back through the exterior security checkpoint.

"Something's been bothering me since we left Greece," Tommy said as they stepped into the warm, spring air.

"You think they kept the device?" Sean passed a sideways glance at him.

"Maybe," Tommy shrugged. "We'll never know that. But what I want to know is, would the SEAL team have blown up the boat if we were still on it?"

Sean kept walking toward the security house on the perimeter of the grounds. When he answered, he faced his friend with a wry smile. "I guess we'll never know that either."

When the assistant closed the door, the president leaned back in his chair and crossed one leg over the other.

"We need him," he said bluntly to Emily.

"I know, sir, but he won't come back. Believe me, I've tried."

Dawkins let out a long sigh. "Well, keep trying. He's the best natural agent I've ever seen."

"Yeah. I hated to lose him. But I'm telling you, he won't come back, sir. His mind is made up. And when Sean sets his mind to something, there's no convincing him otherwise."

Yarbrough entered the conversation. "We'll keep an eye on him, Mr. President, just in case we ever need him again."

"Good. The world needs heroes like him. And I may need his services again at some point."

Emily's face curled into a curious frown. "I'm sorry to ask this, Mr. President, but was the SEAL team able to recover the device?"

Dawkins stared straight ahead, his expression as stoic as ever. Before he could answer, Emily did it for him. "You know, John, you can't bluff a bluffer. Your men were able to recover it, weren't they?" Her eyes stared through him with one eyebrow higher than the other.

"You don't have to worry about the Eye of Zeus, Emily. It will never fall into the wrong hands again."

"Mr. President," she protested, "if that thing can do what you said it can do, it should be destroyed."

"Trust me, Em. It's never going to fall into the wrong hands."

"Didn't our government think the same thing about nuclear weapons?"

Dawkins passed her a pleading glance, wanting the conversation to be over. "Would it make you feel better if I told you the device really was at the bottom of the sea, and that the SEAL team's orders were to destroy it along with Gikas's ship?"

She thought for a second before answering. "No. But I guess it's all I'll get from you for now."

He winked at her. "Good. Now, tell me what's going on with your agent in Paris."

53

WASHINGTON, D.C

Sean sat across from Adriana at a little bistro table just outside his favorite coffee shop. He'd been to the eastern market several times before when visiting D.C. and found several little places he enjoyed grabbing breakfast or an early lunch. He detested using the word *brunch* but found the foods at that time of the day were some of his favorites. Bloody Marys were also a welcome addition to the pre-noon part of the day.

Pedestrians walked by on the sidewalk, busily heading to the shops and crafts kiosks dotting the area. Many of them carried two or three bags from the various vendors. A cool breeze rolled through the sunny city street, carrying a collage of smells: spring flowers, lavender, freshly baked bread, onions, and Bradford pear.

"The Braves are in town playing the Nationals tonight," Sean said, breaking the relative silence of their little piece of D.C. "Want to catch a baseball game tonight?"

"Sure," she responded with a shrug. "Though I am a much bigger fan of football than baseball."

He perked up at this revelation. "You are? Who's your favorite team? I'm a big fan of the Falcons, though that can be difficult sometimes."

"Atlético Madrid," she said cutely.

Sean realized immediately that she was talking about soccer. "Right. Football. I forgot."

She laughed at him, revealing her bright-white teeth. "You don't appreciate what you Americans call soccer?"

He put up a defensive hand. "No, I love soccer. I cheer for Everton in England. But I don't have any allegiance to a team in Spain, so I guess I could root for Atlético."

Adriana smiled at him as she sipped her cappuccino. She'd suffered two cracked ribs from her ordeal in Greece, but other than that she was recovering well. She had relayed the story of the young boy, Niki, to Sean, but they'd never been able to find out anything else about the child. Adriana hoped desperately that the boy had made it to safety. That piece of information, however, would likely never reach her.

"He's with good people who will watch over him," Sean reassured her.

She stared into her milky espresso drink. "I hope you're right. I would hate to think something bad happened to him."

Sean sympathized. "If he had stayed, Gikas would have probably brought him along on the boat. You saw how that ended. I'm sure he's in the care of a saintly person now."

The last sentence brought back the grin to her face that she'd lost while thinking about little Niki.

Sean's phone buzzed on the table. He glanced down at it and entered his four-digit code to unlock the device. He read the message quickly then placed the phone back down on the table. "Just got a text from Mac," he said. "It sounds like he and Helen are finding some interesting things over in Denmark."

Adriana's expression turned quizzical. "What are they doing over there? And why are they texting you? They work for Tommy now?"

"Some excavation for the IAA. Seems someone stumbled upon a few really old artifacts near Kronborg Castle. They aren't really sure what it is. Actually, no one is really sure what's there. The Danish government requested IAA to check it out. So Tommy sent Mac and

Helen on the case. As for why they texted me, I guess they just figured I'd be interested."

"That sounds interesting."

"It is..." Sean caught himself. "Though, it's nothing I'd want to get into."

She eyed him suspiciously, but said nothing.

"It's probably just a bunch of digging and cleaning and sifting through thousands of years of dirt. Wouldn't be any fun."

Adriana took another sip of her coffee and continued to let him go on.

"I mean, Copenhagen is really nice this time of year. It's one of my favorite places to visit. Wouldn't hurt anything if we popped by to see Mac and Helen. You know, just to say hello."

"What about your shop in Florida?" Adriana asked with a playful grin.

"Right." Sean had nearly forgotten about his kayak and paddleboard shop in Destin. He'd been gone for several days and hoped everything was okay. "I guess we can go to Copenhagen some other time." He thought about it for a minute, remembering the last time he visited the Danish Riviera, across the waterway from Sweden. On a typical summer day, you could easily see the Swedish city of Malmo just on the other side of the inlet.

"I'm not stopping you," she said.

"No, you aren't." He leaned across the table and kissed her softly on the lips. "And I would appreciate it if from now on you didn't go off on your little adventures without me. You get into too much trouble on your own."

Her dark eyes gazed into his, their lips nearly brushing against each other. "I might just take you up on that, Sean Wyatt."

"Might?"

She nodded. "Might."

THANK YOU

I just wanted to take a moment to thank you for reading my book. You could have chosen any number of books, and you chose mine. I'm honored by that fact. I work hard to make sure I never let you down with any of the books that I write, and am always doing my best to make the next a little better than the one before. I hope that hard work comes through in the best reading experience possible.

Once again, thank you. You are the reason I tell stories.

Ernest Dempsey

OTHER BOOKS BY ERNEST DEMPSEY

Sean Wyatt Adventures:

The Secret of the Stones

The Cleric's Vault

The Last Chamber

The Grecian Manifesto

The Norse Directive

Game of Shadows

The Jerusalem Creed

The Samurai Cipher

The Cairo Vendetta

The Uluru Code

The Excalibur Key

The Denali Deception

The Sahara Legacy

The Fourth Prophecy

Adriana Villa Adventures:

War of Thieves Box Set

When Shadows Call

Shadows Rising

ACKNOWLEDGMENTS

I'd like to thank my incredible editors, Anne Storer and Jason Whited, for all their hard and patient work with me. They make my stories shine, and without them I'd be lost. Thanks, you two.

ABOUT THE AUTHOR

Ernest Dempsey is the author of the up-tempo, Sean Wyatt thriller series. He makes his online home in Chattanooga, Tennessee, and online at ernestdempsey.net. You can connect with Ernest on Twitter at @ErnDempsey or on Facebook.com/ErnestDempsey.

Send him a message if you feel so inclined. He'll be happy to get back to you.

For my amazing family and friends;

thank you for your constant support.

Made in the USA
Monee, IL
25 October 2020

46002659R10198